FRUIT COCKTAIL

FRUIT COCKTAIL

a novel
ARTHUR WOOTEN

alyson books
NEW YORK

Manufactured in the United States of America

This trade paperback original is published by Alyson Books
245 West 17th Street, New York, NY 10011

Distribution in the United Kingdom by
Turnaround Publisher Services Ltd.
Unit 3, Olympia Trading Estate
Coburg Road, Wood Green
London N22 6TZ England

First Edition: December 2007

07 08 09 10 11 a 10 9 8 7 6 5 4 3 2 1

ISBN: 1-59350-047-5
ISBN-13: 978-1-59350-047-4

Library of Congress Cataloging-in-Publication data are on file.

Cover design by Victor Mingovits

To all the full grown
and ripened fruit who
are still hopeless romantics
and a little bit mushy on the inside

ACKNOWLEDGMENTS

To Dr. Neera Kapoor and Dr. Sujana Chandrasekhar, two beautiful women with hearts of gold who literally saved my life in 2006.

CONTENTS

ONE

FOREPLAY

"You were born gay and you're going to stay that way!" my mother hollered at me from Wunderland's Department Store fitting room. "And throw that other dress to me."

I got up off the stool that I'm sure had my name engraved upon it. Here sat Curtis Jenkins for nine years as his mother, Mrs. J., tried on every dress in Bremerton, New York. I picked up the basic knit, short sleeve purple dress and threw it over the changing room door. "But Ma . . ."

"No ifs, ands, or *butts* about it. You're not switching teams on me now."

In 1973 Wunderland's was *the* place for the happening woman to shop for clothes in all of Westchester. A brick monstrosity of a building, the store was once the Peabody Printing Press Building, Bremerton's first and only book factory and outlet. I used to think that reading and writing became such an important part of my life because of the hours I spent in that building. Even though the haphazard and destructive transition converting it into a department store literally raped that beautiful structure of all its important and historical value, I could still find clues to its former glory and heyday. Underneath my throne in front of changing room number three, I could still trace with my finger the circular indentations on the floor caused by the sheer weight of the mighty printing presses. My mind would wander and wonder, dreaming about the books and stories created by brilliant writers, while my mother would try on everything from cashmere sweaters and hostess coats to support bras and tummy-taming girdles.

"Hello, Curtis," our neighbor Mrs. Philpot said as she came around the corner with her arms full of hideous skirts.

"Hi," I said, looking at them with a repugnant look.

She glanced at my face, then at the skirts, and then back to my face. "Is something wrong?"

"You are putting those back on the rack, aren't you?"

She looked at them, worried. "I was going to try them on." She held up a bright orange one. "This one in particular I think is quite fetching." She put the other skirts down and held it up to her waist. "It's a woven embroidered midi column skirt. It's very special."

"Yes, I can see that," I said, careful not to be too condescending.

It was already well known in our town that I had impeccable taste in women's clothing.

Mrs. Philpot brought her face close to mine and whispered, "Curtis, what's wrong with it?"

"It's a midi skirt."

"Yes and?"

"And that's what's wrong with it." I couldn't hold back. "These hideous things should never have been invented. And I'm certain whoever did create them was a misogynist."

"A misogynist?" she asked, frightened.

"Only a woman hater would create something that chops her legs off midshin. It doesn't look flattering on anybody." I touched the fabric, held it out in front of me, and said, "And it's probably carcinogenic. Please, Mrs. Philpot, for your own good, put it back. Put them all back."

My mother hollered from the changing booth. "Did you say something, dear?"

"Mrs. Philpot is here."

My mother stuck her head out. "Connie! How is your diseased ovary?"

"It was a retention cyst and I had it removed," she said, placing both hands on her abdomen.

Mother put on her worried face. "But you're all better now?"

"A little tired but yes, I'm doing quite fine."

"Good," she smiled. "Now please excuse Curtis and I. No time for chitchat. He's picking out my spring outfits."

My mother slammed the door shut as Mrs. Philpot looked at me feebly. "I'll just put these skirts back."

I smiled warmly at her. "I think that's a good idea. You're long waisted with short legs. I'd choose a skirt that comes to just above your knee."

"Thank you, Curtis," she said, touching my arm gratefully. "Thank you for your help."

She started to leave as I said, "And focus more on your upper body."

"My what?" she asked tentatively as she turned.

"Aisle four has some really smart cashmere sweater sets," I said, pointing to the back of the store. "They do wonders for the flat-chested woman."

She blushed and self-consciously looked down at her nonexistent breasts. "Oh my!" she exclaimed as she ran off to aisle four.

Just then, the dressing room door banged open and my mother strutted out, buttoning up the dress. "I love this one."

I turned my nose up at it. "No you don't."

She predictably rested into her left hip as her opposite hand came down aggressively onto her right. "And why don't I love it?"

I threw it and her a dismissive glance. "If it were cut on the bias it would flow beautifully from your hips." I got up off my throne and paced around the room. "But it's not."

Dumbfounded, Mother looked into the three-way mirror and checked herself out. She shrugged her shoulders. "Curtis, you're right. The bias is off." She dashed back into the room and threw on her clothes. "What the hell is a bias?"

"An unfair preference for or dislike of something." I smiled, knowing that she was now standing totally naked and confused. "Mother, it's not that I want to switch teams. It's just that all my friends are dating girls and I like girls and I was wondering if maybe I could be at the very least . . . bisexual?"

I could hear her huff. "A mother knows when her son is gay. I almost went under the knife for your life!"

I shook my head thinking *here we go again*. "Yes, and I appreciate that but . . ."

She bolted out of the room wearing what she came in with: a fuchsia tube top, white short shorts, and mule pumps. She may have had three kids, but at age thirty-three my mother still had the body of a teenager and knew it. "And don't tell me none of your classmates are gay."

Wide-eyed I racked my brain thinking of one of them, any of them who could be homosexual. "I honestly don't think . . ."

"That Blair Crandall is a fag if I ever saw one."

I looked at her with disbelief. Blair was Harry High School. He was the captain of the football team. No one in my mind could have been straighter. "He's dating our homecoming queen, Deleena Blaze."

Mother blurted out a guttural laugh. "Ever really watch him play quarterback? *He's* the homecoming queen."

She went on to remind me of how Blair would wiggle across the field in those skintight, white, see-through synthetic football pants that showed off his jockstrap so beautifully. The way he touched the other teammates' thighs and butts when they were in huddle formation. The extraordinary amount of time he would take to call a play while nestling his hands gently in and amongst Payton Pavlov's hindquarters. I thought to myself, *She might have a point there.*

"Curtis, you do love girls. You adore them. But wouldn't you rather be one than get naked and play with their muffins?"

I looked at her, terrified.

"You're not straight. You're not bisexual." She grabbed her purse and looked around, disoriented. "Where's the exit?"

"On the bias."

She eventually located it catercorner across the cavernous department store floor. "On the diagonal. Now aren't you clever? What would I ever do without you?"

I sensed that my mother feared that if I jumped the fence, instead of gaining a straight son she'd be losing a personal shopper.

"Let's dash over to Ford's Coffee Shop and chow down a couple of dogs." She suddenly spun around and hugged me so tight I thought I was going to burst. "And no more talk of this straight shit, Curtis. Jesus, what would the neighbors think?"

I was thirteen years old.

≷ ≶

Thirty-two years later and I still doubted myself. Not sexually, of course. I'm so gay I've never even had a nighttime sexual dream about a woman. I was questioning my talent. Here I was about to experience the biggest highlight of my writing career and I wondered if I deserved the success.

I had just finished a nonfiction book titled *101 Ways to Collide into Your Gay Soul Mate* ahead of schedule, and my publisher, editor, and marketing team at Carrington Press had created such an insane buzz about it that advance sales were already sky high. A tremendous book launch and party was planned on my behalf at a new trendy gay restaurant in Noho called the Pup Room, with all of the gay media invited. But deep in my gut I had this tremendous fear, this doubt about whether or not I was the right man to help others find their gay soul mate when I myself was still Miss Lonely Hearts? Was I a fake? A sham?

"Curtis, you're the only person who could write this book," Quinn declared as Ricky, the hot little pedicurist at the Oil Slick, massaged the arch of his foot.

I sat next to them with my hands marinating in some sort of slimy broth while wondering who was going to reach orgasm first, and where the hell had my surly manicurist gone to? Located in Hell's Kitchen, the Oil Slick was a chic attempt at creating a gay day spa. A big strike against this less-than-immaculate string of storefronts was that they were decorated like pit stops along the Indy 500. The floors were checkered and scuffed in black-and-white linoleum tiles, the walls were covered in oversized faded photographs of race cars, and they had Quinn and me sitting up in old-fashioned-style barber chairs that had fiberglass shells of race cars mounted onto them in primary colors. Not a typical gay theme in my book. And considering the second-rate manicure and pedicure we were receiving I assumed that they made their money with their spray tanning booths and erotic massages.

I went along with Quinn's wish to treat me to something special prior to the book event, not knowing that he had been into the Oil Slick the week before and had developed a crush on his doe-eyed, eager-to-please practitioner with the light brown buzz cut.

"Yes, oh yes that's the spot, Ricky," Quinn moaned.

Ricky looked up at him and said in a very thick Southern accent, "Your adrenals are full."

Quinn winked. "I love it when you talk dirty."

Quinn Larkin and I had been best friends for over twenty years. Initially we had met in an Uta Hagen acting class down on Bank Street at HB Studios. And although I went on to pursue an acting career before becoming a writer, Quinn always had a burning desire to write for Daytime soap operas. Eventually his dream came true, first working on shows here in New York City and then out in Los Angeles. But sadly, he discovered that by the time he had come on board, Daytime had lost its allure and respectability not only amongst viewers but also within the television industry itself. Or maybe the glamour and excitement of that medium was always just an illusion in Quinn's mind?

Either way, he had recently been fired from his most recent soap gig out on the Coast. Furious when his own producer mistook him for a messenger boy, Quinn threw his cell phone at her and managed to imbed the tip of its antenna into her right cornea. Pending a lawsuit and since Daytime is one of the most incestuous industries ever to exist—and maybe also because Quinn had burned every bridge he had ever crossed—he decided to move back, or more correctly flee the authorities, to New York City and pursue another life-long dream.

"I want you and your mother to come down to the theater and meet Ann."

I didn't know if I should laugh or cringe. Quinn had recently taken on the job of doing the full body makeup for none other than Ann Vermillion, the oldest living stripper starring in the longest running burlesque show, *Puss N' Boots*. With Ann clad only in pasties and a G-string, Quinn had his work cut out for him. She needed as much body paint as possible. Admitting to eightysomething, the sprightly Ms. Vermillion performed daily with shows at 8:00 A.M., 10:00 A.M., and a late show at noon at the last original vaudeville theater remaining in Manhattan, now called the Gentlemen's Desire, located just off of Times Square.

When Quinn said the word "theater," the barely-of-age reflexologist heard his cue and pulled Quinn's toes lovingly. "You must be very creative."

Quinn dug his foot into Ricky's chest. "And how would you know that?"

"Because your second toe is so long." He grabbed Quinn's fingerlike toe and massaged it rather erotically. "It indicates a great appetite."

"He does tend to like quantity over quality," I chimed in.

Quinn smirked at me as Ricky continued. "No, you have an extremely elongated digit." That prompted Quinn and I to look at each other. "Please close your eyes as I help dissolve these crystals."

Quinn winked at me and closed his eyes.

"As I stroke your large man toe think of these big old uric acid deposits as deep pockets of ultimate creativity. I'm going to release the blockage with pure and loving energy, allowing your juices to flow. Feel the hunger. Feel the craving. Release it. Like delicious hot chocolate oozing down over vanilla ice cream, melt that knot of creative congestion. Yeah man, melt that bowl of cream." He paused and looked up at Quinn. "How do you feel?"

"Hungry," I said as Quinn let out a snore.

The boy looked dejected, like he had failed, so I came to the rescue.

"You're actually right on," I whispered. "He's very creative but also very tired."

"What does he do?" Ricky asked as he got up on one knee and placed his porcelain white hand on top of mine. "I was born to be a Broadway star. Is he a producer?"

I could have run with this one but I told him the truth. "He's a Renaissance man." Actually, a Renaissance man without a renaissance.

"Wow, that is so cool. I applied last summer but they said I was too small."

"Too small?"

"Yes, and they were right. I tried on the armor and it was much too heavy for me to wear."

I got it. "Renaissance fair?"

"At Dollywood." He looked over at Quinn. "He has strong ties to the theater?"

Thinking of Ann Vermillion I said, "I'm not sure if I would call them strong, but they are definitely old."

Suddenly, Quinn woke up, choking on his own breath. "It wasn't me!" he exclaimed, kicking Ricky over.

"That's it, Quinn," I laughed. "Start another lawsuit."

"Jesus, I dreamt I was on the lam."

I laughed. "No, you *are* on the lam."

Quinn looked down at Ricky who was picking himself up off the floor. "Could you get me some water, please?"

"It would be my pleasure to get a knight in shining armor his water," he said as he rushed off.

"A what?" Quinn asked, looking at me as my absentee manicurist returned, dried my hands off, and proceeded to massage them rather aggressively.

I studied the man's face, which was somewhat haunting, as if he reminded me of someone I once knew. I wasn't sure if it was his strawberry blond hair and the way the bang scooped down over his high forehead or if it was his nose that was slightly pug and off to the left that seemed so familiar.

Whatever it was, I looked at my watch and realized that we were cutting it a bit close for the book launch. I had my outfit with me but the Oil Slick was located on Tenth Avenue and 47th Street and we had to get to Mott and Bleecker within an hour. And of course this all brought back to my attention my personal doubt again.

"But Quinn, what qualifies me to write the guidebook on finding the man of your life?"

"The same reason you've got to move out of town," Quinn said, smiling devilishly as Ricky returned with his bottle of water and a super-sized tube of lotion.

I looked at him quizzically. "And why is that?"

"Because you've dated everyone in New York City."

Ricky flipped the top of the lotion, preparing to massage it into Quinn's feet, as I gave him my standard sarcastic look. "Very funny, Quinn." I looked at the pedicurist. "I haven't wined and dined and made mad passionate love to you, have I, Ricky?"

He promptly squirted the lotion out past Quinn, hitting my leg.

"No, sir," he smiled.

Sir? Why doesn't he just call me gramps? I glanced down at my practitioner who was chopping my nails off at a record speed. "And I haven't dated this handsome man, either."

He paused and threw me such a look of disdain. Then he continued hacking away, staring at my face. He eventually veered off course and cut a rather large chunk of my right index finger off with his clipper.

My eyes witnessed what he had done before the pain registered in my brain. I pulled my hand away and held it up as blood dripped down my forearm. Then I felt the intense shock.

"Oooooowwwwwwwww!"

The manicurist just sat there looking at me, blankly.

"Curtis, you're bleeding!" Quinn screamed, throwing me a towel.

I looked at the guy, waiting for him to say something, anything. I gasped for breath, blurting out, "You hurt me."

Finally he spoke. "And you didn't hurt me?" He stood up and walked to the front desk.

Quinn and I looked at each other.

"Excuse me?" I shouted as I raced after him. "You just sliced off my finger."

The manicurist turned around and looked at me with such contempt. "You honestly don't recognize me, do you?"

"No, we've never met before," I said, doubting my own emphatic tone.

He poured a liquid into cotton balls and jammed it into my gaping wound as I screamed bloody murder.

"It's alcohol," the manicurist said dispassionately. "It stings, doesn't it?"

My eyes were tearing up as Quinn raced to my side. "He's a very famous author and moments away from a tremendous celebration of his new book, and you're in a lot of trouble, mister."

The manicurist looked at me. "You sold one screenplay that was never produced. You doctored two scripts that were shelved and never released. You've written seven plays. Three of them deserving some merit, the others are a piece of shit. You've written sporadically for television and have managed to eke out one mediocre gay book of fiction every other year. Famous? I'm afraid not."

Quinn looked at me and shrugged. "So he Googled you."

"You have a brother Stewie, a sister Kelly, an incorrigible mother, and your deceased grandmother called you Timmy the last two years of her life."

I looked at him, worried. "You do know me."

"And you should know me since I shared with you some of the most personal moments in my life, too." He paused, waiting for me to say something. "Curtis? What is my name?"

Everyone watched me as I racked my mind trying to figure out who this guy was.

"Don't give yourself a brain hernia. Dale? Dale Callahan? We dated for three weeks and two and a half days."

Quinn came to my defense. "You can't expect him to remember everyone he's dated from the past."

"It was five months ago and if you can't remember the names of the months either, that would be May."

"Geez," Quinn whispered.

Dale looked at me like I was scum. "You're an idiot," he added as he grabbed his coat and headed out of the salon.

"Shit," was all I could say.

Ricky appeared with gauze and bandages. "I'd date you even if you forgot me," he said, trying to make me feel better.

"Thank you, young man." I jumped at what I said. "What am I doing calling you young man? I'm only forty-five."

"I'm used to it. My dad is thirty-eight."

"Oh Jesus," I cried as he and Quinn wrapped up my finger.

At that moment Raul, the Oil Slick's sexy Latin manager, came to my side. "Is there a problem, sir?"

"You bet there is!" yelled Quinn. "That manicurist just attacked Mr. Jenkins here and he's moments away from the literary media event of the century."

The manager looked at my hand. "Oh my, does he need stitches?"

"Dale Callahan?" I whispered, frightened to death because for the life of me I couldn't remember dating that man.

Quinn tied a tourniquet around my finger. "No time for stitches. There must be some way that you can make up for this."

Raul pondered this statement as I felt my hand going numb. "We could certainly offer a discount."

Quinn threw his arms up in the air. "A discount? Newspaper reporters and television crews, not to mention all the gay publications will be interviewing Mr. Jenkins shortly and you certainly don't want him mentioning this incident to the press, do you?"

Raul was sweating bullets at this point. "No, of course not. There will be no charge for Mr. Jenkins's visit."

"Just Mr. Jenkins's? Did I mention that I have deep ties to the theater?"

"And old ones," added Ricky.

Quinn looked at him, confused. "I also work in television and I too will be expressing my thoughts to the industry moguls that will be present."

Raul wrestled with this one as I started to feel faint. "Alright, your treatment is on the house, too."

"And how about throwing in a free spray tanning session?" Quinn added, elbowing me.

"Dale Callahan?" I mumbled.

"It would be the Oil Slick's privilege," Raul grumbled.

He ushered us over to the booths as Quinn looked at his watch. "We're kinda in a hurry."

Still in a daze, Raul and Ricky started stripping me of my clothes. "Curtis, you are going to look fabulous," squealed Quinn.

"I don't remember dating him at all," I whispered, feeling my forehead.

"Curtis," Quinn ordered, "forget about him and step out of your pants."

I pulled one leg out wondering, "Do you think I have Alzheimer's?"

"I don't remember," Quinn laughed as he threw me into the booth.

"Maybe something awful happened and I blocked him out of my mind?"

"Curtis, you probably don't remember him because he was such a bore," Quinn said as he shut the door on me. Muffled, I could hear him yell, "Even his manicure was lame!"

Raul reached for the spray setting and asked Quinn how much of a tan I wanted.

"Think Hollywood starlet on the red carpet," he laughed. "Give him a triple dose."

The manager looked at him hesitantly and then set the timer.

"Hold your arms out to your sides!" Quinn hollered as he gave the signal to Raul to turn it on. "Let her rip!"

But in the booth all I kept asking myself was how could I have totally forgotten a man who I had dated just five months earlier. A man who had already figured out that I'm a fake? A literary fraud? Other than a vague feeling of recognizing him, I could not recall one bit of information about Dale, not to mention having sex with him. What was wrong with me? My God, at the very least I must have Half-zeimer's.

Needless to say, I not only neglected to raise my arms out to my sides but I continued to hold my uninjured hand up to my face during the entire tanning cycle. My handprint was tattooed to my cheek.

⋛ ⋚

What were we thinking? Trying to get a taxi in Manhattan, in Hell's Kitchen, at rush hour is more challenging than a neurosurgeon operating on a brain tumor having consumed a magnum of champagne and wearing oven mitts. Feigning a medical emergency and screaming that my finger had been amputated, Quinn hip-checked an elderly woman with a walker on Ninth Avenue and stole her cab. We managed to get two blocks downtown when I directed the driver to come to a screeching halt.

"Quinn, take my credit card and buy whatever we need to even out my face," I ordered as he dashed out of the taxi and into a drugstore. "And hurry!"

I looked at my watch, realizing that we had exactly four minutes to get to the Pup Room. Located in Noho, which means north of Houston Street, the trip from the West 40s was probably a little over three miles, and in moving traffic that would take about fifteen to twenty minutes. But listening to the driver's radio, we heard that a suspicious package had been discovered in the entrance of the north tube of the Lincoln Tunnel, which connects Manhattan to New Jersey. Streets from West 42nd to 31st and avenues 9, 10, and 11 were blocked off to traffic. Midtown was gridlocked.

"Excuse me, sir?" the cab driver asked in a very thick Indian accent as he slid open the clear plastic divider.

"Yes?"

He turned around and smiled at me, proudly showing his front gold tooth. "Sir, do you have a cell phone?"

I panicked, checking all my pockets, thinking that he heard it ringing and I didn't. "Yes."

His skin was a mahogany brown and he sported a full beard that must have been extremely long because it parted from the middle of his chin and he had it twisted and tucked somewhere up into his white turban. I found the phone but checked and no calls had come in.

"Sir, I was robbed at gunpoint yesterday and my cell was stolen. My mother is deathly ill in the hospital and may I use your phone to call her just for one minute."

He could see that I was holding it in my hand and yet I wasn't offering it to him.

He continued. "Sir, I totally understand. No bother. Who am I for you to trust? I am sure my mother won't die . . . today." He slid the partition back and looked out at traffic. Then his hand went up to the corner of his eye and I swear I saw him brush away a tear.

I felt horrible. How could I be so skeptical? How could I be so callous! How could I be so selfish? I knocked on the plastic and he slid it open again.

"Of course you can use my cell phone," I said, handing it to him.

His face lit up as he lunged for it. "Thank you, kind sir. Thank you from the bottom of my heart. And my mother's, too."

I squinted at his name on the taxi's identification card. "You are Virat Singh?"

"Yes sir, I am and you pronounce it very well."

I wondered what religion he practiced. "And are you a Sheik?"

He looked at me quizzically through the rearview mirror. "A what?"

"Do you practice Sheikism?"

He started to laugh. "Sir, I am Sikh."

God I felt stupid. "Yes, that's what I meant," laughing at my own faux pas. "Please, talk to your mother for as long as you like."

He eagerly dialed as Quinn opened the car door and jumped in, throwing a huge and outrageously heavy shopping bag onto my lap. He closed his door as traffic began to move.

"Curtis, here's your credit card," he said, handing it to me. "Damn, it was crowded in there."

I looked into the bag. "What *didn't* you buy?"

"I picked up a silent ionic air purifier with ultraviolet germicidal protection, but it wouldn't fit into the bag."

I laughed at the joke.

"So, I'm having them send it to your apartment."

I looked at him with a half smile. "You're kidding."

"I am not," he said indignantly. "Your apartment is stuffy and full of your dog's dander."

I threw the drugstore bag onto his lap. "You are kidding?"

He shook his head. "I know you love Emily-Mae." He genuflected. "And Dr. Magda Tunick, bless her soul, I'm sure is looking down on us at this very moment thanking you, but that eighty-two-year-old, toothless, blind, and deaf thing smells to high heaven."

I ignored what he said. "How much did it cost?"

Quinn looked at his watch and mumbled, "Just $499."

"What?" I screamed.

The cabbie slammed on his brakes, reacting to my voice, and we both flew forward out of our seats.

"Hey, it was marked down $100," Quinn said as he knocked on the divider. The driver ignored him and continued to chat on my cell phone. "You gotta get a move on, mister. We're late for a very important date."

"That's just stupid," I said, shaking my head. "If you really bought it, I'm having it sent back."

"Then don't ask me to buy things with your credit card."

I pointed my damaged index finger at him. "You can't use mine anymore. I'm changing my signature."

"You need to," he laughed. "It's so not attractive."

I turned and looked at him. "I beg your pardon?"

"Look at Bette's or Joan's or even Judy's. Now those are signatures. Yours looks like you're in third grade. You've got to work on it."

"God, what street are we at?" I asked as I looked outside the window trying to see a sign.

Quinn knocked on the divider again but the driver ignored him as he talked on the phone.

Suddenly, it dawned on me. At the book launch I'd be signing copies of my book. Hopefully a million copies of my book. "How am I going to write my name?" I asked tentatively. "Quinn, give me a pen."

He dug into his shoulder bag and pulled one out. I gingerly laid it onto my right palm and slowly grasped it as if I was going to write.

"Here, use the charge receipt," he said as he handed it to me.

"Oh my God!" I screamed as the cabby slammed on his brakes again.

Quinn scrunched up his face, feeling my pain. "Does it hurt?"

"You spent almost seven hundred fucking dollars!" I yelled at the top of my lungs.

"We'll send it back. We'll send it all back." He touched my hand. "But can you write?"

I moved toward the receipt with pen in hand and slowly applied pressure to scribble my name.

"Oooooohhhhh!" I dropped the pen and gasped for breath. "It's throbbing."

Quinn shrugged his shoulders and said rather nonchalantly, "Just write with your left. No one will be able to tell the difference."

I was about to slap him with my good hand when he knocked on the divider again.

"Hey, guy?" he asked as the driver continued to talk on the cell, inching through traffic.

"His name is Virat. He's Indian."

"With that turban and hair he must be a Sheik."

"Quinn, you are terrible," I said as I rolled my eyes at him. "It's Sikh, for God's sake."

"It could be hide-and-go-seek for all I care," he said as he dug both hands into the drugstore bag and scooped out a plethora of cosmetics. "We're in damage control now. Let me see your face."

I presented my left cheek to him and he studied the imprint.

"You have surprisingly small hands," he said with a smirk.

"Yes but I wear a size eleven shoe."

He looked at the different items. "I feel like a kid in a candy shop. We have some avocado and oatmeal facial clay masque." He handed the tube to me. "We have a nighttime face cream with almost 10 percent alpha hydroxy acid to minimize your crow's-feet."

"Those are laugh lines."

"I'm not laughing," he said as he handed the jar to me. "We have nose strips because all the world is aware of your blackhead problem." He handed the box to me. "Here's a pumice stone."

"I don't need that."

"Trust me, you are so callous."

I am, I thought to myself.

Quinn continued. "And this product was a tad expensive but if you rub it into your stretch marks they disappear."

"I don't have stretch marks and what's a tad expensive?"

"$125?"

I lost it. I'm sure my face turned beet red as I felt the brain aneurism about to explode. While searching for words to spew at Quinn, he argued in his own defense.

"But if you use the stretch mark cream on your face for six weeks, it'll look like a baby's bottom."

I took a deep breath. "I don't care if it looks like a ninety-two-year-old's ass. I just want this fucking handprint off of my face, now."

He dug deeper into the bag. "Such a diva." He pulled out a concealer brush and four other products: a caramel foundation, a cinnamon sunlight concealer, a liquid carob highlight, and a mocha compact deep powder.

I looked at all four of them. "Quinn, these products all say for the Nubian princess hidden within me."

He rubbed his hands together. "You're going to be America's Next Top Model," Quinn laughed as he started ripping open the products.

"I don't want to be Tyra Banks!" I cried. "I have to be Curtis Jenkins, the white middle-aged gay writer without out a handprint on his face."

Quinn opened the mocha compact, which had a mirror and the caramel foundation. "This should actually match the rather"—he coughed—"dark, um, deep tan that you have."

I frowned. "What's wrong?"

He looked at my face and struggled to keep the corners of his mouth from turning up. "Nothing."

I stared him down. "Liar. Give me that compact."

Quinn tried to cover his ass. "Sometimes these spray tans darken a bit after a treatment but you really look like . . ."

"Shit!" I screamed. I stared at my face. "It's fucking orange."

"More like a dirty rust," Quinn said guiltily. "I don't think anyone will notice the handprint."

"Because they'll just be shocked by my skin tone?"

He opened up the foundation and reached for my face.

"No Quinn." I grabbed it from him. "You've done enough damage for today. I'll do it myself." I poured the liquid into my palms and started slathering it onto my face.

Quinn looked at his watch again and suggested that we call the Pup Room and tell them we were stuck in traffic.

"That's a good idea," I said, desperately trying to cover all of my face. "I look like I've been microwaved."

Quinn looked at me and said, "So, let's call them."

"OK," I replied as I feverishly worked.

He stared at me like I was an idiot. "Curtis, you know I lost my cell."

"Mine's upfront," I said as I pointed to the driver.

Quinn looked at me, then at the cabbie laughing on the phone, and then back at me. "That's not your cell he's talking on, is it?"

I nodded.

"Oh no!"

"His mother is in the hospital and he really wanted to talk to her and . . ."

Quinn slammed the partition open as we heard the driver say, "Oh, ya, you sexy bitch."

Quinn and I looked at each other. I wrote Virat's taxi identification number on the back of my hand with the liquid foundation, and in one quick movement Quinn reached through the partition and snatched my cell phone out of Virat's hand. I grabbed the bags and thank God the cab was standing still in traffic because we both threw ourselves out onto the street. I caught a glimpse of the meter, which read $17.50.

"Run!" Quinn screamed to me as Virat got out of the cab and yelled for his fare.

"You bastards! I want my money!"

"I'm sure it's a lot less than that call to your bitch!" Quinn hollered as he tried to catch up to me.

T W O

I'VE GOT . . . ARASH

We ditched Virat at Seventh Avenue and Christopher Street. Cabs were nowhere to be found so we decided to make a run for it to the Pup Room. In the lead, I chose to go east on Washington Place. The fifteen blocks I knew I could handle; it was Quinn I was worried about. The most athletic thing he could do was run up and down the stairs at the Muenster Bar without once spilling a drop of his frozen margarita. And even though I was in a total state of panic, I couldn't help but notice the stunning leaves turning colors on the trees as we dashed through Washington Square Park.

Autumn in New York is a glorious time of year, but this particular day was exceptional. As late as we were I ran up to and then around a giant maple tree. Facing west, I caught a glimpse of the setting sun shining through its branches.

"Snap out of it," Quinn screeched, hitting me on the back. "You have Manhattan waiting for you."

Always careful to dress seasonally and keeping the décor of the Pup Room in mind for this event, I had picked out a pumpkin, short sleeve button-down shirt and dark brown corduroy pants. I had made a quick trip to the gym earlier in the day and like magic, the shirt and pants knew exactly where to drape and where to cling.

For shoes I wanted something different and hip but not too youthful. And surprisingly I found the most luscious pair of chocolate suede slip-ons with a classic loafer design in one of those trendy gay clothing boutiques on Eighth Avenue in Chelsea. Walking in them felt like I was tiptoeing on a cloud.

Unfortunately, as I raced to catch up to Quinn, my comfy Euro slippers had absolutely no support and the shin splints started to burn up my legs as I pounded against the pavement. I knew that by the time we would make it to the restaurant my very expensive, cool imported shoes were going to break down and look like a geeky pair of cheap Hush Puppies.

Out of breath and drenched in sweat, Quinn and I stopped at the corner of Bleecker and Mott streets to calm each other down and check out the damage. Quinn ran his hand through his thick black mane of hair and felt something attached to the back of his head.

"Curtis, what is stuck in my hair?" he asked, spinning around.

I looked at it closely. "Oh geez," I exclaimed, reaching down to the side-walk for a stick.

"Oh geez what?" he cried.

"Just hold on and I'll get it out."

"Get what out?" he screamed, turning around. "Someone spit on me once from a high-rise. Actually, twice."

"Someone threw beer down on me." I brought the stick up to Quinn's head and carefully detached the culprit. It fell to the sidewalk. "It was really stuck."

"Is it gum?" squealed Quinn.

We both looked down at the ground and then stared at each other.

"A popsicle stick," I said with awe.

Quinn stepped on it and it stuck to his shoe. "Aw shit! How did that fucking thing get in my hair?"

We both looked up at the sky. He spun around, beating at the back of his head as I took a bottled water out of the drugstore shopping bag. Quinn put his head down and I gently rinsed water over it as he shook it out.

"You're fine," I said, trying to pull myself together. "Where's that compact mirror."

Quinn rifled through the bag.

"Curtis, I think we left it in the cab." He practically turned the bag upside down. "We left all the makeup in the cab."

I took a deep breath. "Then you'll have to be my eyes. How do I look?"

Quinn looked at my face and then quickly away.

"What's wrong?" He kept his head down, pretending to look for something in the bag. "I know you, Quinn Larkin, better than you know yourself. What is wrong with me?"

"Nothing," he mumbled as he took out a brush and stroked his hair aggressively. "Curtis, you look great. Your hair is perfect. The outfit is stunning. Now we've got to get in there before they all leave."

He picked up the bag and headed toward the party as I trailed behind trying to find a mint to pop into my mouth.

As we approached the Pup Room a group of four people were laughing as they were leaving.

"Odd that an author wouldn't show up for his own book signing," one of them said.

As they passed, all four gave me a very obvious double take. Quinn must have suspected that I saw this and jumped in with, "So, what are you going to order?"

I looked at him, confused. "Order?"

He pulled a tissue out of his coat pocket and wiped my face a bit. "Food? I'm starving," he said, fiddling with my face. "I think I'll have two entrees."

I grabbed the tissue and swatted his hand away from me. "This isn't a sit-down dinner."

"But there'll be food, right?" he asked in a panic.

"Yes, Quinn, you'll be fed. But probably by stylish waiters carrying silver trays of delicious tidbits."

"I hate tidbits. Sounds like dog food and there's never enough."

I looked at the tissue, which was now stained a burnt umber. "Is the makeup coming off?"

"You look fine," Quinn said as he padded me on the back and pushed me forward. "Now go in there and get them, tiger."

I removed my jacket, rearranged myself, took a deep breath, and walked toward the entrance where a very large and muscular man sat on a stool holding a folder. He got up and stood in my path as I reached for the door.

"Private party, sir," he said officiously. "Name?"

I looked at Quinn and laughed. "Curtis Jenkins."

He opened his folder and scoured the party list, slowly going over each name as if he had just learned how to read.

Quinn whispered to me, "Don't you think you should have had a little more worldly and accessible doorman checking in your party guests?"

"Sorry, sir," he said, shaking his head. "There's no Curtis Jenkins on the list."

"Of course I'm on the list, the party is for me."

"Maybe he doesn't know how to spell," Quinn said under his voice. "How about me? Quinn Larkin." The doorman went down the list very slowly.

"This is just perfect," I exclaimed.

"Here you are, Mr. Larkin. You can enter."

Quinn smiled and walked toward the door. I followed right behind him but as Quinn entered, the pea-brained muscle guard grabbed my arm.

"Sir, you're not on the list."

"But . . . Quinn!" I shouted as he entered without me.

The door shut as I pulled away from the bruiser and ran to the large picture window in the front of the restaurant. The room was jumping with everyone but me. I saw Quinn walking to the bar, obviously about to order a drink when I pounded on the glass. He looked over, gave me the OK signal, and waved to me, indicating to go back to the entrance.

By the time I had met up with Brutus again, Quinn was standing at the door with the restaurant manager. Feeling like a party crasher at my own party, finally I was allowed to pass and gave the lug the dirtiest look.

"Sorry, Mr. Jenkins," the manager said. "But better safe than sorry."

"Why don't you set up a metal detector while you're at it?" I suggested sarcastically.

"We were but your publishing house thought it might be a bit intimidating."

As I walked in Quinn said to me, "You should have them all fired."

The sexy lounge and bar area was packed with people. Every booth, every bar stool, every inch of space was occupied. I felt Quinn right behind me.

"This many people in one space, isn't this against some law?" I screamed to him over the deafening din of the crowd.

"Hope there's not a fire," he hollered back.

The Pup Room lounge was beautiful. Upon entering we were greeted with a huge floral arrangement set upon a marble table. The bar was made of teak wood and the walls were painted a buttery cream. Cocktail tables in the center of the room had been removed to allow more people to stand, however the outer perimeter was enveloped with luxurious semicircular leather banquettes. The lights were low and sexy and the room was happening.

Strategically placed around the lounge were giant eatable fruit topiaries, but the pièce de résistance was free-flowing La Caravelle Brut champagne. Both Quinn and I grabbed glasses of the bubbly as a waiter zoomed by, and then out of the corner of my eye I saw a gigantic easel with my face and the cover of the book on it. Piled high on a table next to it were countless copies of *101 Ways to Collide into Your Gay Soul Mate*. I wormed my way over to it, followed by Quinn, and we both stood there in silence.

After a moment, Quinn said, "I am so proud of you."

"What?" I screamed.

"I'm so fucking proud of you!"

I smiled at him as we toasted and downed our glasses of champagne. That's when I looked over his shoulder and saw her standing with her back to me, holding up the end of the bar.

Quinn saw the blood drain out of my quite colorful face and asked, "What's wrong?"

"What the hell is she wearing?" I asked as I shook my head.

"Who?"

I pointed to her.

"Oh Jesus," Quinn laughed.

My sixty-five-year-old mother was wearing a shimmery satin, chocolate knee-length, spaghetti strap, backless cocktail dress.

"That's cut way too low," I exclaimed disapprovingly.

"I think I can see her tailbone," Quinn added, smiling.

Her sandy-colored hair was tucked up into a classic French twist and she had her feet slipped into a pair of Vera Wang three-inch-heeled bronze evening sandals. She must have stopped by several cosmetic counters at Bloomingdale's on her way down here because instead of her usual makeup, which is strong enough to begin with, today she had on so much war paint she looked like a high-class call girl. In her hand she deftly balanced a full glass of her beverage of choice, a dry Tanqueray martini, up, with three olives. And from the looks of her movements and the dazzling hunk she was flirting with, I was sure it wasn't her first.

I made my way toward her when someone grabbed my arm.

"Well, fuck my ass."

I'd recognize that raspy, foul-mouthed, cigarette-and-alcohol voice any-where. It had to be Darcie Kaye, my editor.

Quinn left me and pushed and shoved to get to my mother as I said, "Darcie, dear."

"Where the hell have you been?"

I turned around and she gasped, falling back a step as she looked at my face.

"It's a long, pathetic story," I said apologetically as she grabbed my arm, dragging me to the bathroom.

Close to seventy, Darcie Kaye was brilliant at her craft and always im-peccably dressed. Today she was wearing her red-and-white checked Cha-nel powerhouse suit with her snow-white hair severely pulled back into a ponytail, topped off with a black velvet ribbon bow. And of course her black Gucci pumps matched her signature oversized black Gucci prescrip-tion sunglasses, which she wore day and night. Without a single wrinkle on her face due to the fact that the sun has never touched it, Darcie wore not a stitch of makeup except for Max Factor's lipstick number 948 called Flaming Red. Appropriate for this evening, I thought.

Her chic style, coupled with the great respect that the publishing in-dustry held for her, was always a shocking contrast to the filth of swear words that would fly out of her mouth. Think Joanne Woodward's class with Wanda Sykes's mouth.

"You shithead," she cursed as she burst through the ladies bathroom door with me trailing behind. Two young women, one Asian and one African-American, instinctually let out a shriek when they saw me, and it wasn't because I was a man.

I looked into the mirror and shrieked, too. "Oh my God!"

My face was the color of my pumpkin shirt. And not only was the hand-print visible, but the makeup had streaked due to my sweating.

"Girls," Darcie demanded, "what and how much foundation do you have?"

Fearful of her, the two women dug into their purses and gave her what they had.

"If we blend these two weasel piss colors together, maybe it will work," Darcie snorted.

The two women shrunk to the back wall as she prepared the makeup to cover my face. She then informed me that *G-Trend, Intuit, Glitter and Be Gay, Bi-Way, ManHOOD, Twinkle,* and *Hombre a Hombre* magazines as well as the GayTV television show were in the room impatiently waiting to interview me. Two reporters from prominent mainstream newspapers had already left. Flop sweat appeared on my forehead.

"Are you Curtis Jenkins?" asked the Asian girl.

"I'm afraid so," I whispered embarrassingly.

"Gosh, so now is this"—the African-American girl pointed to all of us—"all going to be in your next book?"

"At this rate he won't have another shit ass book to write, and stop spritzing, Curtis," Darcie ordered as she applied the cover-up. "I swear it's that friend Quinn of yours. Whenever he's around you get into trouble. Fuck, now I sound like your mother."

I laughed. "No you don't and my mother is a worse influence on me than Quinn."

Back out in the lounge Quinn made his way to my mother's backside and whispered into her ear, "I want that dress."

She twirled around with her libation in hand, not spilling a drop, and wrapped her arms around him. "Thank God you are here, Quinnie, this man is such a ninny."

"A gorgeous ninny," Quinn laughed. "Is he the guy?"

"No," my mother said as she pointed to the rust-colored circular booth in the far corner of the lounge. "He's the one in the middle with the red shirt."

Quinn started to salivate. "Mrs. J, you've outdone yourself. He's . . . he's . . ."

"Magnificent," my mother said, putting words into his mouth.

I'm sure Quinn wanted more than words put into his mouth as he squeezed by people to get a better look at the man. "What's his name?"

"Arash."

Quinn looked at her in disbelief.

She smiled. "I hear it's quite a common name in Iran."

"How does Arash say he got out of Iran?" Quinn winked at her.

"I ran!" they both hollered.

"I've nicked him the Persian Boy," my mother added proudly.

Arash was a mere twenty-two years old and was named after a celebrated hero and archer from Persian folklore. In truth, he was exactly what I pictured in my mind when I thought of Alexander the Great's eunuch lover, Bagoa. Jet-black curly hair, dark midnight eyes, flawless olive skin with an exquisite nose and lips as if an artist daintily painted them on him. The phrase that came to my mind was brooding luminescence. Add to that the body of a strong Greek boy and you had Arash.

My mother pulled out a wad of bills from her clutch and quickly shoved them into Quinn's pocket. "When it's time for the transaction, I think it will look better if you do it."

"How much did he cost?" Quinn asked.

She looked at her watch and calculated. "He's been here an hour and a half and at $350 per hour, at this moment he's costing a mere $525. Double time if we go past four hours."

"Damn, I should have been a prostitute."

"Escort, Quinn," my mother said, correcting him. "He's my son's escort."

"And does your son know?"

Mother looked toward the bar and changed the subject. "Barkeep! Get this brilliant young man his drink of choice." She pushed Quinn in the direction of the bar and then went after Arash as I emerged from the ladies' room with Darcie.

"I want you to talk to the reporter from GayTV first," Darcie said as she dabbed at my face. "She's a cunt but they have a large audience base and she's about to leave. I'll tell the others the order in which you'll meet them. Go be brilliant. I love you, you little shit." She patted my butt and then took off.

I bravely stood next to my beautiful poster and pile of books, girded my loins, and smiled for the camera.

"Mr. Jenkins, I'm Gloria Trumble from GayTV," she said, reaching out for a handshake as the film crew followed her. The aggressive yet diminutive woman grabbed my hand before I could shift a foundation-soaked tissue from my right hand to my left and squeezed it so hard makeup started to drip to the floor. She withdrew her hand and looked at it. I handed her a clean tissue and panicked to shift her attention as my right lopped-off index fingertip throbbed to the beat of my heart.

"It's a pleasure to meet you, Gloria. I love your show and watch it as often as possible."

She wiped her hand clean. "I don't have a show."

I stood there like a deer caught in headlights.

She laughed and actually tried to help me out. "I was a writer for *Lady-L* and I just joined GayTV as a reporter. This is my first assignment."

"Oh good, so you're a lesbian?"

This time she didn't try to help me out nor did she laugh. "No, I am not a lesbian. Do I have to be one to work for *Lady-L* or GayTV?"

"No. No! I mean I just assumed . . . but straight is cool, unless you're bi . . . or maybe you're a trannie?" I was getting myself in deeper. "Um, is the camera rolling?" I asked, feeling the rivers of perspiration gushing down from my armpits.

Gloria looked at her watch. "Let's just get to the interview. I'm running really late for my next assignment." The cameraman turned on his light. "So, Mr. Jenkins, tell us about your book, *101 Ways to Collide into Your Gay Soul Mate*."

I grabbed a copy and held it to my chest for support. "Well, my book is a practical guide to help the gay man find the man of his dreams."

"And how does one do that?"

Her question was just so blunt I was momentarily dumbfounded. "Well, um, that's why you need to read the book. I mean, not you, Gloria, but the gay man. But you could read it too if you like . . . whatever you are." I was choking. "Because it's not only a guide but . . . it's sprinkled with humorous personal anecdotes. Ah, dating and finding your mate and the trials and tribulations are universal. Whether it's a man with a man, a woman with a woman, or a man with a woman, everyone will enjoy *101 Ways to Collide into Your Gay Soul Mate*. I held the book out in front of me, smiled at it and then at the camera, and felt like I was doing a fucking third-rate infomercial.

There was a dead pause as Gloria took this all in. "OK well, I think we have enough. That's a wrap." The cameraman turned off his light.

"But I could tell you more," I suggested.

"Mr. Jenkins, I have enough. I've got to run but I'll let the crew keep filming. If I need more copy I'll call you by phone."

"Thank you, Gloria. And give my thanks to GayTV, too," I said, trying to see how far I could get my nose up her ass.

She turned and left as my mother appeared with Arash.

"Hello my little Chekhov," she said as she threw herself upon me. From over her shoulder I gazed at the beautiful man/boy, who managed to give me a weak smile. She unlatched herself from me. "You're wearing more makeup than I am."

"Don't even go there, Mother."

She grabbed the Persian Boy's hand. "Curtis, this is Arash, your book launch present from me." She pushed us together like those two little figurines of the boy and girl that when they get close enough, the magnet in their faces makes them kiss. Well, we didn't kiss. We just stood face to face holding our breaths.

"Allo," Arash said rather uncomfortably but in a surprisingly deep and sexy Middle Eastern accent.

I stepped back from him and looked at her. "What do you mean 'present?'"

She pulled me aside and tried to speak so he couldn't hear us. "Listen, you've just written the definitive book on how to find your lover and you are still freaking single. He's your partner for tonight. Get it?"

I was confused.

"Curtis, it will look better if they think you are with someone."

Quinn joined us sipping a cosmo, as I looked Arash up and down. "You really are something, Mother. You bought me a prostitute?"

Quinn nodded approvingly. "We came up with the idea together," he grinned as he stopped a waiter walking by with a tray of bite-size toast points covered with caviar and topped with a dollop of crème fraiche. Quinn sniffed one, made an awful face, and put it back. "I don't eat fish."

"Not prostitute," my mother whispered. "He's an escort for your evening."

"This is unbelievable," I said, escaping to find the next reporter to talk to. "You're all insane!"

My mother looked at me as I stormed off. "How could I have birthed such an ungrateful little brat?"

"Do you have any pigs in a blanket?" Quinn asked a waiter as he followed him back to the kitchen.

Darcie grabbed my arm and wanted me to meet Paul Hendren, a writer for *G-Trend* magazine. The mag described itself as being hip, smart, stylish, and perceptive. Heck, that's what I wanted to be.

"He's a massive cocksucker so suck up to him," Darcie demanded as she pointed me in the direction of his table. "Give each one of these bastards a couple of good bite lines and then scoot to the next. We have a lot of assholes to kiss."

"Mr. Hendren, it's a pleasure to meet you," I said, shaking his hand painfully and sitting down at his table.

"Please, call me Paul. My time is a little lean so let's get right down to the interview."

His time may have been lean but his body certainly wasn't. Giving him the once over I calculated his weight at no less than three hundred and fifty pounds.

"OK," I said, nodding. "You look great tonight, by the way."

He gave me a sour look from over his too-small-for-his-face aviator glasses and proceeded to tell me about his background and the type of article he'd like to write.

But my attention was diverted to Julian Zanetti, a tall, attractive, Argentinean male reporter for *ManHOOD* magazine. His trademark was his sexy dark brown hair that tickled the tops of his shoulders. Always dressed from head to toe in black, he had that stereotypical South American look of a matador and I wished he'd wave his red cape at me. I had always had a mad crush on him. Unfortunately, he had just discovered my mother and I strained to make out their conversation.

"Mrs. Jenkins, you look more like you could be Curtis's sister than his mother," Julian complimented, with pen and paper in hand.

"Why Julian, flattery will get you everywhere," my mother cooed as she sipped her martini. "Ask me anything. I'm an open book." She cackled a little too loudly.

"Was your son born to be a writer?"

"Hell, the only thing he was born to be was gay." She laughed, taking another swallow. "I honestly think he would have been a better clothing designer than a writer."

Julian knew he was on to something. "Do you not like your son's writing?"

"The first several pieces of work sucked but don't get me wrong, this book is fantastic. And even though it's nonfiction, you'll find me in it. I work my way into all of his writings. How couldn't I?" she giggled, flirting with him.

I scanned the room and saw Arash talking to a group of people and off in the distance Quinn was emptying a tray of bite-size meatballs into his mouth.

"Mr. Jenkins?" Paul Hendren shouted.

He pulled my attention back to him. "Yes?"

"I asked you what makes you an expert on finding your soul mate?"

I panicked. Expecting these questions, I had answers all ready but with the craziness of the day, the overcrowded room, my mother, and the hooker, I was a bit overwhelmed.

"I have explored many options for meeting gay men and tried all of them myself. From online dating to gay spiritual retreats." Suddenly, I thought of the right answer. "And in my book I describe in great detail the Tunick Technique."

"The what technique?" he asked, writing this all down.

"The late, great Dr. Magda Tunick was a brilliant and eccentric woman who taught me to use creative visualization to help find the man of my dreams."

"Fascinating," he exclaimed. "And have you?"

"Paul, I apologize but I just got here and I need to speak to quite a few other media people and I know your time is short, too. Please call me if you'd like to follow up with this interview. I promise I'll give you my undivided attention."

"Will do, Curtis," he said, but I could tell he felt a bit snubbed.

I got up and shook his hand lightly. "I'd even be happy to come down to your office, if you like."

I left Paul, having diverted his last question, and was working my way over to Arash when Ross Dillon popped up in front of me. Ross, who was now a contributing writer for *Twinkle* magazine, was a man whom I had dated maybe a year earlier for a very brief amount of time. And all I could remember about him was that at our first dinner, he had brought a clipboard and a list of questions. He proceeded to ask me things like "If you drink alcohol, how many glasses do you consume in a week, and have you ever contracted a sexually transmitted disease and if so, how long did you go before you had it treated?" He was a control freak and a jerk.

Not surprisingly, the blond-haired gym rat was holding a clipboard.

"Curtis Jenkins," he said smugly, "isn't this a surprise?" He looked at his list and made a big check mark.

"Hello Ross."

"So, let me ask you this."

I dropped my head knowing what he was going to hit me with.

"Who the hell are you to write the book on how to collide into your soul mate?"

I took a deep breath. "Ross, you have every right to ask that question."

"You bet I do. I don't see a man on your arm."

And that's when I pointed to my by-the-hour lover. "No, he's not on my arm. My boyfriend is talking to reporters as we speak."

Ross looked over at him. "The Middle Eastern guy?"

"Yes." I hesitated a moment, struggling to remember his ridiculous name. "Awash."

"Hmmmm," Ross said suspiciously. "I swear that kid advertises in our escort section."

Thank God Quinn appeared. I grabbed him and with his mouth full of cheese balls I pushed him into Ross's face. "Quinn Larkin meet Ross Dillon."

I left them and worked my way over to my hooker.

Quinn caught up to me. "Curtis, your mother and I had your best interests at heart."

"It's OK. I see your point now and I'm going to use it."

A group of gay reporters and the GayTV television crew surrounded Arash. They were all mesmerized either by his looks or by what he was saying.

"I don't read. I don't like to read. But I did just skim through this book and it's pretty stupid," he confessed to Julian Zanetti.

Only hearing bits and pieces of what he said, I squeezed by more people trying to get to him.

Another reporter asked, "How long have you and Curtis Jenkins been lovers?"

He looked at his watch. "About an hour and three-quarters. Not sure how long we'll be together. Can't imagine he makes much money and I'm pretty expensive."

I entered the literary circle and slipped my arm into his. "Here's my man," I said as I strained to kiss his cheek with affection. "Hey, Abash."

"Arash," he said, pulling away.

I laughed nervously as he continued.

"He makes useless suggestions and pathetic attempts at humor."

"Who does?" I asked even more nervously as the reporters' pens were flying.

Ignoring me, Arash continued. "And the harder Curtis Jenkins tries to be funny, the more embarrassing the book becomes."

I stepped back and turned to Quinn. "I'm going to castrate him."

"And the Persian Boy will officially be the Eunuch," Quinn declared.

"Quinn, why is he being so hostile?"

"He's jealous. He wants all the attention."

Julian turned to me. "And this is your lover, Curtis?"

"Not anymore." I looked at Arash and said, "You're fired!"

I whispered to Quinn, "This is half your fault. Get rid of him now."

I desperately had to grab Julian's attention as Quinn escorted my escort to the front door and started whipping out hundred dollar bills.

"Julian, I just love your writing and have been a huge fan of your work for years," I gushed, looking up at him dreamily.

"Thank you and congratulations on what looks like is going to be a great success," he said, a little too businesslike. "I hear that in this book as well as your works of fiction, a strong mother figure often appears. Is your mother a dominant influence in your life?"

Reporters' ears perked up as the GayTV camera came in for a close-up.

"I wouldn't call her dominant but yes, my mother is a great source of . . ."

Suddenly, my words trailed off as I looked across the room and thought I saw her on top of another person on a banquette.

"Curtis?" Julian asked, bringing me back.

I looked at him and started my sentence again. "My mother is a great source of outrageous material." I looked at the reporters hanging on my every word and then looked back at the banquette. It had to be my mother because no one else was wearing that dress, and at this point it was inching a little too far up on her hips for comfort.

"Please, would you all excuse me for just one moment? Please? I'm sorry. I'll be right back."

I bowed out from the group and ran over to her.

"Mother," I whispered urgently while pulling her skirt back down. "What do you think you are doing?"

She finally came up for air and looked at me with a shit-eating grin on her face. "I'm kissing Harrie."

From underneath her emerged a petite and pretty female. I was speechless.

"Harriet, do you mind that I've nicked you?" my mother asked.

"You can call me anything you like," Harrie said eagerly. "Just make sure you call me."

And with that, they were lip-locked again. To tell you the truth, it didn't shock me that my mother was making out with another woman. Recently I had come to grips with her very open sexuality, but did she have to share it with all of New York City's gay media and at my book signing?

"Mother, please! Everyone is watching," I said, exasperated. "Please stop."

Quinn ran to my side as my mother pulled away from Harrie, rearranging her dress. "Curtis, I can't. I read your book."

"And so did I," chirped Harrie, flashing a dazzling smile of perfectly white teeth as if she were auditioning for a toothpaste commercial.

"God, she's perky," Quinn said critically.

Harrie tossed her long, curly, crimson hair behind her shoulders and looked right at me with her emerald eyes. "Obviously, if two people in a room have read your book and the stars are aligned, they won't collide into each other . . ."

My mother finished her sentence. "They'll crash!" They started to kiss again.

"Someone call in the U-Haul," Quinn laughed.

I shook my head. "But who is this person?"

Mother managed to pull away. "Harrie," she said, touching her cheek tenderly, "is the entertainment director for a gay and lesbian cruise line. Isn't that a hoot?"

The extremely effervescent lesbian with the aerobic instructor's body stood up, straightened her elegant black Armani tuxedo suit, and shook my hand. "Curtis, it's an honor to meet you and I loved your book."

"Oh?" I said smiling. I am a glutton for sycophancy.

"Yes," she continued, "and on behalf of ASAP Cruises we'd like to book you on our ship."

"Really?" I asked as Quinn grabbed my arm.

"Yes, we could do a book signing," suggested Harrie. "All expenses paid and you can bring a guest. We sail from New York City going to the western Caribbean for a New Year's Eve, ten-night cruise."

"Yes!" exclaimed Quinn, jumping up and down.

Harrie continued. "If you like, I'll have my people call your people."

And with that, she sat down and started kissing my mother again.

"OK. Wow. Sure. That's great," I said, having chosen clever and descriptive words to express myself.

"We're going on a cruise! A New Year's Eve cruise!" Quinn sang happily, plopping down on the banquette next to the girls.

Numb, I walked away from all of them very slowly and looked at the long line of people holding my book, waiting for me to sign them. I brought my bandaged, nonfunctional index finger up to my lips and kissed it to make it better.

Magically, Darcie appeared with a pen and gently placed it into my right hand, and walked me over to my admirers as I gracefully grabbed another glass of champagne from a waiter's tray with my left.

"Don't worry, Curtis," she said. "Later you'll need to thank your mother." I looked at her, confused, as she continued. "Trust me, because of her, this event will be carried in every gay rag and on every gay Web site across the nation. All press is good press."

She sat me down at a table draped with crisp white linen, kissed my cheek with great affection, and then stepped back.

I took a deep breath and felt an incredible rush of calmness. I thought of the insanity of the past three hours and gazed across the Pup Room. Like a bad rash that wouldn't go away, I could see Arash talking to Julian out on the street and pointing accusingly at me through the front window. Inside, the party was still going strong. The Gay TV cameraman who was filming guests dancing in the middle of the lounge had swung around and zoomed in tightly on my mother, Harrie, and Quinn giggling side by side on the banquette.

I shook my head thinking I wouldn't have wanted this crazy day to have turned out any other way. I smiled and autographed the first book painfully with my third-grade signature.

THREE

GREAT BLISTERS, SISTER!

Darcie was right. My mother was more effective than any marketing strategy Carrington Press could have come up with. From *Splash Night Life* magazine in Fort Meyers to the *Emerald City Journal* gay cable television show in Seattle to *QX Magazine* in London to Lisa Chiat's *Cape Talk* radio show airing out of Cape Town, word of *101 Ways to Collide into Your Gay Soul Mate*, the book launch, and all its shenanigans had gone global.

I sent a copy of the book tucked into magnificent fruit baskets to every industry person who attended the event. They were chock full of seasonal fruit, a box of biscotti, chocolates, and a bottle of wine, all punctuated with flowers and greens.

I even picked up a copy of *Twinkle*, perused the escort section, found Arash's ad and Web site, and sent him a thank-you note. He replied rather tersely, saying, "I'm dating Julian Zanetti." Reminding myself of karmic boomerang, I wished them both good luck.

And to personally show my gratitude to my mother, I dropped by T. Anthony, Ltd. and bought her their woven leather shoulder bag in a hunter green and hid inside of it a bottle of her favorite perfume, Chanel No. 5.

Just two months earlier she had made a huge change in her life. With my dad having passed quite a few years ago and brother Stewie and sister Kelly off leading their own lives, my mother felt lonely living in our huge house in Bremerton. All of her friends had moved out of Westchester and she was spending most of her waking hours attending to the property and spending way too much money on its massive upkeep. So, on a whim she put our 1920s Tudor-style seven bedroom, five full bath, two-and-a-half-acre property with dilapidated tennis court and cracked cement Olympic-size swimming pool with its own three-bedroom house, on the market for an extremely over inflated price of three million and shockingly the first couple who walked through bought it.

Mother sold some of her furniture, donated the rest to Angel Street thrift store, packed her bags, and set her sights on Manhattan. With a new lease on life and an expensive mortgage on a new apartment, she relocated to a renovated building dating back to the late 1800s located on West Street between 13th and 14th Streets. Originally a mill factory prior to being left abandoned, the new owners gutted everything and created loftlike apartments that she said had phenomenal views of the Hudson River.

It was 8:00 A.M. on the Tuesday after my book launch when I took a cab downtown from my Upper West Side apartment. Before entering my mother's building I stopped and surveyed the building sitting west of it. The sign said THE LIBERTY INN MOTEL. There was something about the three-story building that seemed so familiar and yet I don't think I had ever noticed it before.

I shrugged my shoulders and welcomed the warm rush of air as I entered her massive lobby, which had huge black-and-white photographs of the building taken when it must have just opened as a mill. A very young doorman decked out in a stereotypical uniform greeted me from behind a mahogany desk.

"Can I help you, sir?"

"I'm going up to apartment 5A."

He smiled and winked at me. "A friend of Mrs. J.'s?"

I was slightly offended. "No. I'm her son."

Realizing that he had overstepped his boundaries he quickly snapped back into professional mode and dialed her apartment with great seriousness. "Mrs. J.? Arnold here." He looked at his watch. "No, it's not him. It's your son." He listened to my mother and then looked at me quizzically. "Your name, sir?"

"Oh, for God's sake, give me that phone." I grabbed it out of his hand. "Mother, tell him to let me up."

Arnold took the phone from me, nodded, and then gestured to the elevator. I could tell this was going to be one of those days.

I knocked on her door and waited patiently for a full four minutes and thirty-seven seconds till she finally opened it.

"Good morning, Curtis," she whispered as she enveloped me with her purple satin bathrobe.

"You're not ready," I said, noticing that she didn't have a stitch of makeup on.

"What time do we have to be at the theater?" she yawned.

I looked at my watch and said, "Considering we'll probably get caught in the morning rush, we should leave here in about fifteen minutes. Quinn wants us to meet Ann backstage before her second show."

"Do you want a drink before we do this?"

I did but said, "No." I walked into her apartment and was stunned by the sheer beauty of it. Open and sleek, it had concrete polyurethaned floors, exposed industrial beams, fifteen-foot-high ceilings, and an entire wall of windows facing west. The view of the Hudson River and New Jersey beyond was spectacular.

"Mother, this is just such a contrast to Bremerton."

"Thank God," she said, sipping a glass of champagne. "You sure you won't change your mind." She held out a fluted glass and started to pour.

"You are the worst influence on me," I said, laughing. "I can't get high, I have to write today."

"This isn't to get high, it's to give us the strength." We clinked glasses, took a sip, and I handed her her goodies.

"What is this?" she asked in a little girl voice.

"A thank-you from me."

"For what?" she asked, opening up the tissue-stuffed T. Anthony box.

"For being you," I said as I kissed her cheek. "I'm number one best seller on Amazon in gay nonfiction."

She stepped back and looked at me. "My baby is a star." She ripped open the box and took out the purse. "What urbane sophistication."

I frowned at her choice of words. "Look what's inside."

She opened the shoulder bag, discovered the perfume, and held it up to her chest. "Next to mother's milk." I laughed as she embraced me. "Thank you, dear."

"You're welcome. Now go put your face on and get dressed."

"All I'm going to wear is Chanel No. 5," she giggled as she ran into her bedroom.

"I sure hope Ann Vermillion has more on than that." I walked over to the wall of glass and looked out at the view.

Two floors below us and across the street was that three-story building I had noticed as I entered her building. What was it that made it look so familiar? Down on the street I saw two young men stop in front of the place, kiss briefly but passionately, and then continue on their way hand in hand. Then it dawned on me. Oh my God, that was the Anvil! Of all the clubs I went to in my early years in New York City, the Anvil always stood out in my mind as the definition of unrestrained self-indulgent behavior.

Downstairs at the Anvil were dark tunnels and passageways with things going on that one couldn't even fantasize about. I only went down there once, and just by walking through while fully clothed I got gonorrhea.

I glanced back down onto the street and saw an innocent-looking young straight couple who were obvious out-of-towners climb out of cab and rush into the Liberty Inn Motel with their floral print luggage. Little did they know that they would probably be making love in the same space that some hungry gay soul had had his first fisting. The Anvil—debauchery at its best. Thank goodness it was a thing of the past considering my mother had just moved in across the street. She would have given them a run for their money.

She emerged from her bedroom wearing a black turtleneck, black leggings, and black ballet slippers. An Hermès scarf was wrapped over her head and tied under her chin and she had slipped on a gigantic pair of Jackie O. sunglasses.

She smiled, grabbing her keys. "I'm ready."

"Hello Ann-Margaret," I laughed. "Why are you dressed like that?"

We dashed out of the apartment and grabbed the elevator. "I have a Pilates lesson right after this and then a Rolfing session with Umberto."

I flinched at the thought of Rolfing. "Then I have lunch with this really fascinating woman I met in my painting class."

"Painting class?" I asked as we entered the lobby.

Mother veered off to Arnold's desk where he was holding a copy of today's paper for her and they exchanged a wink that felt just a little too intimate. My stomach said it was happy that I had skipped breakfast.

"I took a beginners watercolor class at the Learning Annex and my teacher said I had talent."

"Mother, you can't even draw a stick figure."

"I know. The class is not aimed at depicting objects. Instead they focus on internal structure and form. Curtis, I'm abstract," she exclaimed with delight as we exited her building.

That I did know. "I have no idea how or where we are going to get a cab down here."

My mother took two steps forward and stood in front of a shiny black Lincoln Town Car Sedan. The driver hopped out and opened the passenger door for her.

"Good morning, Mrs. J.," smiled the large bodyguard-type driver.

"Morning, Paul. This is my son Curtis."

Paul looked me up and down. "Son? He looks more like your brother."

I wasn't sure how to take that.

Mother touched my arm. "Car service, dear. It's the only way to do New York." She slid in as I slowly followed, shaking my head. "Curtis, tell him where we're going."

She opened the newspaper as I said, "41st Street between Seventh and Eighth Avenues. The Gentlemen's Desire theater?"

"*Puss N'Boots?*" Paul asked, looking at me with a sly grin through the rearview mirror. I nodded. "My grandfather used to go to that show. That stripper still alive?"

"Just barely," I replied.

"Oh my gosh!" my mother cried out. She pushed the back cover of the newspaper into my face. "Look."

I grabbed the paper from her and held it far enough away so I could read it. But before I could focus on any print, it was his picture that caught my eye. It's an odd and disconcerting feeling when you feel your heart flutter and sink simultaneously. And my mother was sensitive enough to observe both.

I managed to smile as I gazed at Dell's beautiful face. It was a group photo taken in uniform of him and three of his teammates.

"Was he traded to another team?" my mother asked quietly.

I didn't know. I was still looking at his face. Earlier that spring I had collided head-on into an accordion bus, literally, and Dell was the dashing young man from Paris, Texas, who came to my rescue. He was so kind but the timing was so wrong. We actually met serendipitously again shortly after that incident and dated successfully but much too briefly. Unfortunately, Dell—who is a professional baseball player in the minor leagues—was traded to a team out in New Mexico called none other than the Albuquerque Isotopes.

I'm not sure if Dell was "the one" but he truly was the nicest man I had met in years. I even flew out to Albuquerque a couple of times to see him and considered the possibility of a long-distance relationship, but Dell had been there and done that and he knew it didn't work for him. I brought up the idea of moving out there but he was quick to remind me that he could be traded the next season and then I might have to traipse after him to another city.

My mother sat uncharacteristically quiet as I opened up the newspaper and read the article. Each minor league ball team is affiliated with a major team, Dell's being the Florida Marlins. And he was right. Yet again, he was changing cities. I closed the paper and looked out of the car as we drove uptown on Eighth Avenue and ironically passed a sports club.

During the last phone call we had, Dell had encouraged me to date other men. He himself had admitted to meeting what sounded like *the* guy.

"He's doing great, Mother. He's been named shortstop of the year and is graduating to the majors and joining the Marlins."

She smiled warmly at me as I felt my eyes well up. I let the emotion wash through me before speaking. "He met someone who works for Marsha Mason out in Santa Fe."

"The actress?"

"Yes. She has an organic herbal medicinal farm called Resting in the River and he's the head horticulturalist."

She looked out of her window but I could hear her smiling so hard. She held her tongue and let me say it when I was ready to.

After a very dramatic pause, I turned to her and said, "The farmer and the Dell."

We both burst out into laughter as the car pulled up to the Gentlemen's Desire theater, one block south of Times Square. We had put off seeing Ms. Vermillion in action for so long that I thought Quinn was about to disown us. We both wanted to encourage and support him but nothing prepared us for what was about to happen. At least it took my mind off of Dell.

Paul opened the passenger door for my mother as I climbed out of the other side. Nestled between a fabric and trimmings supply store and a national seafood chain restaurant that I'm proud to say I've never eaten at, was the Gentlemen's Desire theater.

Constructed in 1895 it was originally a vaudeville theater called the Avalon. Out on the street if you looked past the decades of soot, grime, and decay you could still see remnants of the ornate wrought iron decorations, marble gargoyles, and stained-glass windows that framed the entrance to this once magnificent building. The theater's overhang, which in its glory days would have shouted out with self-importance *The Avalon Extravaganza* now whimpered with embarrassment, *Puss N'Boo s.* Some charming soul had blackened out the letter *t* and no one had bothered to fix it.

"Why the hell are we seeing a strip show at 10:00 A.M.?" my mother asked as we searched for the entrance to the back stage.

I found a metal security door that had STAGE DOOR written on it and pressed the buzzer. "Did you want to make the 8 o'clock performance?"

Disapprovingly, she made a *tish* sound from the back of her throat.

"I didn't think so, Mother. We're on Ann's time. We're halfway through her day."

The security door clicked open and we carefully worked our way down the back alley, dodging dumpsters full of trash, when Quinn popped his head out of the stage door and waved to us.

"Welcome!" he shouted.

"We're here to see *Puss N'Boos,*" I meowed.

"Come in, come in," Quinn said, gushing with pride. "I can't believe you both finally made it."

I bowed, allowing my mother to pass first but as she stepped over a black garbage bag, it moved.

"Aaaaaaaah!" she screamed as she fell into Quinn's arms. "For crying out loud, what's in there?"

"Don't worry," he said. "I checked earlier. It's not a baby."

A baby rat, I thought to myself as I hopped over it.

Quinn helped my mother up the stairs to the stage door. "Mrs. J., I love your rehearsal costume. Wait till Ann gets a load of you. Maybe she'll teach you how to do a trailer."

My mother caught her breath. "What the hell is a trailer?"

"It's the strut you do before a strip. She taught me how to do it." Quinn held his shoulders back, pushed his pelvis forward, kept his chin down, slightly bent his knees, and then strutted. Think of Groucho Marx imitating Catherine Zeta-Jones attempting to execute Fosse-like choreography in the movie *Chicago.*

He trailered us down a dank and dreary hallway lit sporadically with bare lightbulbs. Down on the far right of the passageway was an ancient call board—with notices posted on it that were so old the print was illegible—and on the left, Ms. Vermillion's star dressing room. She may have been the star but the star on her door had lost two points and now resembled a broken origami bird.

Quinn stood in front of Ann's door till we caught up with him.

"You're gonna love her," he said beaming as he knocked on her door. "Annie?" We heard something but it didn't sound like a hello. He knocked harder. "Annie!" Quinn cracked her door open and a cloud of cigarette smoke bellowed out.

We allowed the air to clear a bit before we entered. Her entire dressing room appeared to be decorated in sepia. Or maybe the tar and nicotine had just stained everything a piss yellow. Plastered on the walls were decades of postcards, 8 × 10 glossies of Ann, and scores of telegrams full of well wishes for opening nights during her amazing fifty-year tenure at the Gentlemen's Desire. Her makeup table supported dozens of jars and bottles of antique cold creams and lotions. At the far end of the room was a simple divan, except that the red velvet fabric had split up the center. And set up beside it was a dressing screen with the image of the Venus de Milo crudely painted upon it.

A poof of smoke rose into the air from behind it and Ann tried to clear her throat. Quinn smiled at both of us as she hacked even harder.

"She's going to cough up a lung," I whispered.

"What was that?" Ann croaked.

Quinn walked to the screen, glanced at her, and then quickly turned his head away to us as if he had just witnessed a horrible accident. "My friend Curtis is here with his mother and he just said that he thought coffee must keep you young."

All three of us breathed a sigh of relief.

"Coffee enemas, three times a day," she yelped.

I cringed as I noticed three empty coffee cups strewn about her dressing table.

Not knowing what to say next we stood there till Ann broke the silence. "You gotta swell setup."

None of us knew what that meant. Suddenly, my mother screamed and pointed to the Venus de Milo. "The eyes! They're moving!"

Quinn laughed. "She's watching you." He picked up a large plastic bucket full of body makeup and a paintbrush and went behind the screen with Ann.

"A swell setup is burlesque for you got a good figure, doll," Ann explained.

My mother touched her body and curtsied as I laughed at her odd behavior.

"Kids, I don't want you to see me now, it'll spoil the illusion. My best angle is from out . . ."

Out of town, I thought.

". . . in center orchestra, row H. Shit that's cold."

Quinn stuck his head out from behind the screen, showing us his paintbrush dipped in the body paint. "Got my work cut out for me."

"From the sound of it, she's going to need spackle," I whispered.

"What was that?" she screamed.

Mother crossed her eyes at me and chimed in with, "Do you need some sparkle?"

Ann looked through the Venus's eyeholes again. "Great blisters, sister."

Wide-eyed, we glanced at each other as Quinn came to the rescue. "Blisters are your breasts."

I touched mine and said, "Thank you" as I walked over to a wall and looked at one of the many pictures of Ann. An 8 × 10 that dated back to 1962 caught my attention, and I motioned Mother to come look at it. She was decked out in a black-sequined fishtailed strapless gown hemmed with a pile of tulle. She had her then black hair piled high upon her head and was done up in exquisite makeup. Ann could have been a movie star. She autographed this picture with the inscription: BURLESQUE IS THE TAIL END OF SHOW BUSINESS — LOVE, ANN VERMILLION.

"That's it, Quinn. Get it all the way up in there," Ann said appreciatively.

Mother and I looked at each other with fear.

"Damn, the asbestos was down during the 8 o'clock show."

Quinn poked his head out. "Means the audience wasn't responding." He looked at his watch and suggested that we head on out to the theater and he'd meet us in the orchestra section. "Any place you like," he smiled. "It's open seating."

"Nice to meet you, Ms. Vermillion!" I shouted.

There was a bit of rustling going on behind her screen. "Quinn, where's my gadget?" she barked.

"Yes, Ann," my mother added. "The pleasure was all mine."

"Quinn, slap that gadget on my jacuzzi."

Mother and I tiptoed out of the dressing room and after I closed the door, I asked her, "How old do you think she is?"

"Older than dirt," Mother giggled.

"I heard that!" Ann screeched from her dressing room.

We ran down the hallway till we met a stage manager with the worst case of bowlegs. He allowed us to walk onto the stage before the house opened and it was amazing to stand there and look out at this awe-inspiring theater. The stage manager said that when the theater first opened it had the finest toilets and resting rooms and offered the purest artesian well water. He showed us how to get down into the audience, where we discovered carved dark wood paneling, glass pilasters, and I'm certain, Tiffany stained-glass windows adorning the side and back walls of the orchestra level. Hopefully, with the renovation and restoration of Time Square theaters, the Avalon would be saved and brought back to its one-of-a-kind splendor also.

Doors to the theater had just opened and Mother and I peeked down into the orchestra pit before anyone else arrived and spotted a lone, upright piano. Wanting to see Ann from her best angle, we counted up to row H. The theater was so damp and musty I thought I was going to have arthritis before the show was over. Our feet stuck to the floor as we shuffled across our row.

"Curtis, what's that smell? Chlorine?"

I knew exactly what it was but didn't have the guts to tell her as we sat down in the two middle seats. Immediately, we both stood up, feeling our bottoms. We winced at each other as we felt the moistness.

"I'm sure it's just water," I said unconvincingly as I felt surrounding seats. "They're all damp." We tentatively sat back down.

Just then another patron arrived. Carrying two huge shopping bags filled with more shopping bags, I pegged him for about seventy years old. He waddled all the way down to the front row and sat just off center to the left.

Mother laughed. "You can tell that seat has his name on it."

Quinn appeared from backstage and dashed out to join us. "You all ready?"

I looked around the theater as my mother asked, "Don't you want to wait for the other theatergoers?"

Quinn pointed to the man in the first row. "Mr. Rosenblatt is here. It's a good house."

She and I gave each other a glance. The lights went down and a follow spot hit an elderly woman in the orchestra pit.

"That's Babes La Tour," Quinn informed us. "She used to do a high-wire strip act but then she developed oscillopsia."

"That sounds like a venereal disease for some neurotic toy dog," I laughed.

"It's actually quite tragic."

Mother and I switched to our serious faces.

"Head trauma from a fall off the wire and now she has balance problems and her eyes are locked into every movement of her head. She told me that she sees life through an erratic handheld camera. Sometimes she gets real excited playing and slips off the piano stool so I run down and help her back up."

"Poor thing," my mother whispered.

"Babes has a foot-operated drum and cymbals. She's the entire orchestra," Quinn added proudly.

We clapped as she bowed out toward us, lost her balance, and then plopped down onto her stool. Babes La Tour started pounding the keys with a song called "Viva Burlesque." It had a strong left-hand bass beat that complemented the thumping of the drum and her right hand tinkled and teased the keys in rhythm to the cymbals. She was actually quite good. The firewall curtain went up on stage revealing a huge swag velvet curtain with giant gold tassel trim. The music shifted to a sexy vamp and the follow spot hit stage left.

It was obvious that Babes La Tour had come to the end of her music, paused, and then started playing from the beginning again as we all patiently waited for the big moment. At the tail end of the second round of the intro, I saw a leg. Not necessarily a sexy leg, but it was working. Ann was holding onto the side curtain, hiding her face from us, and managed to wrap her leg around it. But as she tried to slide the leg down the drape to the floor it was clear to all of us that the heel of her stiletto was caught in the fringe.

We held our breath as she struggled on one foot to release the shoe. Even Babes slowed down the music as she watched the ordeal unfold. Once her foot was free, the music picked up happily and Ann disappeared altogether. And then in a flash, she was on stage.

Quinn was sitting on the edge of his seat, blinded with enthusiasm while we looked on aghast.

"My God, she's really old," my mother whispered.

I shook my head. "Bless her soul."

Wide-eyed with disbelief we watched as Ann Vermillion held number one of her seven signature poses: knees bent, right hand on right knee, left arm stretched up, back arched and chin forward, huge smile. She was wearing red thigh-high Naugahyde boots, red opera gloves, and a red bustier. Cat ears sat on top of a rat's nest of white hair and whiskers were glued on her face. She was a dead ringer for Bette Davis's twin sister—at the end of her life.

"I applied each of those whiskers. Doesn't she look great?" Quinn asked.

"She's definitely a puss in boots," I said, looking at Mother for agreement but she was speechless, still staring with her mouth open.

Ann pulled herself out of her pose as we clapped. She acknowledged Mr. Rosenblatt and us and then shuffled a few steps to her right. Surprisingly, the stage manager appeared from the opposite wing wearing a large black trench coat and a fedora hat.

"Watch this," Quinn said grabbing my arm. "This is so great."

Ann rolled down one of her opera gloves and then struggled to get it off her hand. The stage manager patiently waited as Babes started the section of music over again. Finally, the glove dropped to the stage and Ann looked away as if not knowing what to do. The stage manager ran to Ann and quickly went down on one knee as he picked up the glove.

"I beg your pardon?" the stage manager said politely as he handed it back to her.

Ann took a huge beat, looked down at him, rested into her right hip, and eventually said, "What are you begging for? You're old enough to ask for it."

"Yes!" hollered Quinn, rising to his feet and clapping as the stage manager bowed and exited stage left.

Mother and I caught on and started to clap too. Even Mr. Rosenblatt whistled, although he seemed semidistracted by a layer of newspaper that he had placed on his lap.

"Now the show really begins," Quinn warned us.

Babes La Tour switched to a song called "Las Vegas Strip!" and that's exactly what Ann started to do. She slid the other glove off with no problem, twirled, and attempted to send it out into the audience. Sadly, it landed about a foot in front of her. Then her hands went to her corset but it was obvious that her fingers just weren't going to obey today.

Frustrated, she worked her way back to stage left and vamped, facing us as magically a pair of hands coming out of an oversized black trench coat appeared and started to unzip her corset. Without warning it fell to the stage, revealing Ann clad only in bright red pasties and a red G-string.

I heard my mother gasp. I had stopped breathing. Quinn was in heaven.

"She lets me put her gadget on," he smiled as I looked at him, confused. "Her G-string."

Ann began to bump to the music and with each bump she limped closer to center stage. Mr. Rosenblatt jumped to his feet and attempted to throw a dollar bill at her, however it fell short and drifted down into the pit, resting on Babes La Tour's piano keys. She looked up over her shoulder, almost lost her balance, and smiled at him. He sat back down and placed the newspaper back over his lap.

Once Ann was center stage she caught her breath and then began to pirouette. She spun slowly and crookedly and as the music began to swell so did what was underneath Mr. Rosenblatt's newspaper.

Like an unseasoned ice skater she came out of her spin facing the back wall of the stage. She turned around, lost her balance as she walked down stage, and with the follow spot glaring in her eyes, she promptly fell into the orchestra pit. Before anyone of us could register what we saw, we heard an ear-piercing crash of the cymbals followed by a dead thump of the drum. Then silence.

Mother, Quinn, and I all screamed with horror. Shocked, even Mr. Rosenblatt jumped to his feet, forgetting that his pants were down around his ankles. We all rushed to the edge of the pit as the stage manager hung over the stage. Ann's fall had knocked out Babe's piano light. Neither of them was moving.

≳ ≲

I called 911 and the two ambulances that arrived wanted to take the girls to St. Doris, but I knew that was more of a morgue than a hospital so I demanded they be taken up to St. Matthews on Tenth and 59th. Mr. Rosenblatt, with tears streaming down his face, talked the EMS crew into allowing him to travel in Ann's ambulance, holding her hand all the way. The stage manager went in Babes's while Quinn, Mother, and I jumped into Mother's car and Paul followed them up to the hospital.

It was torturous enough to have to sit endlessly in the emergency waiting room for their prognoses, but added to that, Mr. Rosenblatt would not calm down.

"What if Ann can't dance again?" he screamed.

Mother put her arm around him. "Let's cross that bridge when we come to it."

"What if Ann is crippled?" he cried.

The stage manager patted his back gently. "Then we will get her the best physical therapy possible."

He grabbed Quinn's arm. "What if she's dead?"

"Mr. Rosenblatt," he said, "if she were dead, they wouldn't be taking this long."

He then spun around to me. "What if she's disfigured?"

I had no response.

Thankfully, a doctor appeared and Mr. Rosenblatt ran to him. "Is she? Is she?"

"She's doing just fine." Mr. Rosenblatt threw his arms around him. "Luckily, her fall was broken by Ms. La Tour. Ms. Vermillion has a fractured hip, but she's going to be OK."

"Can I see her, please?" Mr. Rosenblatt begged.

"Just for a moment."

He dashed into her room.

The doctor looked at the rest of us. "Ms. La Tour is another story."

For a moment we all looked at one another with shock.

The doctor continued. "When Ms. Vermillion's body crashed into Ms. La Tour, the impact must have bashed the piano player's head into the upright. It took thirty-two stitches to close up her forehead." Mother, Quinn, and I grabbed onto one another. "The imbalance and eye disorder that she suffered from was rare enough, but even rarer is that the trauma to her skull due to the fall cured her of her oscillopsia."

From down the corridor we heard "Hallelujah! Praise the Lord! Amen!" Skipping toward us with her entire head bandaged was none other than Babes La Tour herself.

"Oh my God!" I exclaimed. "She's alive!"

Babes was hopping from one foot to the other. "I'm purged! Praise Ann Vermillion! I'm purged of the dizzies!"

Mother grabbed my arm. "This is a miracle."

The stage manager hugged me. "Vermillion cured La Tour!"

"Hallelujah!" hollered Babes.

"And Ann's alive!" I declared. "Broken, but alive."

Mother, the stage manager, and I all embraced Babes as Quinn slumped into a chair.

"But I'm fucked," he whispered.

I pulled away from the group hug. "Why, what's wrong?"

"Curtis, I'm out of a job."

FOUR

LOOK BACK IN ANGER

Still job hunting and having much too much time on his hands, Quinn dragged me downtown to a secret rendezvous to meet husbands but didn't tell me how or where.

"Where are you taking me?"

Quinn turned left on Hudson Street. "Almost there." He pointed to a building on the left, midway down the block. "Here we go." He opened the door for me to an elementary school building. "Welcome to *Petticoat Junction*!"

We walked in and there were close to a hundred people, mostly men, all paired up in groups of eight, square dancing. I immediately did an allemande-left and tried to do sa do out the door but Quinn caught the sleeve of my coat and dragged me back.

"Fucking square dancing? Quinn, this is an all-time low for us."

"We're here for the men, not the dancing."

The perimeter of the school cafeteria had onlookers sitting in chairs who were probably ambushed suckers like myself.

"Quinn, are they gay?"

"Yes. They're called the Washington Squares Square Dancers."

I shook my head. "Square they certainly are."

"Come on. It's an open house and I was told by a very reputable source that these guys are really nice."

He pulled me into the room, kicking and screaming. It turns out that there are hundreds of gay square-dancing groups not just throughout the country but all around the world. And periodically throughout the year they have what are called "fly ins" where a host club invites all others to visit for a weekend of dancing, dining, sightseeing, and whatever else may come up. And annually they have a huge conference of all groups worldwide. Last year it was held in Las Vegas and more than two thousand square dancers showed up. We gays are so organized.

There was a man up on the stage singing out the calls to the dancers on the floor with some nondescript country twanging music blaring from huge speakers. The exhibition dance with the club members came to an end and the dancers in each circle held hands and seemed to spin inside out, twining their arms together and shouting in unison, "Thank you!" Just that move alone confused and frightened me.

"Quinn," I whispered, "let's go now before it's too late."

He stood his ground and the members instantly swarmed us.

One plump middle-aged dancer shook my hand. "Welcome to Washington Squares! I'm Cubby. Who are you?"

Annette!

"I'm Curtis and this is Quinn."

Cubby gave me a huge bear hug. "Are you a girl or boy?"

Quinn and I looked at each other. I touched my chest and said, "I'm a man. I think."

Cubby put his fingers to his lips and giggled. "Silly me. I meant are you dancing the girl's part or the boy's? Lead or follow?"

I still looked at him, confused.

Quinn translated for me. "Top or bottom?"

I shrugged my shoulders. "Can I be versatile?"

Cubby laughed, patted me on the back, and slapped a nametag on my shirt. Unfortunately, I was now an accepted member of the Washington Squares Square Dancing Club. Quinn decided for me that we were both girls because they get to do all the spinning and twirling. And to initiate us virgin dancers the caller had the entire room make one huge circle. We were all told to stand front to back and then every other person had to turn around and face a dancer. To the beat of The Village People's "Y.M.C.A," we did the right-and-left-grand, or as the caller renamed it, the circle-jerk. Grabbing right hands with my partner, pulling through, walking straight ahead to the next partner, we repeated the movement until everyone had shaken hands with everyone else. This was truly the geekiest thing I had ever done in my entire life.

After the circle-jerk, we were partnered up and put into squares of four couples. I desperately searched for Quinn but was then told we had to pair up with a seasoned dancer. I was on my own and panicked but was quickly rescued by Cubby. He was a handsome man but his waist size must have been equal to his age, which I guessed at about fifty. I wondered if that would make dancing difficult with him? His waist size, that is.

While waiting for everyone to pair up I looked around at the other people. "Cubby, I'm disappointed."

He held my hand like we were a real couple. "Why's that sweet pie?"

Sweet pie?

"Where are all the gingham skirts, petticoats, and shellacked hairdos?"

"We just dress in casual clothes but wait till Halloween, it's a hoot!"

I spotted a man and a woman kissing in another square. "And is everyone gay?"

"No. Straight dancers love to come and play with us. We dance fast, strong, and creatively."

But of course. The caller on the stage talked us through several dance steps and then turned up the music. It was "Bow-to-your-partner, bow-to-your-neighbor, allemande-left . . ." and I was lost. Literally, dancers pushed me in the right or wrong direction in hopes that I would end up in the correct position. It felt like gay bumper cars.

Across from me was a couple that somehow I needed to change partners with. Cubby pushed me across the square and as I thankfully managed not to collide into the oncoming girl/follow, a six foot six, dark-skinned boy/lead wearing a large western hat grabbed my hand.

"Swing your partner, do sa do, and promenade home."

Yes, please, take me home.

The tall guy spun me like a top and then the whole square walked a full circle as pairs, then we came to a stop.

Once I had regained my equilibrium and my breath, this new partner squeezed my hand and smiled. "Timber."

I looked way up to his face and shouted, "What?"

"My name is Timber."

Shiver me timbers. I'm not sure if it was his height or his name that shocked me. "Curtis here."

"Now, box-the-gnat," I heard the caller holler out and Timber hurtled me into some move that felt like a jitterbug. And somewhere between slip-the-clutch and girls-sashay-in, I realized that I was laughing my head off.

The song ended and I asked him again what his name was.

"Timber. Kind of a nickname."

"Cause you're tall as a tree?"

"You got it."

Although Timber was nice and very exotic looking, the whole scenario felt extremely awkward, like we were back in fourth grade dance school. I noticed Quinn talking to a cute guy two squares to the left of me. I was going to inch my way over to him, when the music came blaring back on but this time it sounded more like a fast-paced, country-western tune.

"Two-step?" Timber asked me.

"I beg your pardon?"

"Would you like to two-step?"

"Heck, I don't even know how to one-step."

"Between square dances we country two-step. Want to try?"

I threw up my hands. "Why not? I like to live dangerously."

Timber swept me into his arms and patiently attempted to teach me to two-step. In this dance, one partner leads while the follow dances backward.

"I can't even dance forward," I cried.

"I'm going to signal you to spin and turn and the steps we take always start with the right foot. The trick is the rhythm. Think quick, quick, slow, slow."

"And I start stepping on my right, in reverse?"

"Correct."

I've always fancied myself a good dancer but I was so not getting this. I felt like I had two left feet . . . on backward! And you would think that with Timber being so tall and muscular that he might be clunky with his dancing but he was quite the opposite. He was so graceful and elegant it almost looked and felt like he was skating on ice. And two-stepping is sexy. The partner stance is extremely close, hip to hip, almost intertwined and although I stepped on his toes more often than not, I think he enjoyed dancing with me.

Surviving the dance lesson, Timber and I headed over to a table decked out with desserts and beverages and sat down to rest a bit as other dancers jumped up to country line dance. Off the dance floor and with the luxury of not having to stare at my feet in fear that I was going to smash one more pair of toes, I had a chance to really check Timber out. He took off his hat, revealing a head of thick black hair parted in the middle. His eyes were literally black, no color to the iris at all, and although his nose looked like it had been broken several times and was definitely on the large size, it perfectly balanced out his high cheekbones and very full lips. But it was his skin that was so fascinating. A reddish brown, it almost looked like he had been stained with iodine. And he had the most enormous hands with long delicate fingers.

We chatted for a bit and I discovered that he had not only been dancing with the Washington Squares for five years but that last season he was president of the club. It also turned out that he was a bigwig at the advertising firm Saatchi & Saatchi.

"Good for you, Timber. I hear that industry is pretty cutthroat."

"I can take it. Hey, I had good training. I'm the youngest of twelve siblings."

I almost choked on my cookie. "Twelve?"

"All boys."

"And all from the same uterus?"

He elbowed me. "If you're referring to my mother? Yes."

"But twelve? You must be Catholic."

"No, Native American. I'm a descendent of the Klickitat tribe."

I opened my mouth and it just flew out. "The KitKat?"

He laughed, squeezing my knee with his extraordinary fingers. "Everyone does that. No, the Klickitat."

I caught myself an Indian. "Oh, OK."

After the break, I managed to get through another square dance with Timber as my partner and I actually felt a little more comfortable with the calls. As the dancing and the evening came to an end we exchanged numbers and shook hands. Then without knowing he was going to do it, he awkwardly bent down to kiss me and ended up not hitting my lips or my cheek but landing a big one on the top of my head.

"That was weird," Timber joked.

"But nice."

We gave each other a hug and then promised to call. I saw Quinn by the front door and was making my way over to him when Cubby appeared with his business card.

"Curtis, I loved being your top."

"Hey big guy." I hit him lightly in the chest and he recoiled. "Oh, gosh, did I hurt you?"

He took a deep breath. "No. Just a little heart surgery, that's all."

Heart surgery? Grossly overweight? Should he even be dancing right now?

"Curtis, here's my card."

He handed it to me. It had his name and number on it and the logo, 4-H CLUB.

"Hey, I belonged to that when I was a kid."

"Um, I think this is a different kind of 4-H club. It stands for husky, hairy, homosexual, and"—he winked—"hungry."

"Wow, that's a mouthful. And yes, that's definitely a different club."

I shook hands with Cubby and thanked him for dancing with me, then I rushed over to Quinn.

"Get me out of here, now," I said as I slipped my arm into his and we exited onto Hudson Street.

"Curtis, I got several guys' numbers, what about you?"

"I exchanged with Cubby and the other guy I danced with."

"Jack and the Beanstalk?"

"Timber."

"That's his name?"

"As in Timmmmber!" We turned right onto Christopher.

"Is he black?"

"Native American."

"Honest Injun?"

I gave a look of disapproval. "Let's have a beer at the Banger. Quinn, that was the queerest thing I've ever done in my life. The music was queer. The dancing was queer."

"The people were queer."

"Most of them," I said as we crossed the street mid-block to get to the bar. "Shit! Piss! Damn! Prick!"

"What? What's wrong?"

"I think I have to go back."

"To square dancing? Did you forget something?"

I stopped in the middle of the street and looked up at the night sky, waving my fists. "Because I fucking loved it!"

≷ ≶

And I did. I went back to Thursday night square dancing for several classes and must say I was getting the swing of it. And I had several nice dates with Timber. I liked him. I really liked him, but we hadn't had sex yet. I was enjoying getting to know him and it felt good to go slow. But that all came to an abrupt halt when I developed a nasty cold. I had to call and cancel going to the movies with him but was a bit concerned when I never heard back from him after leaving a phone message. I didn't hear from him that night or the next day or even the day after that. I was nervous. I was nervous that Timber had lost interest, but more nervous that something awful had happened to him.

The following Thursday I went down to the elementary school a little before class was to begin to see if Timber was there. And he was. When I walked through the front door he was down at the stage helping the caller set up his music speakers.

"Timber," I called out as I started to cross the large cafeteria.

He looked up, realized it was me, and dashed out the back door. Totally at a loss, I stopped in my tracks trying to figure out why he had just done that. Then Cubby entered through the same door Timber had exited.

I walked toward him. "Cubby?"

He looked nervous and guilty. "Hey Curtis."

We embraced. "What's up with Timber?"

Cubby looked back toward the door. "Up? Not sure what you mean."

"What I mean is, he hasn't returned any of my phone calls and just now when he saw me, he ran out of here like I was the last person in the world he wanted to see."

I pulled out a tissue and blew my nose.

"Curtis, are you still sick?"

"I had a cold but it's way past contagious."

"Timber says to call him when you are feeling 100 percent better. Gotta set up refreshments. Later." And Cubby ran out the back door with his tail between his legs.

I could have stayed and confronted him or even danced but I was angry, perplexed, and thought this behavior was just ridiculous, so I left and vowed never to call him again.

≳ ≲

So, I waited five days and called him again. The mysteriousness of his behavior was driving me nuts. And I actually missed him. He was the first guy in a long time that I had met who shared a lot of similar interests. We had had lengthy discussions about our mutual passion for theater, both current and period. He told me that one of his favorite plays was *Look Back in Anger* by John Osbourne. We both also loved travel, film, museums, dancing, of course, and *food*. And yes, he was one of those very strong, muscular body types that can eat anything and everything and never gain a pound.

When I did call him I was surprised that he picked up, knowing he had caller ID, and even more surprised when he agreed to meet on neutral territory to talk.

"I love Shakespeare's Garden," I said as we approached it from the direction of Central Park's Belvedere Castle. "Have you been here before?"

Timber was amazed. "I didn't even know it existed."

It was a very cold but sunny day as we walked through the cottage rock garden and sat down on one of its rustic benches.

"The garden was inaugurated in 1916 on the 300th anniversary of Shakespeare's death. The flowers and herbs planted here are ones mentioned in either his plays or sonnets." I pointed to a tree down at the bottom of the garden. "And see your namesake in the lower part?"

Timber smiled and followed the direction of my finger. "Yes?"

"It's a graft of a white mulberry tree planted by Shakespeare himself at Stratford-upon-Avon, in the year 1602."

"That is awesome."

"Isn't it? Sometimes I just sit here for hours, trying not to think of anything."

Suddenly, I thought of why we got together. I paused a bit, breathed in the brisk, fresh air, and then dove right in.

"Timber? I thought everything was going great. What happened?"

He hesitated for the longest time and then gently touched my knee. "Curtis, I can't be around you when you are sick."

I thought for a moment and tried to put two and two together. I came up with cancer and then felt dreadfully awful. "Oh my gosh, are you on chemotherapy?"

He shook his head.

I touched his hand. "I'm so sorry. Then is it prednisone? I know people who are on high doses, for whatever reasons, can't come in contact with contagious diseases."

"No. It's not that."

I knew it was something much worse and I just felt horrible that all this time I was so quick to judge and be angry.

"Please Timber, you can tell me."

I looked at his face and it was so contorted, I just couldn't imagine what was wrong. And then he said it.

"Getting sick is a sign of weakness."

I stared at him as I repeated what he said, in my brain. *Getting sick is a sign of weakness.* "You mean, we feel weak when we get sick?"

"No, you getting sick is a sign of your weakness and that's unacceptable to me."

I stared at him as I repeated what he said, in my brain. *No, you getting sick is a sign of your weakness and that's unacceptable to me.* I thought about it for a moment and then while embracing the tranquil surroundings of Shakespeare's garden sanctuary, I addressed him.

"What? Are you insane?" I screamed.

A bevy of sparrows flew out of a tree next to us, chirping their annoyance at my loud outburst.

"Curtis, I'm not going to discuss this if you get unreasonable."

I stood up and faced him. "Me? Unreasonable? OK. OK. Let's say you do have this . . . weird—and you have to admit it's weird—demand? If you can't see me when I'm sick, why didn't you at least talk to me on the phone?"

"Curtis, there isn't a simple explanation." He reached for my hand.

I let him pull me back down onto the bench and he moved closer causing our knees to touch. As nuts as he was acting, I was so damn attracted to him. "I can handle complex."

"I come from a large and poor family that couldn't afford to have anyone get sick. Our tribe . . ."

"The Klickitat," I said, proudly showing him that I was a good listener.

He smiled, approvingly. "We were originally from the Columbia River area in Washington State and were exceptional fur traders. But around the mid 1850s we were forced onto a reservation and the one thing we were good at was taken away from us. By the time I was born my immediate family had moved up to Skagway, Alaska, to take advantage of the cruise ships dumping hoards of tourists into Glacial Bay and its surrounding towns."

I was fascinated by his story. "How do you mean you took advantage of?"

He obviously struggled with his thoughts. "Don't get me wrong. I respect my parents and my heritage. But all twelve of us children, my parents, and my grandparents humiliatingly dressed up as Indians, desperately trying to sell anything and everything to make ends meet. Although it was our choice to exploit ourselves, it was an embarrassing way to survive and make a living."

I squeezed his hand. "I'm sorry you had to experience that."

"And of course we had no health insurance and the cost of hospitals or even medications were out of the question. It was drilled into me from as early as I can remember that we had no time for illness in our lives. We couldn't afford it."

"I understand that."

He looked out over the garden with fierce pride. "It's also what gave me the drive and ambition to be the first person in my family to graduate from college."

We sat quietly for a few moments as two squirrels chased each other up and down and around an old oak tree.

"But Timber, now, as an adult and making what I assume is a good living with health benefits, don't you like friends or family to call you, to make sure you're OK or to ask if they can bring you something when you're not feeling well?"

"It's not relevant."

His response was so illogical I furrowed my brow. "It's not relevant?"

"No one in my family was allowed to get sick."

"But what happened when one of you *did* get sick?"

He looked at me with a straight face. "No one ever did."

Bursting out into laughter I said, "You're pulling my leg, you bastard."

"I am not. I'm serious. No one in my family has ever been sick. I have never been sick."

I looked at him like he was mad. "You've never been sick?"

"No."

Wanting to run away from the stupidity of the conversation, Timber followed me as I raced through the garden. "You've never had the mumps or the measles or the chicken pox?"

"No."

I stopped right in front of the bronze plaque that lists the medicinal herbs that thrive in the garden in warmer months. I pointed to where the echinacea and goldenseal weren't. "Not even a cold or the flu?"

"Never."

I turned around and confronted him. "Are you lying?"

"Are you calling me a liar?"

This was so retarded it was funny. "If you have never been sick, never had a cold or the flu, it would not only be in the headlines of every newspaper but you'd also be listed in the *Guinness World Records*."

"So you're calling me a liar?"

I'm not sure where the humor was in all of this but I came to the conclusion that it was some sort of joke. "You know what, Timber? No, I'm not calling you a liar. I do think," and I took a deep breath, "we should just let this go. It's a dumb thing to let stand in the way of us getting to know one another. Don't you think?"

He looked at me and then started to smile. "Curtis, I really like you and yes, I want to get to know you better."

Suddenly, we both started laughing. He bent down and gave me a hug.

"Thanks, Curtis, for understanding."
Timber, you big liar.

≳ ≲

The conversation Timber and I had was so absurd, so bizarre, so unreasonable that I just threw it out of my brain. Erased it with a desire to move on. All of our dates had been out in public so on the following Saturday I invited him over to my apartment for an early intimate dinner followed by a creative surprise.

I kissed him at the door and looked at my watch. "Eager huh?"

"I'm sorry," Timber said walking in, "I was just so looking forward to seeing you."

"Early bird catches the . . . Curtis?"

"Good," he said as he walked in handing me a bag. "Dry white?"

"Perfect."

And so was the first part of the evening. We drank some wine, listened to some Sondheim, and I gracefully put together dinner.

I knew that Timber loved seafood so I went to my local fishmonger and picked up some beautiful pieces of wild salmon. He sat on a kitchen stool drinking his wine as I did my magic.

"Curtis, I can tell you love to cook."

I was preparing a simple poaching broth for the salmon, which consisted of white wine, peppercorns, sea salt, celery, and fresh dill. "I do when I have the time and energy and someone to share it with. It's a creative outlet for me. And you?"

"I can put things together. Like bottled tomato sauce on pasta, a boiled hot dog on a bun, milk on cereal. I have no cooking abilities and have put all my faith in eating out and dialing in."

"I worked in restaurants when I was a kid. If you saw what goes on in those kitchens, you'd better have faith."

I was about to go into lengthy details about health code violations, chefs dropping food on kitchen floors and throwing it back onto diners' plates, and in particular, one restaurant I worked at that was forced to close its doors due to it spreading hepatitis to half of the population of Bremerton, New York. But considering our Shakespeare Garden discussion, I didn't.

We sat down to eat right on schedule and I was delighted that he found the dinner delicious.

"I could eat a million of these," he said as he stuffed another curried sweet potato fry into his mouth.

"It's so easy, you could do it."

He gave me a sly look. "The salmon is perfect and this dill sauce you made. The sautéed broccoli and garlic. I could get used to this."

I winked at him. "So could I."

"I'm in heaven," Timber said with his mouth full.

I really outdid myself. Both of us gobbled up everything, leaving not a morsel of food on our plates.

"Now for the surprise," I said as I blew out the candles on the table.

"More?"

I got Timber's coat and without telling him what we were doing we left my building and walked uptown on Broadway. I was hoping that he would come back to the apartment after the show for fresh blueberries topped with whipped cream, lemon curd, and me.

He draped his arm over my shoulder and kissed the top of my head. "Thank you for a wonderful dinner. No one has ever gone to this much trouble for me before."

"Trouble? It was fun."

A couple of blocks north, I stopped and he looked up and saw the marquee of the Symphony Space theater.

"Oh, my gosh!" he exclaimed. "You remembered."

I smiled, knowing I had done well. The Peter Norton Symphony Space had recently gone through a wonderful renovation and is beloved in New York City for its annual *Wall to Wall* music marathon and its *Selected Shorts* broadcasts. But one of my favorite events is the staged concert-style readings with Broadway actors. Tonight it was Mia Dillon and Keir Dullea in *Look Back in Anger*.

We found our perfect seats in mid-orchestra and sat down amongst the sold-out house. The evening was perfect. Great food. Great company. And now, great theater.

It was indicated that the performance was going to be done without an intermission so I tugged at Timber's arm. "Last chance for the little boy's room."

He squeezed my knee and smiled. "I'm fine."

When *Look Back in Anger* was first produced in 1956 on the British stage, John Osbourne was tagged as a "kitchen sink" dramatist. Literally that referred to plays that took place in the kitchen and home, portraying a slice of life, a style of domestic realism. But Osbourne in particular used everyday language and speech to shock with its bluntness.

"Timber, look in the program and at the reviews critics gave this play when it first opened in London."

Moments later, the lights went down, the curtain went up, Timber and I held hands like school kids, and the stellar performance began. And brilliant it was until Timber's stomach started to growl so loudly midway through the play that theatergoers around us were looking to see where the noise was coming from. He pulled his hand away from mine and gripped his stomach. Unable to endure the pain, Timber got up out of his seat and without any of the grace and elegance that he danced with, he stepped on people's toes and forced them to stand as he worked his way excruciatingly out of the theater.

Worried to death, I trailed behind him whispering excuses to theatergoers as I tried to step over feet and forced them to stand again to let me by. Once out in the lobby, Timber was nowhere to be found. I ran to the front door and looked out and then I heard something coming from the men's room.

I entered and found him in an open stall, driving the porcelain bus. Timber was down on his knees and his hands were gripping the toilet seat so tightly his knuckles were turning white. He continued to wretch so hard I thought he was going to bring up his kidneys.

I grabbed some paper towels, wetted them with cold water, and brought them over to him but he slapped my hand away aggressively.

"Get away!"

"Timber, let me help you."

He managed to pull his head out of the toilet long enough to say, "I said get away from me!" And then he started in with the dry heaves.

Backing off, I washed my hands and quietly left the men's room. I went out onto the street and decided to wait for him in front of the theater. No less than twenty minutes later Timber emerged, still looking horribly sick. I went to his side but he pushed me away.

"You did this to me!"

I was dumbfounded. "I what?"

"This is all your fault!"

"What are you talking about?"

Timber started to walk away and then came back. "You are the sick one, Curtis! Sick for poisoning me!"

He was being so absurd I started to laugh. "That's ridiculous, Timber."

"You just couldn't stand it that I've never been sick."

"I could stand it, I just couldn't believe it."

He walked away again and then swung back toward me. "I should have known that you were cooking up something more than just dinner."

"I ate exactly what you ate!"

He started to walk off again and then turned around. "I don't ever want to see or hear from you again."

"But—"

"Never again!" he shouted with intense rage.

I stood underneath the theater's marquee, numb, as he stumbled away. I didn't poison Timber, although I'd like to now. Chalking this one up to insanity, I threw my program into a very full trash can. I noticed that it opened to the page that had the critic's review of *Look Back in Anger*'s original production. "Osborne draws liberally on the vocabulary of the intestines and laces his tirades with the steamier epithets of the tripe butcher."

I glanced up and saw Timber turn around one more time while holding his gut and look back in anger.

FIVE

OLD DOGS, NEW TRICKS

That following Sunday was a day that I had looked forward to and simultaneously dreaded for months. A memorial for Dr. Magda Tunick, my friend, shrink, and the former owner of my Brussels griffon, was arranged at the Cathedral Church of St. John the Divine. Mrs. French, who was her downstairs neighbor, had haphazardly thrown together a ceremony for Magda immediately following her death. It actually happened before I had even known that she had died. In fact, so many people had missed it that this more formal ceremony with a complete list of guests was planned.

Upon Magda's death, I rescued her very old dog, Emily-Mae, from euthanasia and adopted her as my own. If you've never seen one, Brussels griffons are extremely odd-looking toys. They have this intelligence, alertness, and humanlike quizzical expression that is at times quite unnerving. They have dark, mysterious eyes, their faces look punched in, and their ears are batlike. My Emily-Mae weighed about five pounds and had a smooth, short, black-and-tan coat.

Most of these dogs live eight to ten years. And although she had some *minor* health issues and was missing all her teeth, Emily-Mae had a huge appetite for life and food and had gone way past her expiration date. I'm sure she broke a record when she turned the ripe old age of fourteen. She also broke in my Upper West Side apartment. She had a bladder issue. Everywhere you took a step, I had laid out doggie pee pads. Actually, I used human urinary incontinence underpads. They're cheaper than the pet store brand and hey, if I'm in a rush or don't want to run to the bathroom I can use them, too.

I lived within walking distance of St. John the Divine and on that Sunday afternoon the sky was moody with ominous-looking clouds hanging above but the temperature was quite mild. And although in the past I was one of those stick-in-the-muds who criticized people for dressing their animals in clothing, I realized it's important to make sure your pet is warm and comfortable, especially when she is a senior citizen. Therefore, keeping the somberness of the memorial in mind I dressed Emily-Mae appropriately.

Of her many outfits, I chose the Glamour Girl hooded jacket. It's a roomy boutique coat featuring a fabulous tone-on-tone embroidered 100 percent wool in olive green. Rolled up sleeves revealed a luxurious red paisley satin lining, and to top it off, I put a double strand of pearls on in place of her collar. And it was only $129.95 plus the cost of the pearls. When I went out with Emily-Mae, PAW was my mantra.

Pride—Attention—Warmth. I dressed myself in basic black, head to toe.

Due to Emily-Mae's blindness and bilateral vestibular dysfunction, which is a fancy way of saying deafness with an equilibrium problem, walking a straight line for her was a challenge. Instead, she constantly made left-hand circles. Fine for about five feet, I would eventually scoop her up in my hand and carry her wherever we went.

St. John the Divine is the mother church of the Episcopal Diocese of New York and the seat of its bishop. They have always valued the life of mind and dialogue with fields of secular study. In fact, Sir Isaac Newton was a clergyman there. And considering that in August of 2002 they chose a gay man to be their bishop and that the current one is now a woman, I found it acceptable to enter their house of worship but not necessarily to practice an organized religion.

As I walked up Amsterdam Avenue with Emily-Mae, everyone wanted to stop and chat with her, making us almost fifteen minutes late for the memorial. The invitation said that it was going to be a moment for Magda's friends and animals to reflect upon her life. Quinn was going to join me but the night before he left a rather cryptic message on my answering machine saying that he was being evicted from his sublet and that that Sunday he had an unexpected but exciting job interview. So, I entered the Holy Sanctuary solo and not knowing a soul.

We rushed down the south wall of the church and at the end of the long passageway was the very last and intimate St. James Chapel. Before entering, I stood for a moment, recognizing Samuel Barber's masterfully crafted "Adagio for Strings." Built on romantic structures, I always felt that it was one of the most moving compositions ever written. I creaked open the heavy wooden door and immediately saw a violin quartet sitting up in a tiny stone balcony, playing live. As I entered the chapel, the music climbed emotionally, intellectually, and I'm sure for some, sexually with a deliriously heightened and vibrating climax of violins. A tad self-conscious, I desperately searched for an empty seat.

The chapel held about two hundred people and it was packed. I managed to squeeze up against the back wall with Emily-Mae in my arms as the adagio was winding down, which gave me a chance to look at the people and their pets that had showed up.

It seemed more like a demented Alice in Wonderland garden party than a memorial. One woman wore a bright yellow dress and matching hat and had wrapped around her neck and torso a giant yellow boa constrictor. It obviously had had its lunch because right next to it sat a small boy in a Buster Brown suit cuddling a tiny white mouse. I also saw an elderly bald man with a raspberry birthmark on the back of his skull that matched a splotch of pigmentation on the back of his totally bald cat, which must have been a sphynx, and a young girl wearing a pith helmet and safari vest who was holding none other than a hooded falcon on her wrist. The San Diego Zoo had invaded New York City.

For some strange reason, during the last several bars of music Emily-Mae decided to sing. I don't mean howl; she sang. It was the oddest thing and it actually sounded like my deaf dog was on pitch. Of course everyone turned around as she continued to do this at the top of her lungs until the "Adagio for Strings" was over. There was a pause and then everyone burst into applause. The only thing I could think to do was to bow with Emily-Mae.

As the room calmed down I saw a flurry of bright orange satin flashing around in the front row but couldn't make out who or what it was. Beyond that was a raised stage with a simple yet beautiful altar with a long white runner flanked with huge floral bouquets of white lilies and purple tulips. And standing proudly in the center, mounted on an ornate gold easel, was a large oil portrait of Magda with Emily-Mae on her lap.

She actually had it hanging in the front salon of her Riverside Drive apartment, over her silver tea cart. On several occasions I had studied it and guessed that it was done about thirteen years ago because Emily-Mae was just a puppy.

I believe that when a person reaches adulthood, we are pretty much who we are going to be for the rest of our lives and as we age, we just become more of that. Sweet people become sweeter. Nasty people become nastier. But on rare occasions one shifts and changes direction and outlook upon one's life. And when I was age forty-five, Magda helped me to do that. In a very short period, she taught this middle-aged dog some new tricks for which I will be ever grateful.

The day she died we had had a very nontraditional therapy session. I helped her prepare her front room to be painted as we discussed some boundary issues I had with my mother. I was also eager to tell her about a wonderful man I had met named Eric. I remembered taking down drapes while teetering on a rather unstable ladder and ironically, one of the paintings I removed from a wall was her portrait that was now up on the altar.

Done in an impressionistic style, the artist captured a haunting essence of Magda. Previously I had only seen the strength in the portrayal. I saw her as stoic and indestructible. But much more revealed itself as I gazed at her likeness in the chapel. Like pentimento, which is the growing transparency of paints allowing underlying elements to show through, I saw a loneliness seep through her eyes and a quiet sadness in the way her mouth turned slightly down at the sides.

I was the last to see Magda alive. Why didn't I stay? Why didn't I insist on helping with the rest of the apartment? Why didn't I tell her not to climb that rickety ladder? Why . . .

"Why?" I asked out loud as the knot of emotion welled up into my throat. Buckets of tears instantly poured out of my eyes drenching Emily-Mae as I held her tightly in my arms. Instinctually, she started licking my hand to calm me down. A thoughtful woman beside me handed me a tissue, allowing me to absorb the blubber that was about to emerge from my nose.

A priest appeared and stood in front of the altar.

"Oh my God!" I thought to myself. I must have thought to myself a little too loudly because several people turned around and gave me a disapproving look.

"That's not God," whispered the woman who gave me the tissue. "That's Father Greg. He oversees weekday evening prayers. Isn't he nice?"

"Is he Latino?" I whispered.

"No. Half Mexican, half Welsh."

"And all man," I said, raising my voice again, causing more heads to turn.

Father Greg stood about six foot one and had a classic chiseled face, black hair, and dark brown eyes. And he happened to look like a famous actor whose name I just couldn't remember. I don't know if it was the emotion of the memorial or the beauty of this man in cloth, but my knees were shaking.

He had on a beautiful floor-length white robe covered with a purple sash, but my mind drifted to what he might be wearing underneath it. Do Welshmen wear kilts? The thought of it made me smile and the desire to unpeel those holy layers just made me want to run to confession. But which actor did he remind me of? What was that great movie he was in?

Father Greg slipped on his black horn-rimmed glasses and opened his mouth.

"Thank you all for coming today to celebrate in Dr. Magda Tunick's life."

His voice was so rich, deep, and sumptuous, my knees buckled and I almost dropped Emily-Mae. He sounded like Sean Connery mixed up with Antonio Banderas.

The kind woman next to me sensed I was losing it. "Sorrow weakens us all."

Or lust, I thought to myself as she pushed me forward, whispering, "There's a seat up front."

The sea of animals and their owners parted and propelled me to the front of the chapel. The anticipation and excitement of getting up close to him instantly created a vascular thumping at the back of my skull so hard I could barely see straight. I saw his full red lips moving but heard not a word the priest was saying as I blindly stumbled toward him. I remember people touching and pushing me forward. And like a lost and broken follower struggling to get to his beloved faith healer, I knew the moment he would lay his hands upon me I would be healed. Well, maybe not his hands.

The pounding in my head became louder as I staggered to the front row. I stood before him straining to read his lips as he said one more thing.

"I want you," is what I fantasized he had said.

Father Greg became quiet and it seemed like eternity passed before I spoke.

Feeling guilty for all my unholy thoughts I said, "Forgive me Father, for I have sinned."

He smiled a little too warmly. "We have all sinned, my son," he said as he placed both of his hands on my shoulders.

Father? Son? I was never into the dad/boy role-playing but I was about to sign up that moment. I'm the sacrificial lamb; do me right now on the altar, please? And what was that actor's name?

He gestured for me to sit and in doing so, brushed the top of Emily-Mae's head. Her adrenals must have been working overtime because her fight or flight instinct kicked in and she decided to fight. Like a Tasmanian devil she started snapping at thin air.

"She'd only gum you to death," I laughed nervously as I turned around and saw a peanut sized woman swimming in orange satin. She was an elderly woman with a bright red pixie haircut, hazel eyes, two-inch false eyelashes, scarlet lipstick, and multidrop Bakelite earrings. She smiled and patted the seat next to her.

"Please, sit," she whispered in a very exotic European accent.

I managed to bend my knees and collapse into the chair.

"Emily-Mae," she said as she placed her hand on my dog's back.

Normally, Emily-Mae would have snapped around at this gesture but instead she squinted her eyes as if she were smiling. They knew each other.

The priest pulled my attention away from her.

"Magda was pragmatically spiritual, hence she enjoyed the services here at St. John the Divine. Having spent many fond moments with her discussing life and its lessons, I had the privilege of her sharing with me some of her deepest reflections upon life and the people who influenced her."

He went on to mention that one such mentor in Magda's life was Sir William Osler, a Canadian-born physician. He recited what he remembered being Magda's favorite quote of his: "Live neither in the past nor in the future, but let each day's work absorb your entire energies, and satisfy your widest ambition."

There were smiles and nods amongst the crowd as he continued. "But there was another side to her. A softer more personal Magda that only a few lucky people knew."

The woman in orange suddenly slipped her hand into mine and squeezed it tightly. I was about to lose it again.

"To quote Sir Osler again truly sums up the whole of Magda: 'There is a form of laughter that springs from the heart, heard everyday in the merry voice of childhood, the expression of a laughter-loving spirit that defies analysis by the philosopher, which has nothing rigid or mechanical in it, and totally without social significance. Bubbling spontaneously from the heart of child or man. Without egotism and full of feeling, laughter is the music of life.'"

I knew that side of Magda and it made my eyes well up.

There was a moment of reflection and then he asked if anyone would like to come up and speak about the Magda they knew.

The woman holding my hand suddenly jumped to her feet and thrust me forward to the altar with Emily-Mae. Father Greg smiled and held out his hand, helping me up the step. The strength and warmth of his palm sent shivers down my spine. Embarrassed that people might notice, I tried to pull away from him but he wouldn't let go. He placed his other hand on my shoulder, grounding me. I'm not sure if it was real or wishful thinking but I swear he fingered my palm.

Feeling flop sweat instantly appear on my forehead I pulled my hand free, almost falling over backward, and proceeded to blather. I felt performance anxiety spread throughout my body like a virus.

"Hello, my name is Curtis Jenkins and I probably didn't know Dr. Tunick as long as most of you, but in the short time that we were together I discovered that Magda was irreverent, unethical, unyielding, unpredictable, stubborn, independent, motherly, grandmotherly, childlike in her sheer honesty, brutal in her sheer honesty, funny, very tall, and she had man-sized extremities."

I pointed to her hands in the portrait and the crowd laughed. This honestly threw me because I was being serious. I looked at the priest for support but he just made things worse by winking at me.

I coughed, swabbed the sweat away from my face with the back of my sleeve, and continued. "In fact, there were times when I wondered if Magda was actually a man."

Somehow, this last comment didn't go over as well. Where was I going with this? I was panicking. My instincts told me to switch gears so I promptly ignored them and continued.

"The only thing my shrink wasn't . . . was a shrink."

Heads were turning as a murmur rushed over the room.

"And after weeks of psychiatric sessions with her it wasn't until her untimely death at the young age of ninety-eight that I found out she was a . . . veterinarian."

I was on a roll, a stale roll, but a roll nonetheless. And a subtle outburst from a man in the crowd let me realize that they weren't on the same page as me.

"Who the hell is this guy?"

I trembled on, clutching Emily-Mae probably too tightly. "It all sounds absurd but truthfully, if Magda were still alive and I found out she was a veterinarian today, I'd still see her as a shrink. In fact, most good vets are shrinks. The easy part of their work is helping and healing the animals." I kissed the top of Emily-Mae's head and she barked on cue. "The problem side, are the humans." I forced a laugh and at that moment mistakenly pointed at the group, which caused several of them to stand up and actually boo me. Boo me? That had something to do with the actor's movie. What was it? What was his name?

I managed to get off the stage as the diminutive orange bomber jumped to her feet. She grabbed a large red velvet bag, slapped my hand like we were tag team wrestlers, and stepped up in front of the altar. Without missing a beat, she saved the ceremony.

"For those of you who don't know me I am Petra Tunick, Magda's *older* sister," she said in a smoky Garbo-esque voice.

The chapel broke out into a cheer.

"I just want to say thank-you to everyone who brought joy and happiness to my sister's life." She pointed to me on the sidelines. "And if you haven't figured it out, Curtis is the sweet young man who has adopted Magda's beloved Brussels griffon, Emily-Mae. And in doing so, I'm sure you thank him for that, too."

She started to clap and a few people in the room followed.

"And to show my appreciation to all of you, and to our friend Curtis, I'd like to sing a song."

There was more applause as she motioned Father Greg to put her chair beside her on the altar. Petra slid the orange satin fabric sensuously up her leg as she placed her tiny foot onto the chair. Surprisingly she was wearing a chic, youthful, and very expensive pair of Manolo Blahnik leopard print sandals. Obviously she wasn't self-conscious of her bunions, and with a three-inch heel she couldn't have been more than four foot ten. She dug into her red velvet bag and pulled out a musical instrument.

I heard a man in the crowd call out, "Zither."

Petra smiled and corrected him. "It's a hammered dulcimer, darling."

And without further adieu, she began to strum and sing seductively, à la Marlene Dietrich, "Falling in Love Again."

Even my jaw dropped. She sung of how love had always been a game for her and then she removed her foot from the stool, slid her skirt up mid thigh, straddled the stool, and faced directly out to the room. Thank God she was wearing underwear.

I guess I had never really listened to the lyrics before but they didn't allude to being bisexual; they stated that men and women were drawn to her like moths to a flame and it wasn't her fault.

After listening to the inappropriate song, accompanied by the even more inappropriate physical behavior, the room was full of deafening silence. Afraid she was going to be hit with something other than applause, Petra threw her hammered dulcimer into her red velvet bag, stepped off the stage, and grabbed my arm and her purple boa.

"Come, Curtis," she said as she pulled Emily-Mae and me toward the back exit of the St. James Chapel. "Let's blow this joint and bubble spontaneously."

Anticipating our exit, the father rushed to my side and in front of the entire congregation, kissed me. Not on the lips, unfortunately, but he did give a peck on my cheek. I was blessed and suddenly, I knew it. I figured it out.

I turned around before Petra dragged me out of the chapel and shouted, "Father Gregory Peck!"

SIX

QUEEN OF WANDS

As incredibly tall and imposing as Magda was, Petra was exquisitely tiny and accessible. Her zest for life was infectious and her endless drive to learn new and different things was exhausting. Exhausting for me that is.

This bundle of orange energy scurried us out of St. John's and onto Amsterdam Avenue. I put Emily-Mae down so she could do her business while Petra spun around and looked up at my face.

"Curtis, do you have a moment to spend with me? I have so much I want to discuss."

Slightly thrown I haltingly said, "It would be my pleasure. There's a nice bistro just an avenue west on Broadway."

"Darling, I want to explore more neighborhoods. Can we jump in a cab and you show me something new?"

"Of course," I replied as she handed me her red velvet bag to carry.

"Oh!" she squealed as she lifted her foot.

We both looked down. Emily-Mae had peed on her left Manolo Blahnik. Horrified, I reached into my pocket for a tissue and wiped her foot. "I'm so sorry."

"Please, I'm honored," Petra laughed. "She's christened me."

I picked Emily-Mae up. "It truly does mean she likes you."

Petra planted a huge kiss onto Emily-Mae's head. "And I *love* you," she said in her low, husky voice that I was so jealous of. Then she unwound her purple boa from her neck and threw it over my shoulders. "Now, let's take Manhattan."

I can't imagine what people thought as the three of us marched out into the street to hail a cab. Actually, in New York, I'm sure no one even looked twice.

I wasn't sure where to go so I initially told the driver to head to the West Village. Then I remembered a place on Grove Street nestled between a piano bar and a jazz club that had a leftover bohemian feel to it. It was a coffee house that served food and wine and I hoped they would allow Emily-Mae to enter.

Petra paused for a moment after getting out of the cab and studied the wooden hand-painted sign hanging outside of the café.

"The Queen of Wands," she read out loud. She turned to me and embraced me with such strength. "How did you know?"

"Know what?" I asked, a bit confused.

"This is my place."

I was still confused but smiled. The coffee house was actually on the second floor and being a Sunday afternoon it was quite busy. I wrapped Emily-Mae up in the purple boa and decided to sneak her in. We climbed up the rickety staircase and entered a large main room dotted with tables, each with its own Chianti bottle burning a colorful candle. Mismatched chairs of all sizes and shapes and the faded prints of Italian operas on the century-old dark paneling gave the place an old world, almost mystical feel.

In front of the large picture windows overlooking Grove Street was a makeshift stage where a clarinetist and a guitarist sat improvising a jazz number. To the left was a wine bar, clinking and clattering with pouring of wine and making of espresso.

We worked our way through the second interior room and then out to the back enclosed sunporch. There was one table free in the far corner, overlooking the garden that was lit up with twinkling white Christmas lights. Petra was so ecstatic I thought she was going to burst. We sat down in overstuffed wingback chairs and I snuggled a sleeping Emily-Mae up next to me. We quickly ordered a bottle of Pinot Grigio and she got right down to business.

"Curtis," she said as she took a blue drawstring bag out of her purse, "this is the reason I am the Queen of Wands." She loosened the bag and took out something covered in a silk cloth. Our waitress walked by and Petra caught her attention. "Dear heart, could we order something to nibble on?"

I suggested their assortment of antipasto appetizers and Petra's face lit up. She took a large gulp of her wine and unfolded the silk.

"These are ancient and precious tarot cards," she said as she laid the midnight blue silk scarf with gold stars and moons printed on it upon the table. "Each of us has a court card that relates to us. Believe it or not"— she searched through the pack and held up one card—"mine is the Queen of Wands."

"What a coincidence," I said.

"No coincidences in life. This was all meant to be." She smiled ominously and continued. "The Queen of Wands is a woman who has an attractive personality," she smiled and bowed her head a bit, "and draws people to her." She grabbed my hand and pressed it against her chest. She took another gulp of her wine and laughed heartily. "And that's me."

I noticed that a few tables were watching us, amused with the cards, intrigued by Petra.

She held the card up to her forehead and closed her eyes. "Fair hair, red hair, eyes of blue; loves her home and nature too." She opened her eyes and put the card on the table. "I have a sensible attitude and can be most helpful with good advice. Don't be afraid to ask me for assistance; I'll help you if I can."

Feeling a little awkward I said, "Well, OK. But I want to know about you. And how long are you staying in New York?"

Petra smiled and started sifting through the cards, removing some and keeping others. "We shall see."

I smiled while examining her face, and after a long pause I said quietly, "I adored Magda."

Caught a bit off guard, Petra looked up from the cards with such a look of sadness. "I adored her, too." She picked up her glass and I followed. "Here's to my little sister." We clinked and took a sip.

"Were you born in Poland?"

Petra raised an arm like she was going to hit someone. "Asch! We are Latvian."

I must have looked surprised. "I'm sorry. I just knew that she was going to visit you in Poland."

"True. But I had just moved there from Prague. Now that is a beautiful city."

I took a sip of my wine and thought hard. "Where the hell is Latvia?"

She laughed huskily. "Latvia is north of Lithuania, west of Russia, and much of our coast is along the Baltic Sea. Magda and I grew up near a city named Jelgava. Many outside people have controlled our country over the centuries, including Catherine the Great. But we finally gained independence when the Soviet Union broke apart in 1991. We've embraced the West and even joined the United Nations."

"Well, you learn something new every day."

I also learned that Petra and Magda and eight other siblings grew up on a dairy farm. It was fascinating to find out that Magda was healing animals even as a child, years before she went to veterinarian school. And after she had become an established and respected vet, she went back to school to be a psychiatrist. It turned out that in moving to America, educational and medical boards approved Magda as a vet, but not as a shrink. So, she outwardly worked with animals and secretively practiced with people.

"So I was her human guinea pig."

Petra laughed so hard. "Now you understand why the people at her memorial were confused by what you were saying."

"Hell, I was confused by what I was saying."

Emily-Mae stirred and looked up, sort of in my direction, with groggy eyes. I slipped my palm onto her tummy, massaged it, and she happily went back to sleep.

Petra gestured to the restaurant. "This is just my second trip to New York City."

"Really?"

"I visited Magda once before about ten years ago. I find it just as exciting now as I did then."

ARTHUR WOOTEN

The waitress placed a large platter of roasted red peppers, mozzarella cheese, hot Italian peppers, colossal green olives, peppered salami, thinly sliced layers of prosciutto, a bottle of olive oil and balsamic vinegar, and a basket of foccacio bread on the table. It was so simple yet it felt like a feast. We looked like two little kids about to dig into Thanksgiving dinner.

"Curtis, this is so beautiful!" Petra exclaimed, throwing her hands in the air. She popped an olive into her mouth and then picked up the smaller grouping of cards and started shuffling them.

Meanwhile, I tore up a small piece of the prosciutto and fed it to Emily-Mae, knowing I was going to regret it later.

"These are the Major Arcana cards," Petra whispered. "I'm using them because it will give you a more focused reading. You will pick three cards and it will offer us a snapshot of what's going on in the moment."

"Why me?" I asked seriously.

She looked up at my face, confused. "You don't want a reading?"

"Petra, out of all those people, why did you grab me in the church?"

She smiled. "When I saw you walking down the aisle like you were about to marry Father Gregory Peck, I knew you and I were two peas in a pod."

I burst out with laughter as she touched my hand.

"He's beautiful, Curtis," she confessed as she looked at me from the corner of her eye and winked her humongous fake eyelash, "but proceed with caution."

I tilted my head like Emily-Mae often does when she's perplexed. "There's nothing to proceed with."

"Let's do your reading," she said, rubbing her hands together. "Concentrate on a question. Although the tarot will reflect the present situation it can refer to the past and help bring clarity to your future. We all have the answers within; sometimes we just need a little nudge."

I sat there trying to think of something to ask but my mind went blank. Feeling a little warm from the wine, I pushed up the sleeves of my sweater and thought harder.

Petra reached out, touched my forearms, and moaned ecstatically. Instinctually I pulled my arms away.

"Curtis, what's wrong?"

No one is really sure if it was fifteen years of me being HIV-positive or the fifteen years of being on HIV medications, but lipodystrophy had robbed my arms and legs of body fat resulting in a very lean look. I've always been self-conscious of it but to some and obviously Petra, it was quite attractive.

"You're so vascular," she said as she reached out for my hands. I was blushing ten thousand shades of red as she dropped her chin and looked up at me with her huge hazel eyes. "I want to do you, Curtis."

I'm sure my ten thousand shades of red turned to white as a sheet as my eyes popped out of my head.

There was a moment and then she cackled so loud. "Not *do* do you. I want to paint you." She saw my relief and then that embarrassed me. She patted my hand saying, "And just for the record, I like the girls."

"Oh my God! You are a lesbyterian?"

Petra looked at me for a moment and then crumpled over in laughter. "Yes, my love of women is a religious experience."

"I caught your reference to men and women when you sang "Falling in Love Again." We *are* two peas in a pod."

"Now back to your body. My next master class I'm sharing you with my students. Like a marionette, with every movement your tendons, ligaments, and muscles make, we can see exactly how the human body operates."

"I'll feel like a living cadaver," I exclaimed.

"No, my dear, on the contrary." She raised her glass, waiting for me. Adding a little drama to the moment, I finally joined her and we toasted. "To life!"

Now I rubbed my hands together. "About this reading."

Petra had me quiet my mind and think of a question or a situation. She also said that the tarot provides a bridge between our conscious mind and our intuitive self, helping us dispel clouds of confusion and fear and create the clarity of mind we seek.

Again, I struggled to come up with a question that felt important and imperative. I shared with her that I was a writer and that my latest book was just released so, as lame as it felt, I came up with a career question.

"Place your tongue on the roof of your mouth, breathe in from your nose, hold the breath for seven seconds, and slowly exhale through your mouth," she instructed me.

She told me not to tell her my question, which actually was, will *101 Ways to Collide into Your Gay Soul Mate* be a success?

Petra checked to make sure that we were sitting north and south, which we were, and then she ran her hand over the wooden table.

"Wood is a good conductor of psychic energy," she said.

She laid out the silk scarf on top of the table and then placed the cards before me. I was instructed to shuffle them as much as I wanted while I concentrated on my question.

Petra then held the cards in her palms and pressed them tightly three times as a ritual of solidification. I sneaked a peek and the entire sunroom of the Queen of Wands was watching and mesmerized. So was I.

She spread the cards out facedown on top of the silk, evenly in front of me. I was to point to three cards, and as I did she pulled them out.

"Like myself, my readings are quick and to the point. The first card represents the past." Petra turned it over and it was The Tower.

I studied the card and then I studied Petra's face, and then I took a large gulp of wine.

She wrinkled her forehead. "Hmmmm."

"What? What does hmmm mean?" I looked at the card again. It was beautiful but a tad upsetting. A huge stone tower was engulfed in flames, assaulted by tidal waves, struck by lightning, and two people were tumbling to their death. This didn't look good.

I finally said something. "Thank God it's the past."

"Curtis, this is wonderful. Excellent."

She went on to explain that this was all about change and to be prepared for things to shift rapidly. And in the card position of the past, it meant that I needed to release old ways of life. Rather than stewing and mulling over the past, I needed to accept change and plan for the future. Clinging to old beliefs and ways of doing things was going to prevent me from accepting new and wonderful opportunities in the future.

She winked at me. "Curtis, learn from your mistakes."

I'm thinking to myself, *What the hell does this have to do with my writing and the book?* Was I supposed to break away from Darcie and Carrington Press?

"The second card represents the present situation and your attitude toward it." She turned it over and it was the Lovers, but upside down.

I touched it. "I like this one."

"Be careful, dear," Petra said as he put her hand over mine. "It represents more than coupling. And in a reverse position, this card is giving you important advice."

I pulled my hand away slowly and studied the card. It was the picture of a woman and a man, naked and intertwined amongst a field of calla lilies. Floating above and behind them was an angel with a hand over each of their heads. And behind the angel was a bright sun. It all looked pretty happy and safe to me.

Petra dropped her head into her hands.

I waited as long as I could. "What? You can't do this to me. Say something!"

"I never give negative readings. They don't exist. But I'm trying to say this in the most positive . . ."

Her words drifted off. As she contemplated, I filled our empty glasses.

"Just hit me," I said, taking a swig. "I can handle it."

"Curtis, in reverse this card indicates that wanting the best of both worlds can cause everyone concerned to feel unstable. It could ruin everything."

I looked at the card, then at her, and then sat back. "Ruin everything? Well, if that's all it means."

She smiled and continued. "You must have control over your temptations within your personal life. There's a lack of willpower. Possibly you're trying to find easy ways out. The card warns one not to abuse other people with power or knowledge. And to look deeper into oneself and the situation."

Again, I couldn't figure out how this was pertaining to my career.

"Let's move on," she said as she touched the third and last card. "This represents your future."

Petra let her hand hover over the card, tapped it, and turned it over.

A group of onlookers who had quietly formed behind us let out a collective gasp. More frightened of them, I turned around with a surprise. They dispersed, I'm sure not wanting to know the awful outcome. The card was Death.

"Oh no!" I cried.

Petra laughed. "It's not a bad card." She grabbed my hands. "Curtis, if you don't resist change, the powers that be will protect you. You'll have all the strength needed to face any situation. But experience is your friend here. It confirms that you must learn from the past. Don't be afraid to open your heart to new opportunities. The past is dead and its beliefs and ways of looking at love and life must be let go of. Have faith in your future because it is very bright."

There was a moment of relief and then the room started to applaud.

"You want to know my question?"

"You don't have to tell me."

"Will my book, *101 Ways to Collide into Your Gay Soul Mate,* be a success."

"But you already knew the answer to that question." Petra smiled.

I looked at her. "Where did you come from?"

"Latvia."

We both laughed.

"Curtis, this is all about love or the lack of it in your life."

I dropped my head. "Oh God, this is so perfect," I mumbled as I tried to gather my thoughts.

She was patient with me as I struggled to find the words. Magda's memorial smacked me in the face with my own mortality and with the success of the new book I had never before felt so alone in my life. All these wonderful things were finally happening for me and I had no one special in my life to share it with.

I thought of Dell. "Petra, I met a great guy but he . . ." My words drifted off as my emotions caught up with me. "And Magda was helping me but . . ."

Suddenly, the floodgates opened up and I started to cry. Tears splashed onto Emily-Mae, waking her up and causing her to stir. I calmed her down and took a deep breath.

"I just feel like on so many levels the rug has been pulled out from under my feet. And do you know what I'm most frightened of? I don't even know, if after being alone this long, if I'm even capable of letting another person into my life, my heart."

"Of course you are. You've let me in. The ember is still glowing inside of you, Curtis."

I couldn't believe how kind and generous this virtual stranger was being to me.

"But now I need you to help *me*," Petra said.

I looked up at her, confused, as she started to shuffle the cards.

"I can't choose my own card. You must do it for me. I trust you."

She shuffled the cards several more times and spread them out on the silk scarf, facedown.

"Just one card, Curtis. Point to one card."

Petra had her eyes closed and was concentrating as hard as she could. I looked over all of them and was about to touch one when a teardrop fell from my cheek and splattered on another. I touched it with my finger.

Petra turned it over and it was the Sun. She put her hands to her face and started to cry, too. The card was upright and showed a child riding a white horse and carrying a large banner. Behind was a wall with sunflowers on top of it and in the sky, a big vibrant sun.

"There is my answer. This is a time to be happy and give thanks. New adventures, good health. It's telling me to grab life with both hands and to go ahead. I'm going to do it."

"Do what?" I asked.

"I'm staying. New York is my new home."

I didn't know what to say. I didn't know what to think. "Can you do that?"

"Darling, I can do anything I want. And with the Sun in my spread, whatever the question is, the answer is yes. Now, I can't upset the Goddesses, can I?"

I threw my arms around her. "Welcome to New York."

"You must help me find a fantastic home. And then promise me something, Curtis."

"Anything."

"Be my life model. I want to paint you. Come sit for me and while you do we can discuss our lives and loves and will call upon the spirits and use the I Ching and the ancient ruins and contemplate quantum physics and induce hypnopompic experiences and . . ."

"Hypno what?"

She laughed. "And if you really want to find him, let me help you collide into your soul mate. You wrote the book, I've lived it! Is it a deal?"

Overwhelmed with her enthusiasm I shouted, "It's a deal!"

I embraced this virtual ray of sunshine thinking, *I've met my new best friend*, and then reminded myself not to describe her to Quinn like that.

Petra smiled from ear to ear. "Atta boy, Timmy."

I pulled away suddenly as I felt goose bumps all over my body. "What did you just say?"

"I'm not sure. It just came out of my mouth."

I stared at her with disbelief. "Petra, you said, 'Atta boy, Timmy.' That's a phrase and name for me only my Granny used to use."

"Used to?" Petra whispered. We both looked spooked and wide-eyed. She finally said, "I guess she's proud of you?"

We both looked up and around the room, deliciously unsettled.

Petra and I ended up ordering another bottle of wine while soaking up more information about each other like a pair of sponges. She was not only an accomplished artist and sculptor but also a musician, entrepreneur, author, and last but not least, belly dancer.

It turned out that she was staying at the Pierre Hotel, and considering rooms started at $650 per night, I assumed that money was not an issue for her. But while enjoying every minute I spent with her and the delicious food, wine, and atmosphere, I had almost forgotten that I had made plans to meet a man who had already read my book and asked if I could sign his copy at a diner located up near my place early that same evening. Petra and I exchanged numbers and she was going to leave with me when the waitress appeared and said that several people wanted to know if Petra would read their cards.

She looked at me for my thoughts.

"You must! Your audience awaits you," I said, giving her a huge embrace.

"Thank you, darling," she said, squeezing me tight. "And to confirm your instincts, the cards said you are as healthy as a horse and you're going to stay that way."

She winked and squeezed me a little tighter.

How did she know about my health status? "Thank you and welcome home," I whispered back.

I picked up Emily-Mae carefully and started to unwind the boa to give back to Petra.

She stopped me. "It's yours. No, it's Emily-Mae's. Now go out there and find the man of your dreams. Is that understood?"

"Yes sir!"

I wound it back around Emily's body and headed out of the sunporch. A sense of déjà vu appeared as I remembered exchanging those exact same words with Magda. I turned around to wave good-bye and a crowd of patrons had already flocked to our table to have Petra read their cards. She was in her element.

I grabbed a cab and rushed Emily-Mae home. As with many animals, she had developed diabetes in her older age and I needed to give her a quick injection of insulin before meeting this guy about my book.

Recently I had had my kitchen remodeled and in doing so—and I know this sounds morbid and probably insanely unsanitary—I had designed a kitchen island that had a hide-a-way IV stand built into it. I've always loved animals and have had many of my own and I justified this odd extravagance by telling myself that there would be many more elderly pets to come.

Emily-Mae was brilliant. I had never had a pet that understood injections and IVs like she did. Most would squirm or fight or even bite, but instead she would wait patiently while I screwed up and made a mistake or got nervous. It was so endearing to hear her exhale a "Huff," as I struggled with a pilling or wrestled with a bag of saline solution that I needed to hydrate her with.

The insulin injection I performed without incident. Placing her on the island, I quickly grabbed the skin between her shoulder blades, pulled it up, inserted the needle gently but firmly till it poked the skin, and then it was a quick injection. She didn't bat an eye. I shook every time.

But with this shot, I realized that I had used up the last syringe. I looked at the clock; I was going to have to swing by the vet's before I met this man. And I needed to feed Emily-Mae.

I took freshly cooked ground round out of the fridge, nuked it for a minute and a half, and stirred in a quarter teaspoon of psyllium husks—Mother Nature's intestinal broom. A dollop of flax seed oil and a shake of Doggie Gourmet Seasoning and it was dinnertime. Hell, she eats better than I do.

Emily-Mae inhaled her food as I grabbed my keys and ran out the door. My vet was located just five blocks south which meant if I speed-walked it, it would take me about six and a half minutes. I was already ten minutes late. I dashed out of my apartment building and headed west. But when I reached Broadway and turned left, I literally ran into a man sitting on the sidewalk at the corner of the building and tripped over his ankle. In an instant I was down on the cement.

I did a full body scan of myself before I moved anything. Although my knee stung, I sensed everything was still intact and was happy to realize I could move all fingers, toes, and limbs. Years of skiing taught me how to fall correctly. Then I noticed the man's sign. Written in black crayon on the side of a box was RIDDLED WITH AIDS — CAN'T WORK — WILL TAKE MONEY OR FOOD. I lay there contemplating this surreal moment when it dawned on me: He hadn't even noticed that I had tripped and fallen because he was so engrossed in reading a book titled *The One Minute Millionaire*.

I managed to get to a sitting position and assessed the damage. Feeling like a nerdy ten-year-old, I discovered that I had skinned my knee and torn a hole in my pants. My bookworm beggar, who looked healthier and more fit than I have at any time in my life, finally pulled his nose out of his hardback, shot me an obnoxious glance, buried his face back down into the book, and then said, "Hey klutz, look where you're stepping."

So, I picked myself up, dusted myself off, and in the most politically correct voice I could muster up, I replied with, "Get a fucking job!"

As I limped to the vet's it dawned on me that I hadn't seen my neighborhood bag lady in weeks. In fact, it may have been a couple of months since I had run into her. She was such a fixture in my daily routine that I feverishly erased thoughts and images of something awful having happened to her.

After purchasing a surplus of syringes, insulin, vitamins, supplements, and IV bags of lactated ringer solution for Emily-Mae, I rushed back to the Manhattan Diner with my large box of supplies. I paused for a moment in front of the restaurant to catch my breath and wipe the sweat from my brow, when suddenly, out of nowhere, a beautiful middle-aged blonde woman, chicly dressed and wearing a French beret, came barreling toward me in a motorized wheelchair. People were jumping out of her path as she tore down the sidewalk, headed right for me. I wasn't sure if I should go left or right, forward or back, so I stood still. And that's when she hit me. She ran right over my foot with her outrageously heavy wheelchair, causing me to drop the box of vet supplies and fall to the ground, again.

"What the hell was that?" I hollered.

Stunned, I sat there as I watched her continue to roar down the sidewalk. She spun her head around and yelled, "Watch where you're going, asshole!"

"Jesus Christ!" I exclaimed. What had happened to my neighborhood? I had recently nicknamed the Upper West Side of Manhattan "suburbia." Maybe I was wrong. This was more like a war zone.

I checked out the damage and discovered that I had torn my pants back pocket. I picked up the box, looked at my watch, and calculated that I was now forty-two minutes late. I entered the restaurant and it was packed.

This man had contacted me through my book's Web site and I was delighted to sign his copy, but all I really knew about him was that he was from Scranton, Pennsylvania, and his name was Huey. Honestly, I'm not one to stereotype but I automatically searched the diner for a big lump.

The hostess was eager to seat me at the counter but I told her I was meeting someone, so I marched myself up and down the restaurant searching for a solo diner. And of course, there was the big lump all the way in the back, squeezed into the very last banquette. I knew it was him because my book was on the table, but facedown. His face was also down. Down on the table. I wasn't sure if he was fat or not. He was layered in so many oversized thrift store clothes I couldn't tell what his body was like. And then there was his hair. Long, black, matted, and unwashed.

"Huey?" I asked tentatively, hoping this serial killer wasn't him.

He slowly turned his head to the side and looked at me through binocular glasses so thick I couldn't tell what color his eyes were. "You came."

I held out my hand to give him a shake but he didn't take it. "Of course I came. I said I would."

Huey, with his head still on the table, looked at his watch. "You're over forty minutes late."

I pulled my hand back and took a deep breath. "You know, it's a long story, and well, I'm sorry and I'm so appreciative that you took time out of what I'm sure is a busy day in the city to say hello to me and let me sign the book."

Huey lifted his head up off the table. "I came in only to meet you."

This felt weird. "OK. Wow. I'm really touched."

I threw my box of vet supplies down on the opposite seat and sat down. He relaxed and extended his hand across the table. It felt cold and damp so I shook it quickly but he held on to me. I dropped my elbow to the table and he continued to hold on as the waiter came by.

"Your menus."

He held them out to me but I had to cross my left hand over my right to grab them. Huey still had me in a handhold. The waiter seemed unfazed.

"Soup is split pea, vegetable is broccoli, and we're out of scrod," he said, leaving abruptly.

I managed to get my hand back.

"So, Huey," I said nervously as I picked up my book, "did you want me to sign your copy?"

He stared me down. "You want to leave, don't you?"

"I just got here. I haven't ordered anything. Why would I want to leave?" God I wanted to leave.

Huey looked at my box. "What's in there?"

I nervously patted the box like it was Emily-Mae. "Just medical supplies for my dog."

He raised an eyebrow suspiciously. "What's wrong with it?"

"She's antediluvian." I winked.

Huey thought very hard as I took a sip of my water. "I don't know that breed," he confessed.

I laughed so hard water sprayed out of my mouth. He picked up his napkin and wiped himself off, not amused.

"What's so funny, Curtis?"

I looked at him seriously. "I'm sorry. I thought you were just making . . ." I shifted gears. "Antediluvian isn't a breed, it means ancient." And then I lost it laughing again.

"You're laughing at me."

I looked serious again. "No. No Huey I'm not. Honestly, I'm laughing at myself."

The waiter returned just in the nick of time. "Ready?" he asked us.

I gestured to Huey to give his order first.

"I'll have the Reuben and Diet Coke."

The waiter looked at me.

"Do you have Maker's Mark?"

He looked across the restaurant and squinted at the bar. "Yeah."

"Good. Chilled, straight up in a martini glass, please?"

Huey looked at me. "Is that all you're having?"

"No," I said looking up at the waiter, smiling. "I'll have a cherry, too."

There was silence at the table after he left. Dead silence. Huey stared at me as I uncomfortably looked around the restaurant.

The next thirty minutes was the longest half-hour of my life. I discovered that Huey was surprisingly Puerto Rican. Surprising only because he didn't look Puerto Rican to me. And of course I opened my big mouth and said that and promptly offended him.

I also found out that he was an independent IT consultant and software developer. And I was shocked when it came time to autograph his book. Shocked because he pulled out four more for me to sign and they weren't copies for friends or relatives. He bought them all for himself. At that point I downed my drink.

Standing outside of the restaurant, I teetered a little as I held onto my box.

"Huey, it was a pleasure to meet you," I said rather officiously.

"Was it?" he asked, doubting my sincerity.

I nodded a little too enthusiastically. "Yes, it was. And please, have a safe trip back to Scrotum." It took a moment before I realized what I had said and then I doubled over in laughter. Once I gathered my composure, I stood up and Huey was gone.

Suddenly, I felt terrible. How could I be so insensitive? Sure I could have blamed it on the Maker's Mark or on the wine at the Queen of Wands, and it was a long and moving and exciting and exhausting day, and yes it was an honest mistake but did I have to laugh?

I tiptoed to the street corner and as I waited for the light to change I noticed that my shoe was untied. I put the box down next to me and bent over to tie the lace. Maybe it was the huddled position I was in or possibly it was the torn knee and back pocket of my pants but suddenly I heard someone call out to me.

"Hey panhandler."

I turned my head. It was the bookworm beggar.

"Get a fucking job!" he yelled as he threw pennies into my box and walked away.

SEVEN

A NEW LEASH ON LIFE

"Darcie, I don't think I can do this book signing," I cried as I tried to turn my head.

I could hear her face contort over the phone.

"You motherfucking cocksucker," she said endearingly. "I work my goddamn ass off to get you Barnes & Noble in Chelsea and then you piss on me?"

"Darcie, I am not pissing on you and I thank you from the bottom of my heart but I can't move my head."

I momentarily put the phone down and tried to look to my left. "Oooooowwww!"

"Serves you right for sucking some dick off in a back alley!" she screamed.

"From your mouth to God's ears. I did it towel drying my hair."

"You girl cock."

I dropped my phone I was laughing so hard. That was truly one of the funniest and best swear combinations she had ever come up with. But reaching down, picking up the phone, and standing back up only magnified my problem.

"Take down this number," she ordered. "He's Tripp with two 'p's.' The best Swedish masseur in town."

"Two p's?" I asked, trying not to laugh.

"Tripp Inwood," she said with a straight voice.

I lost it and started laughing while thinking to myself, *This has got to be one of those new age junkies.*

"He'll put you back together again. You're doing this signing at 7 o'clock or I'm breaking your fucking neck," she warned, slamming down the phone.

Swedish massage for me always felt good but it never really changed anything. And the thought of another man, especially if he's good looking, stripping me down and slapping oil on my loins never resulted in relaxation. The last treatment I had was with a practitioner who said he was half Russian, half Roman and, inevitably, I ended up with a headache from trying to not react to his rushin' hands and roamin' fingers. But desperate for relief, I called Tripp Inwood.

I was pleasantly surprised at how normal he sounded over the phone, was delighted that he could see me right away, and decided to splurge and pay the extra money to have him bring his table to my place. I'm blessed and forever grateful that my living room is larger than the total size of most people's apartments in New York City, but when I slid the heavy antique wooden coffee table to the side of the sofa to make room for Tripp's table, I managed to make my neck even worse.

Thinking that hot water would help to loosen up my muscles and that Tripp might appreciate a squeaky clean body, I drew a bath and filled it with a long forgotten and probably re-gifted Christmas present that was called a bath tea. A blend of lavender buds, orange oil, and chamomile flowers combined with Dead Sea salts, it not only smelled delicious but was also incredibly relaxing. Actually, a little too relaxing.

My buzzer rang in the kitchen, jarring me awake and hurtling me forward in the tub. My neck now felt fractured. I carefully and moanfully crawled out of the tub and threw a towel around myself as I tried to dash, with my head permanently cocked to one side, to the house phone to extinguish the never-ending buzzer.

I let Tripp into the building and worked my way to the front door as he rode the elevator up to my floor. I was so stooped over by this time I must have looked like an elderly man suffering from advanced osteoporosis.

I heard him come out of the elevator and then tried to look at him.

"Nice shoes," I said, unable to straighten up.

"Man, do you need this," Tripp said as I shuffled back inside.

Tripp had brought not only his table but also a wonderful aromatherapy candle, a stick of exotic incense, and some very relaxing new age music. And it wasn't till everything was all set up and I actually lay down on my back onto his table that I honestly got a good look at him.

"Hi," I said, smiling from ear to ear.

"Hey," Tripp said as he took out a bottle of massage oil. "Can I nuke this a second?"

Hell, he could nuke me.

"Of course," I said, trying to get up from the table.

"No, you stay put and relax. I'll be right back."

Miraculously, my neck allowed my head to follow him out of the living room and into the kitchen. Tripp stood probably five feet eleven and had a very nice swimmer's body. His longish blond hair made him look more like a surfer dude than a spiritual weirdo. He wore loose-fitting jeans and a T-shirt, and I guessed his age at about thirty-five.

He made his way back into the living room and I started to tremble. Not because of pain or because I was cold. I trembled at the thought of him touching me. I started counting the minutes till my headache would come in.

"Curtis, you're gonna have to unwrap yourself from that towel or I won't be able to do my job."

I nervously laughed as I allowed him to take it away from me and just as I predicted, there I was saluting him in all my glory. I felt cheap and excited.

I managed to squelch the possibly erotic moment with, "Sorry about that."

"Please, I'm flattered. And it's all part of your energy. And we want to make sure your energy is running smooth."

Oh God, I was in trouble. Tripp was *real* smooth and I sensed my soon-to-be headache would develop into a full-blown migraine at this rate. My vascular system beat so hard I was popping off his table. But Tripp draped a sheet over my body, stood above my head, and started to work his magic with my crippled neck.

I had never felt hands like his before. They were strong but sensitive. I could tell that his fingertips were actually listening to my body: diagnosing the situation and solving the problem. He was good and at one point I drifted off to another place. We didn't speak much as he worked but I do remember him telling me that I was in an alpha state. A brain wavelength frequency we're in during dreaming. The remarkable thing was that I was still awake.

"A lot of my clients creatively solve problems from this place. It's cool," he whispered.

It was. And so was he. In fact, I was extremely impressed. He decided not to have me lie on my stomach for fear of aggravating my neck so he had me lie on my side. He slipped a pillow under my head and sat on the table, supporting my back with the side of his body. He then cradled my top arm with the bend in his arm and worked my head, neck, shoulders, and upper back in this fashion. It was such a comfortable and nurturing position to receive bodywork in; I was shocked when I started to cry. He allowed me to move through the moment.

"Just let it go, Curtis. We tend to store old stuff in our backs. It can go back as far as childhood trauma. Stuff we haven't processed. Stuff we don't want to process. Stuff we don't know we need to process. Just let it go."

He was so good that I emerged from this experience not only without a headache but also without any neck pain. I was absolutely pain free.

"I swear I could do rapid fire jazz dance head turns right now," I declared.

"Please don't," laughed Tripp as he started to pack up his things. "Unless you want another session."

"I do! I do! Tripp you really are talented."

He actually blushed, which I found extremely attractive. "Flattery will get you everywhere."

I smiled as I went to get my checkbook. "I'd have cash for you but I didn't have time to run to the bank."

"Checks are fine. Just make it out to Harold Inwood."

"Nice name," I said as I started to write.

"Scottish here."

"I'm half English, but my mother pleads with me not to mention the other half."

"Which is?"

"Irish." I smiled at him. "So where does Tripp come in."

He kind of kicked his shoe in a gosh gee kind of way. "Do you see me as a Harold?"

I shook my head. "No I don't."

"I'm actually Harold Stanton Inwood III. And being the third . . ."

"Tripp! I get it." I handed him his check and added a little extra.

"Hey, you didn't have to do that," he exclaimed.

"As long as you're not insulted, I wanted to show my appreciation." Awkwardly, I walked him to the door. "Thanks again. Darcie was going to kill me if I didn't make it to this book signing tonight."

"She called me. Barnes & Noble, right?"

I nodded. I wasn't sure if he was *interested* interested in me but I sure knew I was interested in him. I thought about embracing him but he reached out and shook my hand very firmly as the elevator arrived.

"And I'm sorry about the getting mushy with the tears and all."

He smiled. "Not a problem. I think a man who can feel his emotions is very attractive."

OK, now what?

He stepped into the elevator. "Guess I'll be going."

I was so impressed with how professional he was and not crossing boundaries and jumping on top of the massage table and having his way with me, but boy did I want him to lose his integrity right now.

"Well, bye. Have a safe . . " I caught myself.

"Tripp!" he smiled as the door closed.

Damn he was nice. Now I needed a cold shower.

⋛ ⋜

Minutes before I was leaving to do the book signing my phone rang and caller ID indicated Quinn Larkin.

"You better not be canceling," I warned as I answered the phone. Due to the background noise I could definitely tell he was calling from outside.

"Back, get back!" Quinn screamed.

I tried to figure out what was happening. "Hello?"

"I'll be at the Barnes & Noble," he said, sounding like he was wrestling someone to the ground.

I grabbed my coat and checked myself in the mirror. "I'm heading down there now. I need your moral support."

"Let's meet out front. I'll be there and I have news to tell you."

"I do too," I smiled, thinking of Tripp.

I heard a truck horn blast and Quinn scream followed by the oddest sounds.

"Drop it!" yelled Quinn.

Then his cell went dead. I grabbed my exquisite McKlein oversized distressed brown leather briefcase—that is cutting edge enough to have a pouch for my laptop but has that retro feel of your dad's bashed up fifties valise—and dashed out the door. I tried to hail a cab but at six-thirty on a weeknight, none were to be found. During my brisk walk uptown to the subway I called Quinn's cell back several times, only to be put through to his voice mail.

I glanced at my watch and realized once again I was cutting it close as I came around the corner of 23rd Street and 6th. I threw a mint into my mouth, made sure everything was in place as I caught a glimpse of my reflection in a store window, and patiently waited at 22nd Street for cars to pass before I crossed.

Something was creating a commotion in front of Barnes & Noble but a little voice in my head told me it wasn't a mob of hungry book buyers eager to hear me read from *101 Ways to Collide into Your Gay Soul Mate*. A large truck slowly passed and like a herd of cattle, we the masses crossed the street. I stared straight ahead trying to decipher what was going on. The front of the store looked like the Westminster Dog Show and who was the master of ceremonies?

"Quinn!" I hollered from about a half block away. "Quinn!"

He couldn't hear me over all the commotion. Dogs were barking. People were yelling. And Quinn was literally in the middle of it all.

There was a brindle-colored bullmastiff with a head the size of a cannon ball, a snow white Skye terrier with an extraordinarily long torso, a burnt-orange, medium-size mutt, a stunning black-and-tan Gordon retriever standing waist high, a heather-gray Scottish terrier, a dark brown wall-eyed pug, an apricot miniature poodle, and a teensy weensy shivering beige Chihuahua.

"What the hell are you doing?" I screamed.

Pedestrians were not amused with the sidewalk traffic jam he had created and I still couldn't figure out why he was tied up amongst all the leashes. An ambulance zoomed by with its siren blaring, which then triggered off all the dogs to start howling at the top of their lungs.

"Quinn!"

Finally he heard me.

"Curtis!" he cried. "Help me!"

I worked my way carefully into the vortex of canines and started untangling him.

"Whose dogs are these?" I asked, spinning him clockwise. "How did you get mixed up in this?" I asked, spinning him counterclockwise. "Where are the owners?" I asked, spinning him clockwise again.

"Stop it. You're making me dizzy!"

The two of us managed to pull the dogs to the side of the walk so people could at least get by and Quinn took a couple of deep breaths.

"As you know, I lost my job, temporarily I hope, doing Ann's full body makeup."

Just then the apricot miniature poodle snapped at the humongous bull-mastiff.

Quinn jerked her leash. "Stop it, Butch."

I looked down at the creature. "That little thing is Butch?"

"Wait," Quinn said, catching his breath. "The giant mastiff is Brie. And all of these dogs are now in my care. I'm their dog walker."

"How did this happen?"

"Gaye with an 'e'," Quinn declared.

"Gaye Dumont! A voice from the past."

Gaye with an "e" is a smart, single, straight mother of three challenging teenagers. She's a Tony award-winning Broadway actress whom Quinn and I met when we were all in our twenties and studying acting with Uta Hagen.

I shook my head. "I haven't seen her in ages."

"I hadn't either," agreed Quinn. "I ran into her in the subway and I told her of my woes and then she hooked me up with this actress who had to go out of town with a show who was walking these dogs. So, I took over her route."

"Gaye with an 'e' is the queen of *Law and Order* now. I swear she guest stars at least once a month."

"Curtis, it's 'cause she's so emotional."

I nodded. "No one cries like Gaye Dumont."

"But wait!" Quinn exclaimed. "To supplement her income and eliminate the need to do regional, stock, and touring theater, she's gone back to school to become, get this, a licensed acupuncturist."

"Get out!"

Probably to the detriment of society, I thought.

"But, Curtis, there's more. I'm going to be staying at her brownstone down in the East Village."

"Gaye with an 'e' has solved all your problems."

He licked his lips. "And her oldest son is gorgeous."

"And jailbait." I could foresee trouble. "Congratulations," I said patting him on the back, which prompted the wall-eyed pug to growl at me.

"Tulip is quite protective of me already," he said proudly, bending down to pat her head.

I looked at my watch. "But you hate dogs."

Quinn corrected me. "I don't hate dogs. I hate picking up their crap."

And on cue, the oversized Gordon retriever spun around twice and prepped for an evacuation.

"Shit!" Quinn cried.

"That it is," I agreed, realizing that dog must have had one huge lunch.

Quinn searched his pants and coat pockets. "What the hell are these owners feeding these beasts? I'm out of bags! Give me something fast."

I threw my hands up. "Sorry, I don't have anything on me."

Quinn started to panic. "I already got one fine today from a fucking cop on a bicycle."

"A fine for what?"

"Leaving the scene of a poop."

I tried as hard as I could to suppress the smile.

"And I wasn't leaving the scene. I had to get to the corner to grab some free newspapers to pick it up with. Fifty bucks he slapped me with."

"That's some pricey shit."

Quinn's eyes bugged out of his head as he started digging into my briefcase. "Give me something. Give me something now. A cop is coming!"

He grabbed a bunch of flyers for the book signing and started picking up the mess.

"Geez, thanks a lot, Quinn. Now I've got shit on my face."

The policeman stopped temporarily and then walked on by once he was certain Quinn was obeying the law.

"Just doing my doodie duty, officer!" Quinn hollered with a little too much attitude.

The cop looked back at him and I could tell he was deciding whether to call him on it. Luckily, he moved on.

"Quinn, you want another fine? Keep your mouth shut."

And that's when I noticed the Chihuahua. During this brouhaha all the other dogs were nervous and skittish and practically trampling this tiny Mexican dog, so I picked her up. She was barely large enough to fill up my palm.

"Quinn, she's shaking to death."

"Karen shakes all the time."

I looked at him in disbelief. "Her name is Karen?" He nodded. "I'm sorry but she shouldn't be with this pack of dogs."

In truth, I felt she shouldn't be under the supervision of Quinn. None of those dogs should have been.

"I'm a little overwhelmed here, Curtis, and I have to take these things to their respective homes. I can't play nursemaid to Taco Burrito at the moment."

Obviously Quinn wasn't going to make it to my reading. And then I suggested the unthinkable.

"Why don't I take Karen in with me. She'll fit in my bag and then you can scoot around when you are done taking all the other dogs home and pick her up."

Quinn shook his head. "I really don't think that's necessary, Curtis."

"But I do." I opened up my McKlein valise and gently plopped her inside. "Go, do your business."

"Bad choice of words," Quinn laughed.

I turned around and headed into Barnes & Noble. "Hey, I met a guy."

"You what?"

I waved back to him without turning around.

≳ ≲

The book signing was actually, for the most part, a wonderful success. Every author has the fear that no one is going to show up at one of these events. Worse yet, that only two or three people show up. So, you demand that every person you know within a twenty-five-mile radius make an appearance or else. A sprinkling of colleagues came but I was really surprised to see that it was standing room only, full of strangers. And of course, there was Darcie.

"Isn't Tripp the fucking best?" she asked, slapping me on the back.

I stumbled a bit forward. "Yes, but don't throw it out again."

She glanced at my briefcase. "Something's moving in your goddamn case," she declared, falling back a step.

I covered it as quickly as I could. "Don't be silly. Just papers and . . ." I looked up above. "Air conditioning blowing." I quickly closed it up as she looked at me suspiciously.

The manager of the store spoke first and said some really nice things about my book and me. Then I was brought up to the front of the room and was introduced to the audience. I placed my briefcase underneath the podium, opened it up, and gave Karen a sweet pet.

Then I spoke a little about the concept of the book, how closely I worked with Darcie on it, and that I was thrilled that people were enjoying it so much. They had me read a few excerpts, some of which were practical, others that were humorous, and then the room was open to questions and answers.

I was pretty impressed with some of them. Impressed with their questions because I hadn't a clue as to what they were talking about. The first
person to speak was maybe in her late sixties, had her hair done up in a
bun on top of her head, and was wearing a tweed shawl. And she must have
had one too many face-lifts because her mouth had that trout pout.

"Hello Mr. Jenkins. My name is Mona Gaffe," she said, standing up.
"I'm a spiritual metaphysicist."

I heard the entire room think to themselves, "What the hell is that?"

She continued. "And I personally believe that the two of us, in a very
similar fashion, are helping the gay, lesbian, bisexual, and transgender com-
munities immensely when it comes to the physiology of gay dating."

I hesitated for a moment, trying to make sense of what she was saying
and then I responded effusively. "OK."

"Mr. Jenkins, you're breaking new ground."

I looked down at the floor, which created some giggles. What ground? I
was wondering if she was mistaking my book for someone else's. Just then,
Karen popped her head out of the briefcase and I quickly patted her and
nestled her back down into it.

"But I did some research and was wondering, considering you don't have
any educational background pertaining to this subject matter, what makes
you an expert on this topic?"

Shit, here we go again.

I took a dramatic pause and then said in a flat, droll voice, "I'm gay and
I date?" Thank God that made the crowd laugh. I looked over at the store
manager hoping she would give this woman the hook.

She read my expression. "Thank you, Ms. Gaffe. Anyone else have a
question?" The manager pointed to a disheveled young man with longish
brown hair and thick horn-rimmed glasses.

He stood up and was obviously very nervous. He coughed and managed
to whisper out, "My name is Albert."

"Hi, Albert," I said warmly, trying to make him feel as comfortable as
possible. "Thank you for coming to my reading."

"Um, you're welcome," he said, almost embarrassed to look at my face.
"Um, I was wondering, if maybe, um, I could interview you for a college
thesis paper I'm writing that is dealing, um, with the social context of gay
interpersonal communication in the twenty-first century?"

I caught Darcie out of the corner of my eye shaking her head no.

"Sure," I blurted out a little too quickly. I immediately thought of the
meeting I had had with Huey and felt a sinking feeling in my stomach.

This time Darcie spoke up. "We have time for one more question and then Mr. Jenkins would be delighted to sign copies of his book for all of you."

Albert slowly sunk back into his seat as a woman shouted out from the back of the room, "Do you think you did this all on your own or do you credit your mother for your talent and exceptionally good looks?"

I stood on my tiptoes to see her and then asked, "Could you please stand and repeat that question . . . Mother?"

The room broke out into laughter. She stood up, took a bow, and waved to the crowd as they applauded her. I couldn't describe what she was wearing, probably because it was glaringly bright. I know it's OK to wear white after Labor Day but Mother had taken it one step too far. From head to toe she was decked out in whites. A high collared white linen and lace Victorian blouse, a white linen peasant skirt, white boots, a white cashmere sweater coat, and a strand of some sort of white flowers in her hair. She was the White Party.

My mother's grand bow marked the ending of the reading. Still in awe of her bizarre getup, I noticed that she had turned to her left, looked at someone, and then she did a double take. And standing in the opposite far corner of the room, looking like a blond Adonis, that someone was Harold Stanton Inwood III.

I couldn't believe he came. He must want me! But realizing that my mother was now trying to get his attention, I switched into don't-you-dare mode. Before sitting down to sign books I bolted over to intercept her.

My mother stretched her hand out to Tripp. "Well, hello there."

Just in time, I put my hand in hers. "Thank you for coming, Mother." I gave Tripp a huge smile and spun her around, away from him, whispering, "Hands off, he's mine."

"What?" she asked totally confused.

"I just had a massage from him today and he's here to see me."

She gave him the once over. "I wouldn't mind a massage."

I gave her a look that could kill.

"Curtis, when did you become so possessive?"

I brought my voice down even softer. "Mother, he's gay."

She squinted her eyes and scanned him again. "I wouldn't be so sure of that."

At least I thought he was. I guess he could be bisexual. Or maybe straight? No. He flirted with me. He did say to me that he thought a man who shows emotions is attractive. He must be gay. I think?

The Barnes & Noble store manager pulled me out of my doubting inner monologue. "Curtis, your fans await you."

Regrettably, I had to trust my mother but before I went over to the signing table I gave her one more look, hoping to keep her at bay. "Mother, he told me flattery would get me everywhere."

She stuck her tongue out at me.

Most writers would kill to have a line as long as mine of people having purchased their book and wanting an autograph. But my attention kept going back to Tripp and wondering whether or not he liked me. At one point I looked up and he was gone. I was almost relieved to know that I had probably lost him when all of a sudden he was standing before me with a copy of my book.

I sat there just staring at him.

"I thought since you've sampled my work that I should at least read your book."

My God he was sexy.

"But don't buy one, Tripp. Let me just give you one."

"Too late. I already dished out my $19.95," he said, smiling. He handed me the book to sign and I panicked, trying to think of something to write. Most writers have several stock phrases they use but none seemed appropriate right now. So, I just scribbled something, closed the cover, and handed it back to him.

Tripp promptly opened the book and read it out loud. A little too loud. "Tripp, maybe this is the one hundred and second way to collide into your soul mate? Flatteringly, Curtis."

Embarrassed that everyone heard what I wrote, I was scared to look up at him.

"We'll just have to find out."

I shot him a glance, he winked at me, and then walked away slowly with a sultry strut.

Having witnessed all of this, Darcie hit me on the back of head with her hand and then whispered into my ear, "Back to business, cocksucker."

That thought put a smile on my face. I signed another copy, realized there was just one more man left in line, and then looked to the back of the room. Quinn had arrived and was talking to my mother and Tripp had joined them.

"Could you sign my copy to me, Paul?"

Totally distracted, I looked up at the man and said, "Yeah, sure."

It was bad enough that my mother was interested in Tripp. Now I had to deal with Quinn. I scribbled an autograph and thanked the man for buying my book.

As I got up to rush over to Tripp, Paul said, "Hey, wait a minute. You did this wrong."

I looked at him, confused. "What?"

"I said my name was Paul. You wrote this to Paula."

I took the book from him. "Paul, I'm so sorry." I grabbed another book and started scribbling while looking up and down at Tripp. I squinted, trying to see what was going on. Was it my imagination or had he just given business cards to both my mother and Quinn? Shit! I closed the book and handed it to Paul. I jumped up from the table and he caught my arm.

"You got my name right, but you signed yours, 'All the Best, Shit'," Paul said, handing it back to me.

"Damn it." I just grabbed another book and handed it to him. "Here, keep all three."

I rushed to the back of the room but by the time I got to Quinn and my mother, Tripp was gone.

I was about to interrogate them, but Quinn said, "I have to take Karen home."

I stood frozen.

"Curtis, where is she?"

"Who's Karen?" my mother asked. Getting no response from either of us, she announced that she was going to the little girl's room.

Where had I left my briefcase? I ran back to the autographing table, looked underneath it, and then remembered that I parked it at the podium. I dashed over to it and there it was, lying on its side. I said a prayer to all the gods and looked inside. Karen was gone. Quinn caught up with me.

"I'm so late; her owners are going to kill me."

I turned around sheepishly. "I'm afraid they're going to kill me, too."

Quinn studied my face and knew in an instant. "You have to be fucking kidding me!"

"She was here up until . . ."

"You have to be absolutely fucking kidding with me! A Chihuahua somewhere in this fucking huge Barnes & Noble? We will never ever find her, Curtis!"

I was trying not to panic. Quinn would do enough of that for both of us.

I took a deep breath. "Let's just stay calm and look for her right around here."

"When was the last time you saw her?"

I looked at my watch. "Thirty minutes ago?"

Quinn was about to have a heart attack.

"I'm sorry, Quinn, but I had a signing to do."

"You are the one who insisted on taking her!"

I started looking under all the seats. "Let's just focus. The good thing is we're on the street level. I mean if we were up on the second floor she could break her neck falling off the balcony or worse, step onto the escalator and get squashed to death."

Quinn gave me a sarcastic look. "Oh, thanks. That makes me feel a lot better. It's just that being on the street level, she could walk right out the..."

We looked at each other in horror and whispered simultaneously, "Front door."

"Lose something, boys?" Darcie asked as she was about to head out.

We both stood up, looking like the cat that swallowed the canary.

"No, Darcie," I said. "Great signing. Thanks so much for setting it up for me."

She looked at me apprehensively. "You're welcome." She walked toward the exit as Quinn and I stood there smiling a little too hard. She spun around and laughed, "Maybe it was your briefcase that upped and walked away?"

"Honestly, Darcie," I said much too calmly. "Nothing to worry about."

She shook her head as she turned to leave. "Shit-ass liars."

Darcie stepped into the front revolving door and pushed it with all her might. Midway the door came to an abrupt halt.

"Karen!" Quinn screamed.

Stuck halfway out, Darcie jiggled the door, pushed with all her might; it jolted and then started revolving again.

"Oh my God," I whispered as the two of us ran to see the damage as Darcie exited the building.

I looked through the glass as Quinn dashed out the push/pull door, inspecting the door from that angle. He looked at me, reached down, and picked it up. In both hands he showed me a flyer for my reading. It had jammed the revolving door. Relieved that it wasn't Karen, he came back in and we went ballistic looking for her.

Before alerting Barnes & Noble that we had lost a dog in their store that doesn't allow dogs to be brought in, we checked underneath every chair, looked up and down every row of bookcases, and in and out of every open cabinet used for storage.

Frightened and exhausted, the two of us sat down on the floor at the back of the store.

"Quinn, I'm so sorry," I said, putting my arm around him. "I don't know what to do."

He just sat there shaking his head in disbelief when a woman came running out of the ladies' room, hysterical.

"Jesus Christ!" she hollered as she passed us. "Goddamn Snow White is petting a rat in the bathroom the size of a Chihuahua."

Quinn and I looked at each other and bolted to the bathroom. And there they were. Mother was cuddling a trembling little Karen in her hands.

"Aw, you sweet thing. It's OK," she said, trying to calm her down.

"Karen!" Quinn cried.

My mother looked at me, smiling. "So, this is her? She was huddling next to the radiator trying to get warm."

Quinn took her from my mother and kissed her all over her tiny pea-sized head. "*Usted es una traviesa, traviesa pequeña niña exploradora*," he cooed as they exited the bathroom.

My mother quickly went into Spanish/English translation mode. "Did he just say, 'You are a naughty, naughty, little . . . girl scout'?"

"Yes, Snow White," I smiled as we walked out together.

EIGHT

TOUCH AND TELL

Later that evening I called Tripp to thank him for coming to my reading and especially for buying my book. I also wanted to ask him out to dinner. Why didn't I wait a few days and be coy about it? I feared my mother would get to him before me. To my surprise, he was the one who asked me.

I hadn't been on a date since the fiasco with Timber and normally I would have considered wearing any number of outfits that I thought were pretty hip, but considering Tripp was so relaxed and laid back, I opted to go in another direction. I like jeans and wear them once in a while but I'm much more of slacks kind of guy. Way in the back of my closet I found an old, faded, naturally-distressed-over-time pair of sloppy jeans. And considering it was on the chilly side, I layered an avocado-green long sleeve cotton shirt over a white T-shirt. I slipped on black Timberland boots and my authentic, totally worn dark brown leather motorcycle jacket and I was ready to go.

Tripp lived on East 9th Street so I suggested a favorite Italian restaurant of mine, Basilica, located in Hell's Kitchen. He could come uptown while I could go down and it would be meeting kind of halfway. Basilica was a gem. It was tiny, romantic, the staff was extremely friendly but not so much that they were intrusive, and the food was out of this world. It was very popular and considering they could only seat about thirty people I suggested that we have dinner on the later side. And conveniently located across the street was a popular gay bar, Garage. So we decided to meet there for drinks first.

Garage was a gay lounge that wasn't quite sure of its identity. Originally, I think it was aiming at the hip urban gay professional. They had hundreds of models' 8 × 10s mounted on the walls, and on the street-side wall was a glassed garage door. Then a while back they redid the place in a kind of sixties retro—beads and nude female velvet art décor—but kept the glassed garage door. Oops, they did it again. Now they had gotten rid of the bare-chested women and were back to the 8 × 10s. Upon entering, one didn't know if this was a snooty, stuck-up, high-attitude bar catering only to the A-list crowd, or if it was a cool, kitschy, tongue-in-cheek hangout for the artsy-fartsy group. The confusing result was—and hold onto your hats boys—that people at this place tended to be nice. How novel!

The cocktail rush hour was over and I got to Garage before Tripp, so I plopped myself down at the bar and ordered my usual.

"Maker's Mark, chilled, straight up in a martini glass, please?"

The exceptionally attractive bartender smiled. "Want a cherry?"

"Only if the stem is long enough."

He smiled knowing what I was referring to.

Some people may characterize me as a control freak; I prefer to see myself as an orchestrator. Stools at the bar were full, lounge chairs were free, so I eyeballed the room for the best place to sit. I didn't want to be too far front, where hoards of people tend to congregate, nor too far back where no one can see you. Right in the middle was perfect.

The bartender poured my bourbon almost to the rim and held up a bowl of maraschino cherries with moderately long stems for me to see.

"Acceptable," I said as he picked one up and plopped it into my glass. Filled beyond the brim, the smoky-colored liquor now magically danced a millimeter above the lip of the glass.

I took a long hard sip of the Maker's Mark while it was still on the bar, to bring it down to a level that I could at least walk with, but when I came up for air the bartender was smiling at me with his arms crossed, waiting for me to prove my talent.

I nodded to him, accepting the challenge, and delicately fished the garnish out of my drink. I bit the cherry off and took my time eating it while eyeing him. He smiled as I swallowed and took another sip of my drink.

I held the cherry stem up for him to see and then pointed to his watch. He watched the second hand and then pointed to me.

"Go," he said.

I placed the cherry stem on my tongue and knew instantly this was a perfect specimen. Like tying my shoe, I crossed left over right with my tongue and pushed the knobbed end of the stem through the loop. I hooked it in front of my top teeth while pressing the stem up to the roof of my mouth, closing the knot. I then stuck out my tongue presenting a perfectly knotted cherry stem.

Three men sitting across from me applauded.

The bartender shook his head. "Damn, thirty-eight seconds."

"Wait till my second drink. I'll do it faster," I promised as I left him a tip and the tied knot.

"Too bad you're not straight," the bartender said. "Women would love you."

"Men do, too," I replied, very uncharacteristically cocky.

I grabbed a bowl of what looked like goldfish crackers tossed with trail mix, turned, and slowly walked away from my audience, showing off my best side. I chose a love seat located in the middle of the lounge, placing my drink and the bowl on the coffee table. The nibbles weren't for me, I was thinking of my guest. I was not going to eat food that strangers had been double-dipping saliva-soaked fingertips into all night. Actually, for that matter, I didn't want Tripp digging into it either. If things went according to plans, I was going to be kissing this man and much more, so I dashed back to the bar to return the unappetizing bar snacks and promptly bumped into Tripp, spilling the entire bowl all over his crotch.

Time stood still as we both tried to register this faux pas. It was the bartender rushing over with a broom to sweep up the mess that made both of us laugh.

"Great first impression I just made," I said, wanting to brush off the crumbs.

"Great second impression," Tripp corrected me.

Like a puppy dog, I just wanted to follow this man all over.

He turned to the bartender. "Scotch straight up, no chaser."

I wondered if his order was an omen. Did it have a hidden message? Straight up? No, of course he's gay. No chaser? I'm not chasing him. He invited me out to dinner. Still, I switched to less obsessive mode and returned to the love seat. Observing him, I chuckled inside because as much as I was trying to dress for him, he was doing the same for me. Tripp had on a really nice pair of charcoal gray flannel slacks and a light purple button-down dress shirt and topped it off with a really expensive-looking black peacoat.

As he joined me, with his drink, I realized that I had missed the opportunity to kiss or even embrace him upon meeting. I jumped up to my feet for a second chance, and he took a seat. I couldn't orchestrate that, either.

I sat back down and held up my glass. "Cheers."

"Bottoms up," he replied.

"Mine already was," I blurted out, instantly wanting to retract it.

"My turn, next," he smiled.

I felt my eyes get bigger and I was sure the surprise registered on my face. He winked and smiled harder and that's when I noticed that this beautiful Scottish blond with violet-blue eyes and classic good looks was actually missing a tooth. Not that it was a front tooth or even a canine. It was a bicuspid, the tooth with two points that sits between the canine and the molars. It ruined his beautiful smile and for the life of me, I couldn't stop looking at it.

I asked Tripp where he grew up and he went into a lengthy monologue about Southern California and his family and childhood but all I kept thinking about was his missing tooth. I know that replacing teeth can be very expensive, whether it's a bridge or especially an implant. And it's not a vanity thing or that I'm a snob about dental hygiene. My pickiness honestly comes from years of myself having to deal with problematic teeth and Nazi-like dentists when I was a youth.

But every time Tripp smiled, and he did so a lot, all I wanted to do was run back to the bar and grab just one large double-dipped goldfish cracker and stick it up into that vacant space in his mouth. He caught me staring at his black hole.

"I love your smile, Tripp."

He blushed. "A lot of people actually comment on my teeth."

I kept my commentary to myself. Maybe it was a financial thing and he was just waiting to get the money together to get it fixed. There was no reason to judge him on his jack-o-lantern smile.

During that round of drinks Tripp and I played The King and I. ("Getting to Know You"?) But as it got later and later, more people showed up and the decibel level got louder and louder. It was still a bit early for our dinner reservation but trying to speak over the din of the crowd, I was starting to lose my voice and suggested that we head over to Basilica.

Luckily, a table for two was ready for us. Located against the exposed brick wall without another deuce next to us, we had a little more privacy in this very cozy restaurant.

"Are you hungry, hungry, or hungry?" I asked as Tripp picked up his menu.

He smiled. "Hungry!"

I relaxed, feeling he got my sense of humor. "Me too and everything is homemade, fresh, and fantastic."

Tripp unfolded the four-page menu. "This bill of fare is larger than the restaurant."

I nodded. "Wait till you see the kitchen on the way back to the restrooms. It's the size of a closet."

"Anything you suggest, Curtis?"

I looked down the menu. "I know it sounds simple, but their linguini with red clam sauce is out of this world. There's something in the sauce that is indescribably delicious."

"Then that's what I'll have."

I looked up at him. "You're easy."

"In more ways than one." He winked.

I closed my menu, thinking *I like this guy.*

"Curtis, what are you going to have?"

I frowned. "I've heard their veal saltimbocca is exquisite, but I can't get past the idea of eating the flesh of a sweet little calf that has spent its entire short life chained up and force-fed. So, I think I'll be a complete hypocrite and ignore the fact that this fowl probably led a life of extreme hardship in a cramped and filthy cage and opt for this dish, which is wrapped in prosciutto and sautéed in dry white and marsala wines with capers and anchovies."

Tripp searched the menu. "Which is that?"

I paused dramatically. "The well-hung woodcock."

Tripp burst out into laughter. "It doesn't say . . ." He stopped talking as he read the description of the dish. "Well, what do you know? It does say a well-hung woodcock. What the hell is a woodcock?"

"I don't know," I said, closing my menu and winking. "And at my age I thought I had eaten everything."

"Curtis, you make it sound like you're ancient." He leaned in closer to me. "Remember, my hands have been all over your body. You're not that old. I've counted your rings."

"Like a tree?" I signaled the waiter to come over. "And for the record, I'm forty-five."

Tripp sat back. "I'm impressed. I pegged you for mid-thirties, like myself."

I grinned. "Still interested?"

He grinned back. "More so. I like older men."

I looked down at the flickering candle. Tripp may have been a great masseur but that just didn't rub me the right way.

He continued. "Older men who have beautiful hazel eyes, funny crooked noses, intelligent high foreheads, and thick, curly brown hair."

I smiled. Good recovery.

The waiter appeared to take our order and I took the lead. "My friend here will have the linguini with red clam sauce, I'll have the well-hung woodcock. We'll split your mesclun salad, and a bottle of Pinot Grigio." I looked over at Tripp for approval and he nodded.

"Thank you, gentlemen." The waiter bowed and scooted back to the kitchen.

I proceeded to have one of the most romantic and interesting dates I had had in years. Tripp was charming, intelligent, conversational, funny, and so freaking handsome. We covered topics ranging from theater and film to politics (he was a Democrat, thank God) and environmental problems to hobbies and sports (that I know of) to museums and travel. And he was a foodie like myself.

Speaking of which, we not only devoured our food but shared each other's entrees and ended up ordering a second bottle of wine. Time was suspending in animation as we gracefully danced the age-old steps of the mating ritual.

I shared with Tripp my love of animals and that in college I started out majoring in pre-veterinarian medicine. And although I was acing my academic courses, the animal science department pulled a couple of fast ones. To sift and sort through potential doctors, as opposed to those who were half-hearted and lacking in courage and strong stomachs, they had a unique way of finding out who had the guts to pursue this career from those who lost their guts pursuing the career.

"Wait, I need another sip of wine," Tripp said. "What did they have you do?"

I needed a larger sip of wine. "After mastering artificially inseminating chickens and horses, I graduated to sheep."

We both took another swig of wine.

"Tripp, it's a good thing we didn't order lamb."

He put his head down. Something sick inside of me enjoyed doing this.

"Do you know your sheep terminology?"

Keeping his head down, he said, "No."

"A newborn sheep is called a lamb until it is weaned at approximately five months. Then they are called a weaner."

Tripp looked up and smiled.

"I thought you'd like that. When they are nearly one year old they are called a hogget. I said hogget not faggot. A female sheep is called a ewe. A male sheep is a ram. Now, what do you think a ram is called when I am forced—with a huge, rusty, heavy pair of metal scissors—to cut off his testicles without the aid of any anesthetic?"

He dropped his head.

"When a ram is castrated it is called a wether. Snip, snip, and then you follow up with a spray, spray of antibacterial that also clots the blood."

Tripp's head dropped farther.

"I agree! I was so upset I brought the college up on charges of cruelty to animals. And I'm proud to say they had to change their castral procedures."

Tripp looked up. "Is castral a word?"

"It is when I've had a Maker's Mark followed by a bottle of wine. Long story short, I switched over to the next sensible major, theater."

He clinked my wine glass. "Now that makes sense."

I hoped that Tripp was having as good a time as I was, but it was while sharing an order of Basilica's sinfully rich chocolate mousse dessert that I fell head over heels for Harold Stanton Inwood III.

"So how did you get into massage?" I asked, wanting to know everything about this man.

"Surfing injury."

I slapped the table a little too hard, causing a loud noise and the water glasses to spill a bit. "Sorry," I said to others sitting around us. "I knew you were a surfer dude."

Tripp went on to tell me that after a huge wave had wiped him out there was damage to his lower lumbar vertebrae. Western doctors wanted to put him under the knife and insert a rod for structural support. But Tripp trusted his instincts and said no. He went alternative and worked diligently with a chiropractor and an acupuncturist. But he felt that what his shiatsu practitioner offered helped the most.

"The shiatsu changed my life." Tripp circled the rim of his wine glass with his fingertip. "Shiatsu saved my life."

There was a quiet moment and then his eyes started to well up. And then my eyes started to well up. And then he slipped his hand into mine.

"I just had to learn everything I could about this style of bodywork. It's like acupuncture but without the needles, working with the same meridians. I came east to study with Ohashi, a renowned master from Japan. He not only became my teacher but also a dear friend. And once he taught me everything he knew, I learned other modalities like Swedish and Thai massage and created my own blend of style. And it just felt right to stay here in New York City and start my own practice."

"Isn't it amazing how sometimes a horrible situation can turn into such a wonderful life-changing opportunity?"

Tripp squeezed my hand. I can't remember the last time I sat in a restaurant and felt 100 percent comfortable holding another man's hand.

He looked at his watch and was surprised how late it was. "Man, I have to be up early tomorrow."

"Massage?"

"No, I visit Delores. Do errands for her and some shopping."

I was in the dark. "A friend? A relative?"

"Oh no. Delores is an elderly widow whom I was matched up with through a volunteer service. I've been visiting her now for about two and a half years. Everyone in her life has passed, including her kids. So I drop by as often as I can to make sure she's taking her medications and is eating enough food. Or sometimes I read to her or we listen to the radio. Her eyes are pretty shot and well, I just don't think she's going to be around much longer. I don't think she wants to be."

It was all so admirable but sad. I didn't know what to say. "Thank God she has you."

Tripp played with his napkin. "I'm lucky to have her. I never knew my grandparents and in her own special way, she's helping me."

Damn, I really liked this guy. The waiter appeared with the check and I grabbed it before Tripp could.

"Hey, I want to pay for that," he said.

I pulled out my wallet. "Nope."

He tried to grab the check out of my hand but I was too quick. "Can we at least split it?"

I slipped cash into the check folder. "Nope."

"Can we do this again and then I treat?"

"That, Harold Stanton Inwood III, is a deal." I looked at him, thinking *This one is a keeper.*

≥ ≤

"Petra, Tripp is so sweet and sexy and sensitive and he has a sense of humor."

"He sounds like superman." She looked down at a piece of paper. "It says here that we take a left at the next street."

"I bet if anyone could leap tall buildings with a single bound or run faster than a speeding locomotive . . ."

"Or have X-ray vision?" she added.

"Then that would be Tripp," I gushed.

Petra stopped and looked up at me, smiling. "I think you are smitten."

"I am. We've had countless dates now and I just keep liking this guy more and more." I was so happy I gave her a huge hug and then looked around. "Now, where the hell are we?"

It was a brilliant, sunny, crisp fall day and Petra was keeping this Manhattan excursion a total secret. We had taken a cab up Amsterdam to 160th Street, which was technically Harlem Heights. She had shared with me that to get the full and proper effect of where we were going, we had to do it by foot.

"I'm not sure, darling," she said as she looked up at the street sign. "This is all quite a mystery to me, too. I read cards for a sweet woman that night at the Queen of Wands and suddenly I got a visual image about this neighborhood. I shared it with her and she said that she lived up here. So, in a way, she's sent me on this field trip."

"Are we visiting someone?" I asked as we continued walking.

"More like visiting something."

We turned left onto Jumel Terrace and walked north. On the west side of the street were some very nice brown and limestone row houses, on the east side there was a modest stretch of green grass populated with beautiful, stately trees. A lonely plaque standing near the sidewalk indicated that this was Roger Morris Park.

"I've never heard of this before."

Petra took a deep breath. "It's so peaceful up here."

We walked about a half block farther north on Jumel and Petra stopped in her tracks and grabbed my arm. "Oh my dear."

I looked up and there was a magnificent tribute to colonial grandeur, the Morris-Jumel Mansion. How did I not know about this beauty? I pride myself in being one of those New Yorkers who loves to search out hidden historical treasures throughout the city—like the Dyckman Farmhouse, the Little Red Lighthouse, the Merchant's House, and the Swedish Cottage Marionette Theatre in Central Park—but this glorious house was news to me.

I looked over at Petra who was taking it all in. "Is this the vision that you saw?"

"The energy feels right but I don't recall such a majestic building."

Now a public museum, we stood in front of Manhattan's oldest surviving house. Painted white and bare of any shutters, it was of Palladian design, which included a two-story portico, triangular pediment, and classical columns.

"Shall we go inside?" I asked.

"Yes," Petra whispered excitedly.

Petra and I were the only visitors to the museum that day. And thank goodness because as I was walking through Mrs. Jumel's front upstairs drawing room admiring a bed that Napoleon had given to her as a present, my god-awful cell phone rang.

I opened it up immediately, silencing my latest and most embarrassing ringtone, the theme song to *The Brady Bunch*.

"Yes?" I whispered, trying not to disturb the ghost of Mrs. Jumel.

"I can't move my neck!" Quinn cried.

I moved over to the front of the room and sat down on a window seat overlooking Jumel Terrace. "What happened?"

"One of the dogs charged after a pigeon, ripping my arm out of its socket."

"Brie the bullmastiff?"

"No," screamed Quinn as I pulled my cell away from my eardrum. "Butch, that fucking miniature poodle. I've also pinched a nerve or something in my neck. I'm stooped over and feeling nauseous."

Petra joined me on the window seat. "I have the cure. You must call Tripp this instant. He'll put you back together again."

"Do I hear wedding bells even with a bicuspid missing?"

"He could be missing all his teeth, for all I care."

"Then we could call him Gumby. Speaking of which, how's the sex?"

I laughed. "You know I don't kiss and tell."

"Liar!"

"The sex is sublime. And he's so cool about me being positive even though he's not."

"That's great."

"Quinn, I'm uptown with Petra who I'm dying for you to meet but call Tripp now. Honestly, his magic fingers will work wonders." Petra leaned toward the window trying to get a better glimpse of something that had caught her eye. "I know you have his business card. Use it."

"I wasn't going to without your permission."

"Stop it and call me as soon as you're done." I hung up the phone, shaking my head. "Poor guy. But I know Tripp will be able to help him."

Petra grabbed my arm. I looked at her as she pointed out the window. I peered through the wavy antique panes of glass and thought that I had been transported to another time and place.

"That's it," Petra whispered. "That was my vision."

The two of us dashed out of the mansion and pranced down the front steps and along the extended pathway till we reached the street. Directly in front of and across from the Morris-Jumel house was Sylvan Terrace. Petra and I crossed the street and were mesmerized by what we saw.

Flanking a cobblestone street were identical rows of wooden two-story Victorian-style houses with Gothic influences. Every house was painted a buttery cream, all the shutters a bright green.

We walked down the street not saying a word to each other. It was enchanting. How could an entire block of what looked like authentic wooden houses survive this city over all these years? We stopped in front of one and studied it. It felt more like we were on a Hollywood set than a street in Harlem.

Just then, a matronly woman came out of the house looking very upset, and hobbled down the staircase as if a knee or a hip were bothering her. Something very important must have been on her mind because once she made it to street level she was thoroughly startled to see us watching her.

"Oh!" she exclaimed, looking at her watch. "You're late. But I'm so glad you made it. Please, please come in."

Petra and I just looked at each other.

"Do you mind if we go in down here," she asked, pointing to the street level door. "I just can't make those stairs again."

"Whatever you say, darling," Petra said in her sexy Latvian accent.

The woman turned around and looked at Petra. "They didn't tell me you were Polish."

She put the key in the door as Petra was about to correct her. I tapped her arm and smiled shaking my head no.

We entered into a front sitting room that was cocooned in floor-to-ceiling bookcases. Snuggled in there was a working fireplace and beyond this room was the kitchen.

"I had the place done over about ten years ago," the woman explained. "I know I didn't restore it to its 1882 birthright splendor but I think it looks nice and everything is in tip-top shape."

The kitchen actually had a country cottage feel with a farmer's sink and thick wooden planked countertops. The house had three bathrooms, one on each floor. Out the back door was a beautiful garden patio with a water feature.

She took us upstairs to the front parlor. Neither Petra nor myself said a word. The woman just kept showing us the house and giving us more information. It turned out that the cobblestone street was actually the original carriage drive for Mount Morris and working-class residents at that time—which included a postman, a seamstress, government workers, and police officers—who had inhabited the wooden row houses. Over the years, the facades were heavily altered but through the efforts of the Landmarks Preservation Commission, the houses had been restored to their original style.

On the third floor were two cozy bedrooms, each with its own working fireplace. The woman walked us back down to the parlor floor. The entire house had a warm and protective feeling about it, as if it was wrapping its arms around you.

The woman rattled off some important statistics like square footage, lot size, property taxes, and last but not least, her asking price of $566,400.

"Trust me, I'm asking on the low end. Units seventeen and twenty-one are each going for over a million." The woman turned to Petra. "I can't wait to get to Florida. It's yours if you want it."

Petra looked up at me and then to the lady. "I want it."

And she bought the wooden row house. Obviously, the woman was waiting for a potential buyer and mistook Petra for her. And it all worked out very gracefully.

I was stunned as Petra slipped her arm into mine and winked up at me. "This is how all the beautiful and perfect things have happened in my life."

⋛ ⋚

"Curtis, I've never seen you this buff."

"Hey, I have someone to be buff for," I said as I looked over at Quinn in our gym's locker room and caught him spraying himself with Guerlain's Vetiver cologne. "We're working out, not getting ready for cocktails."

Quinn slipped on a teal warm-up jacket that matched his teal warm-up pants and then grabbed a small towel embroidered with a rooster on it.

"You're working out?" Quinn asked. "I'm looking for"—he held up his towel—"cock."

I shook my head. "Even you disgust me at times."

"You're such a prude," he criticized as we went out onto the gym floor. "Curtis, you have to help me find a new job."

"What happened to the dogs?"

Quinn sighed dramatically. "The owner of . . ."

"The miniature poodle?"

He nodded. "They accused me of kicking Butch."

I stopped and looked at him seriously. "And did you?"

"Not technically." I looked at him harder as he continued. "She was snapping at the other dogs again and she just happened to walk in front of my foot as I was taking a big . . ."

"Goose step?"

"Yeah, that's it. And the owners were coming around the corner of the block and saw it and well, they called the other owners and well I was kind of fired."

"I think for the safety of all the dogs in New York City, that's a good thing."

"I'm working on a screenplay but in the meantime I was thinking of becoming a male nanny."

Trying to block out the disastrous thought of him with that responsibility, I sprinted out onto the workout floor to goose my body with endorphins. Our gym is located in Chelsea and I guess for many men like Quinn, and women for that matter, the gym is their favorite place to pick up people. The two activities just don't mix for me. I'm there to get work done plus it all seems too fluorescent. If you're going to try to attract someone, you want to put your best face forward and under that hideous lighting, no one looks good.

"I want you to do bench presses first," Quinn said as he dragged me into the free weight room.

"And what are you going to do?"

"I'm going to sit on that bench over there that is strategically positioned across from that Latin slab of meat who is doing flies and try and look up his trunks."

I tripped, laughing so hard. At least Quinn was honest. With him, what you saw was what you got and he made no bones about it. I slipped forty-five-pound weights onto each end of the bar, clipped on the safety collars, laid down my plain white workout towel, and positioned myself on the bench. I grabbed the bar, took a deep breath, and lowered it down to my chest slowly as I exhaled. I gently tapped my pecs with it when Quinn let out a very loud yelp. Distracted, I struggled to get the barbell and weights back up to the resting stand.

I bolted to a sitting position. "What the hell do you think you are doing?" I asked him in a fierce whisper. He was practically lying on the gym floor trying to see up this guy's pants. "Have you no pride?"

"No, thank God."

I lay back down on the bench. "Well then, peep quietly. I can't afford to hurt myself."

I took another breath, lifted the weights, and lowered them down to my chest when Quinn shouted, "Jesus, Mary, and Joseph."

Again, I struggled to get them back up to the resting stand and sat upright. I was about to scold Quinn but when I saw him wiping the sweat off his forehead with his kitchen towel, I had to laugh.

"You have cock all over your face."

"I swear he's wearing no underwear, no jockstrap. I can see it all." Quinn desperately opened his bottle of water and took a swig. "Damn, this is strenuous."

"I can tell. You're working up more of a sweat than I am." I lay back down on the bench. "I'm going to try this once more and if you cause me to drop this I'm going to force you to do something dreadful."

"Like?"

"Work out."

Out of nowhere, a man whom I had never seen at the gym before and who looked like an undernourished Santa Claus came up to me and asked point blank, "Do you like opera?"

I sat upright.

"Just because he's a queen you just assume he likes opera?" Quinn chimed in. "What a lame pick-up line."

"I didn't know he was a queen and it's not a pick-up line. I work for the Metropolitan Opera."

"Oh?" Quinn asked.

It all seemed so absurd. "Honestly, I'm not really into opera."

"I wasn't asking if you like to go to them; I wanted to know if you would like to be in them. I cast the nonsinging chorus."

"We'd love to," Quinn said jumping to his feet, pinching me and rubbing his fingers together indicating money.

Anorexic Kris Kringle looked at Quinn. "We need Egyptian soldiers for Giuseppe Verdi's *Aida*." He looked at me. "This guy is perfect." He looked back to Quinn, scanning him from head to toe. "Can you pull off a leather skirt?"

"Leather skirt, plaid kilt . . ." Quinn looked at the Latin beefcake, "satin boxers."

I looked at him like he was an idiot. "He means, can you wear one and look good in it?" I turned to the man. "Thanks for your offer but I'm pretty busy."

He took out his business card and handed it to me. "If you change your mind, give me a call. It's two hundred fifty bucks a performance."

The guy left and Quinn grabbed the card out of my hand. "Think of the money? Think of the drama? Think of us onstage?"

"I'm thinking of your legs in a mini leather skirt."

Quinn did a dramatic swirl of his head in exasperation.

"Hey, you did that pretty well," I said as I attempted to do my bench presses one more time. "So, isn't Tripp phenomenal?"

"Oh my God, Curtis, the moment that man touched my neck and shoulders, it's like the pain just dissolved away."

I lifted the barbell and started doing reps. "I told you he was good."

"I went to his place 'cause it's less expensive and while he was working on me I told him what was going on and all with my financial problems and he ended up not even charging me for the session."

That seemed a bit generous to me. "How nice of him," I grunted.

"Nice isn't the half of it. He was so flattering, telling me how beautiful my emerald-green eyes are and that they are a striking contrast to my fair skin and jet-black hair."

"How very flattering of him," I said as I felt my body tensing up.

"He even said I was in good shape for someone who doesn't work out. But he's so fucking handsome I never even noticed that missing tooth you are so weird about. And now I really know what you see in that man."

Up to my sixth rep, I wondered what he was talking about. "What do you mean?"

"Curtis, the massage was the most effective and professional I've ever had. But the happy ending was the icing on the cake."

The barbell was midway between my chest and a full extension when I lost it. My strength drained out of me and my arms started to tremble. Suddenly, the weights came down on my chest, bounced to the side, and crashed to the gym floor. Several people working out came to my rescue, including one of the gym's personal trainers, as Quinn sat there and watched.

"I'm OK," I said, coming to a sitting position. "I'm sorry. I'm fine. It's not too heavy. I just had a moment. Please, everyone, I'm fine."

Slowly, the crowd walked away. I'm sure they all thought my face was red as a fire engine because I was embarrassed. Hardly. I was shocked and confused and I had to know more.

"Curtis, what just happened?" Quinn asked innocently.

"I don't know. You tell me?" I asked, about to explode.

"I'm missing something here."

I took a really deep breath. "Let's recap the story. You had a massage with Tripp, he solved your problem, didn't charge you a fee, told you how attractive you are, and then he . . ." I waited for Quinn to finish the sentence.

"Jerked me off?"

I was so upset I couldn't see straight.

"Curtis, you look like you're going to burst a blood vessel. Did I say something wrong?"

I couldn't believe what I was hearing. "You didn't say anything wrong, Tripp *did* something wrong!"

Quinn truly thought hard. "I should have paid for the session, huh?"

"No, he shouldn't have had sex with you."

Quinn laughed. "Oh, that. We didn't have sex, he just pulled my pud."

"This changes everything." I headed back to the locker room as Quinn followed me.

"Curtis, you're making a mountain out of molehill." I went straight to my locker and started fiddling with the lock as he continued. "Didn't he give you a happy ending after your first massage?"

I spun around and looked him right in the eye. "No he didn't."

"Oh." Quinn pulled back. "Gee, I wonder why not?"

I sat down on the bench. "Here I am, having fallen head over heels over this man who I think is the next best thing to Greek yogurt and I find out he's offering happy endings at the end of his massages to total strangers."

"I'm not a total stranger, I'm your best friend."

"That makes it even worse!" I pulled my stuff out of my locker and threw my coat on. "Do you know what that makes him?"

"Popular?"

"I'm outta here."

≥ ≤

"It's me."

"Hey you," Tripp replied.

The siren of a police car blared by me. "I just finished a workout and being downtown, I thought I'd take a chance and see if you were home and free."

"I'm both," he laughed. "Want to come over?"

"More than you know."

I closed my cell and headed toward Tripp's apartment. I wasn't sure if I wanted the eight blocks to his apartment to cool me down or not. When I finally reached his building and gathered the strength to ring his buzzer, my head was still spinning with every range of emotion. I really, really liked this guy. How do I digest this? How do I deal with him? Am I blowing this out of proportion?

He lived in the back ground-floor studio apartment that happened to be the size of a postage stamp. Honestly, it couldn't have been larger than my dining room. In one tiny room he had his galley kitchen, a fold-up massage table, one chair, and a Murphy bed. Over the period of time we were dating I made a conscious effort to spend time there with him, just so he knew I thought it was cool and terrific even though deep inside I found it totally claustrophobic.

I looked down and realized that I was wearing my old, faded, naturally-distressed-over-time pair of sloppy jeans and felt a wave of foreboding.

Tripp answered the door with his missing tooth smile. "Hi."

He was wearing a sexy tank top and cutoff jeans that I made certain I didn't react to and then he tried to kiss me. I offered a cheek and squeezed by him and then squeezed by the one chair and then squeezed by the Murphy bed that was pulled out and then squeezed over to the hot plate in the kitchen.

"What's this?" I asked rather coldly, pointing to the bed.

He hesitated a minute and then grinned. "You called, I responded."

I didn't respond.

He shrugged his shoulders. "I hear you, see you, and I just want to jump into bed and make love to you."

I took off my jacket. "You know what I would love?"

"What?" he asked with a devilish smile.

"A massage."

Tripp looked a bit surprised. "OK. You a little tense?"

"You could say so."

He walked over to me and tried to put his arms around me. "Then let me *release* your tensions."

I slithered away and said flatly, "If anyone will do it, it's you."

"I see we're playing hard to get today."

I looked out his one miniscule window that was facing a brick wall as he put the bed back up and pulled out the massage table. Laboriously, I stripped down to my underwear and then watched with my arms folded across my chest as he lit the smelly candle and the stick of nauseating incense. Then he turned on that goddamn precious new age music. It's amazing how quickly the sweet little things one does can turn into huge, annoying roadblocks.

"Climb on board," Tripp said as he patted the table.

I stood there without moving. "Is that what you say to everyone who rides your . . . train?"

He laughed as he got out the oil and put it into the microwave. I climbed up onto the table and lay down on my stomach.

"Curtis, you know I can't charge you for our sessions anymore."

With my head shoved into the donut hole, I mumbled, "I hope not. You're certainly not charging Quinn."

"What was that?" he asked, truthfully not hearing what I said.

I lifted my head. "Fine."

He came back with the oil. "Curtis, you're wearing your underwear."

"Oops, forgot," I lied, trying to slip them off lying on my stomach. Tripp tried to assist. "I can do it myself," I said coldly.

"Man, you are tense. Just relax and let me handle everything."

I rolled my eyes imagining him handling everyone else's everything as he draped a sheet over me and started the massage. And it was good. In fact, it was so good I got angry because I started to relax. He poured the hot oil onto my lower back and then started kneading my muscles like they were dough.

I asked myself, *What the hell am I doing? I have sex with this man. I make love with this man and yet here I am on his massage table waiting, wanting, and even choreographing it so that he offers me a happy ending so I can call him on it.* He came up over my butt but was very professional in that he didn't get too personal. So I started to respond a little by moving my ass this way and that, which prompted him to move on down to the back of my thighs.

He made long, luxurious strokes up and down my hamstring and each time he came close to my butt I'd wiggle a little, to no avail. He worked his way down to my calves and then my feet and I almost fell asleep.

Working my upper back, he brought me back to this dimension and I was happy that I could get myself all worked up again. But his fingers working into the knotted muscles between my shoulder blades felt like he was scraping away life plaque and I started to melt again.

He eventually had me turn over onto my back, readjusted the sheet, and started massaging my thighs. Again, I twitched this way and that, moving my legs apart, which sent him over to my left arm. He fiddled with my fingers, swung around to the other arm and hand, and then went for my abdomen. In a clockwise motion he massaged me, rocking my body. I thought to myself, *OK this is the big moment, this is when it happens,* but he just kept circling my stomach. I actually tried to push his hands down farther and then he traveled up to my neck.

Tripp loosened it, stretched it, massaged it, and then did some relaxing face work around my sinuses and down to my jaw. Finally, he rubbed his palms together, placed them on my eyes, and then said, "Thank you."

"For what?" I asked bolting upright.

He was so startled he almost fell over. I wrapped the sheet around me and let him have it.

"What the fuck are you doing?"

He stepped back defensively. "What are you talking about?"

I repeated myself. "What the fuck are you doing . . . giving my best friend a hand job?"

Tripp dropped his head. "Quinn told—"

"Yes, he told me!" He sat down on the table. "Curtis, it's just energy."

"It's just wrong."

He looked at me in a very strange way. "Who are you to judge what is right and what is wrong?"

"Why didn't you give me a release when you came over to my house the first time? In fact, I don't recall you ever giving me a release after a massage."

"I didn't offer you a release at the end because I liked you."

I was confused. "So, you only offer them to people who you don't like?"

He shook his head. "You're twisting my words around."

"You're twisting my emotions." I took a breath. "So, answer me this. Do you offer *every* client but me this specialized denouement?"

He got up and squeezed three feet past me to the opposite end of the room. "Now that's condescending. You knew I wouldn't know what demourment means."

"Denouement! And it means finale, conclusion, climax! And do you?"

"It's just another form of energy."

I threw my hands up. "But you're charging for it, Tripp. Do you know what that makes you?"

He looked down at the floor. "I'm not going to play this game with you."

I was surprised at my anger. "A game? You think this is a game? I'm furious. I opened up my heart to you."

"And I've done the same for you." We both stood there saying nothing until he broke the silence. "Do you want me to stop offering it?"

I was beside myself. "You just don't get it."

"I'm a healer. And that includes being a sexual healer."

"A sexual healer? Give me a fucking break."

Tripp lowered his voice to a whisper. "Don't you feel healthier since I've been making love to you?"

My jaw dropped. Did this man just say what I thought he said? "Do you have a Christ complex?"

He shook his head. "That was uncalled for."

I started to pace the two steps back and forth that I could in his space. "I'm the first to say you are one of the best health practitioners I've ever worked with. But I find it so arrogant when people have the balls to call themselves a healer. At the very least you might encourage their health. But, don't give yourself that much credit. These people are healing themselves."

"That's your opinion."

I stopped pacing and looked right at him.

"And a sexual healer? You want my real opinion?" I thought about whether or not I should say it, and then it just flew out of my mouth. "You charge money for it so that makes you a prostitute."

He went to the front door and opened it. "Get out."

"Gladly!"

Still wrapped in the sheet, I just grabbed my gym bag and my clothes and squeezed past the massage table. Trying to get past him without touching him, I managed to ungracefully trip over Tripp and out the door. I turned to have one last word and he slammed the door in my face.

Dumbfounded for a moment, I tried to collect my thoughts when all of a sudden an elderly woman appeared in the hallway. I clutched the sheet around me.

"Love your dress, honey," she said as she shuffled by with her walker.

Quickly, I threw my clothes back on but realized I hadn't grabbed my pants. My wallet, money, and cell phone were all in my bag so nothing was in them, but I had no pants! I almost rang Tripp's buzzer but my ego wouldn't allow me to. I reached for my cell and dialed Quinn as quickly as I could.

He picked up on the first ring. "Where did you run off to, Curtis? I'm worried about you."

I opened my mouth but nothing came out.

"Curtis, are you there? Curtis?"

Quietly, I started to cry. "I didn't get a happy ending."

≳ ≲

After rescuing me, Quinn and I decided to immediately drown my sorrows and headed over to the Cowhide bar in Chelsea. However, a very young bodybuilder met us at the door.

"IDs guys," he demanded.

I looked at him like he was crazy. "ID? You think I'm under twenty-one?"

Quinn smiled at him. "Please marry me."

"The law. Mayor is cracking down on us. Everyone is carded."

I searched my bag for my wallet and then searched my wallet for my driver's license as Quinn showed the guy his and went into the bar.

"I don't have it with me," I said walking past the bouncer.

He grabbed my arm. "Not without an ID."

"This is ridiculous." I exclaimed, "Quinn, get your ass out of there!" The baby bouncer and I just stood there staring each other down. I finally spoke. "I'm older than your father." He didn't react. I looked at my watch and tapped my foot. "Could you at least open the door and tell my friend to come back out?"

He did so and Quinn backtracked looking puzzled as I grabbed his arm. "We're going across the street to the piano lounge"—I threw the rest of it at the bouncer—"where I know they want my business!"

While waiting at the corner for the light to change I pulled out my cell phone and called Mother. I was supposed to have dinner with her so I asked her to meet us at the lounge. Luckily, she was just coming up Eighth Avenue in a cab.

Once inside, we ordered drinks, and Quinn wanted to surprise me with a song so he whispered the request to Trudy, our bartendress.

I replayed the dramatic confrontation I had had with Tripp step-by-step, inch-by-inch for Quinn and then asked him, "Do you think I overreacted?"

"Overreacted? Not for you." He contemplated for a moment. "Curtis, even I would have some issues with a boyfriend who was jerking people off left and right, never mind if it was under the guise of sexually healing them or not."

I nodded in agreement.

Trudy went over to the piano player and whispered something. Then she smiled at me and sang, "When You're Smiling."

"Curtis, now I know why you like it here."

We clinked the world's largest wine glasses.

"Yeah, they fill them to the top. Quinn, was I wrong? Was I too harsh?" I took a large gulp of white wine.

He actually thought hard about it. "You have to be true to yourself and your feelings."

"So you don't think I should go back and apologize?"

"God no. Your exit was too perfect."

Just then, Mother entered the lounge. I embraced her and then almost lost my balance dashing over to the piano player's tip bowl. I dropped in a wad of money as Mother ordered a wine.

She turned and looked at me. "Now those are some snazzy warm-up pants, Curtis."

I looked down at the teal pants Quinn had lent to me.

"Quite the fashion statement, yes?" Quinn asked.

She raised her glass. "So are we celebrating or commiserating?"

I threw my hands up. "Both?"

"Curtis and Tripp just had a falling out."

"That's a nice way of putting it." I slapped my hand on the bar. "Tripp is history."

My mother touched my shoulder lovingly. "And there's not at chance of the two of you getting back together?"

"Even if I apologized, which I don't think I can, he wouldn't take me back. Hell, I wouldn't take me back."

Quinn raised his glass. "Why don't we toast to Tripp. I don't think I've ever had a better . . . massage."

I lifted my glass. "You do have to admit, he was the best."

My mother lifted her glass. "And now that it's safe to confess this, I finally called him and had a massage, too."

"You, Mother?" I asked nervously as Quinn and I gave each other the eye.

"Well, you all have been raving about his work. You can't be selfish and yes, he is extremely talented and totally professional. So here's a toast."

I relaxed a bit sensing that was a close call. We all clinked our glasses.

Mother continued. "Here's to health, wealth and . . . happy endings. Woo hoo!"

I dropped my head to the bar.

NINE

GAY NUDE YOGA

"Drop the sheet, darling, so I can see your perineum."

I looked over at Petra who was sketching on her canvas. "My what?"

"That glorious place between your scrotum and your sphincter."

I couldn't believe what she said. Slightly embarrassed, I realized what she was referring to. "Oh, you mean my t'aint."

She looked at me quizzically.

I went all out. "T'aint my balls, t'aint my hole. It's my t'aint."

She giggled. "I like that. But please, drop the sheet."

I hesitated. Here I was in Petra's new living room on Sylvan Terrace, feeling like a very coy odalisque spread out on a rather simple divan. She had me lying on my right hip with my upper body supported on my right elbow. My right leg was bent on the cushion, the left was open and upright, and my head was slightly tilted back. She wasn't drawing me straight on, more of an angle from my feet. I was nude but had the sheet all wrapped around my crotch.

"Petra, I feel funny about this."

She put down her pencil, got up from her stool, and sat next to me on the sofa. "Curtis, you have a magnificent body."

I flushed a crimson red.

"Of course my painting of you will be erotic but I promise it won't be cheap or exploitive. You've taken what your parents gave to you genetically, you've sculpted it with hours of disciplined exercise, now let the world enjoy the beauty you have created."

"OK, OK. Go back to your easel and turn around."

She patted me on my head and returned to her canvas, with her back to me. "You are a funny one, Mr. Jenkins."

I dropped the sheet. "Paint my t'aint . . . but make it fast."

Petra turned around and put her hands to her mouth. "Magnificent," she declared as she started sketching again. "And so meaty."

Meaty? I frowned. "You're sure you're a lesbian and not just a straight woman using and abusing me and getting your rocks off?"

She burst out in laughter. "Do you know how lesbian I am?"

"No, how lesbian are you?"

"I own a copy of *Showgirls*."

I thought about it for a moment. "The movie? That's a lesbian thing?"

"Even in Prague, lesbians celebrate the film."

I had to protest. "But it's such a bad, over the top, horribly acted joke of a film."

Petra argued. "You are wrong, Curtis. It is a comedy. We view it as a spoof and the women are stunning."

"Well, what do you know?" I put on my thinking cap. "What was it that Bette Midler said about that movie? Oh, 'Poles saw more action in *Showgirls* then they did in World War II!'"

Petra nearly fell off her stool she was laughing so hard. When she caught her breath, she said that before leaving for the States she had a *Showgirls* party for all her girlfriends and she surprised them with the VIP Collector's Edition.

I cocked my head. "How old are you?"

"Inside this vintage car I am driving, I would say about eighteen."

Petra described her VIP DVD edition of *Showgirls*: It included a lap dance tutorial; a set of *Showgirls* shot glasses; a *Pin the Pasties on the Showgirl* game with pasties and blindfold; a deck of *Showgirls* cards; *Showgirls* party games; and a photo series of Elizabeth Berkley. Damn, that was extensive. I was trying to think of what gay men have. *The Wizard of Oz?*

It took a moment but then it popped into my brain. "*Showgirls!* VIP Collector's Edition! It's the ultimate party in a . . . box!"

This sent Petra into a tailspin of laughter. Between tears and snorting, she staggered over to the bookcase and opened up the bottom doors, revealing a liquor cabinet. She pulled out a bottle of cognac and two brandy snifters and brought them over to me, still laughing.

I curled up in the sheet as she sat next me and placed it all on the coffee table. "Brandy break."

It was my favorite time of day. The last rays of the setting sun were streaming in through her west windows, filling the room with dancing sunbeams. As she poured us each a hefty glass of Courvoisier I studied her closely. I just couldn't believe how young and full of life she was.

"You look at least twenty-five years younger than you are. What is your secret? Is it a special Latvian diet high in goat yogurt or something?"

"Darling, I believe in everything, but in moderation."

She went on to describe a typical day's diet. For breakfast: two fried eggs over easy with one piece of buttered whole-wheat toast, two pieces of crispy, well-done bacon, and a cup of black coffee. For lunch: grilled fish or chicken with a salad. For dinner: red meat, preferably on the bone, two vegetables such as sautéed spinach and a baked sweet potato, and two large glasses of red wine.

"And any dessert?" I asked.

"A snifter of brandy and one cigarette."

I shook my head. "And I bet you've never been sick a day in your life."

"That's not true. When I was sixty-two I had a fever."

We both chuckled.

She continued. "I have good genes and I love life. And you my dear obviously are doing the right thing."

"Petra, I try to eat every color every day." She looked at me confused. "Like orange are carrots, green is lettuce, yellow is squash."

"I like that concept."

"And you know how I feel about fruit. I just can't get enough of it."

She brought her snifter glass up and we clinked as she toasted, "Here's to one-a-day." We both took a sip. "So tell me, dear heart, what happened with Tripp?"

I hesitated, wondering if I really wanted to go there. "You know, Petra, it was a fast, passionate, and intense courtship that came to a crashing halt."

"You said something earlier about other people being involved? You believe in monogamy?"

I explained to her that I did believe in monogamy, once in a committed relationship. "The issue I had with Tripp wasn't that, it was in regard to an element of his work."

"What was the element?"

"His bodywork was exceptional. He just felt he had to add a button to his endings."

Petra took a slow sip of her brandy and thought hard. I saw the light go on. "Ah, I see. And you couldn't accept that?"

I got up with the sheet wrapped around me and paced a bit. "I considered trying to work through it but he did it to Quinn, my best friend, which was weird."

"I can understand that."

"And then I found out he did it to my mother, which was gross."

"Darling, he's not for you. He should have some boundaries."

I confessed to her that I was fed up with men. I thought maybe it was me, that I attracted the wounded ones. Maybe subliminally there's some sort of payoff I get from colliding into these dysfunctional people. But this was the last straw. "I'm out of the stirrups."

She touched the divan, encouraging me to sit back down. "No, Curtis, don't say that. You need to thank Tripp."

I furrowed my brow. "Thank him?"

Petra was so excited that Tripp had fanned the ember inside of me. Yes, he was the wrong guy, but he did make me feel something again. Something that I thought was gone. Passion.

"There's a man out there for you. We just have to find him."

Unexpectedly, she put her brandy down, jumped to her feet, and ran to a bookshelf. Up on her tippy toes she managed to pull down a small box covered with exquisite marbleized Venetian paper. She scurried back and placed it between us on the sofa.

Petra reverently placed her palms on the cover of the box, closed her eyes for a moment, and whispered some sort of incantation, and then gently opened it. I looked inside and saw a red silk drawstring bag. She picked that up and underneath it was a small, very weathered leather-bound book with fascinating markings on the cover that resembled some sort of hieroglyphics. Carefully, she picked the book up and held it to her chest.

"Curtis, this is the ancient *Book of Runes*."

I wasn't quite sure what she said. "Ruins?"

"No, runes."

She said that the *Book of Runes* was older than the New Testament. The runes were an oracle similar to the tarot and were commonly used in Iceland up until about the late Middle Ages. It was kind of like the I Ching for the Vikings. Inside the silk bag were twenty-four stones with ancient hieroglyphics inscribed into them and one blank stone called The Unknowable. You don't ask runes questions, instead one addresses issues. The person whose oracle is being read contemplates an issue in his life, pulls one rune out of the bag, and the interpreter reads it as it is presented to her, either right side up or down.

"Petra, I just don't know what to focus on anymore."

She sipped her brandy and smiled. "That's the beauty of the runes. Focus is good but even if your thoughts are cloudy, it will answer truthfully what is at the core of your questioning, whether you are aware of it or not."

She also said that the runes were like a handbook for the spiritual warrior.

"Spiritual warrior?" I asked, turning my nose up.

She hit my knee. "My definition of spiritual warrior is one who is free of anxiety, radically independent, and unattached to outcomes. One who practices absolute trust in the struggle for awareness and is constantly mindful that what matters is to be consciously in the present."

I nodded. "I like the sound of that."

"Without asking a question, let's just meditate on your current social life."

"Or lack of?" I snickered. "I can't just conjure up my knight in shining armor. I tried that with Magda and it didn't work." I felt awful that I said it with such a sarcastic tone but Petra smiled, knowing I meant no malice toward her sister.

"Let's just have fun with it," she suggested.

I stood up with my sheet. "OK, but I'm getting dressed. I don't want to offend the gods."

I dashed off to the front upstairs bedroom as Petra prepared for the reading. Once dressed I brought my leather knapsack and the copy of the Gay Center's list of monthly lectures, classes, and seminars that I had been reading back down to the parlor and set them on the floor next to the coffee table. I sat on the divan, took a gulp of my cognac, and closed my eyes. I was becoming a pro at this.

We both meditated for a moment and then Petra had me dig into the silk bag and pull out one rune. I handed it to her and she placed it on the coffee table. We both fixated on it for a bit. It looked like an italicized letter "F" with a little extension above the top and it was facing right side up.

Petra picked it up and said, "Fehu."

"God bless you."

She gave me a look as she looked up its meaning in the book. "I'm not as versed in runes so please bear with me."

She read that Fehu was the rune of fulfillment: ambition satisfied, love fulfilled, rewards received. I thought that wasn't too bad. It also said that it calls for self-examination and stresses the need for one to understand whether it is wealth and possessions one requires for well-being or is it self rule and the growth of will?

"I'll take possessions and wealth?"

"Stop," she said, pinching my arm. "This rune also warns you to be mindful of what you've achieved. If things are going in your favor, don't collapse into the success. Enjoy your good fortune but remember to share it."

We both sat there in silence until I picked the rune up. "I'm not sure how this is supposed to help me find a guy." I let out a demonic laugh as I tossed it into the air a few times. "Isn't this ironic? I wrote the book and I still can't collide into him." I threw the rune a little higher, attempted to catch it, and missed. It hit the side of the coffee table and then fell on top of the Gay Center's event calendar. I reached down to pick it up and Petra stopped me.

"Where did it land?"

I squinted, squinted a little harder, and then said, "Gay Nude Yoga."

≥ ≤

"Yes, I'm interested in your gay nude yoga classes?"

"This isn't a sex club."

I actually did that really bad actor thing where you pull the phone away from your ear and look at the receiver, like the person talking on the other end is insane. I had called the yoga place and had been put on hold forever till this man came back on the line and was quite terse with me. A sex club? That was the farthest thing from my mind.

"I didn't assume that you ran a sex club, I was interested in yoga."

"Hold."

I rolled my eyes. Petra had thought this was a brilliant idea. With these classes I could kill two birds with one stone. Reap the benefits of stretching, breathing, and exercising, and meet a spiritually hot gay man.

There was a click on the phone and he was back. "Did you fill out our questionnaire?"

"I didn't know there was one."

"Go to our Web site, fill it out; if you meet our requirements, we'll get back to you."

He hung up.

If I meet their requirements? Gee, that sounds real spiritually based. I was going to trash the whole idea, but this guy was so rude I was intrigued. So, I went to the Web site to find out more information. At the top of their homepage was the declaration: GAY NUDE YOGA — AN EXPLORATION MARRYING THE SPIRITUAL WITH THE PHYSICAL BODY.

There was a description of the type of yoga they taught, Tantra. Basically it said that it offered practical tools for reprogramming the mind and our desires. I paused, thinking *Doesn't that sound a lot like Scientology?* It went on to say that by means of physical and ritual cleaning, breathing exercises, contemplation, visualization, and repetition of a mantra, Tantra yoga helps to unfold your divine nature.

Then there were a multitude of pictures of men, individual and coupled up, doing yoga in the nude. I found the questionnaire and read through it. They required that you either had prior yoga training or that you were in very good shape. I didn't understand the either/or reasoning there. And then I nearly flipped when I read the last requirement.

I got back on the phone and called my spiritually based and pleasantly centered friend again.

He answered the phone with such aggression. "Gay Nude Yoga, Tantra yoga to expand awareness. Hold."

I held the line and my temper. After waiting a total of four and a half minutes he clicked back on. "Who's this?"

"Curtis."

"What do you want?"

I took a deep tantric breath. "I'd like to know what the last question on your questionnaire is all about?"

"Are you stupid?"

I was two seconds away from letting this guy have it so I put the phone down for a brief moment to regain my composure. "No sir, I am not stupid. The last question refers to an age limit."

"No one is allowed into Gay Nude Yoga over the age of forty."

I shook my head in disbelief. "How can you call this . . . group . . . spiritual when there is a cut off for age?"

"Obviously you're over forty."

Obviously, you're an asshole. In the calmest whisper of a voice I asked, "Why pray tell do you not let men in over forty?"

"Because we're naked and we have to look at their bodies and we're doing yoga and men over forty are not as flexible and can't keep up with us."

OK, that's all I had to hear. I was determined to climb over the walls of this inner sanctum and prove them wrong.

"Yes, I am over forty. But I was a competitive gymnast through college, have been working out five times a week my entire adult life, I have 6 percent body fat, and I can still do my full splits."

"Hold."

This time he covered the mouthpiece of the phone and I could just barely make out that he was retelling what I said to another person. The one phrase I heard him say very clearly was "full splits." There was rustling of the phone and then he came back on.

"Go to the Web site and send us a naked picture of yourself."

Did I hear right? "I'm not going to send you a naked pic. I don't have one!" Yes, I lied. "But I do have a picture of myself in a bathing suit."

"Send it." And he hung up.

I dashed to my computer, found their contact info, pulled up my bathing suit pic, and sent it off to them. I was steaming mad and I was surprised that they got right back to me.

Their e-mail said, "Come into the studio and we'll do a complete evaluation and decide if you meet the other criteria."

Other criteria?

Gay Nude Yoga scheduled me to come in a half hour earlier than their next group class, which was the following day at 11 o'clock. They made three requests. If I passed the examination I could take the class but only if I had washed all body parts including my genitals, wore no deodorant or cologne, and did not consume beans twenty-four hours before the class. That night I made certain that dinner consisted of a large plate of sautéed broccoli smothered in garlic and two heaping bowlfuls of black bean soup. And just to make sure, I overdosed on dried apricots just before bed.

Slightly bloated and beside myself, I flew out of my apartment the next morning, late as usual, wearing the most youthful-looking workout clothes I owned. While standing in the crosswalk facing uptown while trying to hail a cab downtown, I heard people behind me on the sidewalk shouting. I turned and saw that they were signaling at me by waving their hands. I stood there for a split second not knowing what they wanted me to do and then I turned around, and it was too late. She hit me.

The beautiful, middle-aged blonde woman, chicly dressed and wearing a French beret, came barreling toward me in her motorized wheelchair, again, and hit me, again. I heard the helpful crowd of people on the corner gasp as she rammed her left wheel into my right thigh and then sped off.

"Hit and run!" I screamed. "She hit and ran me again!"

The wheelchair terrorist flew up onto the sidewalk and made a left turn heading down Broadway, but not before yelling back at me, "Watch where you're going, asshole!"

Yes, I felt sorry for her that she was confined to a wheelchair but what happened to make her such a menace to my neighborhood? A nice woman helped me limp to the corner.

"She hit my husband the day before yesterday and his ankle is sprained."

"That's terrible. What is her problem?" I looked at my watch, cringed, and hailed a cab that was coming toward me.

The woman helped me into the taxi and whispered, "We should put together a neighborhood watch, alerting people as to when she is on the streets."

"We should call the cops and have her put in jail," I said before I closed the door.

The yoga studio was located on the corner of Charleton and Greenwich Streets. If I had Mapquested it and allowed myself enough time, I could have taken a subway. But, I didn't. And I had no idea where these two streets connected. The long and expensive cab ride downtown gave my forty-five-year-old quadriceps enough time to bruise and swell up. Just what I wanted when I needed to impress my spiritual and sacred judge and jury.

It turned out that Charleton Street was just a few blocks below Houston and the studio was on the West Side, a block from the Hudson River. I got out of the cab and sensed I was in no man's land. Flanked by abandoned warehouses, I tentatively searched for an entry to Gay Nude Yoga. I couldn't see a sign or a number to what I thought was the building but as I passed a black metal door, I heard a buzzer go off. I looked up and there was a surveillance camera aimed down at me. I scrunched my face and squinted up at it and then immediately realized what it was. Great, I'm sure it had a fish-eye lens, which made my very attractive expression even more appealing to my audience. I reached for the door and the buzzer stopped. I couldn't believe I was putting myself through this but I stepped back, looked up to the camera, and showed them a sweet and beautiful smile and then counted the endless number of seconds before they decided to buzz me in again.

When they did I jumped for the door, fearing they would change their minds, and I entered a dark, windowless building. It felt more satanic than saintly.

"Hello?" I called out hesitantly. I walked down a long dark hallway leading to the back of the building. "Hello? Is anyone there?"

Then I saw the light at the end of the tunnel. Backlit, a shadowed black figure stood in the far doorway, waiting for me to feel my way down to it.

"Hello? I'm Curtis Jenkins?"

The figure said, "When you enter the outer chamber, remove your clothes and place them in a cubbyhole." And then the shadow disappeared.

For a split second, I was actually frightened. Maybe this wasn't Gay Nude Yoga after all. Maybe it was some sort of trick to get gay men into this warehouse where homophobes first tortured them, sexually of course, before chopping their bodies up into bits and pieces. I felt for my cell phone, decided I was overreacting, and chose not to use it.

I walked through the doorway and into a vestibule. To the left was a closed door; to the right some parted curtains. I walked through them and saw the numerous cubbyholes; two of them were filled with clothing. Slowly I undressed, thinking this was either the most outrageous adventure or the most dangerous disaster I had been on in a long time. I slid my workout pants down and flinched as my fingers brushed against my right thigh. Just my luck, it had swelled up and bruised to the point where it looked like a goiter the size of a small grapefruit was growing out of my leg. Underneath the pants I wore my orange Raymond Dragon looks-like-it's-painted-on-your-body bikini brief bathing suit, which I kept on. Everything else I shoved into an empty wooden niche, except for my glasses, and then walked back out into the vestibule.

Like a nervous teenager waiting for the school nurse to jam her cold fingers up into my balls for a hernia check, I shifted my weight back and forth, from foot to foot.

Eventually, the door seemed to open on its own and I walked through it and into a very large rectangular and totally mirrored room. The old wooden floors appeared to have been recently sanded and highly polyurethaned and at the far end of the warmly lit room was a shrine. There were some flowers, oranges, and a bowl of white rice and above it was a huge picture of Ganesha. This bejeweled Hindu god with the head of an elephant was the remover of all obstacles and ensured success with all human endeavors. I thought that was a good omen.

Three yoga mats, one closer to the shrine and the other two behind it, formed a triangle. Then from behind a hidden door in one of the mirrored panels, two men emerged, totally naked. I must have had some sort of pre-conceived notion of what I thought they would look like because when I saw them I was completely surprised.

Considering how restrictive they were with their membership requirements, I guess I pictured them as Greek gods. I looked up at Ganesha and apologized. One was tall and lanky with tight, curly brown hair and sported an extraordinarily large beaked nose. The other was rather ape-like, short and compact with a five o'clock shadow on his shaved head. Both appeared to be rather unremarkable in the crotch department. I sensed that Big Bird was the alpha dog and that he wasn't pleased that I was wearing my bathing suit.

"No clothing allowed in the sanctum," he said dispassionately. "Take off the Speedo."

"It's a Raymond Dragon."

"Whatever."

Again, why was I putting myself through this humiliating experience? Oh, right, for the sake of all gay men over forty. I hesitated a moment and then slowly peeled off my orange suit. Big bird showed no reaction. The simian salivated. I rolled my eyes.

The tall one pointed to my leg. "What's with your thigh?"

I put my hand over the welt. "I was just hit by a motorized wheelchair. Do you have a name?"

He pointed to the yoga mat directly in front of the shrine. "Stand on the mat facing Ganesha, feet shoulder width apart."

"Nice to meet you, too," I said very warmly, hoping to kill him with kindness.

The simian scampered to one of the two mats placed behind me. It was clear that he either wasn't going to talk, Big Bird wouldn't let him talk, or he couldn't talk.

"Bend over and touch your toes; that is if you can."

I took a deep breath and not only touched my toes but placed my palms flat on the floor without bending my knees. I heard the simian make a snort sound and still in the stretch I looked between my legs, and the two of them were mirroring my pose. We were back to back so as I looked at them, they looked at me. The simian was still salivating, plus he had an erection.

Big Bird ordered me to stand up and then asked if I had done yoga before. When I told him that I had taken classes on and off over the years he decided to test me on some of the basic poses. We started off with the sun salutation.

Thank goodness I have a photographic memory. Actually, I have one when I consciously want to use it, otherwise and obviously, I can't remember the last man I had a date with. Or maybe that is called selective memory? But I did remember many of the yoga poses. The sun salutation was, hopefully, a graceful sequence of twelve yoga positions performed as one continuous exercise. Each position counteracts the one before, stretching the body in a different way and alternately expanding and contracting the chest to regulate the breathing.

Remembering to breathe, I think I got through it pretty well. Then Big Bird asked me to do the cobra, the locust, the bow, and finally a shoulder stand. He then ordered me to come to a standing position.

"What's this about you being able to do full splits?"

"I can."

"Show me."

I'll show him. "Side splits or full Russian?"

He looked at me suspiciously and requested, "Full Russian."

Facing them, to the dismay of the simian, I bent my knees and placed my palms on the floor in front of me, and then slid my feet out to the sides and oh-so-very-gingerly lowered my body down, going into the full split. Once my family jewels touched the floor, I leaned forward and placed my chest on the floor with my arms extended out to the sides.

I couldn't hear it but I felt that Big Bird was impressed. I was too. And then I wondered, *How do I get out of this long forgotten split position and will I be able to walk again afterward?* He crossed the yoga room as the simian brought his face down to the floor, examining me. I pulled forward, was barely able to straighten out my legs, and then rolled onto my side. After a few deep breaths I got up onto my hands and knees and then to my feet.

Big Bird looked at me from across the room. "How old are you?"

"Forty-five."

"Your face is pleasant enough." *What does my face have to do with yoga?* "I'm teaching the next class. You can take it; that is if you can keep up." He turned his back to me.

"What type of yoga is it?"

He looked back and sneered at me. "Bikram."

Big Bird, followed by the simian, vanished behind another hidden mirrored door. I stood in the yoga room feeling rather vulnerable so I grabbed my Raymond Dragon and slipped it back on. I sat back down on the yoga mat figuring students would start coming in soon. I looked up at Ganesha and waved. Then it dawned on me that I wouldn't put it past Big Bird to have installed two-way mirrors in this un-fun house.

Bikram yoga is named after its founder, Bikram Choudhury. It's a series of twenty-six poses performed in a room heated up to about ninety to one hundred degrees Fahrenheit. Heat is used in order to allow you to go deeper and safer into a position. Technically, it also is supposed to eliminate the risk of injuries, promote sweating, and help you release the toxins in your body. My personal concern was that my body ran hot to begin with. Heat and humidity were not my fans.

Any person with half a mind would have left Gay Nude Yoga by now. I had proven my point and was allowed to enter the class. But there was a competitive side to my nature and I wanted to show this exclusive bunch that our chronological age was just a number. I knew for a fact that I looked younger than Big Bird and simian and they knew it too. Plus I reminded myself that I wasn't doing this just for me. I was hopefully breaking ageist boundaries and defending the middle-aged and older underdogs. Oh gosh. I wondered if the middle-aged and older underdogs even cared?

Just when I was having second thoughts about staying, the men started pouring in. And let me tell you this, they were hot. They were A-list hot! It just seemed so odd to me that these gorgeous, buff, and I'm assuming spiritual twenty- and thirtysomething year olds would congregate at a yoga center run by Dr. Frankenstein and his assistant Igor.

They all had their own personal mats with them so I grabbed the one I had been tested on and then slowly walked over to the changing room. I really felt stupid standing there in a bathing suit when they were all stripping down to their birthday suits. I had to get out of mine. Trying not to ogle all of them and their porno-movie-perfect bodies, I desperately worked my way through the little room to my cubbyhole.

"No need to push, guy," one said.

"Sorry."

I bumped another who asked, "Who are you?"

"Uh, Jenkins. Curtis Jenkins."

A third looked at me like I was from Mars. "What do you want in here?"

"I'd like to peel off my suit and just shove it in my hole."

There was dead silence. *Did I just say that?* And then they all burst into laughter. They were laughing at me. So, I tried to laugh too but a little too hard. That just made them look at me like I was an idiot.

Humiliated, I waited till the last one cleared out and then decided to throw my clothes back on and I'd call it a day. I really sensed I was out of my element. I grabbed my pants and then heard the sound of a bolt locking. I looked up and Big Bird was standing there in all his glory and with a grin on his face. "Going somewhere?"

I stared at him without saying a word.

"I think that after taking up my time and energy the least you can do is have the courtesy to stay and participate in my class."

He had me cornered. I put my pants back into the niche.

"Look on the bright side," Big Bird added, "this class is on the house."

He waited as I slipped out of the bathing suit.

"Can I at least keep my glasses on?"

He gave me a sarcastic look and walked back out into the main room.

"Good morning, class," he said as he walked to the front of the shrine. "Today, we're going to take things up a notch. We're going to do Bikram mixed with Kundalini."

I put my mat down in the back of the room as the group of men made sounds of approval. I also noticed they all had large bottles of water with them.

"I want all of you to sit on your mats and as I turn the heat up in the room, I want you to get into full lotus positions."

Big Bird walked over to the corner of the room and flipped on a switch and I heard the hum of the heaters start up as everyone else sat down and easily slipped their legs into the lotus. I may be able to do a full Russian split but my knees are shot from years of tumbling on wrestling mats on top of cement gymnasium floors. This was going to be hard.

My lanky challenger had both eyes on me, just aching for me to fail. Sitting tall and in a crossed-leg pose, I clasped my left foot with both hands and brought it high onto my right thigh past my charming goiter and up into my groin. I took a large breath and said a larger prayer, winked at Ganesha for good luck, and brought my right leg over the left and placed the right foot into my left groin. I stopped breathing for a moment just waiting to hear the pop. I was OK.

I won that first round and smiled smugly at Big Bird. He went back to the head of the class. The big question was how was I going to get out of this pose?

"Kundalini yoga is the most powerful yoga ever known. It centers on awakening the energy, the serpent power which is found at the base of our spine."

I instantly started to feel my right leg falling asleep and shifted the weight on my butt to try to get circulation going. But in doing so, my right ankle started to slip. I struggled to keep it in place.

"Anatomically, Kundalini is located in the region of the body that is between the rectum and the testicles. Do you all remember what that region is called?"

My foot flew out of my crotch and I uncontrollably blurted out, "T'aint!"

Of course, there was a moment before the entire class turned their overly flexible necks around and stared at me in the back of the class and broke out into laughter.

"No Jenkins, it's not the t'aint. It's the perineum."

I knew that, thank you, Petra. Oh Ganesha, please club me right now and put me out of my misery. I put myself into the half lotus position as he continued.

"Now we will do the vishnu mudra breathing technique."

The what? I looked around, trying to see what everyone else was doing. With the right hand, I tucked the index and middle fingers into the palm and with the thumb closing the right nostril, I breathed in through the left on a count of four. Then I held my breath, closing the other nostril with the ring finger for sixteen seconds. We exhaled through the right nostril, closing the left to the count of eight. I inhaled through the right nostril to the count of eight, held the breath for a count of sixteen, exhaled through the left on to the count of four, and I blacked out.

Moments later and surprisingly still in an upright position, I heard Big Bird say, "Alternate breathing uses both sides of the brain and gives us divine prosperity, universal energy, creativity, feelings of love and affection, and eliminates"—he looked right at me—"negative feelings such as depression and jealousy. Breathe deep everyone."

And then it happened. I tried my hardest to contain it but considering the diet I had chosen the night before, I was about to add just a wee bit more hot air into the room. I managed, thankfully, to do it quietly. Although I think I singed some hair off my legs.

"Everyone stand, it's time to pair up."

A bit light-headed, I struggled to my feet and waited to see what would unfold. Well, one by one, each of these handsome, strapping, and naked young men wrestled with each other for their favorite partner. Standing there trying to look nonchalant, I feared that not only would I not be picked but that no one would want to wrestle over me. Turned out, I was right. No one picked me and I was literally odd man out.

Oh, but I was hot. Hot temperature-wise, that is. The room had to have been way over one hundred degrees at this point and for a man who never sweats, I was already drenched and perplexed to be left on the sidelines. Was it because I was the new kid on the block? Or the old one? Or how I looked? How hung or not hung I was? Was my ass too flat?

Suddenly, Big Bird threw a towel at my face, knocking my glasses to the floor.

"You'll need that towel. And keep your glasses off unless they come with windshield wipers. You're going to sweat like you've never sweated before," he smirked. "Do what poses you can on your own. Next class, if you make it back, hope for an even number of people."

As the heat in the room increased, so did my heart rate. I struggled with poses and tried to keep up with the class, but salty sweat was pouring down my face, stinging my eyes and blurring my already blurred vision. I'm not sure but I think it was somewhere between the poses of the plow and the downward facing dog that I felt that I was losing concentration. I really had to strain to see the other members of the class. It appeared to me that in the coupling of men, one man was on his knees with his head bent over and the partner was lying on top of the bottom man's back with his body weight pushing him down farther, giving him an ultimate stretch.

Now, maybe this was the ultimate stretch of my imagination, or maybe it was the painful throbbing from the sweat in my eyes or the lack of wearing my glasses or all of the above, but I swear I saw a lot of stretching going on and it wasn't men's backs. It was more like their backsides. Big Bird was right; the poses used in this style of yoga were physically challenging and the heat allowed them to get into positions that I never imagined you could do. Although the room was fucking hot and my head was fucking foggy, I put two and two together and realized everyone, including Big Bird and the simian, were fucking each other.

About to pass out, I searched the floor for my glasses, miraculously found them, and then crawled toward the cubbyholes on all fours. I knew if I didn't get out of there quickly, at the very least I was going to burst a blood vessel.

I found my clothes and without even putting them on I reached for the front door. But Big Bird was quicker than I.

"Going somewhere?"

"I have to get out."

"No. Bikram rule, no one exits."

He grabbed my hand, pulling me back into the class, but I was so drenched in sweat I slipped right out of his hold.

"You don't understand, I have to get out."

I ran back to the door but he got there before me and stood in front of it.

"If you open that door you'll throw off the climate, the atmosphere, the energy of the room."

I was really not feeling well. "If I don't open the door, I'm going to be sick."

Big Bird stood his ground and said, "You leaving this class now is like taking a shit and not wiping."

Not believing what he just said, I looked up to his face and promptly threw up. No, I didn't throw up, I hurled up any and everything that I had in my gut and projectile vomited it all over Big Bird. And if that wasn't bad enough, I started to pass gas at the same time. Stunned and I'm sure sickened by my sick and fumes, he stumbled away from the door, giving me the chance to escape.

I felt my way down the long, black hallway, gasping for any kind of air. Maybe it was the combination of heat stroke, dehydration, shock, full Russian splits, Big Bird and Igor, the flawless young men having sex, or an overactive imagination, but the struggle to work my way out of that steamy mirrored belly of a room and down that dark, damp, narrow corridor felt like a birthing. Suddenly, I felt liberated, free, and independent. An intense feeling of happiness and gratefulness rushed through my body. I felt so purged of fear and anxiousness I wondered if I should run back and thank Big Bird for this epiphany. No, I didn't feel that good.

I could just barely see light shining in from underneath the front door. Buck naked with clothes still in my arms, I stumbled toward it, anxious to pop out and thirsty for fresh air. When I finally reached it, I paused for a second, then burst through the outside door. In my haste to re-enter into the world, I stubbed my toe on the raised metal doorframe, held onto the cross bar, twisted, and fell through the door, ass first. This was obviously my rebirth.

The contrast of being in total darkness inside compared to the blinding bright light outside shocked my corneas and momentarily blinded me. It also blinded me to the crowd of people on the sidewalk.

Someone held open the door as I managed to get to my feet. I'm sure they were as startled as I was. But what startled me even more was the man who spoke.

"Curtis? Curtis Jenkins, is that you?"

Still trying to adjust to the light, I shaded my eyes. I recognized the voice but couldn't see who it was. Then the cold, crisp air reminded me that I was totally naked.

"It's Julian Zanetti."

With my clothes somewhere on the sidewalk, I covered my crotch with my left hand and my nipples with my right thumb and index finger. Why I did this was a mystery to me.

"Julian," I said as nonchalantly as if we were just meeting casually on the street. "How are you?"

He was unable to fathom what I was doing. "I'm OK but what about you?"

"Oh, couldn't be better. Just took a class," I said as I pointed back into the building with my elbow.

My eyes were just beginning to adjust. With the sun behind him I could only make out his silhouette.

"This is Gay Nude Yoga?"

I nodded. "It most definitely is."

"I'm doing a piece on underground gay activities. The controversy is whether this is Gay Nude Yoga or a sex club?"

"Hate to spill the beans," I said as I passed more gas, "but it's both."

"Thanks." He and several other people dashed into the building as I picked up my clothes.

"Hello, celebrity writer," said a strangely familiar voice with an exotic accent.

My head spun around. He was standing in the darkness of the hallway. "Who is that?"

"Forgotten me already?"

Whose voice was that? Racking my brain I strained to see who it was.

"I'm not only his lover but I'm also his staff photographer."

His flash went off, the door slammed shut, and I realized it was Arash.

TEN

LOOK AT ME, I'M SANDRA DEE!

"You made the goddamn fucking cover of *ManHOOD!*" Darcie screamed over the phone. "It's part of Zanetti's exposé of the gay underground and it says you're coming out of a yoga sex club. The picture is of you standing out on the sidewalk stark naked, hiding your dick with your clothes."

I pulled my cell away from my ear and checked for bleeding. "I'm sorry."

"Sorry my black ass!"

"Darcie, you are not African-American and I haven't seen the magazine yet but truly, I am so sorry this got into the press."

"Stop, it's brilliant," she declared. "Your book is flying off the shelves. Gotta run. Good luck with the book signing."

She hung up and I was confused and distracted. Quinn and Mother were with me at Boston's Logan International Airport. It was Saturday morning and having just taken the shuttle up from New York, we were about to board a plane to Provincetown for just one night. But the two of them had too many suitcases filled with too much junk, making them much too heavy for takeoff.

Quinn squinted his eyes to make out the name on the airline ticketing agent's badge. "Fredericka? Why in God's name is there a weight limit for baggage?"

"Because sir," the very preppy and smiley young woman explained, "even if we managed to fit your oversized luggage," she pointed to my mother, "and your friend's oversized luggage onto the plane, we still wouldn't be able to get off the ground because their combined total weight comes to 212 pounds."

"But Freddie," my mother said condescendingly, "I've traveled with this much weight before."

The attendant's professional smile was starting to crack. "Miss, some larger airlines allow heavier baggage and usually charge a fee and please don't nick my name."

"So we'll pay the money!" Quinn shrieked.

I stood behind both of them. "I'm boarding the plane, with or without you."

"I'll nick whomever I want to," Mother declared emphatically.

Fredericka took a deep breath. "Please turn around and look outside the window. That is your plane."

Both Quinn and Mother looked out and saw nothing. They looked back at the agent and she pointed down. They went to the window, looked down, and saw an eight-seater turbo prop plane.

Quinn turned around. "We're flying in that?"

Both the agent and I nodded and smiled.

Mother un-nicked and asked very timidly, "Fredericka, is it safe?"

Her genuine smile reappeared. "They don't call us Tree Top Airways for nothing."

≥ ≤

The airline was nice enough to hold the plane while Frick and Frack dashed off and bought a third suitcase. They threw enough of their clothes into it to bring the luggage weight down to the acceptable limit and then stored the new piece of luggage in a locker. This also gave Mother Nature enough time to brew up a very dark and foreboding sky.

The plane was so small that we had to walk down a staircase, out of the building, and onto the tarmac to get to it. A very young, cherubic-looking boy had us and the other four passengers line up in a row.

Mother elbowed me. "How old do you think he is?"

"Legal. Maybe?"

He announced that all carry-on bags had to be stored in the wings. He opened up a little hatch on top of the left wing and started putting people's belongings into it. Quinn was at the end of the line.

"Sir," the boy asked, "may I have your bag please?" Quinn shook his head no. "Sir, all luggage must be stowed." He shook his head again, so I tried to grab it away from him but he wouldn't let it go.

"What is your problem?" I whispered. "Give it to the kid."

"I can't."

"Why?"

"My laptop is in there and my new screenplay is in it and I don't have it backed up and I know this is the big money one and what if we crash?"

"You die. If we crash, it doesn't matter if it's in the wing or on your lap. Both you and the screenplay will be gone, lost at sea."

I snatched the bag away from him and smiled, handing it to the boy. He slipped it into the wing, closed it up, and then looked us all up and down.

When he got to my mother she wiggled a little, winked, and whispered to me, "I'd date him."

I looked at her. "Jesus, Mother, he's not checking you out."

"How much do each of you weigh?" he asked.

We all told him our weights except for last and least, Quinn. He wouldn't answer the guy. At this rate we could have walked to the tip of Cape Cod and been there already. The boy asked Quinn a second time what his weight was and Quinn came out with, "One thirty-eight."

Everyone looked at him. Quinn was taller and more out of shape than me and I weighed one sixty.

I kicked him.

"I'm one forty-two."

I kicked him harder.

"One fifty."

"We need to seat you according to your weight so the plane doesn't tip o-v-e-r," the boy said very slowly and clearly to Quinn.

Out of fear he confessed, "One eighty."

We all looked at him.

"Two. One eighty-two. I promise."

Finally, we climbed on board. Mother was lucky enough to sit in the copilot's seat. Two very large and very in love gay men had the next two seats. I was in the third row across from a middle-aged man who could have passed for a straight and normal accountant from Normal, Illinois, and Quinn was in the back row next to his zaftig wife with short brown hair, Mrs. Normal Illinois.

The boy climbed onboard and said as he worked his way to the front of the plane, "Welcome aboard. We know you have a choice in airlines . . ."

"No we didn't," Quinn said from behind me.

". . . so we thank you for choosing Tree Top Airways." And the boy sat right down in the pilot's seat.

There was a collective and laborious intake of air in the cabin.

"I'm Captain Bob."

Mother looked back at me as I felt Quinn's knees shaking the back of my seat. I wanted to laugh so hard.

"Today we are flying in a Comp Air 8 Turbine with, as you can see, a single propeller with three blades."

Quinn put his lips to my ear. "Don't you have to have two propellers in case one poops out?"

"When we reach our cruising altitude we'll be traveling approximately two hundred miles per hour which will get us into Provincetown in about twenty-five short minutes, give or take a few, considering this pretty icky looking weather heading our way."

Did he just say icky?

Mother turned to him. "How old are you?"

"Legal." He looked at her and winked. "Maybe?"

The takeoff was hair raising to say the least. It just didn't seem like we were going fast enough down the runway and yet the nose lifted off. We were airborne maybe ten seconds when a gust of wind under the belly of the craft catapulted us skyward, causing all of us to be pinned incredibly hard down into our seats. Ears were popping left and right as Captain Bob tried to regain control of the aircraft. From where I was sitting, I wasn't sure if he could see over the steering wheel.

The tiny plane dipped continuously side to side as well as front to back, and bounced up and down during the longest flight of our lives. I looked back once at Quinn and caught Mrs. Illinois holding his forehead as he barfed into his doggy bag. I think Mother kept her eyes closed during most of the trip. If she did, she wouldn't have missed much because the entire flight was flown through pea soup fog. Why did we even take off in this kind of weather? Suddenly, the plane banked a left turn that felt dangerously too sharp and my thoughts immediately went to John Kennedy, Jr. *We can't end our lives on a silly trip to P-town.*

As we eased out of the turn, we broke through the clouds and into brilliant clear blue sky and there was my home away from home. The first landmark I recognized was the Pilgrim's Monument. I almost wished we were arriving a bit later in the year because on Thanksgiving Eve they string over five thousand white Christmas lights off the tower, which can be seen as far away as Cape Cod Canal. It is simply breathtaking.

The plane flew above Commercial Street and we could see the numerous wharfs and exquisite Victorian, Second Empire, Gothic, and Greek revival homes built by successful sea captains and merchants. And I could already see the hoards of day-trippers walking up and down the street, popping in and out of galleries, stores, and restaurants.

Original inhabitants were the Wampanoag Indians, but they never made permanent settlements on the tip of the cape but instead came out here to fish during the warm summer months. I think they must have been gay.

The plane banked a right and we flew out over the gay beach, which only had a sprinkling of people on it. We banked one more turn before landing, and I caught a glimpse of Race Point and the national seashore, on the ocean side. I loved Provincetown and had been coming up here for many years but I loved it even more now, off-season.

Once we landed, both Quinn's and Mother's coloring came back and I made sure that they both personally thanked Captain Bob for a safe and enjoyable trip. We jumped into a cab, a 1970s Ford station wagon, and headed off to our lodging.

"Captain Jack's Wharf, please," I said.

"What? Is everyone named Captain around here?" Mother asked.

"Not I, Captain," the rosy-cheeked and rotund female driver said. "But on a good night, you can call me Mistress."

Yup, we were in Provincetown. Beautiful, inspiring, quiet but hopefully not too quiet for my book signing, Provincetown.

"You all here for the festival?"

"What festival?" I asked cautiously.

"Cross-dresser's weekend." The cabbie eyed us from her rearview mirror. "You did bring your chiffon and blue eye shadow?"

We all looked at one another.

"I don't think so," I replied.

She laughed a big fat man's laugh. "Ah, you'll get into the swing of it. Hundreds of them pouring into town. Good tippers, too."

Both Quinn and Mother stared me down.

"Don't you dare," I whispered. "We get to stay here for free, compliments of Carrington Press."

Darcie, upon my request, had booked us at Captain Jack's Wharf. Located in the quieter end of town, I had heard that this was truly the ultimate Provincetown lodging experience. Built in 1884, this former fisherman's wharf and its eleven rustic shacks had been renovated into quaint, bohemian cabins.

And talk about history. In 1916, the twenty-eight-year-old playwright Eugene O'Neill joined a group of young artists and turned a building on Captain Jack's Wharf into a stage, and the Provincetown Players Theatre was born. They even made the scenery and costumes themselves.

The cabbie pulled up to the wharf as I giggled with excitement. It looked just like a picture-perfect postcard. The owners of these condo rentals had retained the original look of the seaside shanties, which stretched out into the bay on the wharf. And next to it was our very own private beach.

I paid our cab driver, leaped out, and ran down to the water as Mother and Quinn slowly emerged from the car and looked at the wharf.

The cabbie dropped our bags onto the sandy driveway. "Nice tip!" she hollered to me as I was coming back up the beach. "You must be cross-dressers."

I smiled and waved good-bye as she sped off. Mother and Quinn had such sour looks on their faces, but I wasn't going to let them ruin it for me.

"Brrrrrr," I said, rubbing my hands together. "The water is absolutely freezing cold. Isn't this fantastic?"

"So where are Popeye and Olive Oyl?" Quinn asked sarcastically.

My mother frowned. "This is going to be damp."

"Keep it up and I'm sending you both back to New York."

"Hello there!" hollered a bearish-looking man with a full red beard. "You must be the Jenkins party?"

I shook hands with Paul, the manager of Captain Jack's. He helped with our luggage as we climbed the staircase to the wharf and showed us to our cabin. He walked us down the public deck, past absolutely charming cabins astronomically named Australis, Borealis, and Mars. We could see into the rentals and noticed that one was decorated with a whimsical nautical theme, another had a 1940s boys club feel to it.

"These sunny decks overlook the dramatically beautiful tidal flats that appear and recede from our West End Bay beach," Paul explained proudly. "And each cabin has its own kitchen and bathroom."

"I love this little one named Venus' Locker," Paul said affectionately as he tapped on the door. We all took a step further and the Venus' Locker door swung open, hitting Mother in the back.

"Did somebody knock?" a man asked.

Mother fell into Quinn and the two of them turned around and found themselves face to face with a smallish guy with an exceptionally hairy body, wearing just a pair of women's nude panty hose and holding a tube of mascara.

"Ooooops," my mother said as Quinn put his hands over his eyes.

"Is it tea time, already?" the man asked.

Paul shook his head. "You still have about four hours, Hank. These are the Jenkins staying out at the end of the pier."

"Oh my, you must be the celebrities. Hope you're going to Club Purgatory tonight. Cross-dressers contest. My name this weekend in honor of my charming abode is, Venus de Locker. Ta, Ta!" And with that Hank disappeared back into the heavens.

Paul turned to us and whispered, "South Dakota senator. Staunch Republican."

Why was I not surprised? We passed another cabin named Orion and then we reached the end of the pier.

"This is Spindrift-Hesperus," Paul said as he unlocked the front door.

Mother and Quinn rushed in as I stayed out on the deck soaking up the view. The tide was coming in and straight out from the pier and across the bay was the very fingertip of the cape. And located on its fingernail was a beautiful lighthouse. Moored to buoys was an assortment of boats ranging from rowboats and small dinghies, to sailboats and Boston Whalers. The clanging of rusted metal clasps against rocking wooden boats in the gentle waves was a symphony to my ears. I couldn't wait to see what it would all look like at night.

Spindrift-Hesperus was actually two units reconfigured to form a spectacular retreat. It had a two-story great room, a loft accessible by stairs with a bedroom, two other secluded bedrooms each with its own queen-size bed, a full working kitchen, and a beautiful bathroom. Its décor was casual but elegant with a nautical theme and it had huge sliding glass doors that opened directly onto the deck overlooking the harbor. We were surrounded on three sides by water, which actually made it feel like we were at sea.

"It's moving," Quinn said in a panic.

I looked at him like he was nuts. "What's moving?"

"The cabin is moving," Mother agreed.

"You're both crazy."

Paul corrected me. "No, they're right. The current is really strong out here under these ancient pilings. It is moving. Next season we're finally replacing them. And wait till the wind picks up tonight—you'll really feel like you're on a ship."

Quinn put his hand to his mouth. "I'm going to be sick."

I ignored him. "Hence the name Hesperus? Longfellow's poem?"

Paul took an exaggerated theatrical stance and recited, "Such was the wreck of the Hesperus, in the midnight and the snow! Christ save us all from a death like this, on the reef of Norman's Woe." He bowed and said, "If there's anything you need, I'm in your anus."

The three of us stood there looking at him.

"Uranus," he said laughing as he made a dramatic exit.

Quinn feigned a severe movement of the wharf and spread his legs wide apart to keep his balance. "I'm fucked."

I put my arm around him. "Maybe you can tap into the creative energy that this wharf generates and work on that brilliant screenplay of yours."

Mother realized I was spinning and smiled.

Quinn looked at me slyly out of the corner of his eye. "What creative energy?"

"One of our most celebrated and greatest playwrights of all time stayed here at Captain Jack's and wrote one of the most acclaimed and successful plays of all time."

"Who and what?"

Mother looked at me suspiciously.

"Tennessee Williams. *The Glass Menagerie*.

It's true, he did. But as fast as Quinn's face lit up, it cooled down.

"And then a drunken Mr. Williams choked on a bottle cap and died in the Hotel Elysée in New York. Is that the life you want me to lead?"

"Actually," my mother said correcting him, "he was murdered."

I gave up.

≥ ≤

That afternoon my book signing was held at the Now Voyager bookshop on Commercial Street, which delighted me to no end considering it was named after one of my all-time favorite Bette Davis movies. Mother and Quinn walked down to the store with me but due to its diminutive size, the two of them were more than happy to ditch me and go bar hopping.

Mother gave me a kiss. "Curtis, we promise to be back by the end of the signing."

"Four o'clock," I reminded them. "And Quinn, now that you have a new cell, use it if you're not going to come back for me. OK?" They were already off and running.

There was a poster sent ahead of me by Carrington Press that had been placed in the bookshop window advertising my signing today from 2 to 4 o'clock and a few copies of *101 Ways to Collide into Your Gay Soul Mate* were stacked underneath it. The store manager was very nice but a bit frazzled and pointed to a tiny table that I could sit at and sign books.

He told me that earlier in the day Scott Pomfret and Scott Wittier, authors of the successful gay romance novel series, *Romentics*, had done their book signing that morning from ten to twelve and had had great success. He felt I could do as well but feared that most of the guys in town were probably busy applying makeup and putting their outfits together for some of the big events that evening.

I forced a smile and sat at my child's-size desk that was located at the back of the shop and prayed that someone would buy my book. One hour and fifty minutes had passed and none of the very many tourists perusing the bookstore had even stopped to see what I had written. In fact, none had even looked at me, I'm sure fearing that if they did they would be guilted into buying a book. So, I sat there pathetically doodling, checking my cell for messages that never came in, pretending to read my own book, just to pass the time away until finally, a woman wearing bright yellow pumps stood in front of my desk. I looked up and up and up and it wasn't a woman at all. It was a man.

He was wearing a gorgeous hand-tailored bright yellow suit with a matching hat and veil. No chiffon but he did have on a heavy dose of the blue eye shadow. He picked up my book with his white-gloved hand and opened it up.

"Love your hat, call you on Tuesday," I said as I winked at him.

He stared back, blankly. "What does that mean?"

I had a weird feeling that I knew this guy but I just couldn't place him. "It's just a saying the famous monologist Ruth Draper used to . . ." I stopped midsentence realizing he didn't have a clue as to what I was talking about.

"What's the book about?" he asked dryly.

"Finding the man of your dreams."

"And did you?"

Not again.

"No, but it's a very entertaining book with some great suggestions as to how *you* can find the man of *your* dreams."

"You're kinda late for that, bud." He pointed to a heavyset person in the front of the store with short brown hair who was wearing a rather plain cream-colored raincoat. "There's my ball and chain."

"Oh, don't call him that. I'm sure he's a very nice guy."

"Guy?" the cross-dresser exclaimed. "That's my wife."

At that moment, she angled toward me and I realized who he/she was. It was Mrs. Normal Illinois!

She joined us in the back of the store and cocked her head to the side, looking at my face. "You were on the plane. With your sick friend."

"Thank you for being so nice to him."

I noticed that underneath her raincoat she was wearing a very suburban-looking brown pantsuit with a contrasting but cool leather choker studded with glass crystals. Sensing an awkward pause, I racked my brain thinking of something to say to them.

"So, you're here for"—I gestured to everything—"the cross-dressing weekend?"

"Yes," she said. "Roberta and I travel all over the States to attend these events. We have so much fun."

The cross-dresser must have seen the confusion registered on my face. "Roberta is my name when I'm dressed. Rob when I'm not."

"I get it," I said, nodding approvingly.

His wife picked up my book. "And you're a writer." She elbowed Roberta. "Dear, we must be supportive and buy a copy."

"That's not necessary," I said.

"Go ahead and sign a copy," he said. "Our son might enjoy it."

I picked up my pen. "If he's gay "

"He's not," he said, cutting me off.

She leaned in close to me. "Our son Carroll is just metrosexual, not that there's anything wrong with being homosexual."

I looked at her husband decked out as Queen Elizabeth. *You bet there isn't.* "Um, whom should I make it out to? Rob or Roberta?"

"Roberta," she said. "When my husband is dressed he's Roberta and I'm Brie."

I'd never known a Brie in my life and now I knew two, a woman and a dog. It was just so sweet of them to do this. They bought the one and only book I sold that entire afternoon and when I handed it to Brie she thanked me to no end. Roberta smiled and then grabbed hold of something resting on Brie's back. We said our good-byes and as they turned to leave, I realized that Brie's cool leather crystal-studded choker was actually a dog collar and Roberta was holding the leash. They happily left the shop as if this was the most natural thing in the world. My mistake. I now knew *two* dogs named Brie.

Mr. and Mrs. Normal Illinois made me look like milquetoast.

≥ ≤

True to form, Mother and Quinn did not show up at the end of the signing nor did they call me. Which was fine with me, I could fend for myself. We were in Provincetown for just twenty-four hours and I wanted to make the most of the visit. Like many other tourists, one of my favorite pastimes was to weave in and out of galleries and shops. Or stroll up and down side streets admiring the beautiful houses and gardens.

But the sun was going to set soon so I decided instead to take off my shoes and walk along the harbor beachfront, to escape the throngs of people congesting Commercial Street. We hadn't made plans yet for dinner and this might give me some alone time in our beautiful Spindrift-Hesperus cabin.

I passed the Lobster Pot and then backtracked, unable to resist their perfect lobster roll. So many chefs ruin this simple and sublime recipe. As far as I'm concerned it should just be fresh lobster and lots of it, Hellmann's mayonnaise (with all the fat), celery, salt, pepper, and overstuffed in a toasted and buttered hotdog bun. Perfection. I had them make it to go and then walked back to the harbor and sat on a piling to enjoy it.

While soaking up the beauty and tranquility of the moment, my thoughts drifted back to a phone call I heard Quinn having that morning with his mother at the airport.

≥ ≤

Catching bits and pieces of the conversation, I could tell something upsetting was going on.

"Mom, this is coming out of nowhere," Quinn whispered. "Why didn't you say something before?"

Quinn looked over at me and I pretended to be engrossed with a freckle on the top of my hand. Actually, I was engrossed and fearful that it was my first liver spot. I wondered if I could scratch it off.

"But why are you so calm?" he asked. "You have to pick up dry cleaning? Wait! Mom don't hang up—"

Quinn slammed his cell shut. Well, he slammed a cell shut as much as you can slam a cell. He looked like he had lost his best friend.

I gave him a few moments and then asked, "What's going on?"

He was about to say something but then stopped. I thought he was confused or maybe even had a frog caught in his throat. He looked up and I realized that his eyes were full of tears. I may have seen Quinn cry out a scream or rant or rave but honestly, I don't think I had ever seen Quinn cry tears before. His vulnerability was totally disconcerting especially since I didn't know how to handle it. So I just lightly put my hand on his back, which surprisingly made him cry even harder.

I remember whispering to him to just let it out. He bent over forward and just sobbed. Thoughts raced through my mind. Was his mother sick? His father? I knew they lived in Nashua, New Hampshire, and then thought maybe they were angry at Quinn for not going up to visit them, with us being so close. But it had nothing to do with any of those things.

Quinn gathered his thoughts and was just about to speak when he started laughing uncontrollably.

It was so infectious and scary that I started to giggle with him. "What is it? What's going on?"

"Mommy . . . " and he stopped to regain his composure again.

Why do some grown men call their mother's mommy? This was not the time to find out.

"My mommy and dad are getting a divorce."

I thought about it for a moment and tried to recall any times that Quinn said they weren't getting along. He was an only child and they'd always seemed to be a close-knit, happy, and surprisingly functional family.

"Quinn, I thought they were like best friends."

He wiped away his tears. "She said they still are. Next year would have marked their fiftieth wedding anniversary. It's my dad. He's moved out but she won't tell me why. She said in time they will tell me and that this is not a bad thing. But I heard sadness in her voice. A deep sadness I've never heard before." This threw him back into uncontrollable crying. I just rubbed his back gently.

≷ ≶

The speed ferry heading back to Boston tooted its horn as it made its way out of the harbor, which pulled me back into the moment. I looked up and noticed a gigantic ship docked on the main pier. When did cruise liners start showing up in Provincetown?

I walked on and picked up some great shells and worn glass in front of the unusually quiet Boatslip Resort, which was closed for the off-season, and then decided to jog a bit to get in some cardio. I was heading back to the cabin but as I passed behind a bar/restaurant I heard a laugh that sounded awfully familiar. I stopped and strained to hear it against the lapping of the waves.

I walked up to the bayside deck and there she was standing with her back to me, cackling like I'd never heard her before. I was about to scream to Mother when she threw her hands up in the air and someone wrapped their arms around her neck.

I scurried through the sand and stood under the deck and shouted to her but she couldn't hear me over the music and everybody talking. So I dashed to the front of the place and realized, as I slipped my shoes back on, that this was the PiedBar.

I walked in and it was packed with women of all ages, shapes, and sizes. There were definitely no cross-dressers here and these gals were having a great time. I squirmed my way back to the deck, trying not to push or shove and there she was, lip-locked, arm-locked, body-locked with a petite and pretty woman with long, curly, crimson hair and the body of an aerobics instructor. Could it be? They came up for air and yes, it was Harrie.

"Curtis!" Harrie shrieked. She pulled away from my mother and wrapped herself around me.

It was quite overwhelming, so I just stood there staring at Mother as this impish creature bubbled all over me.

"Isn't it just too incredible that we have *collided*"—she looked back at Mother—"into each other like this *again*?"

I tried to get out of her octopus grip but couldn't. "Quite remarkable."

My mother was beaming and Quinn surfaced from the bar juggling three margaritas.

"Curtis, it's Harrie!" he screamed over the blaring music. "Can you believe she is here?"

Harrie let me out of her grip, smacked a huge kiss on my mother's lips, and then grabbed her drink from Quinn. For Mother and her, it was as if no time had passed since the book launch back at the Pup Room.

"Why are you here, Harrie?" I asked, trying my hardest to sound enthusiastic.

Mother pointed out into the harbor. "That's her ship. ASAP Cruises."

"I'm here for the cross-dressers!" Harrie hollered.

I looked back out at the monstrosity floating in the bay. "Is that entire ship full of cross-dressers?"

"Of course not. This is our first stop on our New England/Canada cruise originating out of Boston and I'm drumming up business. We docked last night and threw a huge costume party on board for the cross-dressers, promoting the cruise line. And can you believe I was Sandra Dee?"

Yes, I could. She handed her drink to my mother who was smiling ear-to-ear and then started belting out the classic song from *Grease*, "Look at Me, I'm Sandra Dee." And when she got to the lyrics that referred to her not having sex till she was married, Harrie spun around and kissed Mother again. "Will you marry me?" The two of them laughed and started making out.

I shot Quinn a glance and went off to the bar with him trailing after me.

"Curtis, lighten up."

I turned around and faced him. "I'm fine. I'm light." I tried to signal the bartender but couldn't catch her eye. "But does she have to be so happy all the time?"

"What are you ordering?"

"Everyone is having margaritas, right?"

Quinn put his hand on his hip and gave me that look.

"What? I can't have one too?"

"We all know what happens when you drink tequila."

I pulled out some cash. "No. *You* all know what happens when I drink tequila. I don't. And that's the point." I tried to signal the bartender again and then turned to Quinn. "What the hell are we doing in a lesbian bar! Let's go to the A-House."

Mother and Harrie caught up with us.

"So, Curtis, what are you going to wear to Club Purgatory's cross-dressing contest tonight?" Harrie asked. "Your mother and Quinn have been brainstorming with me over costumes."

I looked at both of them like they were traitors.

"You know what, the book signing didn't go too terrific, not that anyone has asked, so I think I'll just pass and head on back to the wharf."

Mother pulled me aside. "Please don't do this."

"Do what?" I said, looking down at my shoes.

"You're getting moody and turning inward and nine times out of ten it's because you're just not speaking your mind. You know how much I love you and I'm sorry I didn't ask about the signing and that it didn't go the way you wanted it to. But it truly would make me sad if you didn't join us tonight. It will be so much fun."

I kept looking down.

"Curtis, please?"

I ignored her and looked at my shoe.

"Curtis, I can see you smiling."

I looked at my shoe harder.

"I think I can see you smiling. Is that it? Is that Curtis's smile I can see? Oh I see a curl! I see the corner of his mouth turning up. Oh, there it is!"

She was treating me so juvenile I found it hysterically funny and started laughing.

"You are too much, Mother." I signaled the bartender again and she finally saw me. I turned to Quinn. "Am I that bad on tequila?"

"I would say you're that good on tequila, all others would say yes, that bad."

I reluctantly acquiesced and ordered a bottle of water.

≥ ≤

Once I was on board with the costume party, my mother and Harrie went on board the ASPA ship to retrieve some outfits. Quinn and I headed out onto Commercial Street to see what we could find.

The only party rule was that you had to be in drag. So, Quinn and I ran into several women's shops and he came up with a sixties mod miniskirt with a bold psychedelic print, a green Day-Glo tube top, and a pair of white platform shoes for him. We went to a few other places but I was coming up empty handed. If I was going to do this, I was going to do it the right way.

In a card and novelty shop, Quinn found a hideous and humongous red Afro wig but I still hadn't found anything I liked. However, on a side street we stumbled upon a leather shop and I did find one item that I'd always wanted to have.

Quinn looked at it and frowned. "A chest harness?"

"Actually, I'd love a full torso harness but these things can get freaking expensive."

"But you need to be in drag for the party."

"It's not for the party, it's for me."

His eyes popped out of his head in disbelief. "This is a side of you I've never seen before."

We walked around the store and I actually found the smell of the leather quite exciting. "See anything you like?"

One item caught Quinn's attention. "Mmmm. A cock harness with an anal dildo pouch. Now that's multitasking."

"It's also two hundred and ten dollars," I said, reading the price tag.

"Never mind."

I actually bought the chest harness but was still clueless as to what to wear to the party. As planned, we were all going to meet back at Captain Jack's Wharf. Since Club Purgatory didn't open till ten and we didn't want to show up till eleven, on our way back I stopped off at a convenience store and picked up a few items so I could actually cook a dinner in the cabin.

And I was right. The nighttime view from Spindrift-Hesperus was enchanting. Up and down the harbor you could see lights twinkling from boats, and the periodic flashing from the distant lighthouse coupled with the foghorn was classic. Inside I lit candles and started making dinner, which was going to be tasty but simple.

I made up a batch of linguini with fresh clams and a white wine sauce, tossed a green salad, and heated up a loaf of garlic bread.

Meanwhile, Quinn emerged from one of the bedrooms wearing his miniskirt, tube top, and Afro, as Mother and Harrie were entering the cabin. We all fell onto the floor laughing.

"You look like Ronald McDonald on crack!" I hollered.

He put both his hands on his hips. "Mrs. Ronald McDonald on crack, thank you very much."

Mother and Harrie had bags full of clothing and started rifling through them.

"Look, look, look," Mother said as she pulled clothing out of a bag. "I have tails and top hat."

And Harrie held up a green outfit. "One of the dancers on the ship gave me this Peter Pan costume. I always, *always* wanted to be Peter Pan."

You are Peter Pan, my dear.

My mother joined me in the kitchen and marveled at the dinner I had put together. "But what are you wearing, dear?"

"I don't have anything."

She dragged me back into the living room and grabbed another bag. "We brought this just in case, for backup." She pulled out of the sack a huge pink poodle skirt with a tulle petticoat and a matching black spandex off-the-shoulder top with pink roses embroidered on the chest. "You can be Sandra Dee."

I tried to smile but I just couldn't see it. "I don't know. It's just not me."

"Wait!" Quinn shouted as he ran to my bedroom. He came out with my chest harness. "Wear this on top, the poodle skirt on bottom, and put on your black boots."

"Do you think they'd let me in as half a woman?"

"Hey, I've worn chest harnesses before," my mother admitted as Harrie smiled devilishly.

Quinn and I grimaced.

I thought about if for a moment. "It's kinda edgy."

≥ ≤

We devoured dinner, rested a bit, and then were off to Club Purgatory. It was located in the basement of the Gifford House Inn, which is perched high on the corner of Bradford and Carver Streets. The ambience and charm of this antique-filled yellow clapboard house bustled with energy and activity yet was devoid of the stuck-up attitude that could easily be found in other Provincetown gay hangouts. There was a piano bar lounge in the front lobby, a bar off of the veranda, and then down below was Purgatory.

For the first Saturday in November, the weather was quite mild. We put on our costumes, added just a hint of makeup, and decided to walk to the Gifford House. Embarrassed to hell by what I was wearing, I suggested that we take Bradford Street, the high road, because everyone else would be walking along Commercial. But no, the others wouldn't hear of it. So, with Mother in her top hat and tails, Harrie as Peter Pan, Quinn as Mrs. Ronald McDonald, and me as a leather-loving Sandra Dee, we set off, hopefully to have fun.

It actually wasn't as mild out as I thought. I had on the poodle skirt and tulle petticoat and underneath that a leather thong. On top I was wearing just the leather harness and I was freezing. Harrie brought with her the black spandex top just in case I wanted it, and I did. I slipped it on over the harness, which took the chill away. I caught myself in the reflection of a storefront and was pleasantly surprised at how pretty I looked. But the leather thong was already irritating me so I dashed behind a tree, slipped it off, and had Mother shove it into her suit pocket. And as stupid as I felt, no one noticed me on the street, considering the bizarre assortment of crossdressers who had invaded the town. Mr. and Mrs. Normal Illinois had brought to my attention, and Harrie had confirmed, that a large majority of cross-dressers are straight. That was news to me.

All of us were out of breath as we made the steep trek up Carver Street from Commercial but once we reached the Gifford House, we realized it was well worth it. Gays, lesbians, bisexuals, transsexuals, straights, and of course cross-dressers from all over the country were swarming in and out and all around the place. You could enter Purgatory from the front downstairs door but we wanted to have a drink first up at the veranda bar before we made our entrance. I was pleasantly surprised when we were greeted with an unexpected round of applause from patrons at the bar.

Mother ordered three margaritas, one for herself, Harrie, and Quinn as I struggled with what I was going to drink. Still feeling nervous and looking like a dope, I made up my mind and signaled the bartender.

"Margarita on the rocks, no salt please?"

Quinn nudged me. "You sure you want to do that?"

I looked around. "I'm sure."

Quinn held up his glass to the room. "Fasten your seat belts, it's going to be a bumpy night!"

≳ ≲

After two rounds of drinks and hearing the beat of the music coming up through the floor boards, we knew it was time to make our appearance and descended down into Purgatory from the back staircase inside the veranda bar. The steep winding back staircase, mind you. Quinn went first and I heard the room cheer as he entered. Mother and Harrie went hand in hand and again, the room hollered. Then it was my turn. And I don't think it was the margaritas, but halfway down I couldn't see the fucking steps because my poodle skirt stuck so far out and I slipped and slid down the bottom half of the staircase, on my ass, and spilled out onto the floor of Purgatory. Quite a grand entrance. The room went insane. I wanted to die.

With my ego bruised as well as my entire backside, I needed reinforcements so I ordered all of us another round of margaritas. The club was packed and some of the costumes were fantastic. Most people looked like your Aunt Loretta from the Midwest but several had dressed up as gay icons. The competition for best-dressed cross-dresser had already begun and one by one the contestants went up onto the stage and were encouraged to dance, strut, show off, and perform in any way, shape, or form that they so desired.

One man was a tribute to Divine, another looked more like Cher than Cher. But there was one who was my personal favorite and one no one else could guess who he was. He had on a light sandy-blonde wig with wisps of gray throughout it. It was medium-cut, gently curled, and flipped under just at the nape of his neck. His makeup was light and unadventurous but cleverly hid all the flaws. He was wearing a stylish but conservative suit and sensible shoes and carried a large black handbag. When he came off stage Quinn guessed first.

"Are you Betty White?"

"Too old," he said.

Mother tried. "Barbara Walters?"

"Much too old!"

"Bette Davis?" Harrie asked.

"Much too dead!"I looked at all of them and smirked. "You're . . . Jean Harris."

He pulled a water gun out of his purse and aimed it at me. "Bang! Bang! You're dead!" He spun around looked for his next victim.

My reward for having guessed correctly? I was pushed out onto the stage by my posse. At the exact same moment, the Pointer Sisters' song "Jump" from the mid-eighties started playing and everyone, including myself, went wild. Caught up in the moment and having shed all my inhibitions with the delicious help of the margaritas, I slipped the black spandex top up over my head and threw it onto the stage. The room roared when they saw the chest harness.

To the beat of the music I then slipped the poodle skirt off, revealing just the tulle petticoat, and the club burst out into laughter. Surprising even myself, I then pulled the huge petticoat up to my chest so it looked like a big baby doll dress.

Mother ran up to me on the stage with her drink. "You're gonna win this one, darling!"

I drank up her margarita and the approval of the crowd. She dashed back to Quinn and Harrie, and with that, I pulled the petticoat up over my head and started dancing wildly to the music. The room went out of control with cheers, screams, and propositions being yelled out to me. What I had forgotten is that I had taken off the thong. Here I was dancing on the stage in Purgatory in the basement of the historic Gifford House, where none other than the Vanderbilts used to stay, and I was in a leather chest harness, black boots, and was bare-ass-and-cock naked.

Quinn turned to my mother and Harrie. "Should I go out there and tell him?"

"No, let's enjoy this," Mother laughed.

"Wow, he's hung!" exclaimed Harrie.

Mother kissed her. "That's my boy."

I was soaking up all the attention when Quinn ran out onto the floor and tapped my shoulder. "Curtis?"

I pushed him away. "Nope, I've got the spotlight, tonight!"

Quinn grabbed my shoulder harness and spun me toward him. I don't know what possessed me to do this and maybe the tequila played a big part, but I shockingly slapped Quinn across the face. And with a knee-jerk reaction, Quinn shockingly slapped me right back and the crowd erupted with screams of joy.

"Fight! Fight! Fight!"

Quinn grabbed both my shoulders, shook me, and then screamed, "Look at your dick, you dick!"

I looked down and truly was mortified when I realized I didn't have the thong on. I covered my genitals, grabbed my skirt, petticoat, and top, and ran off the stage to the farthest, darkest corner of the room.

The gang caught up with me as I slipped the skirt back on. I cut them off before any of them could say anything. "I know! I know! I'm never drinking tequila again!"

No, I didn't run off. I swallowed my pride and a lot of water and also waited to see if I had won the competition. And, low and behold, I had. To celebrate, all of us joined the eclectic group of characters in Club Purgatory and started dancing. At one point there were so many different colors of polyester fabrics flying all over the place it felt like we were floating amidst a rainbow chiffon flag. But out of all the cross-dressers, one in particular really caught my eye and not just because of what he was wearing.

"Look at that guy!" I screamed. "He is as free as the wind and having the time of his life."

We all agreed that he wasn't too bad looking, either.

"He's a bit older than what I usually go for," Quinn admitted, "but what a great dancer. What the hell! Wish me luck." He hiked up his tube top, squeezed down his miniskirt, and tried not to trip over his white platform shoes as we watched him inch his way across the crowed dance floor. And happily, the guy started dancing with Quinn immediately. Everything seemed to be going great but then all of a sudden, the two of them stopped dancing and just stared at one another.

I squinted my eyes and shouted to Mother and Harrie. "What do you think is going on?"

We danced our way over to them as the man looked into Quinn's eyes with a bewildered look and hollered, "Son?"

Quinn did a triple take. "Dad?"

We all stopped dancing, realizing that Quinn had hit on his own father.

Quinn was shocked, stunned, and confused, as he looked his father up and down. "Isn't that Mommy's dress?"

Mr. Larkin held out his skirt. "Yes, but don't you think it looks better on me?"

Tongue-tied, Quinn stood there speechless as Mother, Harrie, and I stood there in amazement.

"I took some of your mother's lipstick too when I left but couldn't find any bright red."

"Dad, Mommy isn't a bright-red-lipstick kind of woman."

"But I am!" howled his father, slapping Quinn on the back. He grabbed Quinn's hands and started dancing with him.

In a flash, Quinn understood why his parents had broken up.

≳ ≲

Instead of coming back to Manhattan, Mother decided to travel with Harrie on the rest of the New England/Canada ASAP cruise, and Quinn went up to New Hampshire to visit his mom and get all the nitty gritty details on his father's "outed" lifestyle. Reluctantly, I was left with the responsibility of dragging their overweighted and lockered Boston baggage back to New York. And the moment I walked into my apartment Darcie called, wanting me to go to her office for a meeting.

She held a large manila envelope in her hand and waved it at me. "When I first saw these I thought I was fucked."

I laughed, not even knowing what she was alluding to. "I didn't do it."

"Oh, but I beg to differ, my dear." She threw the envelope at me. "You did it bigger this time."

"Bigger?"

"Seems as though some photos, some revealing photos, some *more* revealing photos of you are circulating around the Internet."

"What?" I exclaimed, trying to open it up. "That can't be."

"I'm afraid so. Pictures taken at a Club Purgatory in Provincetown? Showing you wearing a leather harness? What the hell does a harness harness?"

I tore open the envelope, dreading what I might find. "It harnesses the beast within? I don't know what the hell it harnesses."

"It sure didn't harness your manhood," she said, winking.

I pulled out the pictures and was horrified. "Fuck me."

"No thanks."

"Damn it! I didn't know there were any cameras at that club." I shuffled through the pictures. "Oh shit! That one leaves nothing to the imagination."

"You took the words right out of my mouth, Curtis."

I dropped my head into my hands. "What are we going to do?"

"Do? Nothing."

"What?"

"Except circulate them more aggressively. Maybe do our own"—she pointed to my penis in one of the pictures—"big photo shoot?"

I sat there stunned.

"Sales are through the roof. Breathe, Curtis. This is a good thing. You've been coming off a little too prudish in your interviews. You're hot and spicy now. Everywhere you turn you're making naked headlines and men are eating you up."

I wished.

"Darcie, I'm so embarrassed."

"Embar*rass*ed is more like it," she said, frowning at the picture of my rear end. "And you'd better start doing more squats."

ELEVEN

TO KILL A MOCKING FATHER

I wanted to thank Petra for stopping by and taking care of Emily-Mae while I was in Provincetown so I invited her over to my apartment for dinner. One of the pluses to living in New York City is that you can have anything delivered at just about anytime of the day or night. I opted to order from my local Vietnamese restaurant, which was delicious. In fact, there was always a line of people around the block waiting to get in.

"This tastes like thit," Petra exclaimed. "I love it!"

I laughed so hard. She was right; it was curry thit, which is sautéed sliced pork with vegetables in coconut milk and curry sauce served with pancakes. After we devoured the meal, I served some ginger ice cream and the two of us sat on my sofa with Emily-Mae between us.

"I almost called you while you were in Provincetown," Petra confessed as she placed her hand on Emily's back. "She was having a lot of trouble breathing."

I picked her up and held her in my arms. Brussels griffons notoriously have breathing problems but it was obvious that Emily was laboring harder for breath than usual. I kissed her forehead and sat her on my lap.

"Petra, I dread the inevitable day."

"I know, darling," she said, patting my hand. "I did some Reiki on her."

I thought for a moment. "That's laying on of hands?"

Suddenly, it felt like someone had stabbed a knife into my intestines. I slid Emily-Mae off my lap and onto the sofa as I doubled over.

"Curtis, what is it?"

It took a moment for me to catch my breath. "This happened earlier today. A pain in my gut."

Petra put Emily-Mae on the floor and had me lie on the sofa. "Is it on the right side? Maybe it's your appendix?"

I touched the left side. "No, it's over here."

Petra rubbed her hands together and placed them on the area. After just a few moments it felt much better.

"Maybe they're just gas pains?" I asked, fearing that it might be much more serious. "I'm OK. I feel better."

I tried to sit up but Petra encouraged me to lie flat as she went to get her bag. "Curtis, are you eating too fast, drinking too much liquid with your meals, eating the wrong foods, or maybe thinking negative thoughts while you are eating?"

I paused while I went through her list. "Yes, to all of the above."

She came back, pulled up a chair next to the sofa, and sat in it. "You should eat bitter greens like frisée lettuce."

"You mean scratchy lettuce?"

She smiled. "Yes, it's in the chicory family and has a calmative effect on your digestion. You could also try drinking raw cabbage juice."

"How about some good old fashioned antacid?"

She gave me a look of disapproval and then took out of her bag a large quartz crystal attached to a string. "Maybe you need an enema?"

"With that?" I asked, exaggerating a frightened look.

"Relax. Before I left Prague I took a course in past life regression. Darling, let me take you back in time, maybe it could give us some answers to health issues going on in your current life."

"Past life?" I asked skeptically.

"I'm going to hypnotize you."

Little did Petra know I couldn't be hypnotized. My first shrink found that out the hard way. But she was so enthusiastic and wanting to help me, I let her dangle her huge crystal over my head as I counted backward in time.

"One hundred, ninety-nine, ninety-eight . . ."

"Yes, Curtis, just relax. Just fall back."

I was counting back but certainly not falling.

"Sixty-five, sixty-four, sixty-three . . ."

"Back in time, back in lives."

"Twenty-two, twenty-one, twenty . . ."

I could feel Petra's frustration. "Nothing? You don't see anything yet?"

Suddenly, I did see something. "It's 1762."

"Yes! Yes! Go on, Curtis."

I described to Petra what I saw. "I see a beautiful mountain. No, it's a rolling hill. And there's something purple all over it."

"Could it be heather?"

"Yes."

There was magnificent heather and there was a sweet little thatched-roof cottage. I could see myself running to it. No, past it to a little barn. I looked through the window and saw my own reflection and to my relief, I was still a man. A handsome man, at that, with a full beard and a funny kind of hat on my head. A Scottish tam! I entered the barn and there was a young boy sitting at a bench and before him was a pile of raw leather hides. The smell of it was turning me on. The boy seemed to be making something out of the leather and suddenly he spoke to me.

Petra was on the edge of her seat. "What does he say?"

"Aye! A wee dunkin dory," I said with a bastardized Scottish accent.

Petra asked, "A what?"

"Ya, dirty bugger. You're makin' pants."

I turned my head from side to side and asked in my own voice, "I make what?"

"Dirty, stinkin', leather, pants!"

I thought in past lives we were all Napoleon or Catherine the Great or at least someone historic and important?

"Ya live in Aberdeen, Scotland. And ya stupid enough to make pants when everyone is wearing kilts."

Petra was entranced. "Darling, you made leather pants."

"Ya make leather pants and passes at me, ya dirty bastard. Ya wife would be ashamed."

Astonished, I asked him, "My wife?"

"If I had a cow like her, I'd treat her like gold. But ya just buggering all us lads on top of the moors behind her back."

At this moment I opened one eye and saw Petra was beside herself with excitement. Then it dawned on her that I was goofing the whole time. She slapped my wrist as we broke out into laughter.

≥ ≤

I did try eating slower and without washing it down with liq-uids, but to no avail. I periodically still had intestinal crankiness. Frightened that it might be an ulcer and ever worse, I made an appointment to see my general practitioner.

Considering all doctors are always behind with their daily patient schedules, I made sure I came just on time and not early. I still had to wait about twenty minutes for my appointment, which gave me plenty of time to daydream back to one particular visit I had made to our family physician, Dr. Cavalier, when I was twelve.

≳ ≴

The eye-tearing smell of alcohol and ethers, mixed with the visuals of dingy linoleum floors and the unsanitary feeling of the dark, musty examining rooms haunt me to this day. The sadistic Nurse Axlerod was always decked out in the traditional uniform of white dress, shoes, and cap. And on this day she prepared my tetanus booster shot in a hypodermic needle large enough to suck bone marrow out of a hip bone. I swear I saw a glint in her eye and a faint smile on her lips as she overzealously punctured my tender little body and heard me cry out with pain.

Born with only one testicle having descended, all were waiting patiently for the other to drop, including yours truly. Well, that ball was happy as a clam to stay upstairs in that warm, safe, comfy space—somewhere. The big decision was whether to let it do its own thing or to surgically drop it.

Even at twelve, I had great reservations about this physician and his medical abilities. I voiced my concerns to Mother but she just brushed them off, saying I'd find anyway to get out of going to the doctor. And to add fuel to my imagination, Dr. Cavalier was just plain creepy looking. He was balding and what hair he did have left at the back of his skull, which was dry, brittle, and white, he would comb up and around and over his dented head. I figured he lacquered it down with hairspray because the scent of Final Net always preceded his entry into the room. And Dr. Cavalier had thick eyeglasses magnifying the slittiest of eyes imaginable.

As usual he did his wide range of weird examinations, blood tests, and probing of my body, just aching to find something wrong with me. And on this visit, he thought he had.

"Mrs. Jenkins, please come in here right away," he said in his scratchy, high-pitched voice.

I slid away from him on the examining table as Mother ran in. "What's wrong, Dr. Cavalier?"

"I've done extensive research and I now know what Curtis's problem is."

"Problem?" I asked defensively.

"Your son here is really your daughter. He is a she."

I don't think my eyes nor my mother's could have opened any wider.

"What!" she exclaimed.

"His hormonal levels are iffy, his genitalia is malformed, and he looks like a girl."

He was so excited it frightened me. "What I propose to do is surgically remove the testicle that has not descended. I'll also remove his normal gonad. We can extricate his penis and create an artificial vagina and with some hormonal supplements we can call it a day and him Courtney."

The only nut that should be surgically removed is that quack of a doctor, I thought as I hightailed it out of that office.

Mother was about to have a conniption. "Are you crazy? My Curtis is not a hermaphrodite. He's a gay!" she cried as she ran after me. "Curtis, I won't let him touch you. Curtis?"

≳ ≴

"Curtis," my general practitioner's secretary said, pulling me out of the daydream, "the doctor will see you now."

Once in his office, he ruled out my HIV medications as the source of my pain.

"Could you have caught something from someone, recently?"

"Meaning?"

"Amebas? Parasites? From say, rimming?"

I didn't have to think about this one. "If I caught something by doing that, it would have had to have been the immaculate infection." Not that I'm against it, I just haven't done it in ages. "Oh, doctor? Amebas, parasites? I did have a McDonald's hamburger recently. Would that count?"

He smiled as he wrote down a phone number and address. "I think you're fine, but just to be on the safe side, let's schedule a colonoscopy."

I know this is going to sound weird, but the thought of it fascinated me.

≳ ≴

You hear everyone say that the worst part of a colonoscopy is the preparation, and they're right. But it's not the salty phospho soda laxative you have to take the day before and the intense and never-ending evacuation it produces that is so excruciating. It's the fact that you can't eat any food the entire day before or the day of the procedure. In theory it doesn't seem challenging, but right about 11 o'clock the night before you're looking at your hand and thinking it looks pretty tasty.

Having survived not eating the stuffing in my sofa, I made it downtown to the gastroenterologist's office, checked in with the female secretary at the front desk, and then was completely surprised to find Father Greg from Magda's memorial sitting in the waiting room. Upon seeing him again I was reminded of how absolutely gorgeous this man was. Shit, of all places to run into him.

"Father Greg." I held out my hand to give him a shake but he jumped up out of his seat and gave me a big embrace.

"Curtis."

He remembered my name.

I went into babble mode. "Fancy meeting you in a place like this." I laughed a little too hard. "Wasn't yesterday a killer? Running to the bathroom and running to the bathroom and running to the bathroom? And starving and wanting to eat but not being able to eat and because you can't eat you just want to eat more and—"

"Actually, I'm just waiting for a friend who's having the procedure. I'm going to help her back home."

I suddenly felt quite unattractive.

The doctor's very tall and skinny assistant appeared. "Mr. Jenkins, my name is Larry. Will you follow me, please?"

I remembered that Petra had encouraged me to find a man who was more spiritually connected and suddenly thought maybe Father Gregory Peck was the answer to my prayers.

"Father, would you like to have—"

"Dinner? You took the words right out of my mouth." He handed me his business card.

I had never thought about it before, but it seemed odd that a man of the cloth would have a business card, but then again, why not? "Pulido. Nice last name, Father."

"Mexican. Originally from Oaxaca."

"I've always wanted to go there."

"Curtis," Father said, embracing me again but more intimately, "call me." He squeezed me tighter. "Sooner than later."

"Yes. Sure. OK. I promise. I will. I will."

The medical assistant, with his spindly arms crossed and his foot tapping the floor, coughed to get my attention. "Mr. Jenkins?"

"Thank you, Father. I'll call. And thank you again for Magda's beautiful memorial even though I ran out and missed the ending."

I waved good-bye and floated away from him, following Larry back into the procedure rooms.

"Curtis, you can slip out of your clothes in this room and put a hospital gown on and then I'll introduce you to the doctor and the anesthesiologist."

Who needed an anesthesiologist? I was so high they could have given me a lobotomy and I wouldn't have felt it. I quickly changed out of my clothes but before I had a chance to put on the johnny coat, Larry entered the room.

"Naughty me, walking in on you like this," he said, smiling as he looked me up and down. He stuck his head outside of the door. "Dr. Pratt, Curtis Jenkins is ready for you."

"Oh, but I'm not. I can't find my dressing gown."

"Please, Curtis. We're all on the same team in this office. What we'll see is going to leave nothing to our imaginations."

Was this legal?

The rather short and stout and looking quite like a teapot Dr. Pratt entered the room. "Curtis, I'm Lou Pratt, your gastroenterologist, and it is going to be a pleasure to do your colonoscopy." He too gave my now naked body quite an embrace. "And look at what I loved." He pulled my book out of his lab coat pocket and waved it in the air.

Both he and Larry escorted me into the colonoscopy room where the anesthesiologist, Dr. Ed Morehouse, was waiting for me next to the examining table.

"There's our little celebrity!" Dr. Morehouse shouted. "Get your ass on this table."

This all seemed horribly inappropriate and frighteningly unprofessional, yet I knew they were one of the best teams in New York.

Hesitantly I got up onto the gurney and was told to lie on my left side. Immediately, Dr. Morehouse checked the veins in my arms. "An anesthesiologist's dream. Look at these veins. I don't know which one to choose they all look so tempting."

Simultaneously, Dr. Pratt was wrestling with the scope that appeared to be at least ten feet in length. Suddenly I felt light-headed.

At that moment, the front secretary came in with a clipboard. "Mr. Jenkins, I'm sorry but we forgot to have you sign these consent forms." She placed it down on the gurney.

"What am I consenting to?"

Dr. Pratt answered for her. "You're consenting not to take me to court if I steer off course." The whole team broke out into laughter. "But don't sweat it, Curtis. Once in a while we puncture the colon and that's not pretty but you're our little star. I promise to drive safely."

Reluctantly, I signed the consent form and the secretary left the room.

"Oh, and please sign my copy of your book, too," Dr. Pratt said, slipping it in front of me.

I scribbled my name as Larry snapped surgical gloves onto his hands. "I can't wait to tell the guys who I prepped today."

I felt a prick as Dr. Morehouse slipped the IV needle into a vein. "This is a Valium drip. You'll feel like you're totally gone but you won't be. Some patients go in and out of consciousness."

"I don't feel any—" And I was out.

Midway through the procedure, I did wake up and saw the monitor that Dr. Pratt was using to hopefully drive carefully along my highway.

"Is that my ascending colon?" I asked, slurring.

"We've got a talker here," Dr. Pratt said. "Put him out."

The next thing I knew, I was in the recuperating room and Dr. Pratt was standing next to me with some photos. "Welcome back, handsome. The coast is clear and what a magnificent coast you have. Look at these pictures, Curtis." He held the photos in front of me. "So fresh and pink."

What a crappy job.

"And thanks for signing your book for me," he said as he left the room.

"No problem," I mumbled, still feeling the Valium drip.

Larry entered with a bottle of orange juice. "Here, this will perk you up."

I sat up on the edge of the gurney and sipped a bit of it.

"Let me help you to your feet." Larry slipped his arm into mine and got me standing. "Take your time getting dressed." He started to leave and then came back and handed me his business card. "By the way, you have the transverse colon of an eighteen-year-old." He winked and said, "Call me, too." He tapped my bottom and left the room.

≳ ≲

I actually solved my nondiagnosed intestinal challenge by heeding Petra's advice and drinking three sixteen-ounce glasses of raw cabbage juice a day. Within forty-eight hours, I was symptom free and free to call Father Gregory Peck and ask him out to dinner.

With both of us living on the Upper West Side, I suggested that we meet at Concheta's Mexican restaurant on 116th Street and Broadway, just an avenue away from the cathedral. It was comfortable and spacious and I wanted to impress Father with what I thought was some of the most authentic colonial Mexican cuisine in New York City. The décor was a bit over the top with dozens of oversized and brightly painted gourd masks tacked up on maize-colored stucco walls. Scattered amongst them were colorful serapes, ponchos, and Mexican blankets. And above the rustic bar that was made of fine alder wood imported from Oaxaca stands a jarring self-portrait of my personal heroine and patron saint, Frida Kahlo.

I arrived a bit early to have a moment to collect myself and order a cocktail, but before I could even get my coat off I heard a man call out my name from the far end of the bar.

"Curtis!"

It was Father Greg. And I was surprised to see that he had showed up wearing his white priest's collar with black shirt and pants. But then, what else would he be wearing? I walked down the long bar and was greeted with an even more intimate embrace than the one he offered in Dr. Pratt's office, and a good dose of tequila on his breath.

"Father, it's so good to see you."

"Please, call me Greg."

I took a good long look at this six-foot-plus priest with thick black wavy hair, strong jawline, and mysteriously dark eyes, who happened to look just like a famous actor, and asked very innocently, "May I call you Gregory?"

He wrapped his arms around me and said, "Hell, you can call me Mother Mary."

I was about to freak when I looked up and caught a glimpse of Frida staring down at me and sensed she would approve of this unconventional scenario. I hugged him back and suggested we sit down at a table.

I signaled the hostess as Gregory gathered his belongings and chugged down his shot and she sat us at a table in the far corner of the restaurant. I'm not sure if it was to give us more privacy or to keep us hidden. She handed us our menus and said our waiter would be right with us.

On each table was a Milagro cross, encrusted with an assortment of tin charms of arms, legs, hands, feet, heads—anything one wanted to pray to have healed or give thanks for having been cured.

I touched it. "I wonder if there's a colon on there?"

"I hope everything was OK with your examination the other day?"

"Yes. Everything is fine but what a great conversation for me to start off a date with."

Gregory looked at me seriously. "Is this what you think this is? A date?"

I felt so put on the spot. "Um, well, I'm sorry. I mean I shouldn't just assume but I thought you were . . ." Embarrassed, I put my head into my hands. "Oh Jesus."

"You thought I was Jesus?"

"No," I said, looking up and saw that he was smiling. "I forgot to ask if you are gay."

"Is President Bush an idiot? Of course I'm gay. And although I don't preach it from the pulpit, many of the parishioners know of my sexual orientation." He slipped his hand into mine. "I was hoping it was a date."

"Father . . ."

"If you keep calling me Father, I'm going to have to call you son."

That's OK. "Gregory, I can already see that you are an enigma."

"Who me? A mystery? A puzzle?"

I picked up my menu. "Let's say deliciously irreverent?"

"I'll accept that."

A very cute and young Mexican waiter arrived with chips and salsa. Gregory looked him up and down so hard I almost told him to leave some clothes on the poor kid or he'd catch pneumonia.

"Would you gentlemen like something from the bar?" Gregory licked his lips. "Do you come in a bottle?"

The waiter blushed as I hid behind my menu.

"Don't worry," Gregory said, "I'm harmless. Bring me a shot of tequila. Will you join me, Curtis?"

"Oh no! One tequila and my clothes are off!"

"Bring him a shot and the check please!" he hollered while winking at the boy.

This was not what I expected from a priest. Albeit he was an Episcopal and they sure were lenient with their organized religion but this all seemed a bit inappropriate. "I'll have the Concheta, please."

The waiter nodded. "Coming right up."

Gregory waited till the boy was gone. "What the hell is a Concheta?"

I smiled. "Vodka, lemonade, and guava juice with a wedge of lemon and lime. It's a smart cocktail."

Gregory muttered something about it sounding too sweet but I ignored his comment and buried my nose in the menu. I couldn't decide what to order. Everything looked so appealing.

"Gregory, I love to eat and everything here is so tempting. I'm such a foodie I swear I'm a fat man trapped in a lean body."

"You're a fat man?"

I looked over at this look-a-like movie star priest and with a sinking feeling in my stomach realized that I had just wasted a great line. He didn't get me. And I was switching back to calling him Father Greg and focusing on food.

Ravenous, I continued. "I've had the chicken Oaxaca with their authentic mole sauce which is outstanding, but I was thinking of maybe the tomatillo enchiladas or the lamb with guajillo chile sauce. And we must order the fresh, made-at-your-table guacamole that is served in a giant bowl of lava rock. I'm so hungry and everything looks so good I could order everything on the menu."

"Here in the States, it's all Texi-mush to me," Father Greg slurred.

I looked up from the menu and just stared at him as the waiter brought us our drinks. Before I could even take a sip of my Concheta, he had downed the shot.

"Ready to order?" the cute waiter asked.

I smiled at him. "I think I'll be adventuresome and order the burria and a side order of the chapulinas."

The waiter looked at me. "You are being adventuresome. And you, Father?"

"Just gimme the steak fajitas. And an extra order of tortillas. Nobody ever gives you enough tortillas."

The waiter nodded and started to leave.

"And another shot of tequila!"

The waiter nodded again and left as I took a sip of my drink. This was getting a bit iffy so I tried to steer the conversation in a safe direction.

"I wanted to personally thank you for the beautiful memorial for Magda."

"You mean the one you ran out on?"

I put my head down in shame.

Father Greg snickered. "Hey, I wanted to join the two of you."

"In particular I liked Sir William Osler's quote about laughter being the music of life."

He took a deep breath and shouted, "Reminds me of a production of *Sound of Music* I did!"

I consciously brought my voice down to a whisper. "You did a production at St. John the Divine?"

He responded even louder. "No! No! I was an actor before becoming a priest. I was Rolf."

"What a coincidence, I was Rolf, too. I love that musical."

"I hated it," he grumbled. "Sound of Mucus is what I prefer to call it."

The waiter whisked by and as soon as he dropped his shot off at the table Father Greg shot it down his throat. He looked at the table and I couldn't tell if he was going to say something or was about to be sick. While hoping it was words that were going to spew from his mouth, the oddest thing seemed to occur. It looked like his face was melting, as if it were a beautiful watercolor painting left out in the rain. This perfect physical and spiritual specimen of a man was transforming into something else. And from that moment on, another side, a very dark side of Father Greg emerged.

As dinner progressed his anger and disdain for the world increased in direct proportion to the number of shots of tequila he downed. Locals recognizing the Father stopped by the table to say hello, and each time he managed to put on a compassionate face and respond with a sweet and charming voice. But as soon as they were out of earshot, he'd turn to me, judging and criticizing each one of them with venomous delight.

Midway through the entrees, Father Greg started in on a story about a female parishioner, a very tragic story of a woman in her thirties. She was married to a wonderful man and they were desperately trying to have children. As hard as they tried conventionally, they couldn't get pregnant, so they turned to the help of doctors and medical science. Just as they were about to undergo artificial insemination, the husband was shockingly killed in a car accident. Wanting more than ever to keep him in her heart and her life, she continued to try to get pregnant with doctors using his frozen sperm. After many tries and massive injections of hormones she still couldn't get pregnant. She eventually gave up and having accepting this fate she discovered that she had developed ovarian cancer. And it was bad. She had to have both ovaries and her womb removed and then courses of chemotherapy and radiation. The woman went to church and turned to Father Greg for prayers of hope but got quite a different response.

"I asked her how the hell could she ask God for prayers when she herself was playing God?"

But I thought Episcopals were the open-minded ones?

"I'm sure she ran off to one of the other priests who told her just what she wanted to hear. Doesn't matter." Father downed another tequila. "God punished her. She's dead now."

I didn't even look at him, I was so upset. Instead, I fiddled with my drink, thinking *Whose school of religion did he graduate from? Pat Robertson's?*

"What's in that thing?" he asked.

"It's just vodka and juice."

"Sounds too goddamned sweet to me!"

I always wondered if a father could use the Father's name in vain? He also was getting drunker and drunker and not paying attention to what he was eating. Yes, he had ordered the beef fajitas with the extra side of tortillas, but underneath the last tortilla was a thick paper napkin. And I watched as he, unknowingly, picked up the paper napkin thinking it was the last tortilla, layered beef, refried beans, lettuce, tomato, and guacamole onto it, rolled it all up, and then started to eat it.

"Father Greg," I said pointing to the paper napkin, "you're eating—"

"Don't interrupt me when I'm talking or eating," he snapped.

Between his condemnation of the world and the downing of another shot, I watched as Father Greg consumed the entire paper napkin.

Sensing it was OK to speak and desperate to change the subject, I asked him about the ongoing renovations at St. John's.

"I noticed that scaffolding is up in front of the church entrance. What are they working on now architecturally?"

He looked at me out of the corner of his eye. "You don't go to my church, do you?"

"Yes, I make a point of attending during certain times of the year."

"So, you're one of the cheap bastards who shows up just for the special holidays like Easter and midnight Christmas Mass?"

"Well, I guess . . ."

"I'm stuck"—he burped and hit his chest, I'm sure, trying to digest his paper product—"in that shit hole. That fucking damp, cold stone box, full of mold 24/7, and you just happen to drop in twice a year. Like you're fucking gonna get into heaven!"

I got up and found the waiter. By the time I had paid for dinner, Father Greg had pulled himself together enough to see me walk out the front door.

"Hey, Curt!" he yelled as he tripped out of the restaurant.

I turned around and he started groping me. People walking by on the sidewalk were shocked and horrified. Unable to control him but feeling responsible for getting him back to the rectory safely, I tried to hail a cab but none going by were available. So, I struggled to make him put one foot in front of the other, down the sidewalk. Like a carrot in front of the ass, I walked backward in front of him, baiting him all the way back to the front of the rectory of St. John the Divine.

"Goodnight, Father." I turned to leave and he started screaming at me.

"That's it! Leave me! Reject this mortal man. Run back to your warm little apartment and condemn me to this dank dungeon that feeds my arthritis! Run you frightened sheep for I truly despise you! You're so pathetic. You can all fry in hell!"

And I did run. I ran all the way back to my apartment with my hands over my ears.

≷ ≶

Three days later while having lunch at Petra's row house on Sylvan Terrace, I shared with her the shocking and awful date that I had had with Father Greg. She sat there, not saying a word, until I was finished. Then she gently handed me her newspaper.

"Page three, dear heart. Read it and weep."

An article said that the Cathedral Church of St. John the Divine and its parishioners were in a state of shock. Two nights earlier their beloved Father Greg Pulido, in the dark of the night, had stumbled into scaffolding in front of the church, which in turn banged into a stone gargoyle high atop the north spiral. The gargoyle fell, hitting Father Pulido in the skull, giving him a concussion. But while recuperating in the hospital he shockingly developed peritonitis. Emergency exploratory surgery revealed that the cause of acute gastric dilation and infection was in fact due to an intestinal obstruction. A large wad of paper product, to be exact. Father Greg Pulido was listed in serious condition.

"Oh my God," I whispered.

TWELVE

WHAT NOT TO WEAR

To take my mind off of my disastrous personal life, I was delighted when Darcie called and said she had lined up another book signing in the city at Rainbows and Triangles, a popular book/card/video store in Chelsea. The turnout was fantastic. Not only did I sell countless books but the buyers were just so nice and complimentary. And I was even more thrilled when Petra dropped by.

"Darling, you are such a celebrity," she said, kissing my forehead and inking it with her signature scarlet-red lipstick.

She always dressed flamboyantly but today she outdid herself. She was wearing a deep purple satin pantsuit that looked like a million bucks even though I'm certain she made it herself. Her hair color was taken up a notch and landed somewhere between Lucille Ball and Bozo the Clown. For a coat she wore an authentic Russian wool shawl and dangling from each ear was a tiny nude woman.

"Talk about celebrity, look at you." I glanced down at her feet and noticed she had on a chic pair of Michael Kors silver metallic moccasins. "Sensible flats?"

Petra brought her lips to my ear. "I have a date. She's a sweetheart but terribly short. I don't want to make her feel uncomfortable."

How short could she be? Petra was under five feet.

"Your first date in Manhattan. I can't wait to hear all about it."

"You will," she said, winking at me. "We met at the Clit Club. And here's another surprise." She put a large bag on the table and pulled out five of my books.

"You didn't buy these Petra, did you?"

"But of course. I want to support you."

I looked up at her beautiful hazel eyes sandwiched between those humongous false eyelashes and felt so grateful and lucky that she had popped into my life. She had no idea how much she was supporting me.

"Stop making eyes at me, Curtis, and sign your books. I'm taking them with me when I visit Prague in December so my girls can read you."

"I'm so jealous of you. I wish I had a hot date to look forward to."

"Be patient, Curtis. Your prince is out there." I signed the last of the books and she kissed my forehead again. "Now I must run and meet Lulu. Wish me luck."

I blew her a kiss as she floated out the door.

About twenty minutes later I was just as thrilled to see Quinn. But he didn't come through the front door, he appeared from the back of the store with his arms full of gay porno DVDs.

"Excuse me mister star? Could you sign copies of your porno films for me?" He dropped them on the table.

"What are you doing?"

He looked at the number of people gobbling up my book. "Admiring your book signing."

"Isn't it great? I really need to thank Darcie and the guys here at the store."

Quinn put his hands on his hips. "And what about me?" I looked at him, puzzled, as he gestured to the room. "I'm the reason this is a success. You should have heard how I've been talking up *101*!"

"You?"

Just then the manager of the store dropped by the table. "Curtis, looks like there's just one more fan in line to get an autograph. Quinn here should be your publicist." He patted Quinn on the back and then said to him, "Keep up the great work."

I bobbled my head side to side. "I give up. What's going on?"

"I work here. The back section, renting movies."

"No way!"

"Yes way." I could see that the last man in line was getting a bit antsy so I congratulated Quinn, but before he headed back to his porno dungeon he asked me, "Where the hell is your mother?"

"She's been with PCD all this time." Quinn shrugged his shoulders not knowing what I was referring to. "Perky Cruise Director."

"And you're OK with that?"

"I'm sure Harrie is history by now. You know how easily mother gets bored and flits from one person to the next."

Quinn smirked. "Like mother, like son."

I ignored that remark. "She's meeting me for a late dinner up at my place."

"Give her a kiss for me."

"By the way, Quinn, how is your mom doing?"

"She's trying to understand my father's need to live his new lifestyle."

"Isn't she mad at him?"

"Yeah, for taking three quarters of her wardrobe." Quinn turned around and saw the striking man waiting for me. He spun his head back to me, raised his eyebrows up and down while sticking out his tongue, and then dashed to the back of the store with the DVDs.

I looked up at this very patient person and smiled. He had that bad boy kind of look. Dressed in tight jeans and an open flannel shirt with a wifebeater under it, he didn't appear to be a gym rat but had a nice proportion to his body. And I thought his blond razor-cut hair was pretty cool. Something I definitely couldn't pull off.

I extended my hand. "Curtis here. Nice to meet you."

He shook it confidently, looking me straight in the eye with his smoky gray eyes. "Hugh."

He handed my book to me and I opened it up to the title page and autographed it. "That's a beautiful name for"—and I looked up at him—"a beautiful man." *I'm so schmaltzy I should be writing freaking greeting cards.*

Without missing a beat Hugh asked me, "Would you like to have a drink sometime?"

I checked to see that no one else was standing in line and then stood up. "How about now?"

I settled things with Rainbows and Triangles and rushed to the DVD section to say goodbye to Quinn, who was in a heated discussion with a young African-American who was trying to return a movie.

"The disk was in the case," the man said as Quinn held it up.

"I don't see one, boy."

"Who you calling boy, Pa?"

"When you go home to your mother's house and you put the DVD back into its case, I'll note your account is even, homey." Quinn then tossed the empty case at the boy, hitting him on the head. Realizing what he did, he quickly waved good-bye to me and ran into the back storage room, locking the door behind him.

"I ain't through with you, boy!"

I don't think customer service is the best industry for Quinn. I dashed to the front and met up with Hugh. "Let's get out of here."

As we walked around the corner and east on 19th Street I was amazed at how spontaneous I was being.

"Want to go to Q?" I asked.

"Never been there."

I pointed up the street. "It's just a half a block over."

It was a weeknight at cocktail hour with a DJ spinning some retro R & B to a pretty big crowd. I ordered both of us frozen cosmopolitans and then found a spot big enough for the two of us to squeeze into along the large circular back wall.

I pushed to project my voice over the music. "I call this bar the rotary."

Hugh yelled back, "Why's that?"

"Well, look at it. There's this round bar, and watch. Men just keep going around and around and around it."

Hugh nodded, understanding. But they needed a traffic cop. The bar should pick one direction for all of them to go in. Instead, they were like salmon swimming upstream trying to get back to the place they were born, so they could reproduce.

"I find it exhausting to watch," I shouted over to Hugh.

He downed his drink. "Let's get out of here."

I downed mine too and followed him out onto the sidewalk. He grabbed my arms, pulled me to him, and then kissed me. No, he didn't kiss me. He *kissed* me! But suddenly I had to push away. My palms shot up to my forehead as I moaned in pain.

"Did I hurt you?" Hugh asked.

"Frozen drink headache."

First, he kissed my forehead and made it all better and then he kissed my lips again and made everything feel better. But then he stepped out into the street and hailed a cab.

"What are you doing?" I asked, hoping he wasn't leaving.

"Taking charge." A cab pulled up. "Get in."

"And I like a take charge kind of guy," I said as I got into the taxi.

The next thing I knew, we were headed for my apartment. This was so unlike me. I felt so liberated, so impulsive, so excited, so slutty. We weren't two feet into my apartment and we were tearing at each other's clothes. But the host in me just wouldn't turn off.

"Would you like a drink?" Hugh had my coat off and was working on getting my pullover shirt up over my head.

"No."

We stumbled into the dining room as I tugged at his belt. "Hugh, do you want something to eat?"

"No."

My pants were halfway down my legs as I shuffled into my bedroom with him kicking off his shoes. I turned on the overhead light and one more thought popped into my head. "Would you like a mint?"

"What I would like is for you to stop talking."

Hugh helped with that by planting his mouth on mine. His lips felt like soft pillows and his breath was sweet. There was no tongue darting in and out like a venomous snake, no teeth banging into mine or scraping my gums, no sucking of my tongue so hard that I thought he was going to yank it out. It was just plain old luscious, voluptuous, sensual, erotic kissing. Where did this man come from?

"Where did you come from?"

Hugh ignored what I said. "Strip down and get onto the bed, facedown."

"Yes sir!"

He grabbed his leather shoulder bag and then stopped dead in his tracks. "What the hell is that?"

He was pointing to Emily-Mae curled up on her dog pillow in the corner of my bedroom.

"It's my dog."

"Is it dead?"

I looked over at her. "No, of course not. She's just sleeping."

He went into my bathroom. "Curtis, I'll be right out."

"OK," I rushed to Emily-Mae. "Emily?" I petted her but she didn't move. "Emily?" I poked her and she didn't move. "Emily!" In a panic, I picked her up and shook her and she finally opened one eye.

"Thank God," I whispered as I kissed her forehead and put her gently back onto the pillow. I tore the rest of my clothes off, turned out the overhead, and dashed about the room lighting candles. I straightened the bedspread on my four-poster bed, grabbed a pillow and placed it in the middle of the mattress, and then lay down on my stomach with the pillow under my hips. Knowing this was my best asset I was deliriously excited to present it to "take charge Hugh" in this fashion.

Actually, I was much too excited. Periodically in my adult life I'd been challenged with premature ejaculation and I was so hot and bothered that I feared I would have one before he even got out of the bathroom. So I flipped over and started slapping the bottoms of my feet as hard as I could. I'm not sure if this is a proven technique but Quinn said nurses would do this to men in hospitals if they got erections during sponge baths. What did I have to lose? I just slapped away.

Hugh must have heard this when he was coming out of the bathroom. "I can hear you like it rough, Curtis."

I stopped slapping myself. "Um?" A bit scared yet turned on, I flipped onto my stomach and held my breath.

He walked into the bedroom. "Curtis, I love your ass."

"Good, I wanted you to," I mumbled into the mattress.

I heard Hugh drop something on the floor and then climb up on the bed but I couldn't feel him. I turned my head to the left and could see him in the reflection of my full-length mirror. He had placed his palms above each of my shoulders and with his feet outstretched past mine and in a push-up position, his entire body hovered over me. He lowered his mouth down far enough so only his lips were touching my nape. I melted as he suckled on the back of my neck. This was one of the most erotic images I had ever seen or experienced in my entire life, and I immediately started tapping the bottom of my left foot with the instep of the right.

And it was obvious that Hugh was hung like a donkey. Now I was scared. What was I going to do? Throw it over my shoulder and burp it? I started to turn over but Hugh sat down on my lower back and grabbed my wrists.

"So, you like a take charge kind of guy?"

"I like you being a take charge kind of guy."

"Good. Don't move."

Hugh climbed off me and the bed and picked up what he had dropped on the floor. Was it a toy? Was it condoms? Lubricant? Then I saw them.

"Hugh, are you going to . . . ?"

"Do you like that?"

"I've never done it before but I have to admit I've thought of it."

"You look so hot like this. I want you so bad." Hugh kneeled on the bed and ran his tongue from the back of my neck down to the tip of my tailbone. "Let's do it."

"Yes!"

In flash I was bound to the bed with colorful bandanas. "Um, you tied that so fast. What are you, a seaman?"

"Nope, but I did use square knots."

Hugh had tied each ankle and each wrist to one of the four posts of my bed, with me lying spread-eagle on my stomach and the pillow hiking my hips up, presenting my ass to the heavens. It was absolutely thrilling.

"Hugh, this is one of the most erotic moments of my life."

"I'm glad you're enjoying it. I'll be back."

Hugh left the bedroom but I couldn't tell what he was doing. Maybe three minutes had passed but it felt like eons. Call me madcap, but suddenly this didn't feel right. I heard him walk back into the room and a flash went off. I strained to turn my head around enough so I could see him. He was dressed and taking digital photos of me. Photos of my body. Photos of my butt spread wide.

He put his mouth right to my ear and whispered, "You like the Puerto Rican now?"

I had no idea what he was talking about.

"Mr. Big Shot writer is confused? Mr. Celebrity signing autographs? Mr. I'll Meet You at Manhattan Diner to sign your book?"

"Hugh-y?"

"That's right. From Scranton. Oops, I'm sorry. From Scrotum, right Curtis?"

I tried so hard to convey that I was sorry that I had said that. "Huey, I felt so bad when you left that day but I didn't know how to get in touch with you to apologize."

"You like me now, don't you?"

"Well, yeah but . . . you look like a totally different person."

"This will probably shock you, Curtis, but I do have friends and family who love me. Love me so much they nominated me for the television show *What Not To Wear*. Ever heard of it, Mr. Writer?"

Heard of it? I loved that show and the fashion stylists Stacey and Clinton. They really did life changing transformations of people. I couldn't believe he was on the show and met them. I couldn't believe they gave him a makeover. I couldn't believe how good he looked.

"How dare you treat our meeting like it was a . . . meeting! So officious. I drove all the way from Scranton to be with you, Curtis. And you shunned me. You ridiculed me. You patronized me. Now let's see how you like rejection."

Hugh threw his camera into his bag and started to leave. "And don't even think of telling anyone about this. I have the pictures."

Actually, those pictures would probably help my career, like all the others. "Huey, I'm sorry."

And with that, he left my apartment.

Who the hell was I going to tell? Mr. Policeman, I let Huey tie me up so we could have sex and then he took pictures of my ass. Could you please arrest him? It was so absurd that I started to laugh. Well, not for long.

≳ ≲

Two hours passed, my candles had burnt out, my ankles and wrists were going numb, and I was exhausted from calling out to no one to untie me. I fantasized that Emily-Mae would eventually get so hungry that she'd figure out how to get up onto the bed, and the headlines in the newspaper would read WRITER EATEN ALIVE BY BAT DOG! However, none of the dramatic scenarios I conjured up even compared to the embarrassment of what had really happened.

My doorbell rang. I had to think of who would be at my door that the doorman would not have stopped and buzzed me to ask if they could come up? Was it a neighbor wanting to borrow something? Was it Hugh feeling bad about what he had done and wanting to release me? No, he would know I couldn't answer the door. The buzzing stopped and the person left.

About fifteen minutes later I heard keys in my front door and two people's voices. As they walked through my apartment I recognized one of them. A flick of the bedroom switch and the overhead light was on.

"Curtis, we had a dinner date!" Mother exclaimed as the super to my building turned his head away from my spread-eagled ass.

"*Oh mi Dios!*" Jose covered his eyes. "*No otra vez!*"

"Jose," she said as she handed him a twenty, "no need for you to suffer. I'll take care of this."

Grateful to be anywhere else but my bedroom, Jose dashed out of the apartment. Mother grabbed my bathrobe from my closet and draped it over my body. Without either of us speaking a word, she untied my wrists and then went into the kitchen as I undid the rest.

I splashed water on my face in the bathroom as she poured us both a Maker's Mark. I joined her in the living room and we sipped in silence.

Finally she spoke.

"One word of advice. Always get tied up at their place, dear. That way they have to *untie* you, eventually." Mother held up her drink, toasted to me, and winked. "Oh, and you have to join me for Thanksgiving at Harrie's in San Francisco."

"Harrie's?"

She nodded. "And bring your tux. Our wedding's going to be formal."

THIRTEEN

THE BOBBIE VIBRATO SHOW, HER SHOW!

"Darcie, they agreed?" I asked as I picked up my itinerary from her desk.

"Yes. You'll fly to LAX tomorrow, Tuesday morning. I have a rental car arranged for you. I've rebooked you on GayTV's live television program,

The Bobbie Vibrato Show, Her Show! in Los Angeles at noon that same day and then you can drive on up to San Francisco for Thanksgiving."

I grabbed my briefcase. "You are brilliant."

"I'm fucking brilliant," she corrected.

I kissed her cheek. "That you are."

"So your mother's marrying that little cunt?"

Interestingly, I didn't flinch when Darcie swore that time. "That's the plan."

I started to leave her office and then turned back and looked at her sheepishly. "Oh, I forgot to ask. Were you able to get Quinn . . ."

"The dipshit is going as your 'entourage.'" She shook her head. "His ticket is in with yours."

I rushed back and kissed her again.

"If you keep kissing me like this people will talk." She pointed her index finger to the corner of her mouth and looked up. "Hmmm. Good idea for a publicity stunt. '*Literary Mogul Harnesses Boy Toy Writer*'."

That made me think. "Darcie, you haven't seen any new nude photos of me lately, have you?"

She studied my face. "No. Should I expect some?"

I regretted even bringing it up. "No. No, of course not. I meant did you see all the photos that you saw. That's it." I was so nervous I tripped going out the door and turned back to wave to her. "Bye. Wish us luck."

She looked at me suspiciously. "Hmmm."

As I rode the elevator down her office building I thought of the million and one things I had to do before Quinn and I took off the next day. But most importantly I needed to show Petra how to hydrate and give Emily-Mae her insulin.

≳ ≴

"You don't know how much I appreciate you doing this, Petra," I said as I flipped the hidden latch and pulled up the IV stand on my kitchen island.

"I'd do anything for the two of you."

I attached a lactated Ringer's solution bag up on the hook and got out a 13-gauge needle.

"Curtis, what's in the liquid?"

"Electrolytes. Sodium, chloride, calcium, and potassium. It's like a super duper Gatorade for Emily. She only needs it twice a week and I'll be back on Sunday. So if you could do it on Thursday that would be great."

"They're having the wedding on Thanksgiving?"

I slipped the needle into the plastic tube coming out of the IV bag, undid the plastic cincher, and let the liquid flow till I had knocked out all the air bubbles. "I'm sure the clever idea was the cruise director's."

"Curtis, what is your issue with Harrie?"

"You'll see when you meet her. Harrie," and I paused wanting to come up with the appropriate description, "is irritatingly self-confident."

"Dear heart, you shouldn't hold that against her."

I stretched a towel across the counter. "She's just so damn weird."

"We're all weird, Curtis. She sounds happy."

"Now that sounds weird to me."

"Why do you feel so threatened by Harrie?"

I was slightly annoyed that Petra seemed to be taking her side. "I'm not threatened, I'm . . . I don't know what I am. It's hard to describe."

"Maybe the issue is with your mother? Although I haven't met her yet, it sounds like the two of you are very close."

I really had to sift through my emotions. "Yes, we are close. And although we tend to butt heads more often than not and it's true that no one can drive me more insane with just a critical roll of her eyes . . . I'm . . ."

"You're what?"

"I'm . . . I guess . . . I'm afraid of losing her?"

She touched my hand and winked. "Curtis, you won't lose her. You're gaining a Harrie."

I rolled my eyes critically. "Speaking of losing, where's Emily-Mae? Wasn't she just here in the kitchen?"

Although she only made the left-hand circle turns, she could travel quite a distance in the apartment in a short period of time. I was tempted to dress her up in chamois, cover her with a dust spray, and let her go at it with the floors, but I'd certainly go to animal hell for that.

Petra searched the dining room as I went into the living room. She wasn't under the coffee table or the stand for the flat screen TV. Sometimes she snuggled behind my freestanding bookcases but she wasn't there, either.

"Curtis, I'll check the bedrooms."

I sat down on the floor and then I heard her labored breathing. I turned my head to the right and my heart sank. She had wedged her head between the steam radiator and the wall and couldn't move. I rushed to her and was thankful that the radiator was cool. Frightened, she was locked in and couldn't turn to the left, and she made a panicked sound I'd never heard from her before. I gently pulled her out, picked her up, and instantly felt my eyes fill up with puddles of tears. I kissed her head and carried her to the kitchen and placed her on the island as Petra joined me. Emily-Mae licked my hand and happily lay down on the counter, knowing the routine.

"Maybe I shouldn't go to California."

Petra put her hand in mine. "Yes, you should go."

"But what if Emily-Mae . . ."

"Then you'll come back."

For some odd reason this really made me fall apart. Not convulsively, just a quiet emotional inner breakdown. Both Petra and Emily-Mae waited patiently for me to pull it together. If there's anything I've learned in my older years it is that when a wave of overwhelming feelings hits me, it's best to let it just wash through instead of pushing it down. I blew my nose, washed my hands, grabbed an orange and a spare needle, and gave them to Petra.

The orange's thickness and resistance to the needle was very close to skin. As a practice run and to feel how much pressure she needed to exert to puncture Emily's skin, Petra slipped the needle into the orange.

"You've got a wonderful touch," I said as I stood on the opposite side of the island.

"Let's do it."

Petra took a deep breath, pulled up Emily's skin between her shoulder blades, placed the needle against her, and gently pushed. The moment it slipped in the solution slowly started to drip.

"That was terrific, Petra," I said as I petted Emily-Mae. "Sometimes I'll have these little liver treats for her during the hydration. It helps pass the time for her."

And to help pass the time for Petra, I distracted her by asking how her date with Lulu went.

"*Sausmigs!*"

I wasn't sure what that meant but it couldn't have been good considering the way she said it.

"That bad?"

Even Emily reacted to it and Petra petted her to calm her down. "I'm sorry, Curtis. That was Latvian for awful."

"I thought you were so excited to see her."

"I was. And I thought she was, too. But Lulu confessed that she wants a *sudrabs* mate."

I shrugged my shoulders.

"A silver mama!"

I thought hard. "You mean she wants you to have white hair?"

"No. She said I wasn't old enough."

You can't get much older than Petra. "I don't understand."

"Curtis, she said that I was old enough in age, but too young in body and spirit."

"It's her loss," I said hugging her. "I'd take it as a compliment."

Petra put her fist to her heart and then threw her arm up and outward, cursing. "*Vards!* Doesn't matter what your sexual preference or your age; finding love can be a *kuce*."

I agreed with her, whatever it meant.

"But what about you, darling? Tell me, have you met any nice men?"

I wasn't going to bring up "tie me up, tie me down." "Finding love can be a . . . *kuce*?"

"Amen," she whispered.

◊ ◊

Bobbie Vibrato was a character, to say the least. Androgynous and rather ageless, she—which was what she referred to herself as—was a celebrity oddity. Visually it truly was hard to tell whether she was a man or a woman. Bobbie always dressed the same: a man's white oversized button-down shirt with a pair of black tights and black flats. She had adopted that fifties movie star rehearsal look and had the most incredible legs. They were athletic and shapely for a woman, defined and flexible for a man.

No one could tell if she had breasts or pecs. She wore very light make-up and her jet-black pixie haircut was always tussled. And although she had small facial features and no beard, the shape of her head was definitely on the masculine side.

GayTV, the pioneer in gay television, took a chance during their first season and produced *The Bobbie Vibrato Show, Her Show!* and instantly she developed a cult following. Her show was part variety, part talk show. She covered current events, which she more often than not got incorrect, she read viewer mail that blatantly insulted her, viewers were encouraged to call in but seldom did, and the ones who did had either gotten the wrong phone number or had called to harass her. She interviewed almost-famous and over-the-hill celebrities and she sang a lot, off key.

And for some odd and obsessive reason, Bobbie Vibrato thought she was the spitting image of the late, great Judy Garland. She not only sang the songs that Judy made famous but Bobbie danced, or tried to, and accompanied herself with the trumpet. Needless to say, *The Bobbie Vibrato Show, Her Show!* was insane.

Although both Darcie and Quinn thought appearing on it was a good thing, I still had my doubts and fears. Her show was live. Sure, I was an actor years ago and I could stand before a crowd now and talk about my writing at a book signing, but live television was a different beast altogether. And when you added to the mix a loose cannon like Bobbie Vibrato, who knew what would happen?

My flight out in business class was wonderfully uneventful once the flight attendants strapped Quinn down into his seat. As we boarded the plane, I was delighted to discover that there was no business class so I was actually seated in first. Having the window seat, I threw my carry-on up into the overhead bin and sat down. Quinn promptly sat in the aisle seat next to me as a very friendly female attendant appeared and confirmed our names.

"Mr. Jenkins?"

"Yes."

"Welcome aboard. Would you like something to drink before we take off? Juice, water, champagne?"

Quinn chimed in. "The champagne is free?"

"Yes it is," she said, looking at her list of names. "But I take it you're not Mrs. Reid?"

Quinn looked at both of us. "I could be."

"Sir, may I see your ticket please?"

Of course Quinn had already misplaced it and wrestled with his own body to find it while we waited. "Here it is."

She read it and then smiled. "Sir, your seat is in coach."

He looked at her, trying to play dumb. "Me? I don't think so."

She stood her ground. "I know so."

"There must be some sort of misunderstanding."

Quinn, you are such a bad actor. "I'm sorry, sir, but your seat is the one all the way in back, in the last row, next to the galley and in front of the toilet."

He looked at me for help. I just shrugged my shoulders and looked up at the attendant. "I think I'll have the champagne."

"Jesus Christ," Quinn muttered. "And send a champagne to me at the back of the bus."

He reluctantly got up out of Mrs. Reid's seat and trudged to the back of the plane, swearing under his breath. *The Bobbie Vibrato Show, Her Show!* was obviously on a tight budget.

Our flight left on time but we actually arrived in Los Angeles early and had to circle LAX endlessly till we were allowed to land. And once we landed, the pilot informed us that another plane was at our gate, that there were no other gates we could dock at, so we had wait on the runway till ours was free. We waited and waited and waited, as I got more nervous and more nervous and more nervous. Forty-two minutes later we were allowed to disembark and then I had to wait till Quinn got off, bringing up the rear.

I begged him not to talk because we had to really, really make a dash for it. I made a pact with myself not to look at my watch again and cursed GayTV for not flying us out the day before and putting us up in a hotel.

We jumped into a shuttle bus to our car rental and of course it was miles away from the airport. And once we got there I was horribly disappointed to discover that my reserved red Saturn Sky Roadster *convertible* was gone and we had to resign to driving a very ugly, very boxy, very unglamorous, mousey gray Mercury Grand Marquis *hardtop*.

With me in the driver's seat, Quinn was delegated to reading the directions. I knew the studio was in Burbank and I knew Los Angeles well enough to know that I had to take the 110 North to 5 North, but once we were in Burbank, the directions fell apart.

"Quinn, where does it say the studio is?"

"Like I said. It's in the former *Jeopardy!* game show studio."

I hit the steering wheel with my fist. "But that's not a direction. Give me a street!" I pulled over into a gas station and rolled down my window.

"Excuse me, sir!" I hollered out to an attendant. "Do you know where the GayTV Network is?"

"The old *Jeopardy!* studio."

I put my forehead on the steering wheel as Quinn got out of the car. Within moments, he was back in.

"It's around the corner."

I finally looked at my watch and realized it was 12:14. The one-hour show had already started. What I didn't know was what time my segment was scheduled for.

We flew into the studio and were immediately taken upstairs to hair and makeup by a production assistant. Two male stylists in their fifties were watching Bobbie on a television monitor.

"Hi, I'm Curtis Jenkins."

"Have a seat, doll," the makeup artist said as he grabbed some foundation. "Didn't think you were going to make it."

"Neither did we," I said out of breath.

I was surprised to find out that I was the only guest lined up for that show. Quinn laid out my clothes as the other stylist fiddled with my hair. Never having seen Bobbie's show before I tried to get a feel for her personality and a look at the set. It was decorated in bright primary colors and looked like a studio apartment, with a full-size bed in one corner and a seating area opposite it. Against one wall was a galley kitchen and on the other was a board of lights that lit up when viewers called in. Depending on what scene was being shot, they placed a kitchen table down center or changed it out with Bobbie's desk.

Bobbie was at the end of the current events segment, was going to sing one song, and then I was on. She looked up from her desk and directly into the camera with sincerity.

"I'm not saying I support the President but we needed to attack Iraq to find Osama Bin Laden."

I looked up at the man doing my face. "Bin Laden in Iraq? Doesn't she mean Afghanistan?"

He shook his head. "She doesn't know what she means."

I was also fascinated that her voice was soft like a woman's but didn't have that hormonal resonance that a lot of transgender people end up with. It was quite pleasant.

Bobbie continued. "Plus Saddam Hussein had weapons of mass destruction."

Even Quinn knew this was wrong and looked up at the monitor. "No he didn't."

Suddenly, a light lit up on the call-in board and we heard the sound of a phone ringing.

"A viewer calling in!" she exclaimed. The phone number to the show appeared on the screen and Bobbie pushed a button on her desk. "Hello? Caller of *The Bobbie Vibrato Show, My Show!* speak. Hello? Hello? Are you there?"

A Chinese woman asked, "Address please?"

Bobbie automatically responded. "718 Bulldog Lane . . . Wait a minute! This is Bobbie Vibrato. You can't ask for my address on the air."

"Number please?"

"734-854 . . . Hey, you just called me!"

"Your order?"

Bobbie looked offstage, confused. "My what? Is this a Chinese restaurant?"

The Chinese woman on the other end of the phone was getting irritated. "Order please?"

"Oh, well, since you're on the line and it is lunch time, I'll have the shredded pork and pickled cabbage soup, the sha cha lamb, and the pork fried rice. And none of that brown stuff. I like the sticky white rice."

Bobbie pushed the button on her desk again and the light on the phone board went out. She got up and miraculously her desk disappeared while she purposefully messed up her hair.

"And now, to all my loyal viewers, I'd like to entertain you with a Judy Garland song."

"So what else is new?" the makeup artist said as he put a light gloss onto my lips.

"It's called 'A New World I See' and I'll accompany myself with . . ."

The two stylists in the makeup room mockingly said in unison, "The trumpet."

Bobbie stepped behind a changing screen that was low enough for us to see her head over the top. She proceeded to set up the song while Quinn threw me into my clothes.

"In *A Star Is Born*, which by the way is the movie Judy was nominated best actress for but lost out to Grace Kelly, but it's neither here nor there cause they're both dead, Vicki Lester aka Esther Blodgett aka Judy Garland has become a huge film star. Her husband, Norman Maine aka James Masson was a big star but is now all washed up . . . in more ways than one as you will soon find out."

As Bobbie continued, the production assistant dragged me half-dressed down to the set.

"Judy has once again rescued James from another bout of alcohol-induced self-loathing, self-destructive behavior. Hey, Judy should have played that part but then that would have been typecasting. But Judy is determined to make James's star shine bright again. But James is too smart for this. If he stays with Judy, he'll just drag her down, too."

I was brought down to the floor and introduced to the director as Bobbie stepped out from behind the changing screen. She had put on a stunning fifties hostess dress/coat in a luscious gold silk with matching pants.

It looked just like something Rosalind Russell would have worn in the film
Auntie Mame.

Bobbie looked into the camera. "So, on this beautiful evening at their
Malibu house, James asks Judy to make them sandwiches while he takes a
dip in the ocean. And as Judy wistfully sings this song of hope and promise,
James very sensitively and considerately . . . drowns himself. I love this
movie. I love this song."

She stood center stage and started singing "It's a New World I See".

The director pulled me to the side and whispered, "Curtis, you're doing
Bobbie's cooking segment called *Let's Dish!*"

"But I'm on to promote my book."

"Hopefully Bobbie will make it work."

Gee, thanks for the vote of confidence. He walked me over to stage left
as Bobbie continued singing.

Then, all of a sudden Bobbie was playing the trumpet. Well, the imita-
tion sound of it she did with her lips, and she was really good at it. I was
positioned on the set within the kitchen area and out of view of the camera. A grip threw a copy of *101 Ways to Collide into Your Gay Soul Mate*
into my hands, and a butcher-block island was pushed in front of me. On
the top of it was a whole raw chicken on a cutting board, bottles and jars
full of sauces and condiments, two huge bowls, and a platter of fruit. What
were we going to do?

The camera pulled in tight as Bobbie finished the song. She bowed her
head and then jerked it up, looking at the camera, and shouted very loudly, "Thank you! Thank you!" and they cut to commercial.

"It's a short one, people!" the director shouted. "One minute."

I was afraid to move as three people descended upon Bobbie. One ripped
off her hostess outfit, the other touched up her makeup, and the third ad-
justed her mike.

"Ooooohhhh!" I yelled as a pair of hands went up the back of my shirt.

"Sorry, mike and battery pack," a soundman said as he attached the gear
to me. He pulled the mike under and up and around to the front of my shirt
and clipped it to my collar. "Remember, don't shout. Just speak normal.
Say something now for a test."

"Help?"

"Perfect," and he was gone.

The director brought Bobbie over to the butcher-block island. "Bobbie
this is Curtis Jenkins."

"Welcome to the show, Curtis," she purred.

Part of me expected her façade to fall and underneath I'd find this deep-voiced football linebacker with a wife and two kids. But Bobbie was the real deal.

"Curtis, a lot of talk show hosts skim their guests' books or an assistant gives you CliffsNotes, but I want you to know I not only read your book but I really enjoyed it. Maybe it will help me to find a friend?"

"I just assumed you had a partner, I guess with the success of the show and all."

Bobbie threw away a look that conveyed such deep sadness. "Maybe the show is my lover. I know I live for it and adore the people I work with. From the producers to the key grips to the guys up in hair and makeup. I love and respect all of them. They're my family."

If she only knew what they were saying behind her back.

"Back in ten!" the director shouted.

I whispered in her ear. "I am so fucking nervous."

She squeezed my hand. "Relax and just follow me. And you're not leaving without signing my copy of your book."

I liked her.

The director shouted, "Four, three . . ." and he pointed two fingers at Bobbie and then one.

"Welcome back to *The Bobbie Vibrato Show, My Show!*" she said in her own inimitable way. "And I have with me today Curtis Jenkins, the gay dating guru. Welcome."

"Thank you, Bobbie, but I don't think I'd call myself a guru."

She took my book and held it up. "Don't be so modest. Here it is folks, the number one best seller in gay nonfiction, *101 Ways to Collide into Your Gay Soul Mate.*" She put the book down and turned to me. "And I have a surprise for Curtis. In honor of him flying all the way out from New York City to be on *The Bobbie Vibrato Show, My Show!* I'm going to cook for him, and for all of you devoted viewers, my special first date dinner, Bobbie's Subway Chicken."

How tempting, I thought as I caught a glimpse of Quinn just to the right of the camera making faces at me.

"And Curtis, while I'm putting together everything for the main dish, I'd like you to make an appetizer."

I what? I have to plug my book, cook, smile, look relaxed, and be on live television all at the same time?

"Curtis, I thought fruit cocktail would be appropriate considering all the double entendres it conjures up and of course all the men you mention in your book and well let's face it . . . gays are fruit!"

I forced a laugh as I felt my bottom lip quiver with fear, and said a little too loudly, "And we all love cocktails."

I saw the soundman sitting on a chair off camera lowering his hand repeatedly at me.

Bobbie elbowed me. "Hell, I love cock."

"You do?" I whispered to her. "Can you say that on the air?"

"It's cable, love."

I shouted, "And I love tails!"

The soundman fell off his chair.

Bobbie explained that her subway chicken was called that because on a trip to New York she had seen an advertisement for a chicken company down in the subway and along with it was this recipe. So, as she was throwing ingredients into her bowl, I was cutting up fruit for the fruit cocktail. I was so nervous I really had to concentrate on not cutting off a finger. I admired how comfortable she was just doing her thing extemporaneously in front of a live camera. But without any warning she asked me the dreaded question.

"So Curtis, do you practice what you preach? Have you found the man of *your* dreams?"

I hesitated and then in a moment of sheer panic, I pointed off camera to Quinn. "Yes, my man is right out there. Quinn Larkin."

Bobbie looked out into the studio. "Oh, then he must come out."

"Oh, he's out, trust me."

Bobbie laughed so hard. "No, I want our audience to meet the man you love."

I couldn't see a monitor but I'm sure my face registered shock.

"Come out, come out Quinn Larkin wherever you are." Bobbie literally walked off camera and dragged Quinn onto the set and squeezed him in between us. "Look at you two. What a perfect couple."

Quinn was as nervous as I was and plastered a fake smile on his face that strongly resembled the Joker in *Batman*.

Bobbie picked up a fork and started clinking the side of the chicken bowl. "Kiss! Kiss!"

We both looked at her, terrified.

She clinked the bowl again. "Yes, I insist. The lovebirds must kiss."

She clinked continuously as Quinn and I, reluctantly, brought our heads close together and then very ineptly, pecked each other on the lips.

"Yes," Bobbie laughed as she pushed Quinn off the stage. She looked right into the camera. "See, Curtis Jenkins's book works."

I just kept cutting up fruit as Bobbie held up the entire uncooked chicken by its legs.

"Let's discuss merkins."

I racked my brain. "Bobbie, what is a merkin?"

"So glad you asked, Curtis. Women in the Restoration wore bizarre genital wigs, called merkins, to disguise the fact that their pubic hair had fallen out as a result of venereal disease."

How appetizing.

Bobbie picked up a steel wool pad and put it up against and between the naked chicken's legs and hooted. She waited for me to put two and two together.

I finally got it. "Look, our chicken has a merkin."

"That a boy!" Bobbie howled, slapping me on the back.

The director signaled Bobbie. "We have to break for commercials but stay with us as Curtis Jenkins and I put together the final touches on your first date dinner for the man you catch with his book."

The director counted down, "And we're into commercial."

Bobbie wiped her hands and gave me a hug. "You really are wonderful on camera, sweetheart." She turned to walk off the set and was met by one of her producers.

"Jake, what's up?" Bobbie asked, putting out her hand for a shake.

Jake didn't accept it. Instead, his head was down and he was shuffling his feet around on the floor. "Bobbie?"

"Yes. I've got to hit the ladies' room, fast."

"Bobbie, there's a problem with the show."

"What do you mean?"

"They're pulling the plug."

Bobbie looked at him seriously as I tried not to eavesdrop. Then she shifted gears. "Very funny. I love it! What is this? One of those surprise ambush reality shows taping us. Where's the camera?"

"Bobbie, damn this is hard. But the show is being canceled."

"You're serious? But why? I've put everything I have into this show. Everything is running so smoothly. No one has complained."

"Well, some of the technicians as well as the big brass find you . . . difficult . . . to work with."

Bobbie threw her arms up into the air. "You think it's difficult working with Bobbie Vibrato? Try *being* Bobbie Vibrato!"

That was so Judy.

Jake looked at his watch. "Surveys have been done, ratings have been evaluated."

Bobbie was cracking. "And?"

"No one is watching your show."

"But that can't be."

He shook his head. "The show's over. Finished. Canceled. Today's episode will be your last show."

Bobbie looked around her for support, any kind of support, but everyone had vanished. She was sinking and they were all going to let her drown. She then turned to me with such a look of desperation but what could I do? Devastated, humiliated, and embarrassed, in a flash, Bobbie dashed off of the set and locked herself in her dressing room. The set went into panic mode as I just stood there with fruit on my fork.

"People!" the director screamed. "We have a show to finish."

I looked at Quinn and he shrugged his shoulders. I started to walk off the stage and the director dragged me back.

"Curtis, you're gonna have to finish the show."

"Me?"

"We're back in ten, people!" the director shouted.

"But . . . but . . . what do I do? What do I say?"

"Just keep it going. Cook! Talk about your book." The director motioned to everyone on the set to be quiet. Then he turned to me and counted, "Five, four, three . . ." and he signaled to me that I was on the air as the red light appeared on camera three.

"Hello, and welcome back to *The Bobbie Vibrato Show* . . ." I hesitated, . . . *Her Show!*" I smiled really hard and tried to dive into finishing the food segment. "Bobbie"—I looked off toward her dressing room—"all of a sudden wasn't feeling too well and I've been asked to finish . . ." I stopped talking and started sweating profusely. I've never had an anxiety attack before but I was sure it was happening, right then and there. I felt lightheaded and shaky and knew that if I was near an open window on the hundredth floor of a building I'd probably opt to jump out.

I took a few deep breaths and stared down at the food and my book and the merkin and made a decision. Slowly I looked up and right into the camera.

"The truth is, Bobbie Vibrato was just told that this is going to be her last show, ever." I shook my head as I heard whispers out on the set. I waited until I could hear a pin drop and then I continued. "They've just told her that no one is watching. That no one wants her. That no one likes her. Personally, I find that hard to believe. I've just met the woman and I'm totally intrigued and impressed by her. And I know that everyone in New York City watches the show and loves her."

Then I had an idea. Like a seasoned PBS fundraiser, I pulled out the stops. "You all know you can call in. I want Bobbie's live phone in number put up on the screen again, please call in to save *The Bobbie Vibrato Show, Her Show!* She's put her heart and soul into this one-of-a-kind extravaganza and we can't afford to see it fall to the wayside. So, call in now and tell us how much you love her. GayTV would be making a huge mistake by giving her the ax. In fact, if you call in now, while I'm on the air, I will send to each and everyone of you a free copy of *101 Ways to Collide into Your Gay Soul Mate* as a token of my gratitude for saving a woman who carved the way for all other gay programming. Please, don't let us down. Please don't let Bobbie down. Call in now."

I rushed to a wall on the set and took down a framed picture of Bobbie, held it up next to my book, and prayed that the phone lines would ring. Each second the clock ticked seemed like hours passing by. I searched for Quinn somewhere near the cameras, spotted him, and he gave me the thumbs up. The crew was on pins and needles but I made a decision at that point not to say another word until at least one phone line rang.

And it did. The director made a swirling motion with his hand and put it up to his ear as a light on the phone board lit up and we heard the sound of a ring.

"We have a caller."

The director nodded.

"Caller, you're on the air?"

"We're from Canton, Ohio, and we love the show. We love Bobbie."

I was thrilled. "Stay on the line and we'll have someone take your info so I can send you a copy of my book." The director motioned me again and the phone was ringing. "I think we have another caller." The director pointed to the phone board. "I'm corrected, I believe we have close to twenty calls lined up?"

Suddenly, like people clapping their hands to save Peter Pan's Tinkerbell, we could hear the phones ringing right and left on the set.

"Next caller, please?"

"Yes, we listen to the show all the time."

I nodded. "Thank you. Next caller?"

"They can't cancel the show. We have *The Bobbie Vibrato Show, Her Show!* parties. We all get together to watch."

"Thank you. Next caller?"

"This is Bobbie's mother. Tell her we forgive her."

"OK, Mrs. . . . Vibrato? I will. Next caller?"

"Hello? I would like to be the Bobbie Vibrato fan club president."

"Aw, that's sweet."

The phones kept ringing as Bobbie slowly appeared on the set. She said nothing as she walked up and put her arms around me. "Thank you, so much," she whispered into my ear.

Thinking fast on my feet I said, "Song! Song! Sing a song!"

Bobbie pulled herself together and said, "I know, we'll stay here all night and I'll sing 'em all!"

The entire crew applauded as Bobbie took my hand and walked us to the back of the set. Out of the corner of my eye I even saw the hair and makeup guys smiling down on the floor from the catwalk. She sat cross-legged on the edge of the bed and patted the mattress encouraging me to sit next to her.

She proceeded to sing a cappella, with her mascara running and her hair disheveled, a beautiful and touching rendition of the most classic Garland signature song.

Gone were the affectations. Gone were the gross and overstated gestures. Gone was the forced and exaggerated vibrato. And with genuine tears of gratitude streaming down her face she sang movingly and sincerely, "Over the Rainbow." And when she was done, there was not a dry eye in the house.

The Bobbie Vibrato Show, Her Show! was saved and the sales of my book quadrupled that day.

FOURTEEN

MOTHER SQUARED

Immediately after the appearance on *The Bobbie Vibrato Show, Her Show!* Quinn and I jumped into our armored rental tank and headed up the coast to San Francisco. I think the reason we chose not to fly was, number one, Bobbie's show wasn't going to pay for that side trip, and number two, the thought of driving up the coast sounded like fun. Well, it would have been if we had done our math. Los Angeles to San Francisco by car is approximately six hours if you take the quicker and more boring Interstate 5 North. But of course we didn't do the practical and ugly route. We opted for the scenic and dramatic if not time-consuming Pacific Coast Highway 1.

From Burbank we took the 110 South to 10 West to Highway 1 and drove north. It took one solid hour to get from Venice Beach to Malibu.

"Quinn, at this rate we will get to San Francisco next year!" I screamed while we crept along in bumper-to-bumper traffic.

"Let's follow Highway 1 up to Santa Barbara and then we can pick up the 101. That'll go faster."

I looked at my watch and it was already 2:17 P.M.. That meant it was really 5:17 New York time and I had been up since 4:30 in the morning. And considering the GayTV ordeal, no wonder I was exhausted. I regretted not having paid the extra money to insure Quinn to drive.

Thirty minutes later we made it to Santa Barbara and we cut over to the 101. Quinn opted to take a nap knowing we'd be on this course a long time, while I enjoyed soaking up this beautiful West Coast scenery that I had never seen before. The landscape reminded me of Tuscany, in particular when we passed vineyards near Santa Maria. But surprisingly, just north of there, the rolling hills felt more like Vermont mixed in with a little of the Scottish Highlands. I found it breathtaking.

But right around San Luis Obispo I was starting to have problems. The highway and its markings and Quinn snoring and us forgetting to eat lunch and me running on adrenaline had a hypnotic effect on me. I was fighting to stay awake at the wheel. I thought I had a handle on it until I heard the horn of another car blare at us.

"Jesus fucking Christ!" Quinn screamed as I swerved into another lane.

I just missed hitting a car and then put on my right blinker, got onto the shoulder, and brought the car to a complete stop. I rested my forehead on the steering wheel.

"Curtis, what happened?"

I couldn't believe it myself. "I feel asleep."

Quinn opened his door and got out. As he walked around to my side a car zoomed by honking its horn. He opened my door.

"Move over."

I looked up at him. "You aren't insured."

"I'm not letting you kill yourself and me. Move over."

I reluctantly scooted over to the passenger's seat as Quinn got in.

"Please drive carefully."

He gave me a very sarcastic look as I looked at the map. "Maybe we can stop in San Simeon and have lunch at Hearst Castle?"

"Sounds good to me," Quinn said as we buckled up and headed north again.

Within moments I was fast asleep. And although there were several different versions of what actually happened next, I choose to believe the version that Quinn told me after he had consumed an entire bottle of wine himself later that night.

Quinn continued to drive north on the 101 till we got to Route 46. As I was in a deep coma with my brain wavelength frequency hovering somewhere around delta, he made a decision to go west on 46 and get back onto coastal Highway 1 at the town of Harmony. Harmony to San Simeon was about thirteen miles and then we could have lunch. But as he was waiting at a light to turn right onto Highway1 North he noticed an eighteen-wheel tractor-trailer in the left lane, waiting to do the same. The light had just turned red and Quinn happened to look up to the cabin of the trailer and saw the lone driver look down at him from the passenger's side window.

As if the man had thrown something at him, Quinn ducked out of view. Fascinated, he slowly looked back out of the window and up at the trailer and the driver was gone. Quinn dropped it and waited for the light to change. Then out of the corner of his eye he saw a movement, looked back up at the truck, and the driver had his pants down and was stroking his enormous cock in the window, for Quinn's benefit.

Ducking again, as if he had been hit with something harder, he first checked to see if I was awake. I was out to the world. He then checked the rearview mirror and there were no cars behind him. He looked back up at the driver, who was grinning while stroking with one hand and giving him the thumbs up with the other. Within seconds, Quinn's pants were down to his ankles and he had a throbbing hard-on. The trucker drooled, stuck out his tongue, and then looked forward. The light had turned green. Quinn checked the rearview mirror again and there was a car just pulling up. Both he and the trucker had to make a decision. Quinn moved first and took a right onto Highway 1. He slowed down and let the car behind us pass and then he saw the tractor-trailer coming up our ass.

Supposedly, for the next ten or so miles, Quinn and the trucker played jerk-and-drive. Highway 1 at this point along the Central Coast continued north as a winding, two-lane road with occasional passing lanes. The trucker, having the higher vantage point, chose opportune moments to ride up beside Quinn during these passing lanes to allow them to watch each other stroke. Mind you, they were recklessly speeding along a scenic highway that at unexpected moments took severe turns, kissing the outer rim of dramatic seaside cliffs.

Just north of the quaint town of Cambria, Quinn's eighteen-wheeler lover gave him a clear signal that his time was about to cum. Quinn, overwhelmed with excitement, jerked at his own dick while his trucking lover blew the truck's horn in celebration of blowing his own horn. Startled out of his skin, Quinn came with his left hand while jerking the wheel with his right. I woke up and discovered that, unfortunately, Highway 1 wasn't in tune with these two horny bastards and had decided to twist when Quinn thought it was going to turn and in a flash, we were off the highway, speeding out of control into a ditch. The car flipped completely over once, the air bags exploded, and we slid into a soft marsh of sea grass bordered by wild eucalyptus trees.

The scent of the eucalyptus and the shock of the accident were both overwhelming. I consciously moved every part of my body to see if anything was broken. Then I heard Quinn mumbling something behind his air bag. Thank all the gods that we were both wearing our seat belts. When the car flipped, my window broke out as did the windshield, but I couldn't open my door. I managed to squeeze my way past the safety bag and out the window. I sat on the ground for a moment and touched my face. It hurt, but it wasn't cut. I had a burn from the explosion of the bags.

I got up and surprisingly could walk and made my way through the marsh to the driver's side. I opened Quinn's door and he looked at me.

"Are you OK?" I asked, scared of his answer.

"Yeah, but I'm pinned to the wheel."

I looked around and grabbed a splintered part of a broken eucalyptus tree and jabbed it into his air bags, causing them to deflate.

"Are you in one piece?"

"I think so."

I grabbed his left arm and pulled as hard as I could. Slowly, he squeezed out from under the broken steering column and fell out onto the wet ground.

Exhausted, I sat next to him. "What the fuck happened?"

"Um, the highway swerved like out of nowhere."

I pointed to his dick. "Why is that out?" Quinn's pants were still down around his ankles.

"Ah, damn. Must have been the force of impact?"

I looked at him skeptically. "Fuck!"

"Curtis what?"

"This was a rental. You were driving. You weren't insured. We have to pretend I was driving, or I won't be covered. And now I'll have this accident on my record. Shit!"

"Aren't you glad we got the tank instead of the convertible?" Quinn asked hangdoggedly.

≷ ≶

"No Mother, we aren't hurt but the car rental company can't get me a replacement car till the morning so we are spending the night in San Simeon."

A waiter came by our table. "Sorry but the cook said the kitchen is closed."

I covered the cell for a moment. "I'll have another Maker's Mark."

He looked at Quinn. "Can I at least have a bowl of cereal . . . and a bottle of white wine?"

The waiter did a double take, nodded, and left.

"Curtis," Mother asked, "you will be here in time for the wedding rehearsal?"

"Probably."

"Are you going to visit Hearst Castle? I hear it's beautiful and they let the staff swim in the off limits pool once a year."

I closed my eyes. "Mother, we just spent three hours at the hospital for no other reason than to make sure insurance covered the accident. We've been drilled by police over and over again as to what exactly happened and Quinn and I were clever enough to change our stories only four times. I'm surprised I'm not talking to you from a jail cell. It's dark out. And our drive tomorrow is going to take four hours minimum. I don't think we're going to dillydally at Hearst Castle."

I heard her huff. "You don't have to get testy."

The waiter arrived with my drink and Quinn's cereal and wine.

I took a needed sip. "Not testy. Just tired."

She was straining to ask the right questions. And she failed. "Is your dinner nice?"

"As nice as you can get at a Motel 6 when the kitchen is closed. And thank you for asking about the TV show."

"How did it go?"

"Fine." I shook my head. "We'll call tomorrow from the road."

"Bye dear."

I closed the cell.

> ≷ ≶

After Quinn finished his cereal dinner and I downed my smart cocktail we headed back to our ever-so-charming Motel 6 room with his unfinished bottle of wine. And don't get me wrong, I'm all for reasonably priced rooms with no frills as long as they're clean. This one wasn't.

Without speaking, I brushed my teeth, stripped down to my underwear, and climbed into one of the two full-size damp beds. It's not often but I have been known to get a bit moody. And tonight I had a full moody.

Quinn sat on the edge of his bed, drinking the last of the room temperature white wine out of the bottle while reading a town directory. "Hey, there's a gay bar in Cambria. Want to check it out?"

I rolled over and looked at him. "Do you want to walk the nine miles there and back?"

"Oh, right. No car."

I looked at him and went over in my mind again the image of him jerking off with a truck driver while driving no less than sixty miles an hour on a two-lane road that was riddled with Princess Grace deadly turns.

"What were you thinking?" I screamed. "We could have died from what you did!"

Quinn looked down at the floor and very quietly said, "We could have died from what you did."

I had totally forgotten about falling asleep at the wheel. I looked over at him and wasn't sure what he was doing. "Quinn?"

He looked away.

I got up out of my bed and sat next to him as he turned away. His body started to tremble and I realized he was crying. My God, the man never cries in twenty years and then he hits me with it twice in one month.

I put my arm around him and whispered, "But we didn't die."

He turned around and hugged me. "You know I would never ever do anything to harm you. You're my best friend in the world. You're all I've got."

"And you're my best friend and you're all I've got."

"We've had some incredible adventures together but I think today was one of the wildest."

I wiggled up to the pillows, put my head down on one, and patted the other one for him to join me.

"Quinn, can you believe we did Bobbie's show today?"

He put his head down on the pillow and we looked at each other. "I bet you saved her show today."

I thought about it. "I did good."

"You did great. It was so funny when you told her that I was your lover and she dragged me onto the set."

I pinched his side. "And she told the whole world we were lovers."

He kicked me. "*You* told the whole world we were lovers."

We both chuckled and then looked at each other. I mean we really looked at each other. And then, as if it was the most natural thing in the world, we slowly moved closer. There was a moment of hesitation and then it happened. Our lips met and we kissed. Not a guy/guy kiss. Not a friend/friend kiss. We kissed as two lovers—deeply, passionately, and completely.

And when we pulled away we looked at each other for a tender moment and then bolted out of that bed.

"What did we just do?" I screamed, running into the bathroom.

"Oh my God! Oh my God! Oh my God!" Quinn repeated as he wiped his lips.

I threw cold water on my face as he stood in the doorway. I looked at him through the reflection of the mirror.

"Curtis, it was the alcohol."

I rushed past him and jumped into my bed. "And the stress of the day."

Quinn turned out the light, slipped into his bed. "And we mustn't speak of this to anyone."

"Ever."

"Curtis, if we do, we will have to kill each other."

"Agreed."

≥ ≤

The next morning the car company dropped off a subcompact Chevrolet Aveo.

Quinn furrowed his brow. "Aveo. Isn't that a soap?"

I had never heard of Aveo before either but it didn't matter. I just wanted to get to San Francisco in one piece. Prior to the road trip, Quinn and I had talked about driving through Big Sur but with the time constraint and the fear of either of us veering off that treacherous road again, we opted for the safe, fast, and inland route.

We left San Simeon just after 8 o'clock, and stopping only once for fast food and gas we made it to San Francisco with no drama and right around 12:15. I had booked us a stay at a boutique hotel that I had found online. Each guestroom in the Silverscreen Hotel was named after a motion picture shot in San Francisco and was decorated with original movie stills. A double feature of San Francisco-based films was screened each evening in the Silverscreen Theater, within the hotel. Plus it was centrally located just a block from Union Square. It all sounded fantastic, as did reviews on the Internet from people who had recently stayed there. And considering the fact that Quinn was fired from Rainbows and Triangles the day he threw the DVD at the customer and now was facing assault and battery charges, he was tight for money. I was footing the bill so the ninety-nine-dollar-per-night room with two double beds sounded good. Almost too good to be true.

Checking into the hotel, all my fears melted away. It was fantastic. The room was beautiful, light, and airy. The bathroom was spa-like and clean. There wasn't much of a view but we weren't going to be spending much time in the room anyway. So we threw our bags down, splashed water on our faces, and headed out to do some really fast sightseeing before the 4 o'clock wedding rehearsal and dinner.

As we dashed out the front door of the hotel Quinn suggested we hit the Castro first.

"And walk in and out of skanky bars in the middle of the day?" I shook my head. "You totaled my car and ruined my driving record. We are doing what I want to do."

"And that is?"

"Fisherman's Wharf," I said as we headed east one block.

"You're such a tourist," Quinn muttered under his breath.

With time being an issue, we jumped into a cab at Union Square and headed over to the historic waterfront.

"Curtis, what are we going to do there? It's just a wharf, right?"

The cab clung to Powell Street as we crept up its steep incline. "You've been to this city probably a dozen times in your life and you've never been to Fisherman's Wharf?"

"Are there any gay bars there?"

"Quinn, there's lots of fun stuff to do. We can see them make chocolate at Ghirardelli Square or we can go to the wax museum or walk through the Cannery shops or . . ."

"Are there any gay bars?"

I looked at him. "No, I don't think there are any gay bars."

The cab climbed up over the highest crest on Powell and I pointed to our right. "Look, over there. You can see Hoit Tower."

"Is that a bar?"

"What are you, trash?"

"We're all trash," he said without hesitation.

I couldn't argue with him on that so I sat silent till we reached Jefferson Street. I paid the driver and got out of the cab.

"Sir, are there any gay bars down here?" Quinn asked him.

"I don't know."

"The one time I forget my Damron Guide," Quinn said as he got out of the cab.

I had an idea. Knowing that Quinn was currently operating with the attention span of a Chelsea boy, I continued to play alpha dog and led him over to Pier 43.

"Two tickets, please," I asked an attendant in a booth.

"What are we doing?"

"Perfect timing," I said as I looked at my watch. "Come on."

"Ugh," I heard Quinn utter as we ran down a ramp and jumped onto a boat just as it was about to disembark carrying no fewer than fifty German-speaking tourists.

Upon entering we had the option of listening to an audio recording of the trip. I put a headset on and turned it on as Quinn read the sign. "Eight different languages. Hmmm." He looked up and elbowed me as a German was reaching for a cassette player. "I think he wants me."

"Why didn't I have you neutered? What is it with you?"

"Curtis, we're in San Francisco."

"Quinn, we live in New York City."

I tuned my audiocassette to English and went out onto the deck and sat on a bench in the front of the boat. Eventually, Quinn joined me as the trip began. We left the wharf and headed west past Fort Mason and the Marina district, which was devastated in the 1989 earthquake, and then past the former army instillations of Crissy Field and the Presidio. The boat went under the Golden Gate Bridge and turned around, and there was a phenomenal view of the man-made wonder. I had crossed the bridge before but never sailed under it. What an incredible perspective it was.

I looked at Quinn and elbowed him when the audiocassette was telling us how many lives were lost during the construction of this monstrosity. Quinn ripped the headphones off and threw them down.

"What's wrong?" I asked.

"It's all Latin to me."

I picked up his headset and listened to it and then looked at him with disbelief. "Quinn, you're listening to it in Portuguese."

He threw his arms up. "How was I supposed to know?"

Well, if he had stopped cruising the straight tourists for one second and read the instructions he would have known. I switched his channel to English and gave it back to him.

The narrator pointed out the exotic and beautiful harbor town of Sausalito and the wildlife reserves farther out in the Marin Headlands. Then the boat came up really close alongside Alcatraz. As we swung around, heading back to the piers, the view of the city made me think back to the last time I had been here, which was in 1998.

While he was vacationing in New York City, I had met a really sweet man named Tommy Cavanaugh who was a native of San Francisco. He had never been to the Big Apple before, was traveling alone, and we connected down at the Muenster Bar in the Village. I offered to show him the New York City I knew and loved.

Tommy enjoyed museums, theater, ballet, parks, and *food* as much as I did and it was truly a week of fun and romance. He was almost ten years younger than I and was an aspiring clothing designer. After he returned to San Francisco, I flew out for a week and he showed me the city he loved. I not only really liked him but also thought he was a talented designer with a great future ahead of him.

Wanting to pursue a career in the fashion industry, we seriously discussed him moving to New York but as so often happens, time and distance took its toll and gradually we grew distant and lost touch. For a short while I saw his clothing line, *Tommy Cavanaugh*, show up in New York. It looked wonderful but all of a sudden it disappeared. I feared his company was too similar sounding to another Tommy.

To this day, whenever I thought of him my heart skipped a beat and I felt all warm inside. I actually considered looking him up on this trip but then decided that I should just let it be in the past and wished him well.

The boat gently idled by Pier 39 and we were amazed to see the number of sea lions barking and basking in the warm afternoon sun. Once docked, Quinn and I jumped off the boat.

"And?" I asked.

"I liked it."

I decided to treat him to another surprise as we walked over to Beach and Hyde Streets.

"Quinn, I hope you went down below on the boat."

"No, why?"

"They had a gay bar down there."

"Did they?" he asked, honestly believing me.

I shook my head. "Hey, but at least you can tell everyone that you cruised the San Francisco Bay."

"Ha! Ha! That was bad. What are we doing now?"

Pleasantly surprised that there was barely a line and one was actually waiting for us, we jumped onto the Powell-Hyde cable car.

Neither Quinn nor I had ever ridden one before so I was deliriously excited. And as the car took off, the conductor started ringing its bell rhythmically. I was really impressed with his talent. I think Quinn was too when I saw him talking to him. Hopefully he wasn't asking if there was a gay bar on board. The ride itself I thought was really cool. I was standing on the running board on the front outside of the car, soaking it all in. But when we were between Sacramento and California Streets the conductor switched from improvisational bell clanking to Bobbie Vibrato's favorite clanging. It was too perfect to hear him play Judy's "The Trolley Song." I looked back at Quinn who gave me a sly smile.

"This is so queer!" I shouted back to him as we both joined in with the lyrics.

The cable car ride ended perfectly just two blocks from our hotel and it was close to 3 o'clock. We ran up to the room, took respective showers, threw on some clean clothes, and headed back out to catch a cab up to Golden Gate Park. The breathtakingly beautiful Japanese Garden was where Mother's wedding was scheduled to take place.

Quinn and I got to the garden early enough to give us a chance to check it out. The pagodas, bronze Buddhas, clipped hedges in the shape of Mt. Fuji, pavilions, and statues were gorgeous. But what really hit me hard emotionally was the configuration of plants and trees. Except for a small Zen rock garden, this was what was called a wet garden. I had never felt this in my life but I sensed I had been there before. Petra would have been delighted. Whether it was a past life or not, all I know is that I had an intense emotional reaction to the garden itself, separate from my mother's wedding.

Of course there were Japanese maple trees, beautifully landscaped ponds filled with huge eye-bulging goldfish, wooden bridges, and exquisite lanterns all around, but it was the giant redwoods that moved me most. I found them to be to majestic yet hauntingly sad. It was truly a nonreligious religious experience. I touched one, thinking it was sheer brilliance. It was over a hundred years old and had its roots firmly planted in the soil while its branches reached for the sky. It was flexible enough to bend in the wind yet strong enough to build a house with. It could flower, seed, and reproduce itself and didn't even need a coat in the middle of winter. Hell, I couldn't do all that.

Upon entering the garden, Quinn and I went our separate ways and considering it was about five acres in size it was remarkable that we met up at the same moment in front of a nine-thousand-pound bronze lantern of peace.

"Curtis, this is beautiful."

"Isn't it?"

"Oh boys!" Mother hollered as she and Harrie walked through the impressive Hagiwara Gate.

Harrie ran ahead of her and nearly knocked me over with her embrace. She kissed me on the cheek and whispered into my ear, "I want you to call me Mother Squared."

I pulled away from her, confused. "You want me to call you what?"

Harrie leaped up and down as if she was teaching her high impact step aerobics class. She looked like a Jack Russell terrier trying to jump over a ten-foot fence.

"After tomorrow, I'll be your mother, too. Or two. So, you must call me Mother Squared. Like in algebra?"

Mother to the second power?

Having embraced Quinn, Mother joined us. "He gets it," Mother said sarcastically. "He's just playing dumb."

She hugged me and I honestly didn't get it.

≳ ≲

The wedding party consisted of a dozen of Harrie's closest and most energetic friends and Quinn and myself.

At one point Quinn turned to me. "I feel like we are in the middle of a taping of a Richard Simmons exercise video."

"Except that all of these people lost the fat," I added.

The rehearsal went very smoothly. In the middle of the ceremony they wanted me to get up and speak. I knew what I wanted to say; I just didn't know if I could say it. So, I got out of reciting it by telling them that I wanted to keep it a surprise.

Afterward there was a reception down the road at the Strybing Auditorium, and keeping in tune with the theme of the garden, the dinner was catered by one of San Francisco's most acclaimed Japanese restaurants. It mainly consisted of an elaborate and awesome-looking, if not limiting, sashimi bar.

Mother came over to my table as I pushed some seaweed around my plate.

"Don't play with your food, dear."

"I'm not playing, I'm trying to find something to eat."

She gestured to the gigantic table of food. "Curtis, there's maguro, toro, ebi, saba, ika, and tako!"

"Yes Mother, I know there is tuna, fatty tuna, prawn, mackerel, squid, and eel. But it's all raw." I pushed my plate away.

"I'm so disappointed that you never developed a sophisticated palette."

I was shocked. "Mother, I would love to eat these delicacies. But it seems that you've conveniently forgotten that I'm HIV-positive and you, more than anyone else, knows that I've been begged by my doctor not to eat any raw fish."

She was shocked by her own oversight. "Curtis, I'm sorry. Sometimes I forget because it hasn't seemed to make any difference in your day-to-day life and you've never been sick."

"Knock on wood," I demanded.

We both tapped the table. "Would you like me to go out and get you a sandwich or something?"

"Don't bother, I've lost my appetite." I stood up to find Quinn.

"Curtis," Mother stood and held my hand, "Harrie's inviting a few close friends over to her house and she'd love it if you and Quinn would come."

"I know Harrie means well but I just can't be around her for long periods of time, Mother."

She was momentarily appalled. "I'm not asking you to." She looked across the room at Harrie talking to Quinn. "*I* want to be around her for long periods of time."

I had to ask her *the* question. "Are you sure?"

She looked at me cautiously, wanting to make certain she understood what I was asking. "Am I sure of what?"

"Mother, are you sure she's the one? You've just met. You barely know one another and I think you could do so much better."

She slapped me across the face.

We were both stunned and stood there paralyzed. Finally, she spoke. "How can you be so cruel?" She raised her voice and noticed Harrie was watching us. "This is the night before my wedding and you ask such an insensitive question? Can't you just be happy for me?"

My mother started to cry genuine tears. "That woman, that woman standing over there," she pointed to Harrie, "is sweet and kind and loving and pretty and upbeat and successful *and* she adores me."

"Mother, please."

"Don't Mother please me. You're the one who started this. You know what I think your problem is? First, you're jealous. Second, when you meet a man you just keep thinking someone better might come along. I'll bet you anything, not once but many times, you've met the right guy and you didn't even know it. And third, sometimes, like right now, you can be an arrogant little snot. But I can't worry about that. I'm about to marry the love of my life and I'm not going to let you spoil it. Either you give us your blessing and be a part of this beautiful ritual tomorrow, which I hope you will, or leave. But if you leave, I don't want you to come back. Ever! Is that understood?"

Mother ran out of the rehearsal room crying, with Harrie following her, as I called out to her, "Mother?"

Quinn came to my side. "What happened?"

"I was an arrogant little snot."

≥ ≤

Quinn and I went back to the Silverscreen Hotel. He pleaded with me to go out to the Castro with him but I opted to watch an old movie down in the hotel's theater. Surprisingly, he went out by himself. I was fast asleep at whatever time he dragged himself back in.

The next morning I woke up early, showered, got dressed, and set the alarm so Quinn wouldn't be late for the 11 o'clock wedding. I left a note saying that I wasn't sure if I was going to show up, but I encouraged him to go anyway. At 8:15 I quietly slipped out the door, skipped breakfast, and left the hotel not knowing where I was heading.

I took a right on Mason Street and walked aimlessly until I collided into the Civic Center. There I bought a coffee and started walking again. I passed the Opera House and continued down Grove Street, trying to sort things out.

Lucky for Mother, there wasn't a cloud visible for miles and the temperature was a mild fifty-eight and promised to get up to sixty-five. I tried to put all my thoughts and emotions into perspective but I felt numb. Shell-shocked. I continued walking until I ran into Alamo Square. I strolled through it and came out on Scott Street and kept walking until, surprisingly, I was standing at the east entrance of Golden Gate Park.

I entered on Middle Drive East and walked past the tennis courts that were already full with energetic players, batting balls at each other even on Thanksgiving morning. I continued on and stopped in front of what looked like a specially designated area. Before me stood a large stone and engraved upon it was NATIONAL AIDS MEMORIAL GROVE. I had never heard of it before.

Still being quite early, I seemed to have the sanctuary all to myself. There was a plaque that said that this was a dedicated space where people directly or indirectly touched by AIDS could gather to heal, hope, and remember. This living memorial honored all who had confronted the tragic pandemic; both those who had died and those who had shared the struggle, kept the vigils, and supported each other during the final hours.

I sat in a very peaceful and moving fern grotto that was dedicated to all those who were lost to AIDS and were unidentified. Then I passed through an aromatic pine forest, a section of redwoods that instantly made me feel small and humble, and an open meadow where healing circles took place.

I walked a bit farther and then went through a woodland path and a circle of dogwood trees and wound up at the entry to the Circle of Friends. Engraved into the crescent flagstone floor were 1,524 names to date of those who had succumbed to AIDS. In the past I had been incredibly moved when I visited the Vietnam Memorial in Washington, D.C., but my reaction to the Circle of Friends was even greater.

Slowly, I walked the circle and with reverence chose to read as many of the names as I could. It was the very least they deserved. I was one of the lucky ones. Granted, I'd had the best doctors from the onset. And I'd inherited strong genes and always taken good care of myself. My hope had been to hold on long enough and pray that successful drug cocktails would come along. And they did. But there were thousands of people who had had the same odds on their side and had died. To this day, I wondered why me? Why had I made it this far? By 1994 and at age thirty-three, I had lost and buried most of my gay friends.

After I had spent close to half an hour there, I turned to leave the memorial when an inscription caught my eye. At first all I could see were just a few letters, the rest being covered by leaves. But in my gut, I knew instantly who it was. I stood frozen, looking down at it. A slight breeze blew the leaves away and unable to support my own weight, I dropped to one knee. There wasn't a sentence or a phrase or even a date of birth and death. It was just one person's name. Tommy Cavanaugh. My heart broke as tears fell from my eyes, soaking his engraved name.

I don't know how long I sat there with him, but it was a lone bicyclist who quietly stopped by that stirred me out of the moment. He got off his bike, kissed a name, and then vanished.

I kissed Tommy's name and left, too.

≥ ≤

I approached the wedding from the southern wishing pond and in doing so I had to cross a rustic wooden bridge. Midway I stopped and looked up the hill and saw billowing pieces of ivory silk blowing in the wind. The backdrop for the wedding was the impressive sixty-foot Treasure Tower in the Japanese garden. Landscaped around this brilliant red Buddhist pagoda were azaleas, camellias, oriental magnolias, cherry trees, dwarf pines, cedar, and cypress, all carefully positioned and living in harmony amongst one another.

As I reached the end of the bridge I had to climb a series of stone steps to get up to the shrine area. Maybe a hundred guests were seated in chairs covered in off-white linen slipcovers and positioned in a semicircle, facing a Japanese-style altar table that was flanked on either side with enormous topiary-styled arrangements of pale yellow peonies. Just peonies and hundreds of them. Some closed, some just opening, some in full luscious bloom.

No one could see me as I watched from the back of the ceremony. I had learned earlier that throughout the tea garden both black and red pines existed; the black represented male energy, the red, female. And I thought it was perfectly fitting that the two pine trees guarding the entrance to Mother and Harrie's wedding were both red.

Mother was wearing an Elie Saab A-line off-the-shoulder beige silk layered gown with silk lace appliqué, beads, and a built-in bustier. Harrie was in a Vera Wang off-the-shoulder ivory silk organza with a heavily beaded bodice of pearls and sequins with a chapel length train. Suffice it to say, they both looked astonishingly beautiful and happy.

All of Harrie's friends were present. Quinn was my mother's lone guest and the ceremony was more than half over. Mother and Harrie had already spoken their personally written wedding vows and exchanged their rings.

The elderly white-haired officiant stood at the center and outstretched her arms to the witnesses. "Friends, we are here this day to share with Harrie and Mrs. J. the most important moment in their lives. Over the course of time they have grown to know and love each other and now they have decided to live their lives together."

A friend of Harrie's played Rodgers and Hammerstein's "Some Enchanted Evening" on the harp. Although cornier than Kansas, that song actually did sum up their initial meeting at my Pup Room book launch, albeit theirs was the X-rated version.

Scheduled to speak next was Harrie's best friend. She jumped up out of her seat, bounced down the wedding aisle in her voluminous Bo Peepish dress, and stood in front of the crowd.

"Hi! I'm Happy!"

And she was.

"I'm Harrie's best friend and former lover."

I put my head down.

"In fact, my new lover is here with me. Janice, stand up!"

She stood up and the group applauded.

"And Janice was lovers with Stella who is now blissfully wed to Charlie. Girls, stand up!"

They did and the group applauded.

"Charlie and I shared two wonderful years together, but before that she met Lisa."

She motioned Lisa to stand up.

"Who is now lovers with Sammie!"

Sammie waved her arms and stood up.

Eventually, everyone was standing but Quinn.

"We, all of us women, want to share in Harrie and Mrs. J.'s love."

I think they had.

Happy happily took her seat and then it was my turn to get up and speak. And of course I didn't, which brought the wedding to a dead halt. Both Harrie and my mother searched the crowd for me but I was nowhere to be found. They indicated to the officiant to continue and then she was cut off.

"I have something I want to say!" I hollered out from the back of the crowd.

Startled that I had shown up after all and not knowing whether I was there to give support or condemn the wedding, Mother, Harrie, and Quinn exchanged quick glances as the entire wedding party turned around to see who I was. With the sternest face I could hold onto, I walked the distance down the center aisle, past all of Harrie's bubbling friends, to the front of the ceremony.

I gently motioned the officiant to step aside and then took Mother's hand in my right, Harrie's in my left, and whispered to both of them, "Please forgive me." They smiled and squeezed my hands.

I looked out to the crowd. "In this fast-paced, unpredictable, short ride of what we call life, it's a true blessing when two people, whose hearts are so in tune with each other, can take the unbelievably scary risk and have the guts to say 'I do' and commit their lives to one another, even when they live on opposite sides of the country." I looked at both of them. "You're bigger men than I."

The crowd laughed.

I turned to Mother. "I am so lucky to have you as my mother. You are not only a great source of inspiration but an even bigger source of writing material."

Mother curtsied. "Thank you very much. And I'll take my 10 percent."

I kissed her and turned to Harrie. "I've never met anyone who could tame my mother. You are the true definition of a kitten with a whip."

Harrie jumped up into the air and mimed snapping a whip at my mother.

I couldn't help but chuckle. "If you want her, she's yours."

"I want her!" she screamed.

The crowd laughed.

I put my mother's hand in Harrie's and gazed out over the crowd. "I look at this beautiful gathering of people and the only one I recognize is my best friend Quinn. But I hope in time, I'll get to meet and know each and every one of you who are so dear to Harrie, because she's now," I hesitated for just a fraction of a second, "part of my family."

There were cheers and not a dry eye in the garden. I kissed them both and sat down next to Quinn to watch the rest of the ceremony.

"You always were a better actor off stage than on," Quinn said out of the corner of his mouth.

"Hey, I meant most of what I said," I whispered back.

The officiant took over once again. "We leave here full of hope and joy. May we remember always this couple with affection and love. And so it is. Mrs. J. and Harrie, will you seal your marriage with a kiss?"

Mother and Harrie lovingly kissed each other completely and unselfconsciously.

"I now pronounce you wife and wife."

The crowd cheered and applauded.

The officiant continued. "These two married women want me to introduce you to them as each other's spouses. Ladies and gentlemen, it is my privilege to introduce you to . . ."

Quinn nudged me and whispered, "I don't think I even know your mother's first name."

"My God, and I don't think we know Harrie's last name."

The officiant put her hand on Harrie's shoulder. "This is Mrs. Esther—"

She was cut off by Quinn howling, "Esther?"

The crowd turned and stared at him as the officiant resumed. "This is Mrs. Esther Jenkins."

I laughed, "Oh, this is so *A Star Is Born*."

The officiant put her hand on Mrs. J.'s shoulder and said, "And this is Mrs. Harrie Merkin."

The crowd applauded as Quinn and I looked at each other for a moment and then shouted out simultaneously, "Hairy Merkin!" We doubled over with laughter.

≷ ≷

Back at the County Fair Building everyone was joyously celebrating. The food was fantastic, the wedding cake delicious, and the honeymoon was set to be the same ASAP cruise Harrie booked me on, which would sail out of New York City for ten days, traveling down to the western Caribbean, departing on December 29.

After dinner I danced with Mother as Quinn danced with Harrie.

"Curtis, you do know how proud I am of you."

"Yes, but you can say it again."

"Thank you for showing up. You know I couldn't live a day in my life without you."

She kissed me and spun me around. Then we switched partners and I was dancing with Harrie.

"Curtis, I want you to know that I will do everything in my power to make your mother the happiest woman in the world."

"Oh, she's already happy enough. Work on me, Mother Squared." I kissed her on the cheek and she spun me around.

Then we switched partners again and Quinn and I were dancing together.

"Curtis, I always thought you'd be walking down the aisle with Eric, the one in the wheelchair."

"Me, too," I agreed. "Well, I'd be walking, he'd be rolling." I spun him around but held on.

"He just seemed like such a perfect fit."

"Do you have to rub it in?"

"I'm sorry, I just don't know what went wrong with him."

"Neither do I," I said as I dipped Quinn, held on for a moment, and then dropped him.

At the end of the song, wedding guests were beginning to leave and Quinn and I decided to head back to the hotel, take a quick nap, and have a fun night out on the town.

I went over to Mother and told her of our plans and then asked her when she'd be coming home.

"Curtis," she said, "this isn't the best time to talk about this."

"Why not?" I asked, puzzled.

"Dear, I'm not coming home. I'm going to live here in San Francisco."

My face must have turned white because I certainly felt all the blood drain out of it.

She continued. "I mean I'll come back and sell the apartment and all but Harrie and I want to make our home base here."

I couldn't speak.

"Curtis, you yourself have said that San Francisco's such a charming city and what a great destination for you to visit and—"

I cut her off. "But Mama!"

Both of us were surprised at what I blurted out. I hadn't referred to her as Mama since I was a very little child. No one drove me more nuts than she did but losing her to San Francisco and to Harrie just made me think of the day I'd lose her forever, which in turn hit me in the face with my own mortality. On the outside I was holding it together but on the inside I was falling apart. One negative thought was cascading into another, turning into an avalanche of suffocating anxiety.

"Curtis . . ."

Suddenly, my cell phone rang, cutting off Mother. I looked at the caller ID and it was my home phone.

"Petra?"

"Dear heart, how is the wedding?"

"Everything is fine. Is that why you are calling?" She hesitated too long. "Emily-Mae?"

"Yes. She's having trouble. I took the liberty of taking her to the vet. She has stopped eating altogether and they want permission to put a feeding tube into her neck."

"You mean a feeding tube down her throat?"

She paused. "No, they would cut a hole in her neck and push it through and you would have to force-feed her."

I started to tremble. "No!" I hollered. By this time Quinn, Mother, and Harrie were around me. "I can't let them do that to her."

"I agree with you, darling." I could tell she was crying. "Curtis, they let me bring her home but I think her time is near."

"Petra, let me call you right back."

I closed the cell, looked at the three of them, and burst into tears. I managed to calm down and told them what was going on and then the flood-gates opened up again.

Mother put her arms around me. "I'm sorry, dear."

Through sobs I choked, "I don't know how, but that scrappy little sorry excuse of a dog has burrowed its way so deeply into my heart."

I questioned whether I should stay or leave and they all agreed I should fly back to New York City, immediately.

And Mother reminded me, "Curtis, I probably won't see you again until the cruise."

I kissed her good-bye as well as Harrie.

I threw my arms around Quinn and he said, "You're doing the right thing. Oh, and I forgot to tell you that when I went out last night, a dozen guys recognized me from *The Bobbie Vibrato Show, Her Show!* Curtis, you were a hit and they all loved you."

I squeezed him and took off.

≷ ≷

It being Thanksgiving evening and last minute, the only flight I could get onto and that would get me into New York City the fastest was one that departed San Francisco at 6:30, stopped off in Los Angeles for three and a half hours, and then would arrive at Kennedy International at 7:41 the next morning. The flight arrived a half hour late and after getting my luggage it was about 8:45. I checked my cell as I headed back into Manhattan in a cab and picked up a message from Petra.

"Curtis, it's just after 8 o'clock. I called Dr. Stanton's emergency number and she's meeting me at the office. I'm sorry, Emily-Mae was having tremendous trouble breathing due to a nosebleed and I had no other choice."

A nosebleed? I knocked on the cabby's Plexiglas divider. "Excuse me? I need to change that to Broadway and 84th Street?"

"No problem."

My only fear as we sped along the Van Wyck Expressway was that I wouldn't get to Emily-Mae in time. I had the money and an extra tip all ready for the driver, who made it in a record time of thirty-five minutes. The moment we stopped, he popped the trunk and I dragged my suitcases into the vet's office. There was no receptionist at the front desk and the waiting room was already full of animals and their owners. But there was no sign of Petra. I was about to ring the bell on the front desk when Dr. Stanton appeared.

Several of the pet owners called out her name hoping to see her next but she came right up to me and embraced me. I started to tremble as she took me back to an examining room.

Dr. Barbara Stanton was exceptional. She was not only a talented vet but she was a beautiful and compassionate person. I had been bringing all my pets to her over the past twenty years. We stopped in front of the closed door.

I turned to Barbara. "Is she?"

"I think she waited for you."

Dr. Stanton opened the door and there was Emily-Mae, splayed out on the cold stainless steel table with Petra wiping blood off her face and body. I kneeled down and placed my hand on her side. Her body was limp but upon feeling my touch she opened her eyes and struggled to bare her teeth.

I smiled at her fighting spirit. "Just relax, sweetie. Time to rest," I whispered.

Petra put her hand on my back. "Her nose started to bleed and I just couldn't stop it."

Dr. Stanton cleaned up her face a bit. "I've cauterized it."

I looked up at her. "Why is it bleeding?"

"My guess is a tumor of some sort."

I shook my head in disbelief. "Damn, after all she's been through and all she's survived? Now a tumor?"

Dr. Stanton touched my arm so gently. "Curtis, I'm sorry. You've been so good to her."

"I just fear that I've put her through too much."

"I would have told you if you had. You really didn't," soothed the doctor. "She was never in discomfort."

Petra added, "Her spirit and appetite was always healthy. In fact up until yesterday, she growled and snarled at me."

I smiled at Petra, "I don't want her to go through anything else." I paused before I said it. "Let's let her go."

Dr. Stanton touched Emily-Mae's front right leg. "I thought that would be your decision, Curtis, and I took the liberty of inserting a shunt into a vein. I'm going to get the sedatives and I'll be right back."

She left the room and Petra quietly stood next to me as I took off my coat. I pulled my sweater over my head and gently lifted Emily-Mae up as Petra slipped it under her. I circled my arms around her and felt her heartbeat faintly ticking. My thoughts drifted back to Magda and the time the three of us shared together.

Dr. Stanton returned and patiently waited for me to give her the signal. As remarkable as it was, with all my other pets, I had never been present when euthanasia had taken place. I looked up at the doctor. "Will it hurt her?"

"Not at all. The first injection is a sedative to make her unconscious. The second injection will stop her heart."

I nodded and she inserted the first needle into the shunt, but before she injected it, I broke down with tears pouring down my face.

"Just let me know when you're ready," Barbara said.

I had discovered earlier on that if I put my lips right onto her forehead and spoke, Emily-Mae could feel the vibrations of my voice.

For the last time, I connected with her. "Emily-Mae, I love you and I'll never forget you."

Feeling my voice, she tried to bark. Her mouth opened but nothing came out. I looked up at Barbara and she injected the sedative. Within seconds her head tilted onto my arm, with her eyes still open. The doctor injected the second serum and I felt her heart stop. Within seconds she had turned cold.

"That's it?" I asked. "She's gone?"

Barbara nodded.

I looked at Petra. "It was so peaceful. It was so humane." I glanced back at Barbara. "That's how I'd like to go."

There was a moment and then we all smiled.

≷ ≶

I had Emily-Mae cremated. The next morning, Petra and I rolled a shopping cart down to Riverside Park. Although it was a gloriously sunny day it was absolutely freezing out. We walked along the Hudson River, which was strangely calm, till we reached the boathouses around 79th Street.

The northernmost pier at the boat basin was the only one open to the public. During warmer months there was a seventy-eight-foot old world classic schooner with two majestic masts that offered day trips up and down the Hudson. But in the off-season, the dock was empty both of boats and tourists. Petra and I walked out to the end of the wharf and set up camp on a bench facing New Jersey.

In silence, she removed from the cart a dark blue rectangular piece of fabric with bronze ornamentation on it called a villaine. Petra said that this Latvian shawl was her great, great grandmother's and was adorned to protect the wearer from the outside world. We placed it carefully on the bench as I took out a picnic basket full of fruit, cheese, crackers, and two wine glasses. I grabbed a bottle of red wine that I had opened earlier and had recorked. She set out the food on plates as I poured the wine.

Petra then gently removed a wreath of fresh pine bows that she had made herself the night before as I carefully pulled out a small wicker basket and a tied bundle of muslin fabric full of Emily-Mae's ashes. Petra picked up the glasses of wine and we both walked to the edge of the pier. I snuggled the basket into the center of the wreath and put the muslin into the center of it. I grabbed a handful of rose petals that I had in my pocket and sprinkled them all over the basket and then lay down on my stomach, leaned over the wharf, and carefully placed the wreath onto the river.

I got back up to my feet and Petra and I clinked our glasses.

"To Emily-Mae," I toasted as we watched her basket and wreath gently drift out into the Hudson River. "I can't believe we lost Magda and Emily-Mae in the same year."

Petra slipped her arm into mine. "Energy cannot be destroyed, darling. They are together now. You were a good friend to both of them."

I watched the current pull the wreath farther out as Petra held up her glass to me, saying, "The character and intent of a man's heart will be known by his treatment of animals." She touched my glass. "And so shall you be known, Curtis."

We both took a sip and Petra went back to the shopping cart. Suddenly, the wreath, basket, and the muslin full of Emily-Mae's ashes disappeared. It was as if something from the dark waters below knew how precious it was and had reached up and grabbed it. I was about to tell her how sad it made me feel when suddenly I heard music.

I turned around and Petra had pulled out of the bottom of her cart an accordion of all things, strapped it onto herself, and was playing it. And not very well, I might add. In a very high-pitched voice she sang a very odd song.

"*Gotin mana raibalina, tu man saldu pienu dod; tapec tevi apdziedaju, tapec tevim kroni viju.*"

"That was beautiful," I lied. "But I don't know what you sang."

She repeated it in English. "Oh, my cow, my dappled cow, you give me milk, sweet fresh milk; that is why I sing of you, why I weave a wreath for you."

We were silent and then I broke out into laughter. "A cow?"

She shrugged her shoulders. "I'm sorry, Curtis, it is the only Latvian animal song I know with a wreath."

All of a sudden from behind us there was a *kirchink*. She and I turned around and a passerby had thrown money into Petra's cart.

FIFTEEN

BRUISED FRUIT

It had been over a month since I had seen Mother. She was happy playing house with Harrie in San Francisco and after the New Year's Eve cruise she was going to sell her place in the Meatpacking District and move out to California permanently.

It had also been over a month since I had seen Quinn. Without work, money, or men keeping him in New York City, he stayed on in San Francisco at Harrie's house and finished writing the screenplay that he thought was going to bring in the big bucks. Well, it didn't bring in the big bucks yet, but he flew down to Hollyweird in the middle of December and shopped it around. A fledgling production company read it, felt it had potential, and secured it with a hefty option fee. So, my best friend had re-relocated, hopefully temporarily, back to Los Angeles.

I had continued to promote *101 Ways to Collide into Your Gay Soul Mate* and without the distraction of my mother, Quinn, or any dates for that matter, my life seemed quite calm and uneventful. Even Petra was out of town, visiting friends in Prague for the month of December. And although there wasn't a day that went by that I didn't miss and think about Emily-Mae a dozen times, there was an element of freedom, not having to be responsible for her daily medical requirements. So, with my life quiet and in order, I decided to take a stab at writing a novel. One that centered around the theme of a gay man on a quest to find the love of his life and all the crazy dates he has along the way. Hell, if anyone could write that book, it would be me.

December 25 landed on a Sunday and for the first time in my life, I spent it alone. I feared that I might be horribly lonely or even depressed but I actually really enjoyed it. I slept late, went to a matinee of a play Off-Broadway with an audience full of Jews, and then took myself out to an early dinner and came home to work on the novel. A perfect day.

But as December 29 approached I became more and more excited. Not only was I going to see Quinn and Mother and Mother Squared again, but I had never been on a cruise before. Plus this was a free cruise traveling through the Western Caribbean where I was one of the celebrity guests on board. And considering this was a gay cruise, I couldn't go without buying a surplus of tropical and appropriate outfits so I had a ball running around town and spending a fortune.

But around noon the day of the trip, I realized that with all the stuff I had purchased, I needed an additional suitcase. So I ran up Broadway to a shop that sold luggage, picked up a hefty piece, and headed back home to finish packing. As I was waiting for the light to change at 93rd Street I heard people screaming behind me, shrieks of fear coming from innocent bystanders.

"Look out!"

"Heads up!"

"Watch it!"

"Oh God, it's her!"

I knew before I turned around whom it was. I also knew this had been going on far too long and if I didn't stop her or at least confront her, some-one had to. I spun around and chose to defiantly stand directly in her path. I watched as people narrowly escaped being hit as she headed straight for me. But as she quickly approached I saw out of the corner of my eye an el-derly man crossing the sidewalk. He had on very dark sunglasses, was walk-ing with a cane, and if he kept on his course he was going to walk right into her. I hollered out to him to stop but he didn't seem to hear me.

I saw the neighborhood terrorist swerve just enough to miss him and then yell out, "Watch where you're going, asshole!" But she had miscalcu-lated.

He stepped toward her and it was his metal cane that jutted out and got caught in her wheel. And as if in slow motion, it snapped out of his hand and locked up her wheelchair, instantly hurtling the beautiful, middle aged blonde woman, chicly dressed and wearing a French beret, skyward. All of us on the sidewalk watched as she flew at least ten feet through the air and then crashed upon the cement sidewalk. She didn't move.

I didn't say it. I didn't hear anyone else say it. But we all heard each oth-er wonder if the wicked witch of the Upper West Side was finally dead. And then . . . she got up! She not only got up, she stood up! My first thought was she was healed! My second and correct thought was . . . the bitch was never paralyzed to begin with.

She ran back to the deaf, practically blind elderly man.

"You goddamn fucking idiot!" she screamed.

Well, that's all it took. Like an angry mob tracking down Frankenstein's monster, my lovely neighbors descended upon her. I looked at my watch and if time hadn't been so tight I would have gladly joined in. They didn't kill her although I'm sure they wanted to. And I was certain she'd be mov-ing out of this neighborhood soon enough. But before I left I couldn't re-sist putting in my own two cents worth.

"Watch where you're going, asshole!" I hollered at her.

I rushed back to my apartment, over-packed my suitcases, watered the plants, checked to make sure all lights, stoves, ovens, toasters, microwaves, and irons were off, checked them again, and then walked out of my door at 2 o'clock. The cruise was set to sail at five but we were requested to be on board and checked in at least three hours prior to departure.

I exited my building, and between the time that I had left my proud and local rabble and now, it had started snowing. I knew it was in the forecast but it was really snowing. I mean huge, wet, thick snowflakes where you could barely see your hand in front of your face. I slid my luggage down the street to Broadway and prayed that I could find a cab. After about fifteen minutes I really started to panic. It was not that all the taxis were taken, none had come by.

At that moment, my favorite cashier from the grocery store on the corner plodded up to me.

"Hey, Curtis." She smiled, looking at my luggage. "Off on a holiday?"

"Hi, Serendipity." I looked at my watch. "If I can get a cab I will be."

"Where are you going?"

"Twelfth Avenue and 55th Street."

She signaled me to follow her. "I've got my car. I'll take you there."

She lived up to her name.

On the ride down to the ship she talked about the trials and tribulations of working at the store. In particular, she mentioned a huge problem that they were having with one panhandler.

"Curtis, he's a sweet, harmless man but hasn't taken a bath in months."

"He isn't the one with the foot and a half long matted beard is he?"

"Yes. He manages to sneak into the store and then it's hard to get him out. You can imagine what the customers are screaming."

"I'm probably one of them." Then it dawned on me that Serendipity might know the answer to my question. "Whatever happened to the bag lady?"

"Which one?"

"'Any change, sir? Any change today?'"

She started to laugh.

I didn't find the humor in this. "What's so funny? I haven't seen her in months. I'm so worried. She might be hungry or hurt or . . . what if she died?"

"Curtis, you didn't hear? She's in Florida."

I was puzzled to say the least. "Florida?"

"She saved up a fortune and bought this really expensive condo in West Palm Beach. Curtis, she has more money than God."

I was silent for the longest time taking all this in and then burst out into laughter.

Serendipity was a godsend to take me down to the ship and I thanked her profusely as I grabbed my luggage out of her car and made my way through the snow to Pier 711.

And patiently waiting under a huge heated awning at the dock for me were Mother, Harrie, and Quinn. I gave them all a huge hug and a kiss but as I looked over Quinn's shoulder I was shocked to see Petra.

I ran to her and threw my arms around her tiny body. "Are you coming?"

"I wouldn't miss this for the world."

I kissed her so hard. "What a way to meet my family."

"Everybody, this is Petra, Magda's sister."

They all introduced themselves to her with huge hugs. I was so happy that everyone was going on the trip. I couldn't think of any other people who I'd want to ring in the New Year with. And then I looked up at the ASAP fourteen-story cruise ship.

"Damn, it's as big as my apartment building."

"Probably bigger," Harrie said. "What you don't see are the many decks underneath the water."

Quinn asked very guardedly, "And I won't get seasick?"

"No," Harrie assured him. "The ship has huge stabilizers in the water to help it stay straight and upright."

"Keep your voice down," I whispered. "If Jerry Falwell finds out, he'll attach stabilizers to gays."

The five of us cackled as we checked in with our luggage. Once on board we found our respective cabins and unpacked. Quinn and I had a balcony stateroom on Deck 8, Petra had the identical cabin one level up on 9, and Mother and Harrie had the Owner's Suite on Deck 10 to celebrate their honeymoon. We had all decided to meet at Mother and Harrie's suite at 5 o' clock as the ship set sail.

Our cabin was great, much nicer than I had anticipated. It featured a bedroom/living area, a TV, refrigerator, and bathroom with shower. Plus we had our own private fifty-four-square-foot balcony with table and chairs.

"Look," I said laughing, reading a note about the beds. "It says here that at our command, they will convert into a queen."

Quinn waved an imaginary magic wand over them. "I always wanted to be a fairy godmother."

We both decided to get dressed up for our first night at sea and just before five we dropped by Petra's and we all headed up to Mother and Harrie's. What I kept forgetting was this wasn't just a cruise, this was a cruise filled to the brim, or should I say rim, with gays and lesbians. And everyone seemed just as excited to be there as the three of us were. Just walking down the corridor we passed scores of gorgeous men and women. Quinn's head and tongue were spinning around so much he looked like Linda Blair in the *Exorcist*.

Quinn caught his breath. "Oh God I hope I have sex on this trip."

Petra whispered, "Me too."

I elbowed Quinn. "When is the last time you had sex?"

He almost fell to the floor in exaggeration. "It's been so long, I don't remember how to do it."

"Darling," Petra said, slipping her arm into his. "You don't forget. It's like riding a bicycle."

"It better be," Quinn sighed, "'cause I've been riding a unicycle for months."

Arm in arm, the three of us laughed our way down the hallway. We knocked on the Owner's Suite's door, Mother opened it, and all three of us spoke at the same time.

"Wow!"

The first thing we saw when we walked in was a grand piano. Then the panoramic ocean views from the multitude of picture windows surrounding the space. They also had a separate bedroom with a king-size bed and walk-in closet, a living room with a CD and DVD library, a TV/DVD player, a personal computer with printer, a dining room, and a luxurious spa bathroom with separate shower and whirlpool tub. And to top it off, they didn't just have a balcony, they had a terrace with a garden.

Harrie opened the glass doors and we all went out into the snow and toasted to the New York City skyline with Veuve Clicquot as we set sail to the Caribbean.

"Bon voyage!" we cheered.

We had opted for the late dinner seating and the food was surprisingly delicious. We had a round table all to ourselves and afterward we explored the ship. Everyone who had ever been on a cruise before told me what to expect but it was so much more. And yes, it was like a floating city. It had everything from casinos and chapels to hospitals and Internet cafes.

And I don't think Harrie was fibbing about the ship stabilizers. They were like huge fins that jutted out on either side of the ship below the waterline, which cut down on seasickness. However, our first night at sea was a rough and tough one. Even with stabilizers, during that type of severe weather the sea itself swelled. I woke up in the middle of the night in the most shocking manner. Not only was the ship rocking side to side but also front to back. I had literally rolled out of the bed and onto the floor. I turned on the light and Quinn was gone. I even checked under the queen for the queen but then I heard him throwing up in the bathroom. That night, everyone on board the ship was sick.

My book signing was scheduled for the next afternoon while the ship was still at sea, heading for Key West. Down on Deck 7 in the lounge area of the main lobby was my typical book signing setup. There was a large poster of the book and me displayed on an easel and of course a stack of *101 Ways to Collide into Your Gay Soul Mate* piled high on a table. I was really excited, because everyone on the ship had been sent a list of the day's events to their cabins and my book signing was included. And an hour before it started there was an announcement over the PA system to remind everyone to come on down to the lobby for a chance to meet me and get a signed copy of the book. And thank goodness, the sea was calm.

I arrived at 12:45 for the 1 o'clock event and already there was a huge crowd of people in the lounge. I really felt like I was in my element. Here I was promoting a book specifically written for these cruisers. This was a no-brainer and I was excited.

I had asked Mother, Harrie, Quinn, and Petra to drop by a little after one-thirty when things might be a bit slower and then we could chat. So with a tall glass of ginger ale and a dash of bitters to calm my queasy stomach from the night before in my left hand, and my mighty pen in my right, I was ready for the onslaught of avid readers.

And there was an onslaught, but not of readers. A constant parade of some of the most beautiful men on this planet, mostly clad in the skimpiest of bathing suits, continually marched past my table. They weren't ignoring me. They just didn't even notice me or my humongous sign or my tower of books.

At 1:01 the huge crowd in the lounge left for a volleyball game on the upper deck.

At 1:02 a gay couple stopped by the table, read my poster, smiled at me, and then left.

At 1:05 a gaggle of gorgeous men piled out of one of the elevators and promptly ignored me as they passed by on their way to a couples massage class.

At 1:10 a lesbian stopped by and picked up my book. She read the back cover, smiled at me, and said, "Nice pic." And then she put the book down very carefully and left.

At 1:15 I was sweating.

At 1:18 a man by himself who was maybe sixty-five years old stopped by and asked, "Are you single?"

"Ah . . . no." The man started to leave. "Wait, yes! I am single."

He looked at the poster and then at me. "Is that you?"

I looked at him like he was nuts. "Ah, yes."

"And you wrote this book?"

"Yes, I did."

He picked up a copy and thumbed through it. "Is it any good?"

What does he mean is it any good? No, it's awful. Of course it's fucking good!

"I think you would enjoy it, sir."

He looked at the back cover and read some of the quotes. "Will you have a drink with me while we're on the cruise?"

"Will you buy my book?"

He looked at me and pondered the question. "If you have a drink with me."

"I get off at three."

"Champagne Bar, Deck 6 at three-fifteen?"

I swallowed hard. "It's a date."

He bought the book and I was a whore.

At 1:35 Quinn arrived.

"Where the hell have you been?" I whispered to him.

"You told me to come at one-thirty."

I pointed to my watch. "And look at it." I pushed it into his face. "It's one-thirty-five."

"What's wrong with you?"

"I sold one book!" I shouted. I brought my voice down. "I sold one fucking book and I had to prostitute myself to make him buy it, is what's wrong. Get in line."

Quinn looked around. "Get in what line?"

I was panicking. "Make a line."

"How can one person be a line?" Quinn stood tall and to the side of the table.

I pointed to the stack of books. "And buy a copy."

He put his hands in his pockets. "I don't have any money on me."

"Here's a twenty." I slipped him the bill. "Now walk around the lounge and come back and be animated and buy a damn book."

"But I'm supposed to be in line."

Petra, Harrie, and Mother exited the elevator together and walked over proudly.

"How's it going, Mr. Best Seller?" Mother asked.

"Get in line," Quinn said out of the corner of his mouth.

I begged them. "Everybody please, just pretend to buy a book."

One by one, each of them came up to me and shook my hand. I grabbed a book and pretended to autograph it and then I thanked them. Like herded sheep, they huddled at the end of my table not knowing what to do next.

"Now go away," I whispered.

They all started to leave as a group.

"But come back."

They all started to come back.

"Not now. Come back and get in line again in about five minutes." I busied myself pretending to sign a book.

Quinn walked away saying, "This is so sad."

"I heard that!" I said, not looking up.

The book signing, to say the least, was a complete disaster. I think it out for almost an hour and then closed up shop. I told them to meet me at three-thirty at the Champagne Bar to rescue me from my prostitution and surprisingly, all of them showed up on time.

"Where's your john?" Quinn asked as they saw me sitting alone at the bar.

"He stood me up," I answered pathetically. I pointed across the hall. "Let's hit the casino."

The four of us lined up at slot machines as Harrie watched.

I shouted over the dinging of a winning machine one aisle over, "These people don't read, never mind *buy* books. What were we thinking?"

Petra sat beside me feeding quarters into her machine. "Curtis, you've written a terrific book."

Harrie placed her hands on my shoulders. "Wait," she said as she jumped up into the air. "I have an idea."

Team cheerleading?

Harrie suggested that I take over hosting MaleBox at 5 o'clock, which she was going to do. It's a game based upon Mailbox. Each member in the group has a number and that number corresponds to a mailbox. And each person stands up and tries to sell themselves.

Harrie added, "If you like a person you leave a message in their box."

Petra let out a low, throaty laugh. "How sexual."

"I've played the game before," Quinn said as he hoped his nickel machine would hit.

"Curtis," Harrie suggested, "we can set up a table with your books and you can talk about it and how it will help them with their dating skills, and then start the game."

I was hesitant.

"Dear heart, I think it's a great idea," Petra said.

"I don't know," I said, fearing the worst.

Quinn shrugged his shoulders. "You've already bombed, Curtis. What do you have to lose?"

"Gee thanks." I looked over at Mother who was unusually quiet as she played her dollar slot machine. "Mother, what do you think?"

She was just about to speak when her machine hit. Not only did it ding; sirens went off.

"I just won eight hundred dollars!"

≳ ≴

I agreed to do it. The game took place down in the more intimate cabaret lounge on Deck 5. Fearful that MaleBox was going to be a repeat performance of the book signing, I was sick to my stomach I was so nervous.

Harrie had her staff set up my table of books in the center of the stage and on either side were two very large wooden boxes with 125 numbered cubbyholes in each of them.

Scheduled for 5 o'clock, I showed up backstage fifteen minutes earlier wearing a button-down shirt and jeans that showed off my butt and wondered what the heck I was going to say. I had never done anything like this before. In some ways, I hoped that maybe at least twenty or so people would show up and we could goof on game and sell a book or two. And I had Petra and Quinn planted at the back of the lounge at the bar as backup players in case not enough people showed.

Mother appeared backstage and rushed to my side. "Do you hear it?"

"What?" I asked as I popped a mint into my mouth.

"The crowd. It's a full house."

A full house? I did my math. "That's two hundred and fifty people."

Harrie jumped over to us holding a microphone. She was wearing low-rise jeans that hugged her narrow hips and a cute camisole that stopped just above her pierced navel, showing off a six-pack more defined than mine. And she had quickly hot-curled her gorgeous red hair. Damn, she was perky.

She tested the mike. "I'm so excited I think I have to do a split right this very second."

"Save it for later," my mother whispered, giving her a kiss.

I pretended I didn't hear that one.

Harrie gave me a hug. "Curtis, break a leg!"

"You too, Harr—"

She cut me off. "Ah, ah, ah."

"You too, Mother Squared."

"I love it!" she hollered as she hopped out onto the stage.

I gave my mother a look.

The audience applauded as Harrie took center stage. "Hello everyone!" She looked at them disappointedly. "Oh, that was so enthusiastic," she said sarcastically. "Hello, everyone!"

"Hello!" They all screamed and applauded louder.

"Now that's more like it."

And with no warning she did a back flip, which sent the room into a frenzy with screams and clapping.

I turned to Mother. "Great. Now how am I supposed to top that?"

"She was a gymnast, you know."

"So was I but I can't do that anymore."

Mother looked at what I was wearing and started unbuttoning my shirt.

"Hey, I just ironed that," I said as she pulled the shirt off, revealing a skintight, white V-neck undershirt.

"This will top that. Get down and do push-ups, " she said, shoving me to the floor.

"I'm Harrie, your cruise director. So, if any of you need direction on how to cruise . . ." she turned to her side, licked her finger, touched her butt, and made a hot sizzling sound, ". . . come to me!"

The lounge resounded with whistles.

"Not only are we here to play MaleBox and hopefully match up all of you hot and sexy people together, but we also have the funny and gorgeous and smart author of *101 Ways to Collide into Your Gay Soul Mate* to host the game for you."

I sat up from doing push-ups. "Mother, she's building me up too much."

"Give me ten more," she said, pushing me down again.

"And so are you," I said out of breath.

"So, please give a huge round of applause for one of the nicest and sexiest guys on this planet who also happens to be my stepson . . ."

Oh God!

"Give it up for Curtis Jenkins."

I got up off the floor, hugged Mother, tried to catch my breath, and strutted out onto the stage all pumped up. I didn't know if I could top her, but I sure felt top heavy.

The crowd went bonkers as I kissed Harrie. She jumped into the air, did a full straddle leap, and then ran off.

"Yup, that's my stepmom. And she's younger than I am." The crowd laughed. "She and my mother just got married last month in San Francisco."

There was a thunderous applause and whistles.

"I was concerned at first that the name of this game was geared toward the guys, until I saw the double entendre. MaleBox. Split it up and you have male and box. Actually, I think there are several entendres there."

The room was loving it. "In fact, I just found out I was going to host MaleBox, and if I had had more time I would have shown up as my alter ego drag persona, Chick Pee, who does have a male box."

They screamed and I realized I was going to be OK. I quickly explained the rules of the game, purposely ignoring my table of books. My gut told me to offer them a good time and in return, maybe some might buy a copy, just because they had fun. They each were given a nametag when they entered the lounge with a number on it that corresponded to a numbered mailbox on the stage. They also had a pad of paper and a pencil to write a message to anyone they were attracted to.

"Considering this fantastic turnout, we really need to make the introductions short. I mean really short or we'll still be playing MaleBox three days from now when we're in Cozumel. So let's go in order of seating, starting with the front row left, and just stand up, face the crowd, and tell us a little about yourself."

Some people were funny. Some were sexy. Some were really nervous.

A cute young man about twenty got up and spoke first. "Hi, I'm Dirk, number eighty-two and traveling on the cruise all by my lonely self."

The only thing louder than the guys whistling was the sound of them writing down his number.

A buxom woman in her thirties who got up midway through the game said, "My name is Delilah and my number says it all . . . sixty-nine."

The room screamed as women scribbled her number down.

And I think the funniest and scariest one of all was a very nervous and average-looking man about my age who was dressed like he was going to a funeral. "Ah, um, my name is Merv and . . . uh, I'm number," he looked down at the nametag on his chest to remind himself, "number forty-two and I like hugging, reading, romantic walks on the beach, kittens, and firearms."

The crowd went nuts with laughter, but I'm sure he was serious.

When everyone had had their turn, I encouraged them to have cocktails, mingle, and talk to each other as they filed up onto the stage to put their messages into corresponding cubbyholes. With the ice having been broken, people were really enjoying themselves. And after messages were delivered, they then came back and checked their own boxes for notes, and cruisers were pairing up, tripling up, and even quadrupling up. Not only was the event a huge success, but I also sold every single copy of my book.

Petra and Quinn joined Mother, Harrie, and I on stage when everyone had left, and we decided to celebrate up on the pool deck when Petra noticed there was one message left in a box.

"It's box number one," Quinn said as he removed it. "I hope it's a funny one." He read it to himself first. "Oh my God!"

"What?" we all asked.

"Curtis, I'd love to buy you a 'complimentary' drink. If you're game, meet me in the Admiral's Lounge at eight. An admirer."

I looked at everyone. "Who do you think it could be?"

"And they quoted complimentary," Petra said.

Mother asked, "How can someone buy you a complimentary drink?"

"It doesn't make sense," Harrie added.

My mind was spinning.

≥ ≤

Both excited and nervous, I entered the Admiral's Lounge absolutely not knowing whom I was meeting. Maybe it was the hunky guy who I thought was making eyes at me who was sitting in the second row of MaleBox? Or was it the man who was cruising me earlier in the day when I was working out in the gym? Or could it have been the waiter in the main restaurant who had bent over backward to find me organic grain cereal for breakfast?

Not knowing who it was, I dressed hot but not too hot. But even to enter the Admiral's Club I needed to wear a jacket so I put a black T-shirt on underneath my black suit. The Club was way up on Deck 13 and could be accessed by either elevator or spiral staircase. I chose the drama of the stairs. When I reached the top step there was a small vestibule and then I entered the lounge area. It was packed and I recognized no one. Then I laughed to myself. Of course I wouldn't recognize him, I had no idea what he looked like.

I went to the far end of the bar where there was just one seat left and before I sat down the bartender placed a martini glass before me. I watched as he smiled, shook his shaker, and then poured a chilled amber liquid into the glass and then plopped in a cherry.

"One complimentary opposite cocktail for the gentleman. Maker's Mark straight up, chilled in a martini glass." The bartender winked at me.

I was amazed. "But how did you know?"

"I didn't," he said as he pointed to the opposite end of the room. "He did."

I turned and the admirer held up his martini glass. I was stunned. It was Eric.

As I staggered toward him, a couple who had played the game stopped me. "Dolly Levy!" one of them called out.

I smiled as the other one said, "We met at MaleBox."

"That's great, guys. Have fun," I said in a half stupor.

The walk to the back of the lounge felt like it took forever and then there I was, standing before Eric, who was seated in his wheelchair. I had forgotten how beautiful he was. I snickered to myself, remembering the first time I described him to Quinn, saying he reminded me of a straight Ricky Martin.

"How . . . how . . . how . . ." I stuttered.

"How are you?" Eric said, finishing my sentence.

"That and how did you get onto this ship?"

"I wheeled on?" he said, laughing.

I gave him a smirk. "No, I mean . . . how . . . I don't know what I mean."

He put his hand on the seat next to him. "Sit down and join me." Eric signaled the bartender to bring over my drink.

A million thoughts were going through my head, not to mention the fact that this gorgeous man I was sitting next to had dumped me like a hot potato earlier that year.

"What a coincidence to run into each other on this cruise," I exclaimed.

"No coincidence, Curtis. I knew you were going to be on board."

He explained that having traveled with ASAP Cruises in the past, they had sent him their current brochure and newsletter. It mentioned that I was scheduled to be on the ship to talk about my book.

"I went to your book's Web site." He held up his glass. "Nominated for three awards, I see."

We clinked glasses. "Just nominated."

"And maybe you'll win," Eric said as he put his hand on my knee. "I'm so proud of you."

I shifted my position so that he had to remove his hand.

Eric said that he had gone down to the main lobby at two-thirty to surprise me at the book signing but was disappointed that I wasn't there.

"Yeah, I was disappointed, too. No one was there."

"But I was thrilled to see you at MaleBox."

"How did you know I—"

"Pure coincidence."

I heard Petra's voice in my head. No coincidences in life.

"And I just watched you take over that stage with such charisma. You're a natural, Curtis."

What was going on here? I picked up my glass and took a sip.

"Still complementary opposites," he winked as he sipped his martini.

And why was he being so complimentary? I was confused and fumbled to keep the conversation going. "You came on this cruise with friends?"

"No," he responded. "I came to be with you."

OK, now I was really confused. Why the big turnaround?

Eric took hold of my hand. "Curtis, have dinner with me tonight?"

I almost said yes. Then I explained to him that I was traveling with Mother and the gang.

"They'll understand if you miss this dinner."

I paused for a moment. "Yes they would understand but I want to have dinner with them. Today was a tough day that turned out brilliantly and I owe it all to them."

"Well, my day has turned out brilliantly and I owe it all to you."

God I felt uncomfortable.

"Curtis, will you at least meet me for the midnight dessert buffet?"

I looked at him seriously, knew I should say no, and then said, "Yes."

⋛ ⋚

"Is he still in a wheelchair?" Quinn asked as I joined them at our dining room table.

"Of course he's still in a wheelchair! He didn't just spontaneously heal," I laughed. "He's paralyzed."

Both he and Mother were shocked to find out he was on board, never mind interested in me again. And they couldn't wait to fill Petra and Harrie in on all the dirty details as we ate dinner.

"How does he look?" Mother asked.

I paused. "Fantastic."

Quinn hit his fist on the table. "You can't go back to him!"

"I'm not going back to him. I'm just having dessert."

"Be careful, Curtis," Mother warned me. "Think of what I would do and then do the opposite."

≳ ≲

I was intentionally late for the midnight buffet. Something had shifted within me. Fascinated to know the truth, yes, desperate to reconnect with him, no. This was the man I was crazy about and who left me high and dry in a torrential downpour with no explanation.

I took the elevator to the pool deck. The large enclosed lounge area was converted into a magnificent dessert buffet, including a chocolate bar. Gays and lesbians were gobbling up the goodies . . . and each other. I scanned the room and then noticed Eric who was directly across the lounge, sitting at a table by himself. Not noticing me, I observed him for a moment. My brain fell prey to my heart and I was flooded with a rush of emotions. Why was I suddenly remembering all the fabulous moments we had together? I even quickly fantasized what it would be like to get back together again. I slowly walked over to Eric as he gazed out the window.

"Penny for your thoughts," I whispered.

"Hey, sweet man," Eric said, turning his chair around. "Thought I was being stood up."

He waited for me to acknowledge the pun. I got it but chose to let it go.

"You know I'm not the kind of guy who would stand someone up."

Eric gestured to the buffet. "Care for a coronary?"

I smiled. "It's kinda noisy in here. Let's go out on the deck."

I opened the door and Eric wheeled out. Although it was chilly, the night was magnificent. There was just the sliver of a moon and a gentle breeze as the ship worked its way down the Atlantic Coast. I strolled and Eric rolled as we moved along the deck. We passed two lovers kissing and then stopped a bit farther at the ship's railing and looked out. I gazed up at the cloudless sky and the million and one stars twinkling up in the heavens. Neither of us spoke for quite awhile.

"I know what you're thinking," Eric said, smiling.

"What?"

"That this is straight out of one of your favorite actress's movies."

I thought for a moment and then smiled.

Eric continued. "*Now Voyager*, am I right?"

I nodded. "You know me too well."

"But this reminds me of our own movie," Eric added. "Or should I say reality."

I looked at him, perplexed.

"Curtis, our first date? When we strolled along the Hudson."

How did he remember?

"You said it reminded you of what you thought Paris would be like."

And it did. The twinkling lights of New Jersey, a tugboat chugging by, the romantic starry night.

Suddenly, Eric slipped his hand into mine and pulled me down, close to his face. Without speaking, we kissed. I felt myself falling. It truly was one of the most unique feelings I had ever experienced during a kiss, like I was going up and over the top of a Ferris wheel and then floating deeper and deeper into Eric.

Eric nuzzled his head against my chest and whispered, "Spend the night with me."

I stood up and looked out to sea, and after a long pause I asked him, "Why?"

Eric genuinely seemed surprised. "Why what?"

"Why did you leave me?" I looked at him seriously. "Why did you leave me the way that you left me?"

"Curtis, why ruin the mood?"

I wanted to scream. *Ruin the mood? You devastated me!* But instead, I remained silent. Something inside of me didn't want to let him know how hurt I was.

"Curtis, I always knew that you carried a silent and sometimes not so silent prejudice toward me, my wheelchair, and the paralysis."

I was flabbergasted. "That is so not true. Yes, in the beginning I felt awkward but only about the chair. I wasn't sure when to help you, when to talk about it. And I had questions about your paralysis but it was never a prejudice."

Eric shook his head. "Remember our last date at Le Boeuf Neuf?"

"How could I forget it?"

"You said you didn't even notice the chair anymore."

He didn't have to remind me of what we said because every single word was imprinted permanently in my brain. "And you compared that to telling an African-American that I don't see them as black. Which is so unfair. Saying that I didn't see the chair was a way of conveying how comfortable I was with everything. I wasn't being politically incorrect."

"Well, that's the way I perceived it."

I hesitated for a moment and then said, "Eric, you are an incredible man. You're a very successful lawyer. You're a designer whose apartment has appeared in *Architectural Digest*. You're an athlete. A chef. You've succeeded in so many arenas and you are a paraplegic."

Eric interrupted me. "You don't have to bring my paralysis into it."

I stopped for a moment realizing what was going on. "Eric, I'm damned if I do and I'm damned if I don't."

"I'm not following you."

"Here you say I have a silent prejudice toward your chair and your paralysis and yet whenever I do acknowledge your situation you shoot me down."

"But I can't be with someone who is uncomfortable with me being paralyzed."

"But I'm not uncomfortable!" I said, raising my voice. "But I am uncomfortable with you telling me what I'm feeling."

I wondered if Eric was playing the passive/aggressive victim? As much as he wanted people to accept him like any other man who can walk on two legs, at the same time, was he throwing the wheelchair in people's faces? Was he manipulating me with it?

We both took a deep breath and looked out to sea. Eventually, I asked him, "So why are you here now? Correct me if I'm wrong. Why are you wanting to start things up again?"

"I realized that I chose the wrong man."

I closed my eyes, trying to follow his logic. "What do you mean you chose the wrong man?"

"I should have chosen you over Paul."

I was still in the dark. "Who is Paul?"

Eric nonchalantly said, "I was seeing Paul at the same time that I was seeing you."

My jaw dropped.

"Curtis, I told you about Paul."

"Trust me, Eric. You didn't tell me about a Paul. I would have remembered." I struggled to sort things out in my mind. "I thought you and I . . . we were a . . ."

"Curtis, we never said we loved each other."

That came out of Eric's mouth so smugly that I just wanted to slap him silly, but instead I took another deep breath. "You're right, Eric, we never said we loved each other. But I assumed that we were dating exclusively."

"Curtis?"

"No, Eric, I need a minute."

I needed a minute because I was shocked, truly shocked, and felt like such a fool.

He paused for a moment and then continued. "Dr. Paul Bellows was a wonderful, charming, attractive, and sexy neurotologist. Curtis, a neurotologist is—"

I cut him off. "I *know* what a neurotologist is," I said, lying.

"He and I met just after my first date with you."

I put my head down, feeling like I was going to bring up my dinner.

"I can see you'd rather not hear."

Agreeing, I nodded my head. "You made your point."

"Actually, the point being, Paul left me."

I looked at him long and hard. "So I'm second choice? I'm plan B?" I started to walk away.

"No, Curtis. Ultimately Paul and I just weren't meant to be together."

I spun around and I walked right up to him. "Oh, but now that he's dumped you, we are meant to be together?"

"I realize that I didn't give us the chance we deserved."

Just then, I figured it all out. "You used it!"

Eric looked at me, confused.

"You used the wheelchair as a crutch." No pun intended.

"What are you talking about?"

"Eric, the reason you gave for breaking up with me was the wheelchair and my inability to deal with it. But in truth, it was because you liked Paul more than me? Shame on you! Shame on you for using your paralysis *and* me like that!"

"Curtis, I did not—"

"But it's the truth, Eric. Admit it."

He was caught off guard, put on the spot, and panicked. He looked me straight in the eye and said, "The truth is you came to me somewhat . . . bruised."

"Excuse me?"

"Curtis, you came with a lot of baggage."

He thinks I came with a lot of baggage then? I was tempted to tell him how much I brought on the cruise but didn't think the moment called for humor.

"And now?" I asked. "I have less baggage now?"

Eric confessed, "I'm willing to put up with it, now."

Forget slapping him silly, I was one moment away from throwing him overboard, wheelchair and all.

"So, I'm damaged goods but you're willing to put up with my baggage. How big of you."

"Curtis, stop."

Eric tried to hold my hand again but I pulled it away. We both looked away.

"Curtis, I'm not perfect. You're not perfect."

"Eric, I don't want perfection."

"And I just want to give us another chance."

"OK, so I'm not perfect, I'm damaged goods, and I'm second choice. Why would you want to come back to me?"

"Well, you've written a terrific book."

I stared at him. "Writing a book makes a difference to you?"

"Yes, Curtis. I've not only read the book but also your great reviews and interviews and I even saw *The Bobbie Vibrato Show, Her Show!* And watching you host MaleBox tonight, you're more confident, centered, and pulled together. I think the book and its success has been good for you."

I thought for a moment. "So, that's what's different? The book? The career? Eric, I am neither defined by my book nor the success."

I literally pulled back and took a good, long look at him. I was shocked and embarrassed to think that I had ever allowed myself to be so intimate with him. And deep in my heart, I knew that Eric was right. I was different but not because of the book or the success. I had grown because of the extraordinary people in my life and in particular, the one I had lost, Magda.

We both stared out into the ocean and after a long pause, Eric smiled, knowing he was going to win me over with his quote. He gestured to the night sky and said, "Oh Curtis, don't let's ask for the moon. We have the stars."

He waited for a response as I looked up into the night. I finally answered him. "Oh, but Eric, I want the moon. And I want the stars."

I looked back at him and his face had turned serious. "What do you mean?"

"I mean that I'll hold onto the good memories we had."

"But Curtis—" He sounded desperate as I cut him off.

"I wish you all the best from the bottom of my heart. I truly do. But we're not meant to be together. Good-bye, Eric."

He watched me as I turned and walked away. I know Eric waited patiently, sensing that I was going to stop, change my mind, turn around, and run into his arms. But I never looked back.

≷ ≶

The next day was New Year's Eve and the ship docked in Key West. I held off telling Quinn, Mother, Petra, and Harrie what had happened between Eric and me. I wanted more time to digest what had transpired. I had been to wonderful crazy tropical Key West a dozen times before, and even Mother had come down for an opening of a play I had written that was produced at the Waterfront Playhouse a few years back. So, I had no need to do the town again but I did make up my own personal itinerary of the best of the best things to do and see and sent them off on their excursion trip. I really needed to be alone for a while.

I waved good-bye from my veranda as they disembarked and then gazed out over the small colorful island, trying to pinpoint familiar landmarks. I was just about to head back into my cabin when I saw someone else get off the ship.

Without him seeing me, Eric rolled off the ship with his luggage. Apparently he had decided to fly back to New York City. All the while that I, *and Paul,* were dating Eric, this handsome and successful man—who unselfconsciously lived a vital life in what he called a two-wheel drive—now exuded sadness and loneliness and seemed trapped in a wheelchair. I wanted desperately to run down to the dock and put my arms around him and kiss him passionately and tell him everything was going to be OK but . . . I didn't.

I whispered to myself, "Sorry, man of my dreams."

≷ ≶

Later that evening, the ship set sail for Cozumel, Mexico. New Year's Eve was celebrated at sea and a late-night gala, black-tie dinner was held in the formal dining room timed with the ringing in of the new year. Everyone was dressed in formal wear. I had put on my Perry Ellis tuxedo. Mother looked stunning in a Christmas red Caroline Herrera asymmetrical full-length gown. Harrie was striking in her Armani tuxedo, and Petra looked majestic in her hunter green satins and silks. Without a tuxedo to his name, Quinn borrowed my Bill Blass that was a tad too small and then accessorized it with a gold lamé bow tie.

As the big moment approached, I poured champagne into glasses for me, Mother, Harrie, and Petra.

I looked at my watch nervously. "Quinn's going to miss it." He had dashed off to the Internet café about twenty minutes earlier and had still not returned.

"I'm back!" he hollered, rushing to the table.

"And the late Mr. Quinn Larkin," I said as I poured him a glass, too.

He held up a printed e-mail with a surprised look on his face. "You will not believe this!"

"What?" we all asked.

"I just got a message from the producer of *Puss N'Boots*."

"Oh Quinn!" my mother exclaimed. "Ann didn't . . . die, did she?"

"Die, hell no! The theater went bankrupt and some big conglomeration was going to buy it, tear it down, and put up some sort of high-rise building."

"That theater is a treasure. They can't do that!" I cried.

"Wait," Quinn said. "So, Mr. Rosenblatt? Remember him?"

"The lone stroker in the front row?" Mother asked.

"Yes. It was obvious to all of us that he was crazy in love with Ann so . . . he married her."

"Bless his heart," I said.

"It gets better. Turns out that Rosenblatt is a billionaire and has purchased the theater and is going to restore it to its former glory."

We were all moved to say the least, and then the room started the countdown to the New Year.

In unison we shouted, "Ten . . . nine . . . eight . . . seven . . . six . . . five . . . four . . . three . . . two . . . HAPPY NEW YEAR!"

With everyone in the room singing *Auld Lang Syne*, the five of us held up our glasses and Quinn shouted out, "Here's to Ann Vermillion and Mr. Rosenblatt!"

"Dear hearts, here's to *101 Ways to Collide into Your Gay Soul Mate* becoming an even bigger success!" added Petra.

"Here's to all of you finding the loves of your life, like we did!" Mother wished as she kissed Harrie deeply.

Harrie held up her glass. "Here's to exotic and romantic voyages throughout our lives!"

"And I'd like to propose a *final* toast!" I said in my best Elaine Stritch voice. "Here's to all the gays and lesbians who have ever been put back up on the shelf because someone felt they were damaged goods."

"Hear! Hear!" they all shouted.

We held up our glasses as I continued. "Cheers to us because everyone knows that slightly bruised fruit always makes the best preserves."